Praise for M

The Lost Garden
'. . .had me laughing out loud' *Ireland on Sunday*

'Complex and elegantly written' *Sunday Independent*

'A beautifully crafted story by a very gifted writer' *Sunday World magazine*

'Stanley's sensitive, heartfelt writing shines through' *Newsletter Special Supplement*

Searching for Home
'Settle down to a deeply satisfying, reflective read' *Evening Herald*

. . .a well-written novel that will grip you to the very last page' *Ireland on Sunday*

'This novel is one of the best books I have read this year' *The Irish World*

'A gripping read' *Belfast Newsletter*

Revenge
'[T]his is a woman [who] once she's embarked on something, moves into top gear and, well, stays there' *Sunday Tribune*

'A gripping story. . . The characters are likeable, funny and real. A great read' *The Irish Times*

'A compulsively different read…This imaginatively and stunningly written novel. . . is warm and poignant. . . Thought-provoking and compassionate. . . once again Stanley has proved herself as a spell-binding author' *Irish World*

Missing
'A perceptive and poignant novel exploring the ramifications of loss and abandonment with compassion and a wry, perfectly pitched wit. . . Stanley writes with a lightness of touch reminiscent of Jonathan Coe' *The Big Issue*, Northern Ireland

'A gripping and mesmerising novel. . . Skilfully written with bursts of humour' *Glasgow Evening Times*

'Touching, intriguing and often humorous' *Sunday Business Post*

'Stanley's writing is alive – witty, moving and engrossing. . . The characters of the three girls are richly portrayed' *The Sunday Times*, Malta

Retreat
'Mary Stanley's atmospheric novels tend to draw you in from the first page and haunt you long after you have turned the last. . . This book is beautifully written, achingly poignant, dark-edged but tempered with humour' *Irish Independent*

'A deeply satisfying, reflective read. . . Lively conversation and richly varied settings' *Evening Herald*

'A fresh new voice in Irish writing' *The Irish World*

'The pages turn with ease' *Observer*

'Warm, and even at its darkest, never entirely black. An engrossing read. . . .A deeply satisfying, reflective read. . . Lively conversation and richly varied settings' *Sunday Independent*

THE
UMBRELLA TREE

Also by Mary Stanley:

Retreat

Missing

Revenge

Searching for Home

The Lost Garden

An Angel at my Back

Mary Stanley

THE UMBRELLA TREE

NEW ISLAND

THE UMBRELLA TREE
First published 2009
by New Island
2 Brookside
Dundrum Road
Dublin 14

www.newisland.ie

Copyright © Mary Stanley, 2009

ISBN 978-1-84840-048-1

British Library Cataloguing Data. A CIP catalogue record for this book is available
from the British Library.

Printed by

New Island received financial assistance from
The Arts Council (An Comhairle Ealaíon), Dublin, Ireland

10 9 8 7 6 5 4 3 2 1

For my children
Steffen and Sophie Higel

Acknowledgments

The author acknowledges with love and gratitude her pillars, Diana O'hUid and Ann Sheppard; Sophie Higel for reading and reading; the kindness and generosity of her siblings Fergal and Lucy Stanley; and Steffen Higel, Jeroen Lodewijks and Willem Mevius for their computer expertise and assistance. Thank you to Caroline Montgomery, and everyone at New Island, in particular Edwin Higel and Deirdre O'Neill.

Thank you Justin Corfield for the animal stories, for your support and for being there.

'Earth and sky, woods and fields, lakes and rivers, the mountain and the sea, are excellent schoolmasters, and teach some of us more than we can ever learn from books.'

John Lubbock (1834–1913)

Prologue

'Miss Helayna,' Kulu is calling me.

It is my first real memory. I am three years old. He calls me by my name and he makes the middle vowel very long, even longer than usual. He takes my tiny white hand in his. His hand is black, as black as his face and his bare legs, but the palm of his hand is pink like mine. We walk to the gates.

'They're coming,' he says.

We must have done this before because I know what is coming and I am both frightened and excited. I hold his hand tightly.

We stand inside the closed gates and he lifts me up so that I can see.

The baboons are coming across the scrubland. Some of the babies are on their mothers' backs, some are clinging to their chests.

'The rains are coming,' Kulu says.

Luther has come with us. He stands beside us. Like me, he is little but he can already see over the gates.

The baboons stop and look at us. Some of them sit down and the little ones hold the older ones' hands. One of the bigger ones holds out its arms to me. I hold tightly on to Kulu.

Luther makes a noise and the baboons look at him.

Kulu's hair is thick with tight, dark curls. I lean my head against it, and I hold on to his shirt just as the babies hold on to their mothers' fur.

The big baboon drops his arms and they move on. Kulu swings me back to the ground. Holding my hand, he brings me back to the farmhouse.

On the veranda steps, I turn to look and I can just see across the gates into the far distance. I watch while the baboons pass the umbrella tree and disappear.

Horace comes out of the house through the wooden beaded curtain hanging in the doorway. He sits on the ground. He is writing his name in the dust with a stick.

I sit beside him. 'Baboons,' I say.

'They have gone to the trees,' he says. He knows things I don't know. We sit there under the bright blue sky, two little children, side by side, caught in a moment as in a photograph. Kulu has disappeared and Luther stands in the shade of the lean-to, watching us.

Childhood days. They are the 'once upon a time' days.

Long ago.

Once upon a time, a long time ago, there was a girl called Helena. I was that girl. Somewhere, mixed in with the bark of trees and the dried-up riverbed, we grew up, my beloved brother Horace and I. He used to talk with me. He loved everything to do with nature, and he loved me. He spent countless hours telling me about birds and animals, about the way they all behave. He instilled in me a love of the world, from the wide open sky to the parched earth, and all of the things on, above and beneath it. He told me about nature and instinct, evolution and survival. He told me such wonderful stories.

And then, once upon a time, I left my homeland and went to live in another place, a place where the winters seemed long and cold, where the sky seemed closer to the earth, where I fell in love and married.

Once upon a time ...

One

There is a tree, a single acacia tree, on the hill beyond our farm, before the horizon meets the sky, but etched into the firmament in its solitary starkness.

In October 1978, I left the farm and this tree we called the umbrella tree. I left everything that was familiar to me and I came to Dublin.

I find it difficult even now to describe what I was like, or indeed what that time was like. Photographs, if there were any, would show a thin, healthy girl with sun-bleached hair and tiny freckles scattered across her nose and cheeks, smiling shyly at the camera. They would not show what was happening inside, the feelings of anguish and fear, the awareness that there was no going back to a place of happiness, that all was changed. They would not show the shell of a human being, someone who was fragmented and who was struggling to survive. They would not show the inner strength or the reserves that we all have, that we must have, simply to go on.

My father had studied at Trinity College, and so had my brother Horace, and now it was my turn. I was given a room in Front Square and I settled into my small surroundings. I was eighteen years old and I had never been outside Kenya, and although my brother Horace had described the weather and the bustle of Dublin in great detail, I was not prepared for the reality, though part of that, I am sure, was to do with a general feeling of disorientation.

The trees in the square in front of my window were turning. There was a splash of reds and oranges and russets outside, and when I opened the window I could hear voices as students walked past or sat on the steps of my building.

There was a sound like a horse whinnying right outside my door. This did not seem very likely, and I forced myself away from the window to see what it was.

In the corridor was a tall girl with a grin on her face. She was laughing.

'Hi,' she said. 'I'm Daisy. I'm from Delaware.' She had a slightly long face, almost equine, but she looked friendly and welcoming.

It became apparent that the whinnying noise I had heard in the corridor was a sort of trademark of Daisy's, and I was soon able to identify whenever she was within fifty yards of me. But I'm being unkind. Her laugh still makes me smile, and I learned very quickly to love it, just as I learned to love her.

'I'm Helena.' I said almost tentatively, because I did not really feel like me.

'Hi, Helena. We share a kitchen,' Daisy said. 'Have you found it yet?' I shook my head. 'Come on, I'll show you.'

It transpired that on our small corridor there were three bedrooms, a bathroom and a kitchen. Daisy, unable to believe there was no fridge, had gone out and bought one. It left little room in the kitchen, but she had designated a shelf in it for each of us.

'Let me show you my room,' she said enthusiastically, and grabbing my arm, she pulled me with her. Her room was full of stuffed toys and scarves draped over door handles. Her bookshelves were full.

'Did you bring all of this with you from Delaware?' I asked, wondering how many cases she had brought with her and where she had stored them.

'No,' she said, 'I went shopping yesterday. Let me see your room.'

I was impressed at what she had managed to do since her arrival only a few days earlier. Not only had she managed to buy a fridge and have it delivered, but she had also managed to make her room look like she had been there for a year or longer.

I felt slightly embarrassed showing her my spartan room. All

4

I had were two suitcases, the contents of which fitted into the wardrobe and the drawers of my desk.

'Oh, hey!' she yelped. 'Your view is better than mine.' She stuck her head out the open window. 'Hey, Fred! Fred Wolff!'

I stood beside her looking down as a tall man with dark, brushed-back hair waved up at us with a tennis racquet. He was dressed in whites with a blue sweater tied across his shoulders.

'Hi, Daisy,' he called. He waved at us with the racquet again and jogged out of sight.

This was more like it. It was what Horace had described, feelings of camaraderie and jollity. I immediately admired Daisy. She said she had only arrived two days earlier, but already she had found her bearings and she knew the first person we saw through the window.

'He's in his final year,' she explained to me. 'He has rooms in the next building and is going to play tennis in Botany Bay. I think the Irish only get rooms in their final year, whereas we foreigners get them in our first to help us fit in.' She seemed older than me, not just more assured, but in other ways.

I had the feeling she would fit in anywhere. I also had the feeling that I was lucky to have her on my corridor. In those first five minutes with her, I had not once thought about the past, and that was encouraging.

'Are you in your first year?' I asked, slightly puzzled.

'No, I'm here just for the year, I'm doing a diploma,' she said. 'What about you? You're first year, right?'

I nodded.

'Come on,' Daisy said. 'I'll show you around.'

'I probably should get some food,' I said. I was tired from the journey and the unpacking, such as it was, and I really wanted to get into bed, but I knew that by the time I woke it would be dark and that I would be hungry.

'We'll stock up the fridge,' Daisy said. 'Then we'll make dinner and we can go to the Buttery for a drink.'

I remembered the Buttery from Horace's letters. Botany Bay was alien to me, though I did remember him saying that everything in Trinity had a name that identified a place, and so it was that I set off with Daisy to explore my new world, an autumnal world full of coloured trees and grey buildings and smiling students.

It was still daylight when we made it to the Buttery and I sipped a shandy while Daisy downed a pint of Guinness. Through the windows we could see Fred Wolff playing tennis as dusk began to fall.

This is Horace's world, I thought to myself, looking around at the gathering students and breathing in smoke and beer and laughter. Everyone seemed to know Daisy, and if they did not, she simply introduced herself, and me too. I had the feeling that we stood out in some way, the loud, laughing American and the quiet Kenyan with a slightly clipped accent.

Fred and his tennis partner came in and joined us and he slung his blue sweater over a chair. For some reason, that sweater stays clearly in my mind. It was so very blue and soft, and when it slipped to the floor I picked it up and put it back on his chair. He kept looking at me, and once he casually touched my arm while describing something, but I was so tired I could hardly take in his words.

'Helena plays tennis,' Daisy said to him. I had told her as much earlier. In fact, tennis was the only thing I was any good at; well, tennis, reading and thinking. That sort of summed me up.

'The bowerbird is blue, a deep, dark, magical blue,' I heard Horace's voice in my head coming from far away. I knew I must concentrate.

'Will you play with me tomorrow?' Fred asked me.

'I don't have a racquet,' I said by way of procrastination.

'I'll bring two,' he said.

He was lovely to look at, with his broad shoulders and his

strong, tanned arms. He had brown eyes and a grin, and I suddenly thought of Charlotte Brontë and a line from *Jane Eyre*: 'Reader, I married him.'

By now I was tired beyond reason and I felt slightly sick. I agreed to play, although I was not sure I really wanted to, and then I said that I had to go to bed.

'But it's only eight o'clock,' Daisy objected.

'Helena said she's been travelling since yesterday,' Fred said. 'Let me walk you back to your room,' he said to me. 'You probably still don't have your bearings.'

He was right about that. I was glazed with tiredness, having spent the previous night dozing fitfully while slumped on a seat in Heathrow Airport on my stopover. Fred slung his sweater over my shoulders as we made our way back to Front Square. I was too tired to talk, and at one point I stumbled on the cobblestones and he took my arm and steered me home.

Home? Yes, I already saw my room as home, a place that was mine, where I would sleep and read and find a way to live. Fred said goodnight to me, and it wasn't until I was in my room that I realised I still had his sweater around my shoulders. I buried my face in it and breathed it in. It smelled nice. It smelled of him. I folded it neatly and put it on a chair where I could see it while lying in my bed.

'The bowerbird is blue; a deep, dark, magical blue. He builds a bower to entice a mate. It's a sort of nest, only it's more like a lair than a nest. These bowers can be several feet across. Once he has finished building a suitably impressive bower, he starts collecting blue things. Blue plastic spoons, blue paper, blue foil, blue bottle tops, blue jewellery, blue feathers, blue clothes pegs, blue pen tops. The progress of civilisation has suited the bowerbird very well. Once he had to make do with feathers and flowers and things like that, but now there are all sorts of blue things out there if you know where to look. And bowerbirds spend most of their time learning where to look.

'Sometimes he will raid another bowerbird's bower and steal a blue object. Occasionally he even trashes another bird's bower if it looks too attractive. Eventually, when he has enough blue things to make a really impressive bower, he lays them all out on display in the hopes of attracting a mate. Come to me me me. It's your lucky day. Your search is over. I am the bowerbird you have been looking for.'

'How many things?'

'Blue things? Hundreds of them. Finding blue things is a full-time job. A bowerbird won't make do with a handful of blue things; he wants hundreds. He has to compete with all the other bowerbirds, you see. They get quite fanatical about their bowers. I read that if you wait for a bowerbird to leave its bower, and then you move one of his blue objects, he will always move it back to exactly where it was when he returns. Hundreds of blue things in there, and he knows where each one of them ought to be. Sometimes when a female approaches, the male will pick up one of his favourite blue objects to entice her in, and to present it to her as a gift. Amazing, isn't it?'

'Why do they like blue things so much?'

'I don't know. I don't think they know either. A bowerbird just knows that he's a failure if he doesn't have enough blue things in his bower. Success as a bowerbird means getting blue things for your bower, so that's what he does.'

'And he doesn't know why?'

'No, he doesn't know why. Animals don't know *why* anything.'

'Can I see this happening, Horace? I want to see a bower-bird.'

'No. Bowerbirds don't live here in Kenya, Helena. They

don't live anywhere in Africa. The world is a big place. Bower-birds haven't found their way here yet.'

'But I want to see one.'

'Don't be silly, Helena.'

'Maybe if we left lots of blue things around?'

As I fell asleep that night, I thought about Horace, and about the umbrella tree, and the sun long since set over the horizon beyond the farm. I thought of my father standing in the dark on the veranda and I wondered if my mother missed me. I slept the longest, deepest sleep I'd had in almost four months, and when I awoke to my new world I had the feeling I was being given a second chance.

When we were little, my mother used to read an eclectic variety of poems and stories to us. One of those poems was 'A Frog He Would A-wooing Go', a poem whose rhythm appealed to me. I am reminded it of it now when I think back to that heady first term in Trinity. I had gone with no expectations. It had been one of those things decreed at home in which I had no choice. I was allowed to choose my degree though, and I see now that my choice of Fine Arts and Italian was clearly an effort to get my mother's attention. At the time I just thought they were subjects that would interest me, and indeed they did.

Fred Wolff now wooed me, although at first I did not realise what was happening. I thought it was just my heart that beat faster in his company, and that it was just I who was afraid of doing or saying something foolish. Fred gave the impression of being completely in control.

Impressions can be deceptive, and that was something I was only beginning to learn.

My upbringing had been so isolated, so incredibly singular, that there were things of which I had no knowledge. In many ways, I was very naïve. Daisy told me later that I appeared completely at ease and very confident and that she envied me that, and all the while I envied her ability to chat to people and to fit in, and how she appeared to draw people towards her. In all my life, I had only ever chatted to my brother Horace.

Of course I had talked to my father and sometimes had faltering conversations with my mother, but that was the sum total of my ability to interact. On the rare occasions when my parents had visitors, I was briefly brought in to meet them, and I hovered, shifting from foot to foot, waiting until I could escape back outside.

When Horace and I were little, Kulu, who was one of the men on the farm, used to come with us when we went out on the horses. We were forbidden to leave the farm unaccompanied until Horace was twelve and could use a rifle. Until then, Kulu came with us wherever we went, but he seldom spoke to us other than to advise us of the time.

I was a year younger than Horace and completely under his spell. He was my friend and confidant, the person from whom I learned the most. I loved him with all my heart and I hung on his every word. Horace's main interest was animal behaviour. By default, so was mine. His pastimes were reading and tennis, and so were mine. When we weren't reading or talking under the umbrella tree with the farm below us, we were hammering a ball across a makeshift net on the dusty clay before the house.

Fred wooed me on the tennis court. When I won a game, he jumped over the net in an act of enthusiastic *bonhomie* to congratulate me.

'You're a good player, Helena,' he said.

I know I beamed in pleasure. I could hold my own against Horace, who occasionally had let me win. To win a game against Fred was an achievement, but his words were sincere and I knew that I was not letting myself down. At first I was embarrassed being out on the court, as it seemed so exposed to the windows around it, the rooms and the Buttery, and to the occasional student who stopped to watch. My tracksuit bottoms and T-shirt were old and no longer as white as they had once been, but I remembered Horace telling me in a letter that people didn't seem to worry about clothes and I told myself that it didn't matter. The important thing was that I would play my best, and I did.

Fred beat me easily. Much later he told me that he had thought of letting me win but knew that I would see through it and he wanted honesty between us. Honesty and openness were definitely two of his attributes. When we shook hands at the end of the game, which I had lost 6-1, 6-2, I felt quite exhilarated.

'Great stuff, Helena,' he said. 'Will you partner me in a mixed doubles on Saturday?'

Out loud I said, 'I would love to.' Inside my head I thought 'I would partner you to the ends of the earth.' I thought he was wonderful, which he was, but of course the truth was that I did not know many people, let alone individual men.

If I had difficulties during that first term in Trinity, they were not to do with meeting people and socialising, which is what I had feared the most. Between Daisy, Fred, lectures and seminars, I kept meeting people and I gave the impression of fitting in.

My problems were issues that I had not foreseen.

I loved getting books from the library and following my coursework, but I found it almost impossible to sit in the library to study or write essays. I tried reading while lying on the grass beneath my room, but the weather was chilly and of course I found it colder than most would. I missed the sun and the heat of Kenya; I missed the dry dust which the horses' hooves churned up as Horace and I rode out; I missed the gentle creak of my mother's rocking chair on the veranda as she sat and read under the canopy.

Most of all, I missed Horace and the seemingly endless days of childhood spent under the umbrella tree on that little hill beyond the farm. I even missed my father's study door, always closed, while he worked inside on his mathematics books.

I wrapped myself in a blanket and wrote my essays in front of my open window, a scarf around my neck and a glove on the hand that was not holding the pen. The sky was constantly changing, white clouds sometimes still, sometimes racing along in the wind; grey clouds rolling in and hovering before shifting to show tiny patches of blue that seemed high up and far away. It rained often, and, when it did, I wondered if it would ever stop. Sometimes it was a grey, misty haze, and other times it was heavy and relentless. It was cold and bleak.

As I struggled with the weather and a bit of claustrophobia, Daisy was struggling with the medical student who shared the kitchen with us.

Daisy's fridge was, after all, her fridge. I was delighted to have a shelf in it. It meant we always had fresh milk and our meagre store of food was kept chilled. The medical student, whose accent was so unfathomable that most of what she muttered made no sense to me, introduced herself to us as 'I'm a doctor.' That was in reply to our greetings of 'Hi, I'm Daisy' and 'Hello, I'm Helena.'

'Doctor', as we called her for the whole of that year, had some pretty odd notions of hygiene, even odder when one considered that she was, after all, a medical student. One would imagine that soap and water would play some role in her existence. Instead, Doctor never washed a dish, and kept some very odd things in Daisy's fridge.

The first time Daisy called me in to take a look at Doctor's shelf, I stood there with my mouth open.

'What are they?' I asked. They looked like specimen dishes with some pale orange fluid in them, but instead of lids they were draped with slices of bacon.

'I fear the worst,' Daisy said. I did too.

Daisy dealt with Doctor as best she could. The specimen dishes were banned from the fridge and Doctor refused to speak to either of us for about a week. I did not mind as I could not understand anything she said anyway. Our paths seldom overlapped, as Doctor worked nights in the hospital and then came home and drank.

Bearing in mind that I had only ever dealt with a few people in my life, and animals, I was unaware of how selfish human beings can be. Doctor's behaviour was atrocious. I left Daisy to deal with her, with the dirty dishes in the sink, the rowdiness from her room when she was not on duty, and the pile of empty bottles that built up in the kitchen.

While all of that was going on, I fell in love with Fred. I thought about him at all hours of the day, and in my dreams he sometimes appeared with Horace.

Autumn came to an end and the real biting cold kicked in. If I had found it chilly before, it was nothing to how it now was.

Daisy had found her way around Dublin with ease, whereas I would come out Front Gate and stand in panic looking up Dame Street and wondering which way to turn. She found this funny and often wondered what would happen if I went out by myself. I thought of buying a compass, but she reckoned a map would be a safer bet.

She took me to the Dandelion Market on St Stephen's Green, where I found a winter coat, furry and warm with the lining somewhat torn but not difficult to repair. She bought an afghan coat for herself and took me to Switzers, where she sprayed us both with perfume to douse the musty second-hand smell of our purchases, and I could not help but feel that we were like two strange animals in camouflage.

Routines evolved. I went to my lectures and my seminars, I picked up my books from the library and I studied in front of the window, though by now I had it closed. Daisy and I ate together most evenings and during the day we met up between lectures or during reading breaks for coffee in the Buttery, where Fred often found us. Like Daisy, he seemed to know everyone, and like Daisy, strangely, he seemed to enjoy my company.

'He likes you,' Daisy said to me one evening after we had returned to our rooms and were hovering outside our bedroom doors. Fred had walked us back and said goodnight to us on the steps, and we had gone upstairs and let ourselves into our tiny corridor.

'Really?' I asked hopefully. I wanted her to say more.

'The way he looks at you . . . ' she said.

My heart beat faster. 'Really?' I said again.

'How do you feel about him?' she asked curiously.

I had thought it was obvious. I had thought that I was wearing love on my sleeve. 'Can't you tell?' I asked her.

She looked at me carefully and then she said, 'You should let him see that you like him.'

That night I looked at myself in the mirror in the bathroom. I tried to see what he saw. I thought that the emotions inside must be showing, but it occurred to me that while my heart was thumping away in my chest, maybe my exterior was frozen. I cannot think of other words to describe it. I knew that I was caught in moments from the past that would not really go away. I could cover them up from time to time – more and more, in fact, as time went on – but they were there last thing at night and first thing in the morning.

The following day Fred tentatively said to me, 'I'm going up to visit my parents for Thanksgiving. My mother is American, you know.' No, I did not know. 'Would you like to come with me?'

I wanted to say, 'Yes, I'd love to,' but I thought of Daisy and that maybe she would be alone for Thanksgiving.

As if he were reading my mind, he said, 'Daisy has a date for

Thanksgiving, some invitation from friends of her parents at the embassy.'

'Then I'd love to,' I said. 'But would I not be intruding?'

'Not at all. My parents will be delighted.'

It transpired that Fred's mother had been a big tennis player in her day. She married Jackson Wolff having met him somewhere on the tennis circuit and they had come back to his family home in County Meath. Fred explained all of this to me as we drove up to Meath in his car later that week.

I was more than a little apprehensive. This was the first time Fred and I had really been alone, and we were about to face his family. I wondered if there were any implications, and also how they would react to me. I had no idea what to expect, as Fred was slightly vague about the whole set-up. We would have dinner, turkey and pumpkin pie, he had told me, and we would stay the night. I kept wondering what we would do and what we would talk about and if I would be able to find anything interesting to say.

I need not have worried.

Fred had got his charm from both his parents. Jackson Wolff was quite eccentric but clearly had a heart of gold. He had two passions in life. The first was six Mullingar heifers, which he watched adoringly while leaning on a fence. The second was his wife, Marjorie, whom he worshipped. Having shown me the Mullingar heifers, he promptly whisked me away to admire Marjorie's tennis trophies, all perfectly polished in custom-made glass cabinets.

'This one,' he used to say to some unsuspecting guest, and in this instance that guest was me, as he pointed to one or another of these silver monstrosities, which some poor housemaid cleaned and polished once a week under his supervision. 'This one was won in 1955. Four down in the third set. She inched back, every point a struggle . . . ' He paused for dramatic effect. 'And then she was five-four. She served two aces in succession, then she served long but her second serve was so short it only just popped over the net, taking her opponent by surprise. Forty-love. My God, it was touch and go. Her opponent . . . what was her name? I'm getting old, I can't remember. I recall her face. Square. Curly hair. Well, she managed to return the next serve and there was a rally of at least twenty shots back, forward, right, left . . . one ball clipped the net. I thought she wouldn't get to it. But she did. My God, she did. A flip of her wrist and a lob to die for; it looked like it was going out, but no, it landed in.'

It was exhausting following his tennis reports. He seemed to remember every game his wife had ever played. If I had not known anything about tennis I would have been totally bewildered; as it was, I struggled to keep up with his commentary.

Marjorie, as I was invited to address her, was tall and athletic and in her mid- to late-forties. She ruled the house much as my mother ruled ours, but in a more obvious way. She called the shots, so to speak, and she did it quite openly. The big surprise was that she was pregnant. She saw me looking at her stomach. I had not meant to stare; in fact I hoped I was not staring.

'Yes,' she said with a laugh, 'I'm pregnant, unless I'm harbouring a gigantic tennis ball.' She and Jackson both rocked with laughter and he put his arm around her shoulders.

'You didn't tell me your mother is expecting,' I said to Fred as he showed me to my room.

'I guess I'm still coming to terms with it,' he said ruefully. 'Having been the only begotten child for twenty-three years, it feels a little odd to find that I'm about to acquire a sibling.'

'I think it's quite exciting,' I said. I would have hated to have been an only child. No matter what had happened and no matter how I now felt, I could not imagine my childhood without Horace.

'Disconcerting is the word,' Fred said.

During those two days while Jackson entertained us with tennis stories and Marjorie prepared fantastic food and embraced me like a long-lost friend, Fred and I talked. I was drawn out in a way I had not expected.

Part of this was to do with Marjorie's questions. They were quite forthright. 'Where do you come from? What do your parents do?' she asked.

'I come from a farm in Kenya,' I said. I wanted to say, 'There is an acacia tree on a little hill beyond the farm, and I was brought up there with my brother Horace.' I wanted to say, 'When the sun goes down, there is a heavy glow and the sky seems to splinter with shots of light, and when the darkness comes the sky is sprinkled with stars.' But instead I politely explained the facts that would satisfy her.

'My father's family moved there early this century. He is a coffee farmer, but he has men to run the farm so that he can concentrate on the mathematics books that he writes. He is contracted to various publishing companies in several countries and he produces series of schoolbooks. My mother is Italian. She runs the house and reads a lot.'

'What language do you speak at home?' Marjorie asked.

'English mostly, but also Swahili and Italian.'

'Where did you go to school?' she asked.

'We were educated at home,' I said. 'Once my mother talked of sending me away to a boarding school, but my father overruled her,' I added.

'How intriguing,' Marjorie said. 'Did you have friends?'

'Well . . .' I hesitated. It was a bit difficult to describe the isolation of our situation and the fact that my mother wasn't too keen on other people. 'I had my horse, Tiger, and of course there were the dogs. And Luther.'

'Luther?'

'He's an elephant. My mother found him the year I was born.

A baby elephant back then,' I explained. 'He had been abandoned, which is not what elephants usually do, but there had been a drought and my father said his mother probably died and the herd couldn't care for him. There was probably no choice. Anyway, my mother found him and brought him home.'

I had no idea they would find that so interesting, but they did. Later Fred said to me, 'You never fail to surprise me. Anyone else would have long since said they were raised with an elephant.'

I laughed. It had been surprising, and gratifying, that they were so interested. Luther was as much a part of my life as anything or anyone had been. I had never known anything else.

'Are you going back to Kenya for Christmas?' asked Marjorie.

I shook my head. There had been no suggestion from my parents that I would or should. 'No,' I said, suddenly hesitant as I thought of the loneliness of my room when everyone else would be gone.

'Great,' Marjorie said. 'You will come to us.' She smiled at me. 'It won't be the same as being at home, I know that, but we'll give you as good a time as we can.'

Such kindness, such generosity, such acceptance. I was grateful.

Their house was very warm; Marjorie liked to keep it at Florida-style temperatures. I had the bedroom window open, and in the morning, looking out, I could see Jackson standing with his arm around Fred's shoulders. His voice drifted up.

'Game, set and match, son.'

For a moment I wondered what they meant.

Two

I worked out a number of things during that visit and the drive back to Dublin.

Fred valued his parents' opinion and approval above almost everything else. His relationship with them was very important. He talked to them about things in a way that I had never done with my parents, but then, of course, I had had Horace.

He was also a person who liked individual company rather than large groups. I was aware that people liked him and he had no problem in holding forth in a group. He was like Daisy in that regard, but I knew that given the choice he would sit and talk with one person, and more often than not that person was me.

Fred held my hand in the car on the way back. At first it was a light touch, but I opened my hand and he grasped it. Keeping his eyes on the road, he brought it to his lips. I looked at him, then he turned his head and our eyes met. Neither of us said anything. He smiled at me before looking back at the road. We drove in silence for the next fifteen minutes or so, until he suddenly pulled the car over and stopped.

'I can't wait until we get back to Trinity,' he said. And he kissed me.

My first kiss. Ever. I almost swooned. I felt myself melting in his arms. After he kissed me, he held me. It was awkward in the car, with him caught behind the steering wheel and I, somewhat twisted around, in the passenger seat. I could feel his cheek on my forehead and his arms around me and I thought that any discomfort I felt was worth this sensation.

Daisy took one look at my face when I got back and whinnied. She hugged me and danced with me around the kitchen, in so far as we could because of the fridge, while all I really wanted was to go to my room and think. My mind was in a riot of disarray. I wanted to think about Fred's kisses, and I wanted to think about how I felt, because I did feel. I actually felt a real emotion. Happiness.

'You look alive,' Daisy said gleefully.

My ice maiden. That was what Fred had said to me in the car. I wondered again how I really appeared. I had no notion. If I was as frozen as I had felt, and had obviously appeared, why did they want to be my friends? I tried asking Daisy that and she brushed it aside. 'You're lovely,' she said. 'You're funny and you're kind.'

I was on the road to some kind of recovery. I even managed to write to my parents.

> *Dear Papa, Dear Mama,*
> *I am getting on fine, good marks for my essays, and enjoying my work. I'm spending Christmas with friends. I miss you. Tell Kulu he would hate the weather . . .*

I would have liked to have mentioned Horace in my letter, but I really did not know how. His name had become silent.

'Animals always love their children, don't they, Horace?'

'Usually they do.'

'Are there any that don't?'

'They are all different. Did I ever tell you about giant African bullfrogs?'

'No. How giant are they?'

'They aren't all that big, just giant compared to other frogs. This big,' he indicated with his hands.

'The female lays her eggs in a tiny pool near the river. The eggs are very fragile, and something might come along and eat them, so she doesn't want to lay them in the river. But then, after laying her eggs, she deserts them.'

'Why does she do that? She should stay there with them, they might need her.'

'Like I said, not all animals are very good parents. But bullfrogs are one of the strangest. After the female has gone, the male stays around, watching the pool with the eggs in it. In time, the eggs hatch into tadpoles. You know what they are? But the hot sun starts drying out the pool of water the tadpoles are in, so there is less and less water. If the tadpoles don't get into the river quickly, they will die because the water disappears.'

'How do they get out of their pool?'

'They can't. But then an amazing thing happens. The male frog—'

'Their dad?'

'Yes, their dad, he can see what is happening, and he can see they are drying out. He goes to the river, and he starts digging a channel so it will join up the river and the pool.'

'How can a frog dig anything?'

'They dig with their back legs, kicking the hard earth out of the way. Time is against him. He has to dig very quickly, because if he doesn't his tadpoles will die. Somehow he manages to splash water from the river onto the hard earth, and then kick it away, forming a channel. When the tadpoles have just moments left to live, he gets the last of the earth out of the way, and they all flow into the river.'

'Where they will turn into frogs?'

'Yes. Well, some of them will. Isn't it amazing? If he starts digging his channel too early, the tadpoles will be too small when they go into the river and something will eat them. But if he leaves it too late, they will run out of water. He always knows just when to start.'

'Where is their mother?'

'She doesn't wait around for that part of the process.'

'Well, she should. She could help dig the tadpoles out of there.'

'Different animals have different ways of dealing with their young. It's because of variety. Do you know how a llama is born?'

'No. I saw Tiger being born. Remember? It was scary.'

'When a llama is born, they just sort of plop out of their mother, and then run off, just like that. They land on their feet—'

'On their hooves?'

'Yes, on their hooves, and they just run off.'

'But they wouldn't know how to run.'

'Llamas do. Horses don't. Horses take a bit longer learning how to stand up, and how to walk, then how to run. Llamas just instinctively know how to do it. They don't need their mothers to show them how to do it, they just know.'

'What animal spends the most time with their mothers learning things like that?'

'Elephants and humans . . . '

I had wanted my mother. I had loved her when I was little. I needed her attention, but I never seemed to get it. Frogspawn may get along fine without their mothers, but then, frogs never knew they had one and had lost her. Llamas know their mothers, but don't seem to need them much.

But what about me? I knew my mother, and I needed her, and I felt she did not love me. Whatever feelings she may have had for me, they were surely gone now. I rebuilt my life with reading and essays, with Fred's growing love and with Daisy's laughter and fun. I began to see my new existence as a form of therapy, and the longer I lived it, the more I would become this other person, one who could give and receive love, who could find fulfilment in some way she had not expected, and who could give and receive happiness.

Fred slipped into my room late that night when the university had quietened. He had thrown pebbles at my window to attract my attention. I had been sitting up in bed reading about the Renaissance; Fine Arts and Italian were two subjects that overlapped beautifully. I was startled by the pebbles on the glass and got out of bed and peered out from the side of the curtain, not sure what to expect.

Earlier we had been drinking in the Buttery with Daisy and he had been open in his affection for me in front of her and the others who were with us. I had been both pleased and embarrassed. I believe it was the first public display of affection that had ever come my way and I wanted to get under the table and hide, but I knew that I must try to behave as he was, at ease with our situation and with each other. When Daisy and I were leaving he had whispered to me that he would see me later, but I had not thought he had meant at this time.

We did not make love that night. We lay in my narrow bed, sharing my single pillow with the blankets barely covering us. I lay in his arms and we talked. I could feel his need for me and I was nervous, but he said, 'There is no rush, Helena. I am in no hurry.'

He told me more about his home life, the constancy of tennis in his family, the endless pushing to turn him into a tennis star long after he knew he had neither the talent nor the ambition. He told me of his struggle to be allowed to go to Trinity to study and not to be sent back to Florida for more tennis. He told me he had been christened Fred Perry Wolff. 'That says it all, doesn't it?' he said to me.

Yes. It did.

And just as he opened the door for me into his life, I tried really hard to do the same. For my part I told him a bit of my past

– of the sounds of home, of the creak and the click of the ceiling fans, of the generator that broke down from time to time, my tennis playing, such as it was, and my love for my horse, Tiger. I told him as much as I was able to and I fell asleep in his arms. I woke before him, listening to his even breathing, and as daylight came I could see his dark hair on the pillow. I was so grateful. I had no idea what would happen to us, but I promised myself never to hurt him. I promised myself to learn from everything I had experienced and to try to take the positive and to carry it with me.

It would be wrong for me to say that I did not know what love was. I did. I had seen it in many different ways; the love between my parents, the love Horace and I had shared, the love I had seen between Fred's parents, the love Kulu had for his children, the eternal bond that Luther had with my family. I would find and hold the best bits of all of that, and as long as Fred wanted me, I would give him love.

Fred was full of surprises. It was not just the Thanksgiving dinner; it was everything that followed. It was as though we had bonded and I had no idea how it had happened. Our relationship evolved over the coming weeks. He liked studying in the stacks beneath the 1937 Reading Room and asked me if I would work there too.

I tried, but I needed windows, air and space and with regret I had to tell him that I preferred being above ground. I should have been more honest and explained that I did not like being inside a library at all, other than to fetch books, because he promptly moved his study place to upstairs on the gallery, and I felt obliged to try to work beside him there. I stuck at it for a week, fidgeting beside him as he read and wrote, until eventually I told him that I preferred to sit at the window in my room.

'You should have said. I did not mean to push you into the library. I hadn't realised. I'm sorry.'

'Please don't be sorry. It's me and my problem,' I said to him.

'But it's not a problem,' he said. 'If that's where you work best, that's where you should be.'

He was like that, understanding, kindly and supportive. So we studied apart and I think we both benefitted from that. We met between lectures, drank coffee in the Buttery, shared a slice of chocolate biscuit cake, then went to study separately. Sometimes in the afternoons we walked up Grafton Street to Bewleys and sat and drank lemon tea amid the clatter and the buzz. He said he had never worked so hard or so satisfactorily and loved when the day was done and the library closed and we met up again.

I thought about him all the time when I wasn't studying. I couldn't wait to see him when we were apart, and when we were together we were comfortable with each other, looking out for each other, in some ways absorbed in each other.

'I have never felt like this before,' he said to me with his arms around me as we stood looking out my window. My heart ached with love.

I spent Christmas with his family. Daisy was there too. It was wonderful fun, with a Christmas tree and crackers and a sprinkling of snow outside on the ground. Marjorie, who had been vague about her due date, went into labour the following day while stacking the dishwasher.

'Dammit,' she said. 'I should have done this last night.'

Daisy and I were washing and drying the glasses. 'What's up?' Daisy asked.

'Better get me to hospital,' Marjorie said.

Fred's brother Freyn was born that night. He weighed over twelve pounds and the hospital said they had never seen such a child.

Jackson was ecstatic and moved into the hospital to be with Marjorie, while Fred, Daisy and I scraped up what snow there was and threw snowballs at each other.

'Will you marry me?' Fred asked me as we raced across the snow-covered tennis court with Daisy chasing us and the

Mullingar heifers staring at us through the half-open barn door.

I was not sure if I had heard him right. I stopped and looked at him as Daisy's snowball hit me on the head.

'You will, won't you?'

'Yes,' I said. 'Yes, yes, of course I will.'

I thought he was going to cry. He looked overcome with emotion, this giant of a man with his dark hair and his handsome face. 'I love you,' he said.

'I love you too,' I whispered. He picked me up in his arms and swung me around.

Daisy stopped beside us. 'What's happened?' she asked.

'Helena is going to marry me,' Fred said.

She roared with laughter and hugged us both.

'Good,' she said. 'If ever two people should be together, it's you two.'

Jackson and Marjorie were equally delighted. Marjorie was home from the hospital within two days and she took me aside. 'I am so pleased,' she said. 'I know you are young, but you make my Fred happy. That is all a mother can ask.'

I wondered if it was. I had no idea. I was amazed that they accepted me so easily. I was nervous thinking about my own parents and whether there would be any reply to this new development in my life. I postponed telling them and decided to put it on hold until Easter.

I received one postcard from them in my father's cryptic script.

> *Good to hear study is going well. All is well here, quiet*
> *but well. No sign of Luther. Your Father*

Do I need to add anything to that? Do I need to say how I felt?

Fred, as I said, was full of surprises. I had no idea how to make plans. Until I had come to Trinity, my life had followed a particular pattern of doing more or less what was expected of me. I let Fred take the lead in our relationship.

'Let's talk plans,' he said to me back in Dublin a few days later. 'Come, let's go for a walk.'

It was the last day of the year, a clear December day, by which I mean no wind or rain, although it was already dark in the early afternoon. We wandered up Grafton Street, hand in hand. We stopped for coffee in Bewleys, and then he took me around the corner to a jewellery shop and showed me a ring he had picked out for me.

'Do you like it?' he asked.

Like it? I loved it. I loved its simplicity, its tiny stone and its slim band, and most of all the fact that he had come and chosen it. When he slipped it onto my finger I could barely speak for emotion. I had only known him for three months, but already I could not imagine my life without him.

'Thank you,' I whispered. I did not want to put my gloves back on, but it was too cold outside and Fred insisted.

We walked up to St Stephen's Green with the cold stinging my cheeks. I had one of my hands in his hand inside his coat pocket. He did things like that. He didn't care about what people thought; he was just himself. I got that feeling that I had sometimes had since leaving home, of being transported and being someone completely different. I felt I bore no resemblance to the girl I had been. There was something strange about being this man's betrothed, with his ring on my finger, and my hand in his pocket, and our hips bumping together as we walked along. He was a good bit taller than me, and every so often he would stop and lower his head so that he could kiss me.

'I had a godfather,' he told me. We were by the pond now in St Stephen's Green, and he dug in his other pocket and pulled out a bag of bread. We stood there in the biting cold and fed the ducks. 'He died about five years ago and he left me quite a lot of money.

My parents suggested at the time that I buy some land with it and build a house.'

'Oh,' I said. 'I see.' I had no money. I had nothing.

'They really wanted me to buy somewhere close to them, but while I wanted to live in the country rather than the city, I thought it would be better to be a couple of counties away; mutual space, that kind of thing.'

'I see,' I said again.

'Anyway, two years ago Dad helped me buy some land in County Wicklow. Not much, mind you, about half an acre. I got it at a good price because of some problem that had arisen with boundaries or something. And an American friend of my mother's who is an architect designed a house and it will be finished soon. It has a nice garden and a great view, and I think we should move there when this academic year is over. I'll have my degree, I hope, and you will be out of rooms anyway.'

I had wondered what to do about the coming year. Daisy was going back to the States and I needed to find somewhere to live. I had put it on hold, knowing that I could deal with it in June, after exams.

'So, we finish up in June, get married and move into the Wicklow house,' Fred said. 'What do you think?'

'It sounds great,' I said. 'Um, Fred? Where is Wicklow?'

He laughed. 'Sorry. It's a county just south of Dublin. We can commute to Dublin fairly easily. You'll get on with your degree and I will work my ass off to support you in a lifestyle to which I hope you'll become accustomed.'

'I have an allowance from my father,' I said. 'It covers my rooms, fees and living expenses, although there isn't much left over.'

'That's okay. We will only have a bit of a mortgage. I'll get work. Dad has interviews lined up for me for June. We'll be fine.'

I had this feeling of being swept along by a tide, caught in a current that was bringing me farther and farther away from my roots. Before I make it sound like I had no choice, I did, even if I could not see what that choice might be. But I loved this man. And I loved his love for me, and I was content to fit into his life and to let him map out mine.

The next Sunday we drove down to County Wicklow. I was not sure what to expect, as Fred had emphasised the American nature of the architecture and I kept thinking of the White House or a skyscraper, which were the only two American edifices that sprang to mind.

As we drove south, the Wicklow Mountains came into view and then we turned off and passed through Enniskerry, a sleepy, picturesque village with a particular charm and sloping roads. A few miles later, Fred turned the car into a leafy laneway where the land was flat although the mountains rose in the visible distance on higher ground.

Our house, as I now began to see it, was the first on this laneway. The gateway had no gates as yet, and Fred drove us in, going slowly up the short driveway so that I could take in our new home.

The house was long and low and had a style of its own. We drove in, down a slope, so that the car was parked beneath it. It had two storeys; this basement, in which we were now parked and which consisted of a drive-in garage, a laundry room and a decent-sized games room, and the ground floor, which comprised a family kitchen, an open-plan living and dining area, three bedrooms and a bathroom. There was a front door, but I could see that we were more often than not going to enter the house through the basement, with its winding staircase up to the ground level.

'We could use one bedroom as a study,' Fred said as he showed me around.

'We could use two as studies,' I said.

He stopped and looked at me. 'What's wrong?' I asked.

'Helena, we haven't discussed this . . . but do you want children?'

'Yes,' I reassured him. 'I was joking about the rooms.'

In truth, I was in no rush to have children. Yes, I probably did want to have one, or maybe two, but I wasn't sure, not yet. I had not really thought about it. I was not lying to Fred by so readily agreeing because I knew already that I would do whatever he wanted.

'We'll wait until you've finished your degree,' he said.

'I don't know that I want to. Finish my degree, I mean.'

'What? I thought you were really enjoying it.'

'It's not that. I do love it, it's just that we will probably need two salaries to support us and I don't know if my father will go on supporting me if I get married.'

'I hadn't thought of that,' Fred said. 'Have you asked him?'

I shook my head. It was time to come clean. 'I haven't actually told them that we're getting married,' I admitted.

Fred stopped in his tracks. 'Why ever not?'

'It just didn't seem like the right time,' I said slowly. It was difficult to explain. The shortness of my father's one postcard, the silence from my mother since I had come to Dublin; I simply could not bear any more rejection and I did not know how to tell him.

Fred looked at my face thoughtfully and then said, 'Let's look around the rest of the house so that you get your bearings. It's all very empty and cold right now. We'll look around and then go and sit in the car or find somewhere warm where we can talk.'

I nodded and followed him through the open-plan living and dining room, and into the very bare kitchen.

'I have to choose a kitchen. No, we have to choose a kitchen. I have brochures I'll show you later. Come,' he said and opened the kitchen door, which led on to a wooden terrace that stretched across the length of the back of the house.

'It's wonderful,' I said.

'My mother said we had to have a deck. With good weather, it will be like another room.'

'Like a ship,' I said with excitement.

We looked down over the garden. To the left, we could see the Sugar Loaf Mountain rising majestically into the sky. Beyond our house was a field. 'There's a river down there,' Fred said. 'Let's imagine warm summer days with our feet in the water.' He hugged me. By now I was shivering in the cold and he put his arm around me and we went back into the house. We spent another five minutes going from room to room before going back down the staircase to the garage and the car.

'It's wonderful,' I said, wondering if I had already said that. 'I love it.'

He seemed relieved. 'There's a hotel in Enniskerry, the Powerscourt Arms, we'll go there for a drink and warm up. There's an open fire and I think that's what we both need right now.' He was right.

'My parents are old-fashioned,' I said as we thawed out before the fire.

'And you think they'll want me to support you once we're married?' he asked.

I kept thinking of how open he always was with me. I knew that I needed to be more like him, but it was so difficult to put it all into words. 'It's partly that,' I said. 'And anyway, I'm happy to get a job so that we can be together . . . ' I hesitated.

'Please continue,' he urged. 'You said "it's partly that". What else is it?'

I was afraid. If your own mother can't love you, how can you expect someone else to? I think I feared that if I put it into words, he would stop loving me.

'They haven't really communicated with me since I left,' I said.

'But they wanted you to come to Dublin, you told me that,' he said, puzzled.

'Yes, it was their idea. My father had studied in Trinity, and it was always their plan for me and Horace,' I said.

'I see,' he said thoughtfully. 'Look, I don't want to diddle either you or your parents out of your education. We could postpone our wedding until you've finished. Or you could tell them and see what happens. We'll get by either way. What's the worst that could happen?'

The worst that could happen was that they would not reply, but I could not bring myself to tell him that.

'I think you should write to them. Tell them we are planning on getting married but that you hope to finish your degree. Be frank with them. At least you will know where you stand, and they can make plans to come for our wedding. Will we get married here? Or maybe you would prefer to get married in Kenya?'

He made it sound so reasonable, but then, he had no idea what rejection was really like. 'Here,' I said.

I wrote to my parents that night, simply because Fred made me promise that I would. I told them about him and our plans, about my concerns over whether or not I could continue at Trinity, and asking them for advice. In truth, I did not expect to hear back.

Dear Helena,

Your mother and I were surprised to hear your news. Obviously we are happy for you if you feel it is the right thing to do. We had always planned on paying for your education and will see that through regardless of when you decide to marry. The money will continue to be transferred to your bank account in Dublin until such time as you complete your degree.

As you know, your mother does not like to travel so I am afraid we will not be able to attend your wedding. If there is something in particular you would like as a wedding gift, please let me know and I will send you the money to purchase it.

We are quiet here.

Always,

Your Father

I did not ask them for a wedding present. I wrote back thanking them and saying that I would marry in early July and would continue my studies until I had my degree.

Daisy gave us her fridge as a wedding present. She was my witness at our small wedding, which comprised only Jackson, Marjorie and a sleeping baby Freyn, Fred, Daisy and me. We married on a Saturday morning with the sun shining. Fred wore a blue suit with a bright blue tie and I wore a white Indian cotton dress that Daisy helped me choose in the Dandelion Market. We married in the chapel in Trinity and I felt a true sense of belonging.

'I do, I do,' we said. 'To love and to cherish . . . to honour and to hold all the days of our lives . . . till death do us part . . . ' Such a cruel phrase.

We came out the doors and into Front Square and people stopped and clapped. Jackson and Marjorie hugged me, and Fred kept his arm around my waist. The hands of the clock above Front Gate met at twelve and I tried not to think of time.

Daisy left that evening and we drove her to the airport. She and I held each other as Fred took her bags from the car.

'Write to me, Mrs Wolff,' she said.

'I will. You do too.'

'Have a wonderful life,' she said to us. And then she was gone. I hate goodbyes. Once, I saw them as a doorway; a space you went through, and through which you would return. A bit like Luther

33

when we thought we had said goodbye to him, but he came back. Back then, I saw goodbyes as a blip before reconnecting. Beyond the goodbye was the expectation of some fulfilment or discovery. But I did not think that way any more. Now goodbyes had a terrible finality to them.

Three

Fred and I began our married life spending a luxurious and unlikely night in the Shelbourne Hotel, paid for by my new parents-in-law. I was nineteen years old, and I kept having this feeling that I might wake up and find that I was either back at home with Horace and Luther, or that I would find myself in my rooms in Trinity.

Instead, Fred and I had dinner in Captain Americas before retiring to the hotel and our bedroom, with its view of St Stephen's Green on a warm summer night.

Fred was more romantic than I was. By that I mean that I was not sure how to behave other than from the books I had read and my limited observations of romance, whereas he took my hand and looked into my eyes and said things like, 'I'm the luckiest man alive.' I wanted to behave romantically, but it did not come naturally.

I had no idea if I was supposed to respond similarly. For me to feel that I was lucky to have been brought up on a remote farm with a brother and an elephant for company might well not match up with someone else's notion of luck. The truth is, I did think I was lucky. I thought I had always been pretty lucky – on the whole, that is. I knew I was lucky now to have this man's love, to be sitting across a table from him with a small candle flickering and his handsome face looking into mine. But I sometimes did not have the words to respond to Fred's affection.

'Tell me you feel lucky too,' he said as he kissed my hand.

'So lucky,' I replied. I could feel he wanted more. 'I love you.'

He smiled at me. 'I know,' he said.

I wondered how he knew. But he was right. I did love him, and I was glad we were married, and I was looking forward to starting our life together.

We had breakfast in our hotel bed. I had never had breakfast in bed in my life before that morning and it struck me as being a rather uncomfortable event, because after we had finished, Fred and I made love and I felt every crumb from the toast caught in the sheets.

'Let's do this every week,' he said.

'What? Make love?'

'No, silly, we'll do that every day. I meant have breakfast in bed, lie in and just hold each other.'

'Yes,' I said. 'We must do that.'

I decided I liked the idea of it more than the actuality, but I did not want to ruin the moment.

Our one-night honeymoon was perfect and then we moved to our new home in County Wicklow. Daisy's fridge had gone ahead of us, and I had packed my two bags of clothing and would collect them and my books from Trinity the following day.

Sometime during the course of our one-night honeymoon, Fred started peppering our conversation with tennis scores. Over dinner while we were talking, he said 'fifteen-love' if he felt he had scored a point, 'fifteen-all' when I balanced it, and so on. Where someone else might have said 'touché', he said 'deuce'. It was something I had occasionally heard his parents doing and it had struck me as being a little eccentric, but suddenly I was doing it too, not because I thought it was funny or interesting, but because I did not know how to tell him not to do it. I wanted to be cheery and encouraging and what better way than to fall into his way of speech and to give him the repartee he enjoyed? Like many little things, it began to form a pattern, a way we spoke to each other when no one else was around.

'Fifteen-love,' he said when he put me down in the hall of our new home, having carried me over the threshold.

'You get a score because you could carry me?' I asked.

'No, because I've finally got you here in our home, all to myself,' he chuckled happily.

'Fifteen-all then,' I said. 'I score on that one too.'

Our home was perfect. Everything was so new and clean and neat. We stored our things, bought equipment for the kitchen, made up our new bed, showered in our new bathroom and basked in each other's company for three short and happy days.

Then Fred went to work.

He had landed a job as a junior sports journalist with a newspaper. I spent that summer making our home just the way we wanted it. I took pleasure in little things, like putting our socks and underwear into drawers, hanging up my few items, changing the bedclothes. Some days I dropped Fred to the railway station and he commuted by train, other days he took the car and I was housebound.

I had time on my hands again. It reminded me of the period just prior to my arrival in Dublin. Having done my daily chores, there was this feeling of empty time and I knew from my experience of the last year that being occupied was the only way for me to cope. I missed Fred during the daytime, but I also missed Daisy. She was the first friend I had ever made. I used some of that summer to read in advance of my next year in university. I did not want to be just waiting for Fred's return every day, so once a week I travelled with him in the car to Dublin and borrowed books from the library.

From the wooden deck at the back of the house, I could see into our neighbours' garden. Fred had told me that the house was owned by Joe Martin, a successful barrister, known among his colleagues as both the wizard and the magician. He had married Carolina dei Fiori, whose father was the Count dei Fiori.

Obviously I was unacquainted with anyone who might move in high society, but I had come across Carolina dei Fiori's name and photograph earlier in the year while I was at the dentist. I had been leafing through a magazine and had seen her picture and something about her had caught my attention. I remember looking at the date on the magazine and seeing it was almost two years old, and I had admired the wedding dress she was wearing, which was a far cry from the simple dress I subsequently wore on my wedding day.

It was clear, even to me with my limited knowledge of architecture, that our architect had based the design for our house on our neighbours', but he had added to it, or perhaps architecturally he had subtracted from it, by a form of simplicity.

Later I could see there were internal similarities too, but the Martins' house, in its larger grounds, gave a more sprawling impression as numerous playrooms were added on at the side. Their basement, in contrast to the large games room that we had, was divided into a number of separate rooms with a bathroom. Their house had an extra storey to it, but the tall trees that surrounded it kept it partially hidden from the road. Sitting on the deck in the afternoon sun, I sometimes saw a tall, thin, elderly man pottering in their garden among their plum trees. He was often accompanied by a woman of ample girth and a baby in a pram.

Their story was an intriguing one, which I later learned in some depth. The elderly man was a count, the Count dei Fiori, and he had fled Italy at the end of the war with the downfall, or more precisely, the stringing-up, of Mussolini. The world as the Count had come to know it had fallen apart. It was no easy thing to come to realise that everything you knew, or everything you thought you knew, was being rejected. His ideology, if that is the word for it, had been torn apart, and he found himself having to deal with a new world, on new terms.

In the circumstances of his undignified exodus from Florence, he was forced to leave rather abruptly, bringing with him only the essentials – his name, the clothes he stood in and Alessia, his cook. They escaped on a motorbike with a sidecar.

Before the outbreak of the war, his money had been buried in a variety of different bank accounts, most of them in Switzerland, in case of this very eventuality. This ensured that the apparently destitute man who arrived in Dublin in the fifties was due to enjoy a prompt change of fortune.

Along the way he met a girl and they had a child. The girl's subsequent disappearance left the now-ageing Count to raise the baby, Carolina, alone. He called Carolina his contessa. The name stuck, so much so that by the time she married Joe, some twenty-three years later, all her friends knew her as Contessa, or Conti for short.

Conti quickly became accustomed to a life of luxury. She was brought up with love and attention lavished on her, taught to speak fluent Italian at home and English at school, and generally wanted for nothing. Despite her enviable financial position, Conti had a job working for a fine arts catalogue. This gave her an outlet for socialising and provided respite from her somewhat fairytale home life. She lived with her father and the cook in a grand old house in the most affluent part of Dublin Four.

She met Joe while working in the same building where his law office was situated. A drunken Christmas party that overlapped from one floor to the next begat an unfortunate incident involving a video camera and the unconventional use of a photocopier, long before such usage became a cliché. Conti was rather avant-garde and pioneering in this respect, and in many others.

A series of disturbing memories the following morning found Conti, who was sporting the kind of headache you can only get by mixing whiskey with brandy, making her way uneasily up to the law firm's office in a valiant effort to find and destroy any incriminating evidence. She was greeted by Joe Martin, who was sitting at his desk, watching exhibit A, with his head on one side and a surprised look on his face.

'Oh.' Conti, horrified, stared at the screen.

'I wonder who that is,' Joe said, somewhat bemused.

It was then that Conti realised she was, for some unknown reason and completely outside her memory, wearing a mask on her face in the video.

There was a God all right, she thought, and He was obviously fond of her.

'It's a girl from downstairs,' Conti said. 'I can't tell you who because I'm sworn to secrecy.' Conti tapped the side of her nose in a flirtatious, conspiratorial way, or as near to that as she could muster under the circumstances. 'I promised her I'd retrieve it. May I?' She deftly removed the cassette out of the video recorder before Joe could say or do anything.

'Joe Martin,' he said by way of introduction.

Not every man who has, to all intents and purposes, just been discovered by an attractive young woman watching a particularly sleazy porn film would confidently stand up and introduce himself, or at least not with his real name. But Joe Martin was made of stern stuff. Years of legal training had resulted in a man very sure of his ground, and who, if startled, would never show it.

Conti already knew that. Everyone in the building knew Joe, if only by reputation. He was an arresting man, good looking with his dark hair swept back from his clean-shaven face. He stood to shake her hand.

'Carolina dei Fiori,' she replied. 'My friends call me Conti.'

Joe took Conti to lunch in a restaurant around the corner. He bought her a large bouquet of flowers later that afternoon and had them delivered to her office.

The fine arts cataloguing publishers, Conti's employers, had on their premises that particular day a very valuable sixteenth century vase. It was there to be photographed for an auction catalogue. Conti's boss, enchanted by the bouquet of flowers, arranged them in the vase for the photograph. Conti, returning to the office from one of her many coffee breaks, found the flowers in the vase and a card propped up in front of them: *'Lunch was magic. You are magic. Dine with me tomorrow.'* Misunderstanding, a delighted Conti took the flowers and the vase home.

'Bellissima,' said the Count in delight as he studied the vase, giving his seal of approval.

That Conti still lived at home with her father often came as a surprise to those who discovered it, but as she said, 'Why would I move out? This way I have all the comforts of my childhood and as much freedom as I want.' She could wrap the Count around her finger, and, indeed, she had been perfecting this very art since the day she was born and now had it down to a tee. For his part, the Count indulged her in every way imaginable. No man had yet lived up to him in her eyes. This time, it was different.

Six months later, Joe and Conti married and the vase was never returned.

Joe bought the first house to be built on our lane in County Wicklow, and it was here that the now-elderly Count moved with his daughter. The Count's marginally younger cook came with him, and Joe feared that he might be expected to carry all three across the threshold.

'Don't be silly, dear,' Conti had said to him with a confident shake of her streak-blonde head and her perfectly poised neck. 'It's me you're marrying, not Babbo or Alessia.'

Joe was not completely confident of the truth of this statement, considering that 'Babbo', as Conti lovingly called her father, had accompanied Conti on most of her dates. This did not make things any easier for Joe and Conti, and their 'working lunches' had a much more romantic atmosphere to them than the official dates that the Count accompanied them on, as possibly the strangest gooseberry in the history of unwanted guests on dates.

It was evident to Joe from an early stage that the ageing Count was besotted with his only daughter, and that his appropriateness as a suitor was constantly being sized up by the old man. At one point, on an unofficial date at lunchtime, Joe had joked to Conti that if he ever did anything to upset her, the chances were that he would be gunned down in a mysterious, unexplained drive-by shooting. If he were lucky. If not, perhaps a gruesome garrotting in a café, while the other patrons just continued with their drinks as if nothing ever happened . . . Joe had not just read but also taken on board every message from *The Godfather*.

'Or maybe just poisoned by Alessia,' Conti said, laughing.

For Joe, there was, disturbingly, a hint of possibility to this. On his visits to the Count's house he had found Babbo himself to be very welcoming, in an Italian sort of way. Joe knew from the Mafia movies, and from the antics of some of his clients, that in one scene they hug them, and in the next scene they 'whack' them. In fact, the more enthusiastic the embrace, the more gruesome the subsequent 'taking care of' tended to be. He was only too aware that he was stereotyping his father-in-law-to-be, but there was something about the Count and his protective behaviour towards Conti that slightly unnerved Joe.

Alessia had given him the impression of being both menacing and powerful in her own way. No doubt about it, she loathed him. This had the potential to throw a sizeable spanner into the works of his honourable intentions towards Conti. It was Alessia who lovingly prepared all the meals in the house, who tucked the Count's napkin on his lap or into his shirt collar, who hovered until he tasted the dishes she had prepared, and who pretty much held the place together. The menacing glances she threw Joe's way might germinate into a disapproving comment to the Count, who might then veto the forthcoming marriage.

'Don't worry about Alessia,' Conti had said to him when he mentioned this. 'I'm sure she doesn't hate you. She's just very protective of Babbo and me.'

A couple of weeks later, when it had become apparent that Conti was either coming into his life as one third of an unholy trinity or not at all, Joe tactfully tried again.

'I really don't think Alessia likes me,' he said.

'Oh no, she loves you.'

'I'm not so sure that she does,' Joe persisted.

'She's probably afraid of being separated from Babbo and me. After all, she has been with us – well, with Babbo – all her life. She's uncertain about what's going to happen, even though Babbo has told her she's coming too. She may worry that your cook . . . '

'But why would I have a cook?' Startled, Joe interrupted her.

He could not imagine where Conti might have got the idea that he employed a cook. The full impact of the fact that the object of his affection would naturally assume such a thing was something he had not properly digested. If he had, he might have considered that as far as his betrothed was concerned, the world was a place where it was more normal to have a cook than not.

Joe had just bought the house in County Wicklow, but was still living in his small studio apartment near his office in the centre of the city. Tucked away in a corner off the main room of his apartment, there was a tiny kitchenette, into which he seldom ventured. He had a cupboard full of snacks, facilitating his lifestyle of continuous grazing rather than eating meals as such. There was nothing in Joe's kitchen that Alessia would have been able to identify. And no, Joe did not employ a cook, as he now informed Conti.

'Oh,' said Conti, surprised, the possibility of Joe not employing a cook never having crossed her mind. 'Well, that's all right then. I'll tell her.'

On Joe's next visit, the weight of the world appeared to have been lifted from Alessia's shoulders. The heaviness of her bushy eyebrows lifted and she occasionally smiled at him as she placed his soup in front of him with a certain amount of care, unlike the slopping that had occurred on previous occasions. Joe was unsure how reassured he should feel at this turn of events. There was something almost as menacing in her newfound affection.

Joe had been brought up in the slums of Dublin, in an area long since demolished. His mother, a poor country girl, had been widowed when Joe was a mere nine months old, shortly after she and her husband had decided to move to Dublin. Now, with just her baby for company, she moved to the city anyway, hoping that a new start would bring more luck and happiness.

As he grew up, Joe managed to use his brain, and his considerable flair, to think his way out of the mess they were in. He stood out in his class, won an impressive series of scholarships and made his way into law. He was something of an outsider there, a working-class boy made good but now surrounded by the wealthy and privileged. He worked hard to neutralise his accent. In time, all of this began to seem normal to Joe as he rubbed shoulders with the great and the good. The world had not changed, but Joe had, and, bit by bit, what was once strange became normal.

Conti was everything he admired. He loved her confidence and her background, her youth and her vitality. Although there was a ten-year age difference between them, their dream was the same. She, like him, was ambitious and demanding, and together, he felt, they could rule the world, or at least the world in which they resided. He never took her back to the edge of the slum from which he had emerged, and rarely spoke about it. She never knew he had lived on the dirtiest floor of one of the dirtiest buildings in the city, never knew that his cot was a drawer with a blanket in it, never knew about the abuse he had been forced to suffer at school, and never knew about the revenge he later got on the people responsible. When she asked him where he was from, he just said 'the city centre', not wishing to be specific. The way Dublin was changing, there would soon be no trace of the awfulness of his background as the area evolved from a slum and abandoned area into a new artsy location.

The truth was, in a way Joe did have a cook at one point. His mother was his cook. She worked two jobs, one in a shop and one in a café, and still found the time to cook him a meal of sorts every day, using leftovers from her places of work. Everything she did, she did to keep him clothed and with shoes on his feet and to feed him as best she could. She kept nothing for herself. She died just before he started practising law. He knew that he owed everything to his mother, but tried only to look forward towards the future. That is what she would have wanted him to do.

A handsome man, he had now connected with good old European blood and found a wife who wanted what he did – a nice home, children, family and the good life in general. These were his aspirations, learned from a hardworking mother in a one-roomed flat where the toilet down the dilapidated hall was shared by four families. His life had been spent trying to get as far away from that as he could.

Conti brought money with her, but by the time they married he was already ahead in his field and his salary was such that even without the dei Fiori inheritance, they would have had a comfortable life. Her wealth just meant that they would have the best. He never resented Conti's wealth and privileged upbringing; quite the reverse, in fact. She was what he pretended to be, and her natural energy and style thrilled him.

He sometimes wondered whether Conti loved him as he loved

her. During their whirlwind courtship they made love in his studio apartment, and he was aware that his passion outweighed hers. It did not bother him. He admired what he saw as her sophistication and her somewhat languid moves in bed. He saw her as a temple at which to be worshipped, and she, used to the Count's admiration, felt nothing unbalanced or unusual in this.

Joe and Conti Martin moved into their country home, with the Count and his cook, Alessia, in tow.

The Count, now in his seventies, brought his furniture and art with him, items he had purchased since his arrival in Dublin, obviously chosen for their resemblance to his lost world – heavy gilt-framed paintings of people neither he nor Conti knew, but which had been picked up in various auction rooms after the war, together with old-fashioned heavy Italian furniture.

All of this arrived at the same time as Conti, the Count and the cook, and when it became apparent that the Count was incapable of being separated from these items, Joe got rid of the various pieces of modern furniture that he had bought and allowed the Count to take over the house. With the Count came an old-fashioned gramophone with a loudspeaker that looked like a gigantic trumpet through which opera music played, always louder and louder as the Count claimed he was becoming increasingly deaf, although in actual fact his hearing was superlative.

Joe would have preferred a more minimalist approach to décor and furniture, but he held his tongue, wanting to indulge Conti in whatever way he could. Most people did.

On a bleak winter's morning, Lorina Martin was born to Joe and Conti.

The Count and Joe paced the hospital corridor outside the delivery room, while back at home, Alessia looked up the cookery book into which she had written notes when Conti was a baby.

The notes were a mixture of Italian and English. *Zucchini con* milk. *Uovo con latte. Latte con aglio.* Garlic with *melanzana.* She had little recollection of how Conti had responded to her early cooking, but there was Conti now, reasonably tall and glowing with health, and Alessia knew that her baby-oriented culinary skills were about to be utilised again.

She thought of the Count's disappearing teeth and realised that she could change her cooking patterns to accommodate both him and the new baby. Conti would probably enjoy now what she must have loved as a baby. And Joe, or Signore Martin, as she addressed him, well, he would learn to like mashed and mulched-up food. There followed a period in which Conti had to placate Alessia, trying to convince her that milk was what baby Lorina needed for the foreseeable future, and that a return to classic Italian cooking – pasta, fish, vegetables, gnocchi, salads – was what she, the Count and Joe would most like.

To the Count's consternation, Conti returned to work and he and Alessia cared for Lorina during the working week. Alessia rose to the occasion, reverting to the role she had once had.

Conti told me later that she had been meaning to drop in to introduce herself but that she was so caught up in the business of her life that she just had not found the time. She and Joe each had sports cars and during that summer I often saw them setting off in the mornings with the tops of their cars wound down. They were glamorous people who appeared in control of their lives.

I did not meet her until late September. I was returning by train from a trip to Trinity to collect some papers, and I had just found a seat when she came towards me and sat on the other side of the aisle. I recognised her immediately and her eyes had met mine before she sat down. I did not think that she would know me as her neighbour, but as the train pulled in to Greystones, she spoke to me.

'We live next door,' Conti said by way of introduction as we pushed through the bustling train to get off at the station. 'I'm Conti Martin. Can I give you a lift home?'

'I would love a lift,' I said, having planned on catching a bus and then walking, as Fred had the car that day. 'I'm Helena Wolff. I've been meaning to say hello for weeks now.'

Conti pushed back her well-cut hair in a glamorous gesture. 'Me too, me too,' she said. 'I always promise myself I'm going to make the effort to meet people, but I just never end up doing it. Hopeless, isn't it? I'm parked out the back.'

I was swept along by her laughter and gaiety and what appeared to be a strange mixture of sophistication and sincerity. With the roof of the convertible down and the wind blowing our hair, a new friendship was formed as we drove back to our rural paradise.

'Babbo will love you,' Conti said.

'Babbo?'

'My father.'

Ah, I thought. The Count.

'He's going to be so pleased,' Conti continued. 'We've hardly done any entertaining, you know, what with my baby, Lorina, and work and pressure...you know! But you must come to dinner, you and your husband. Babbo will be so happy.'

'And your mother?' I asked tentatively, wondering where Conti's mother featured in this scenario and recalling not seeing her in the wedding photos I had seen in the magazine.

'Mamma died when I was born,' Conti said with a wave of her hand, pronouncing 'Mamma' with an Italian accent. She found it easier to dismiss her mother by saying she had died than to admit that her mother had abandoned her. 'No, don't be sad for me. I never knew her, and what you don't know, you can't miss.'

I was not so sure. I felt there must be an awareness of absence, but Conti clearly did not think so. She seemed quite content with the Count and the cook, having known nothing else.

'Is it difficult having your father living with you?' I asked.

'Not at all. I would hate living without him. I've lived with him all my life and can't imagine not having him with me.'

I found myself being swept along in Conti's way of thinking, and for a long minute felt that I missed my parents, which indeed I did, and that I should have brought them with me into the marital home before remembering that no, that was not how it worked in my world and that Fred and I valued our space and our privacy. And anyway, my parents would not have come. I don't know what I was thinking even entertaining such an idea.

They say that you can choose your friends but you can't choose your family, but it isn't really true. You tend to choose neither. Your friendships just have a way of happening to you. You look up one day and find you have a group of friends. Who ever really consciously decides who their friends should be?

I didn't.

Four

Fred and I went to dinner at the Martins'.

Time had passed and Alessia was still being encouraged to return to normal cuisine, especially since Lorina was now a year old, although by now the Count preferred having everything blended or liquidised. Conti had told me this with one of her carefree laughs.

'But don't worry,' she said. 'We'll have real food too.'

Fred and I dressed up for the evening in our best clothes only to discover that Conti was in designer evening wear. She was wearing a long gold lamé dress with black gloves that went up her arms past her elbows, and the Count was in a dinner jacket with a gold cummerbund that complemented Conti's dress.

'Oh,' Fred said in embarrassment, glancing at me. 'I don't think we're correctly dressed.'

With that, Joe emerged. Like Fred, he was tall and dark though his skin was pale.

'Not a bit of it,' he said with a laugh, introducing himself. 'The Italian side of my family likes to dress up at any opportunity.' Joe, for his part, was in a white shirt and dark trousers with very bright purple socks. I was relieved to see how he was dressed.

The Count was charming, bowing slightly when he was introduced. Lorina, the baby, was brought down briefly by Conti to meet us. She lay back in the Count's arms at a precarious angle. I feared she might slip from the old man's hands, but surprisingly she did not wriggle or move, possibly having learned from previous experience. She was an odd-looking child with a shock of dark hair and Conti's beautiful skin. Her eyes darted from face to face and then looked back at the Count. She appeared more at home in his arms than in her own mother's.

'She adores Babbo. Don't you, Lorina?' said Conti happily.

'Because she spend more time with me,' the Count explained to Fred and me with what appeared to be a tragic shaking of his head. 'Is no good. A mother should be home minding her baby.'

'Now now, Babbo,' Conti said. 'You know I have to work.'

'You no have to work,' he said. 'I have money for you all. Joe too. We have all the money you want.'

'Babbo, not now,' said Conti, winking at Fred and me. 'It's good for me to work.' In an aside to us, she said, 'I would go mad alone here all day.'

I smiled politely at her, but did not agree. When we had a baby, I would stay at home in order to spend as much time as I could with it. I would not want someone else raising my child and to have my baby being more at home in their arms. I also found the idea of the Count and the cook in the role of surrogate parents during the day to be a very odd concept. Neither looked capable of doing much at all, let alone taking care of someone else.

Although I felt slightly critical, I was also filled with admiration. Conti, on that speedy trip home from the station in the car, had spoken briefly about the situation being a little stressful, and said that she felt she was under pressure. Nevertheless, she managed to look effortlessly beautiful and energised while she was saying it. Whatever way she ran her life, it certainly suited her, and I could see that whatever I might think as being the right way to raise children, it might only be the right way for me.

We had dinner, probably the most sophisticated meal I had ever had, with one course just seeming to follow on to the next and then the next. We had soup, pasta, fish, vegetables, cheese and an ice cream torte. I was still getting used to what was available in Dublin, which at that time seemed very limited, but their table abounded with simple yet perfectly cooked food.

'What a wonderful meal,' Fred said as we drank coffee and listened to music. The Count, so ponderous earlier in the evening, had become animated and spoke of the difficulties of getting the right flour for the pasta, which Alessia had made on an instrument that looked a bit like the strings of a guitar. He asked Alessia to bring it in to show to us and we were both bewildered and impressed. Alessia proudly beamed at us from the doorway.

The leaves were falling from the trees as Fred and I walked home that night. The moon was bright in the sky, almost like a second sun but without the heat. We walked down their driveway hand in hand, then along the narrow path that led to our gates. And I was happy, invigorated by the strangeness of the evening, the foreign nature of the Martins' home, the balance of age and youth within its walls.

Maybe I envied Conti then. I would not have changed what I had, but our house was very quiet as we let ourselves in the front door and went to bed. Fred was laughing about the Count. He said he was like a typical Italian godfather, a *padrone,* in his dinner jacket and his cummerbund. He was not mocking him, but I felt oddly protective. My mother was Italian and I suppose I felt defensive, the way we do if someone picks on some aspect of our race, even though I did not feel remotely Italian myself.

But I laughed too, as I knew it was not unkindly meant, and at the same time I envied Conti having her own family around her, enhancing her, loving her, fulfilling her. Whatever about the weirdness of these people who lived next door, I could see that there was a lot to be said for a family living together like that. Their family was the most important thing to them. We all talk like our family is the most important thing, much more important than our work, but we don't really mean it and we certainly don't act like it. This family did, and I admired that. I hoped, when my baby arrived, that somehow we could all be like they were.

I also realised for the first time that I was ready to have a baby. It seemed to me that my feelings on that front had moved forwards in leaps and bounds. I still was in no rush, but I was receptive to the possibility.

After we left their home, Conti helped her father up the stairs to bed. He had lasted the evening surprisingly well for someone who often nodded off at the table.

'Lovely people,' he said.

She was surprised, she told me later in that way she had of putting me down without having any idea of what she was doing. Lately the Count had shown little interest in anything other than the weather and Lorina. It occurred to her that maybe he was bored. She noted now for the first time how he had dressed for dinner, the black tie and the cummerbund, and how his hair, which had thinned only recently, was sleeked back with some product. She briefly saw some vulnerability in him.

'Babbo,' she said, 'we should go out more often. You would enjoy that.'

'Ah, I am old man,' he said as he opened his bedroom door.

'But not so old that you can't enjoy yourself,' she said. 'I think you need a new interest.'

'I have all I need.'

On the surface, it was true. He lived in comfort. He played his music loudly. He had Conti, Alessia, Lorina and Joe, though he had no real feelings towards Joe other than concern that he would look after Conti properly when he, the Count, died. He liked walking in the garden when the weather was clement, and he had even learned to adapt to the long, drawn-out winters, the short daylight hours and the bitter cold and damp. Muffling himself in scarves and a woolly hat, he brushed the leaves in autumn, and come winter, he would try to shovel a bit of snow from the path. When the war had ended he had encountered such a climate while in hiding and he had loathed it. But now he felt they were in a land of opportunity, opportunity for Conti, his only child.

He would have liked to speak more Italian, but while Conti obliged when she thought about it, she was more inclined to revert to English. He had made Italian friends when he had emigrated, but now, in their country home, he was cut off from the city.

Alessia and he always spoke their native language, but lately Alessia spoke more and more about orchards of lemons and oranges that he could not recall, about the knobbly olive trees and the vineyards laden with grapes. Happiness filled her voice as she spoke of these things, which he identified as her rose-coloured memory filled with the verdancy of nature and abundant crops that he had little memory of having any authentic bearing in reality. His memories were of his leader and the power he once had.

It was a week later when Fred announced his parents were coming to visit us for the weekend.

'Of course Freyn is coming too,' Fred added, knowing full well how my face would light up. I loved his baby brother. We saw them at least once a month and Freyn, now ten months old, was an enormous, cuddly baby who busied himself with bricks and fur toys and screamed only when he saw anything that looked like a tennis ball.

'I wonder if your mother has him playing tennis yet?' I mused, grinning.

'I wouldn't put it past her,' Fred laughed. 'If he's old enough to hold a rattle, he's old enough to hold a tennis racquet.'

'What do you bet that they'll start on us again about clearing the trees and laying a tennis court?'

'A whole set if they don't,' Fred said.

'No, make it forty-love,' I said. 'It's too difficult for me to claw back a whole set. I wish you'd tell them there is no way a tennis court would fit. And anyway, the ground slopes.'

'I have told them,' Fred said, 'but they only hear what they want to hear.'

'Shall I ask Conti and Joe to join us?' I continued. 'Just for one meal, I mean, maybe the Saturday?'

'Sure,' he said. We looked out the window. The weather was clean and crisp, autumn having suddenly arrived, and the forecast bode well. 'I could barbecue and we could eat inside,' he suggested.

I smiled at him. I had noticed this trait in my husband. The only visitors we'd had to date had been his parents and brother, but in common with many males of the species, cooking was something that suddenly required his attention any time guests were coming round, as if I would suddenly panic and forget how to do it. He found the Neanderthal appeal of making fire, then throwing chunks of meat onto it and prodding them with the nearest thing he had to a spear, hard to resist. My father had been like that too.

'I wonder if Joe likes old-fashioned barbecues,' Fred said thoughtfully. I could see that he was looking forward to seeing Joe again and relishing the prospect of a male conversation over the relative merits of the old-fashioned coal versus the newer propane-guzzling barbecue. I understood this. It was a man thing. I was learning.

'A barbecue sounds like a great idea,' I encouraged him.

I did not see Conti on the train over the next few days, so I called her on the Wednesday. 'Conti, hello, it's Helena next door.'

'You're the only Helena I know,' Conti laughed. 'Well, what's up? Or is this a call for a chat?'

I had not thought of that possibility. Chatting on phones was not something I knew much about. In fact, it was something I had never done in my life.

'Well, no, not really,' I said, though I suddenly quite liked the idea of a chat. 'I wonder if you and Joe are free this coming Saturday. It is short notice, I know, but Fred's parents are coming for the weekend and we thought . . .'

'Oh, that would be lovely,' Conti said. 'I'll check with Babbo and get back to you.'

After we hung up I puzzled over what it was that Conti was going to check with Babbo. I wondered if it was to see if Babbo was free to babysit, or did she always run her invitations past him, maybe out of courtesy? I meant to mention it to Fred when he came home that evening, but then I forgot until the phone rang and it was Conti.

'Darling,' Conti said happily, 'Babbo is delighted to come too on Saturday. We're thrilled, all three of us. And Alessia will look after Lorina. This is such fun.'

'Oh, great . . .' It was all I could think of saying. At no point had I intended to imply or even to hint that the Count was welcome too. It was not that I didn't like him, it was just that he had not been included in the invitation.

'That's great,' I said again. 'Umm, about six or six-thirty? We thought early would be best, as Fred is going to barbecue.'

'Oh, won't that be very cold?' Conti asked. 'I might bring a rug or two for Babbo.'

'I meant that he would barbecue but we would eat inside,' I reassured her. I felt slightly put upon and I did not know how to handle any of this.

'Right, see you then, if not before.' And Conti was gone.

'Fred,' I said, coming back into the kitchen, where he was sitting reading the newspaper, 'I'm sorry about this, but Joe and Conti are coming on Saturday and they're bringing the Count.'

'What's wrong with that?' he asked.

'Well, nothing really. It's just that I didn't invite him.'

'Maybe we should have.'

'I know, but that's not what I meant . . .'

I felt slightly perturbed.

Fred seemed to think that we should have invited the Count, and maybe he was right, but that was not the point and I knew it. I just didn't know quite how to explain. We could just as easily have been inviting a colleague or boss from Fred's work to dinner and I had the feeling that Conti would have done the same thing.

But I liked Conti and I found myself making excuses. Perhaps Conti was thinking about the Count and his lonely life, which she had mentioned to me on that first day we had met. Or maybe I had in some way suggested that the invitation was meant for the three of them, for Conti, Joe and the Count, and maybe this was my own fault. I tried running the words through my head as to how I would phrase future invitations to dinner. 'Dinner, just you and Joe,' or 'We're having two friends to dinner on Saturday and wonder if you and Joe would like to make it a six-some.' Eventually I pushed it aside. I was wasting time on something that could not be changed. But what I really didn't like was that I had appeared mean to Fred. I felt slightly wrong-footed, maybe too tense or worried about something that was not important in the grand scheme of things, and it upset me more than it should have.

Now I started to worry about what to serve the Count, as he clearly could not manage a barbecued steak if the previous dinner had been anything to go by. I asked Fred.

'Oh, he'd probably love a steak. Look, it's not our problem. It's up to Conti to say if he needs anything particular.'

'But we saw him sucking his food that night,' I interjected.

'Take it easy,' Fred said. 'You're making a mountain out of this. Maybe it was rude of us not to invite him after we went to their house. I think it's nice of Conti to include him in the invitation. We'll work something out about the food on the night. God knows the world would be a better place if more people cared for their elderly relatives like she does.' He returned to his newspaper in the knowledge of a job well done.

For some reason I wanted to pull the newspaper away from him and say, 'You're not listening,' but instead I leaned over and kissed the top of his head. He reached up and patted my hand, but he stayed focused on his paper.

He had become obsessed with his work and spent all his spare time reading the sports pages in every newspaper. This suited me, as it meant I could study in the evenings without feeling I was locking myself away.

Jackson and Marjorie arrived on Friday night with Freyn asleep, clutching a tennis ball between his hands. He woke just after they arrived, screamed in disgust when he saw what he was holding, and dropped the ball immediately.

'We just can't get that child to like the feel of a tennis ball,' his mother said, hugging Fred and then me, and leaving Fred's father to untie the screaming child from his car seat. I took Freyn from my father-in-law and soothed him with gentle words and little whispers. His screams presently stopped and he put a chubby hand up to touch my face.

'Your mother made a tape recording of tennis balls bouncing,' Jackson said, 'but the little fellow hasn't taken to it yet.'

'What? Why?' asked Fred in surprise.

'To help Freyn get to sleep,' his father explained. 'Only it does not work. Not yet anyway.'

'Oh, that,' Fred said, remembering a similar recording when he was a tiny child. He and I caught each other's eye and we tried to hide our smiles. I loved when Fred and I shared moments like this one, little things that were like a secret between us that made me feel close to him.

'It would be hysterically funny,' I said to Fred later in the kitchen. 'I mean, if it worked it would be fine, or if it was someone else's child, but not little Freyn. Poor little Freyn.'

'*Alternative Approaches to Parenting,* by Jackson and Marjorie Wolff,' said Fred, laughing. 'I can see it now. They probably torture people like that in some countries. It might be better entitled, *How to Mess Your Kids Up for Life in Three Simple Steps, and Spend the Rest of Your Life Paying for Shrinks.*'

I laughed.

'It's amazing I turned out as well as I did, really,' said Fred, flexing his biceps and thumping his chest. 'Never did me no harm.'

'Poor little Freyn,' I said again. 'I do hope he's all right. He's starting to look the wrong shape for tennis.'

'Oh, he'll probably get used to it,' Fred said. 'I did.'

If I felt anything about the way Jackson and Marjorie were raising Freyn, it was only a feeling of being intrigued. People did things in their own way; I knew that. It just happened that it was not the way I wanted to do things. I was not sure my way would be right, if and when the time came, but I hoped and believed it would be better than what I saw around me, between Freyn screaming at the mere sight of a tennis ball and Lorina being more comfortable with the Count and Alessia than with her parents.

'We'll have our own baby soon,' Fred said to me, and I realised that he must have thought I was brooding over that.

I had stopped taking my contraception because I wanted to make him happy. I wondered if he felt like some kind of failure, or how he really felt about his parents having a baby in their late forties and still nothing happening on that front with us. It was early days and I was in no rush, but I knew that he might well feel differently.

I hugged him. 'We'll have a baby,' I said to him. 'It just takes time, and lots of practice,' I added with a smile.

'Lots and lots of lovely practice,' he grinned happily and I knew he had moved on from whatever he had been thinking.

The following evening, Joe, Conti and the Count arrived, bringing flowers and wine. Conti was wrapped in sweaters. 'Against the cold,' she explained.

'Oh, no need,' I said. 'We're eating indoors. I thought I had said.'

'But someone needs to keep the chef company while he barbecues,' Conti said with a laugh. 'Oh, a bambino,' she added, seeing Freyn on the rug. 'I didn't realise you had a baby. We could have brought Lorina with us.'

'If you want to go and get her,' Fred suggested, 'that would be fine. But this isn't our baby. This is my little brother, Freyn. Bring over Lorina. They could be friends.'

Conti laughed. 'I think not, Lorina is asleep. Better to leave her like that.'

'And Alessia, she like to babysit,' added the Count.

Fred poured drinks and then went outside, followed by Conti. I watched them briefly through the window. Conti managed to look like a model for winter wear as she stood beside Fred at the barbecue, with a glass in one hand and the other gesticulating as she spoke. I smiled and turned back to the company in the room. Freyn had dozed off on the rug on the floor.

'Lorina no sleep like that ever,' said the Count. 'She likes her bed.'

'Lorina is Joe and Conti's little girl,' I explained to my parents-in-law, unsure if they had heard the original conversation.

The talk was polite, if somewhat stilted. Out on the deck, I could see Fred and Conti laughing and I wished they would hurry up and come back in.

Prompted by Marjorie, Joe began talking about his work and I left them to check on the baked potatoes and to put the salad together. I could hear Joe's voice through the door talking about some case he had just finished, having successfully defended someone who sounded like the scum of the earth.

'You must find that difficult,' I heard Jackson saying.

'It's just part of the job,' Joe said. 'You get used to it.'

'But who pays for a drug dealer like that? Or does he have that much income from his work?' asked Marjorie.

'In this particular case, he belongs to a family with money.'

'And they are happy for him to be back on the streets?'

'It's that kind of family. Not the kind of family you invite around to dinner, I can assure you,' he said with a laugh, but it carried no warmth. 'Most of them have no money, and that's half the problem. Some of these people have had a hell of a life. Drug problems, in and out of care homes. I mean, none of us really know who we would be if our life had been like that.'

It was clear that Joe knew rather more about this subject than he was prepared to discuss. I later learned that more than once he had seen somebody in court he recognised from his schooldays and had already successfully prosecuted two of his old classmates, boys who had made his childhood hell.

'But don't you think that there comes a point in everyone's life where they must take responsibility for themselves?' Jackson said. 'I mean, a point where the individual must stop blaming the past?'

'I totally agree,' Joe said, 'but brains and determination help.'

'We must leave the past behind us,' the Count interjected. 'In this changing world, it is better to move on.'

The wine seemed to have warmed him up and his English had improved with every sip, even though I was not sure what he meant.

Hearing all this through the open kitchen door, it occurred to me that perhaps he could not be bothered speaking proper English the rest of the time. I could hear him now talking about the problems of bringing up a child in today's modern world, and he sounded quite animated. Glancing through the door, I could see him gesticulating, much as Conti was doing outside. It made me think of things that one learned from one's parents, things that stayed with one always, not just mannerisms but also manners and morals. Generally we are what we are because we are just built that way, I thought. The choices we make matter, and what we do matters, but none of it matters nearly as much as what we are, our natures.

It was one of the things I loved about Fred, that we were so similar. Even though we had been brought up in different countries, indeed, in different continents, our basic morality and conscience were similar. Our values coincided. We did not argue about things that divided us. In fact, we did not really argue about anything.

The fact that he had been brought up in an environment of sport meant that he had a clean-living approach to things. And my upbringing, strange as I was beginning to realise it was, meant that I too had a similar approach. We both believed in good sportsmanship. His home had evolved around it. Mine, on the other hand, had known virtually nothing about sportsmanship, but neither had it known the opposite. My father's hard-core values had been fostered in me, and it was these I identified in Fred. Work hard. Think calmly. All of that helped to give me the security I felt with Fred.

I went outside to ask Conti if there was anything I should do with the Count's food to make it more palatable for him. It was not the kind of thing I would feel comfortable asking such an elderly man.

'Oh, I wouldn't worry,' Conti said to me. 'Do you have a blender? Well, that's fine. If it looks like he can't eat his dinner, you can just take it out to the kitchen and liquidise it for him.'

I nodded. For a moment I felt almost as though Conti was dismissing me. It was an odd feeling, but in the next instant, Conti had put her arm around me and said, 'I just love this deck. We'll have to get this done too. Right now we just have a patio area out the back where Joe keeps the barbecue. We have this huge long table out there. But this is great, with a door into both the kitchen and the dining area. We'll get rid of the patio and eat on the deck instead; when it's just the family, I mean. Actually we should probably keep the patio. Then there are two options.'

'It's always interesting how similarly built houses can be so completely different,' Fred contributed as he turned the steaks on the barbecue.

It was cold and I found I was shivering, so I returned inside and put the food on the table before checking with Fred to see if he was nearly ready.

'Bring everyone in to the dining table,' he said. 'I'm on my way.'

We sat at the table and I felt happy, as if Fred and I were doing something successful, bringing these people together, feeding them, talking, having fun.

Jackson was interested in buying a cabinet in which to display more of Marjorie's trophies. 'So many of them are still in boxes or exposed on shelves where they attract dust,' he said. 'Helena, this is the kind of thing you know about,' he continued. 'I don't mind how much it costs. I want the best. Where would I look?'

I realised that Fred must have told them that I had taken to looking in antique shops and at auction rooms between lectures if I had too much time on my hands. I was about to suggest a place on St Stephen's Green when Conti said, 'This is more my area. I work for a company that catalogues *objets d'art* and in the very catalogue I'm putting together at the moment there are about ten pages of such cabinets that are coming up in a fine arts auction in about three months' time. I can send you a copy of the catalogue and if you are coming up to Dublin I can bring you to the showrooms so that you can look at any that interest you. And then if there is something you like, I could go to the auction for you.'

'That's kind of you,' Jackson said. 'Terribly kind.' He had a stilted way of speaking when he did not know someone well.

There was a little laughter and Conti preened with delight. 'It's my pleasure,' she said.

If I felt a momentary pang of jealousy, I suppressed it immediately. It was nice of Conti to put herself out like that, and it was nothing but mean of me to think otherwise.

'Helena,' Marjorie said, 'tell us how your studies are going. Do you have essays to do this term? What are you enjoying the most?'

In the kitchen afterwards, Marjorie insisted on helping to stack the dishwasher, which they had bequeathed to us when they upgraded theirs. She busily scraped the plates into the bin and I was struck, as always, by her energy. She was a lean, lithe woman who carried Freyn under her arm much as she might have carried her tennis bag, and her organisational skills were exceptional. Her motto off the tennis court, as she often told me, was 'get a job done, and it's done'. On the court, her motto was 'win, win, win'.

'But we can leave this till tomorrow,' I said.

'No, no,' Marjorie said, closing the door. 'Let's do it now and save you in the morning.'

'Thank you,' I said.

'Now, Helena,' Marjorie said quietly in a tone that I had not heard her use before. 'Is this Conti a new friend? Of yours or of Fred's?'

I explained how the Martins lived next door and how I had met Conti on the train. 'But why do you ask?' I asked, puzzled.

'Because I don't like her. Forgive me for saying so, and excuse my bluntness, but she's one of life's takers, high on her own agenda. Just be careful.'

This directness from my mother-in-law was new to me. Was it possible that this was something I should be listening to? Surely not. After all, what did Marjorie know about Conti? She had only just met her. Conti had been nothing but nice to her, and I would be friends with whomever I wanted. But Marjorie was always so kind, especially to me. I did not know what to think.

Then I thought of Conti and Fred earlier, outside on the deck at the barbecue. 'Do you mean I should be careful of . . . ? I mean, Fred . . . ?'

'No, that's not what I meant. I think I meant you should be careful of you.'

With that the door opened and Conti put her head around. 'So this is where you're hiding. Aren't you coming inside?'

'We're just tidying up here.'

'Oh, leave it,' Conti said. 'It can be done tomorrow.'

'You can come and help us if you like,' Marjorie said. 'Get a job done, and it's done, but we'll do it now. This is our way of doing things. I don't like to think of Helena facing this in the morning.'

There was a certain firmness in her voice that I had not heard before. I could see that Conti had heard it too because her eyes narrowed fleetingly and almost imperceptibly. I had the feeling that some battle was being fought, but for the life of me I could not work out what it was. Conti was used to Alessia cleaning up and did not understand the practicalities for those without help.

'Then of course I'll help,' Conti said with a smile. 'I'll bring in the plates and things from outside.'

'No, don't worry,' I said.

'I insist,' Conti said, giving me a hug as she went out the deck door. 'Oh, Helena,' she called from outside. 'Come out at once, I simply must show you something.'

I looked at Marjorie, who was watching me carefully with something like concern in her face, then I went out on to the deck.

'Look,' Conti said, pulling me by the hand so that we were at the edge. We rested our elbows on the wooden rail and I looked up at the sky, where the moon seemed even lower and brighter than the previous weekend. 'It's beautiful, isn't it?' Conti said, slipping an arm around my shoulder. 'Isn't that just heavenly?'

I smiled, thrilled by her friendship. 'I'm so pleased that we met,' I said.

There was such a warm feeling standing there with Conti, sharing the moment. It was a good feeling, like I used to feel with my brother when we shared something, a feeling of intimacy that was completely safe because it was with a sibling. That was what I felt now and I smiled at Conti, and the sense of diminishment I had felt at the table evaporated. Conti was my friend.

'We better go back in,' Conti said. 'It's very cold out here.'

She made for the kitchen door as I went to the barbecue and collected the plates and bits of equipment Fred had been using. Marjorie was wrong. Conti was so lovely and vivacious and friendly to everyone.

I could see Marjorie looking at me through the kitchen window and I wondered what she was thinking. It occurred to me that maybe she felt that if I became too friendly with Conti I would somehow not put the same time and effort into my marriage. I wanted to reassure her. I knew she liked me and I had always seen that as a blessing.

When I went back into the kitchen with the bowls and tongs, Conti had disappeared and Marjorie was putting powder in the dishwasher.

'In some ways you two look very alike,' Marjorie said, almost casually.

'Conti and me?' I asked. I didn't think so. We were about the same height, but I was thin while Conti was curvaceous and she wore clothes to enhance that. I had plain blonde hair while Conti's was expensively cut and streaked. I suppose we did both have similar neat, straight noses, but the similarity ended there.

'A bit,' Marjorie said. 'But you're not a bit alike. Not inside. She's the kind of person I would admire on the tennis court.'

She must have seen my face, as I felt slightly shocked. She

appeared to be saying that she wouldn't admire me on the tennis court.

'No, you've got me wrong,' Marjorie said quickly. 'I admire you greatly on the tennis court. I've seen you playing with Fred and you've got lovely style and determination, and next summer I'm hoping you'll play with me. I meant that Conti's personality would do well on a tennis court, but it's not so appealing off the court. She's a shark,' she added.

'I really like her,' I said. I didn't want to have this conversation. I found Conti to be great fun and I felt that my friendship was being undermined.

'Don't let her use you,' Marjorie said.

'I won't.'

It was the first time my mother-in-law had interfered and I did not like it.

Of course, I see now that I was flattered that someone like Conti would want to befriend someone like me. She was not really interested in me for my own self. In all that time, she never asked me what I was studying, and I never told her I spoke Italian. It seemed to me that I would be intruding by speaking in Italian to the Count, or maybe that it would be rude because the other people around us would not understand. Instead, we talked about her – her life, her clothes, her parties – and I enjoyed that.

It was fun.

Those family evenings were repeated occasionally, but there were other times when Conti and I found time to sit together and chat, sometimes with Lorina playing on the floor between us, and sometimes outdoors when the weather was good.

'I don't know much about you,' Conti said on one such day. 'I know you're a student, but I don't know about your life, about you. Tell me about you.'

And I, basking in the warmth of newfound friendship, told Conti everything.

Five

There is a tree – a single acacia tree – on the hill beyond our farm, before the horizon meets the sky, but etched into the firmament in its solitary starkness. In the evening, when the light changes and transposes into the deep colours of sunset, there is a moment when the tree is completely black just before the light falls. That moment, that umbrella tree, that seeping changing of the light; that for me is home. Not just Kenya, where I was born and raised, but the whole of my life, where all my thoughts and hopes and dreams had once lingered.

I told Conti about my time there, about my childhood, about my home. It was as if I had wanted to speak about it for a very long time.

'My brother and I were raised there. It was like it was our heaven. I remember it all so vividly, as if it had just happened yesterday,' I began.

We often saw a herd of giraffes on the horizon beyond our tree, undulating about in their giraffe-like way. Horace, my brother, used to imitate that loping movement, and it reduced me to fits of giggles, giggles that I had to repress in a valiant effort to prevent my mother from hearing me. It sounds so otherworldly, but that, for us, was just how life was. We didn't know anything different. But we did know even then that we were lucky. I wouldn't have wanted to live anywhere else. It sounds so idyllic, doesn't it, but it wasn't always like that. Sometimes it was hard, very hard. But I wouldn't have changed things for the world.

My relationship with my mother was always difficult. She just didn't really seem to love me. Sometimes I wasn't so sure she even liked me, and I had no idea what I could have done wrong.

When I was little, because I knew no other emotion from her, I was used to her harshness or her coldness. I don't know which word is right. Maybe neither. It was more that I didn't really feature in her concerns or interests. Looking back at it now, it was like she was going through the motions, but her heart wasn't really in it.

I didn't know why, but I did know there was something unfair about what was happening. She used to direct all of her affection, all of her attention, towards my brother. He was worth her effort and I was not. And somehow it ended up that he directed his affection towards me. He was my protector, my guardian and my best friend in the world. He was everything a brother should be.

My mother didn't like the idea of my brother being far away, so we were never sent off to school abroad, like the neighbours' children were. Back then, our neighbours lived several miles away, down a dust road. Since my brother was not being sent off to school, she couldn't very well send me away, though one time I remember she suggested it. I can't remember where, but she said it would be better for me. But my father, who rarely had time to pay any attention to either Horace or me, refused point blank to have me sent away to school.

He said, 'If here is good enough for Horace, then it's good enough for Helena.'

I'll never forget it. I don't know what would have happened to me if I had been sent off abroad somewhere, or what difference that might have made to me.

He set my mother straight, and he said it standing up, military style, legs apart, shoulders back, chest out, hands behind his back. He used to do that occasionally, when he wanted to pull rank in the house.

At the time, I didn't know how to feel about what was happening. I'm still not sure. Maybe he just didn't want to spend money on my education, like it didn't matter, but maybe he knew how much it mattered to me to live there with my brother. He used to make these pronouncements periodically, which sort of became law. But that was the only time I can remember when one of them concerned me and what was going to happen to me. And that one time when it mattered, he said I must stay where I was. I've never forgotten it. I still feel grateful now when I think about that day.

So the way it turned out was that I got to stay at home, with my brother. That was all I wanted.

We didn't go to school like we would have done living here. We used to go to a tutor once a week. Horace started first, of course, and I was so jealous of him. It was all so exciting. Our handyman, whose name was Kulu, used to drive us to see our tutor. Kulu sort of helped out around the place, and he was always good to us both. We felt safe around him. The trip took over an hour in each direction. That was why, when Horace had started but I had not, I used to hate the days he was gone and I was left alone. I would be by myself all day. It cannot have been more than four or five hours once a week we would see the tutor, but it seemed like such a long time by myself.

I know a few hours a week doesn't sound like much, but the rest of the time we were taught at home. I say taught, but we weren't really taught. We learned everything at home. The books were all there for us, and we would have work set for us each week to do.

At an early age we learned to ride and it was pure joy to take our horses out on the land beyond the farm, racing each other in the direction of the umbrella tree. It was there, under the branches of that solitary tree, that my brother read to me, taught me how to read, gave me words for everything we could see, instilled in me a love of language and a love of our life. But more than that, much more. A love of nature.

70

We had to be home before nightfall and so it was that as the African sunset unfolded in the western sky and we moved slowly homewards on horseback that I would look back and see the tree like a strange, flat, black umbrella painted on the hill, connecting sky and land.

'Horace, Helena.' My father was waiting for us. 'You're late.' He was holding his rifle and his face was angry. By now Horace was old enough to look after both of us and Kulu no longer came with us.

My father stood there, his stance both angry and perturbed.

I looked back. The tree had disappeared and the night was immediately black behind us.

'Your mother was getting worried,' he said.

It was unclear if he had been about to come looking for us with his rifle, or if the rifle was there as some kind of threat.

'Sorry, Dad,' Horace said.

'Don't be late again. It upsets your mother.'

He was a man of few words and little time, a quiet, contemplative man, intrinsically kind although appearing cold. He was a mathematician and spent most of his time locked up in his study. However, he enjoyed his land. I suppose it absorbed him just as numbers did, and yet it was he who would try to entice our mother into town for parties or an evening out. It was with even more difficulty that he convinced her ever to have friends over for dinner. He farmed coffee, a business that was quite successful, but he left most of the everyday work to a farm manager and oversaw it from a distance.

My mother was the silent type, more silent than he. Still, deep, maybe emotionless . . . I don't know how to describe her.

I liked when they had friends over, rare and all as it was. Those evenings were always great fun. My parents sort of came out of themselves. They were the only times my mother showed any interest in how I appeared. She chose my clothes, brushed my hair, told me how to come in and say 'good evening' and shake hands, and then to leave when she nodded her head in my direction. I didn't really like being brought in to say hello, but I liked the fact that my mother gave me some attention on those evenings.

I wanted my mother to love me. I wanted her care and attention. I wanted her praise and affection. I tried to please her, but I never succeeded. My mother didn't like the dogs on the farm much either, but they managed to learn faster than I did that it was better to keep out of her way. She wasn't unkind to animals, not at all, but she liked the dogs to keep their distance. I remember a pup once coming over to her to lick her hand. She was sitting in a chair with her hands on her lap, and the puppy put his paws on her knees and tried to lick her. She pushed it away. It came back again and then she kicked out at it. It didn't come back after that. It came to Horace and me for cuddles and hugs.

I, on the other hand, did come back. Perhaps that is the difference between humans and animals. Humans are more optimistic. Or we just won't accept the way things are sometimes, but want to change them, whether or not we actually can.

It must sound like I hate my mother, but I really don't. She was a good woman in many ways. Still is a good woman. But she and I just never clicked like we should have. We just missed each other somehow.

She wasn't always cold and hard. She could be very caring. She certainly loved my brother. And she loved Luther. Luther was a dwarf elephant, a runt of nature she had rescued when he was abandoned as a baby. Luther lived with us at the farm, sleeping in a kind of lean-to. It had once had four walls, but Luther knocked one of the walls down when he grew too big to get in the door. He loved my mother, and I loved Luther. He would tap on her bedroom window in the morning to get her attention. I was never able to attract her like he did.

At one of those dinner parties, where I was temporarily in favour, the usual conversation was going on:

'How she's grown.'

'Lovely to see you again.'

'How pretty you are becoming.'

'My goodness, I would hardly recognise you.'

But then, like a bolt from the blue, one of the women at this party asked my mother why she had not seen her lately in town. My mother was not interested in town. I remember her smiling politely through gritted teeth.

'You really should bring Helena into town. I know it means staying overnight, but it would be nice for her. I know what we could do. Horace and Helena must come over to our place to play tennis. Would you like to come and play tennis?' This question was directed at me.

And so, in due course, Horace and I did just that. We went on horseback with our tennis racquets strapped to our backs.

It makes me laugh now, thinking of us just riding off on horses to play tennis miles away from home like that. But it really did happen.

It transpired that I was very good at tennis. You might not believe it now, but I was. We both were. We played more and more, and got better and better. We started playing in a club, then on teams, and eventually we ended up playing in something or other almost every weekend. They said if only we had started earlier we could have been tennis professionals, playing mixed doubles tournaments around the world. They said we had the potential, and there was even talk of us going on the circuit, but it was just talk. We were good, but not that good. We passed hours and hours at home playing tennis together, on the scrub grass before the umbrella tree, or on the dust in front of the farmhouse.

When Horace turned eighteen there was no longer any

question of his staying at home with us. He would have to go to university, and he was accepted into Trinity, here in Dublin. My parents saw education as being important, and also my father felt that whatever we decided to do with our lives we would be enhanced by going abroad and getting a degree. Horace was so clever that he would obviously do very well at whatever he turned his mind to.

I was so sad when Horace left, so desperately lonely.

My father spoke about coming with him to Dublin to help him settle in, but my mother wouldn't go with them. By that time, she wouldn't leave Kenya. She said it was her home, and nothing would get her away from it, despite my father's best efforts. She did not want my father to leave her, so Horace left alone.

A long, lonely year stretched before me. Initially, in Horace's absence, my mother did not appear to notice me at all. I played a little tennis, but only when there was a tournament. The rest of the time was passed either with my tutor, or riding with Kulu, or studying under the tree, keeping an anxious eye on the light from the west. Sunset was the curfew.

The rains were late that year. I remember riding out to see the dried-up riverbed with its cracked and arid basin, a trip my brother and I used to make sometimes with sandwiches in our backpacks. He always marvelled at how hard the ground was in the dry season, how the earth baked in the sun until it split like an enormous jigsaw puzzle. Horace showed me how life, which had seemed to disappear from the landscape in the drought, was hiding, waiting beneath the surface for the rains. I walked the riverbed that afternoon, with my horse at the end of the rein beside me. In the distance, the sky darkened and I could feel the change in the air long before the first drops of rain suddenly fell. The temperature changed and huge clouds came rolling in like waves. Kulu was on horseback, on the bank, watching me. He called to me to hurry, that we should return.

I was late getting back to the farm and I feared my mother's wrath, but with my brother's absence she appeared to neither know nor care that I had not kept to the curfew. She was inside reading. That was her favourite pastime. She was kept busy with running the place, but as soon as she had some time to herself she used to sit on the veranda or disappear into her study and bury herself in some book or other. Books kept her utterly absorbed, often for hours at a time. I learned that from her. Books became my friends too. Without Horace there with me, I read and read.

My mother had books sent to her from town. She read avidly and I discovered that if I talked to her about them, then I could in some remote way, through them, catch her attention. It was lonely without Horace, and, finally, in that loneliness I discovered that my mother and I actually did have something in common. We both missed my brother.

I suppose she was quite a lonely person even before Horace left. We lived in such an isolated place; it would be lonely for anybody. Maybe it was my father's fault. He had chosen to move them both out there, to this farm in the middle of nowhere. But then, I think she knew that in advance. He had been raised there and she married him knowing what sort of life it was that he wanted. She bought into that too. I think it suited her.

There were no books that did not interest her. She tended to get her books in groups. She would have a fad of reading everything she could find about one thing, and then would choose something new upon which to become an expert. Her latest interest was books on art. She had been reading with determination through all manner of different books on art, the history of art, biographies of famous painters, literally anything she could get her hands on.

This was something of a new departure. Previously the books had usually been different varieties of novels. She would read the complete work of one writer, then another, then another, and eventually move on to a different period, or a different country.

I, of course, read a lot of the same books that she did. I used to 'borrow' one by sneaking into her study at night, and would return it to the exact same place on the shelf before she got up in the morning.

So this one day I arrived back, soaking wet, and I could see her through the window, sitting in an easy chair with a book open on her lap, staring at the wall. I ran around the back of the house and let myself in, drying my hair and changing my clothes before going to join her.

She was still sitting with the book on her knees, but now she was peering at a picture in it.

'What is it?' I asked rather tentatively. She was never easy to talk to. I might have just been ignored, or attacked in some way. I tended to be quite cautious with her, mainly to protect myself, as I did not know how she would respond.

It was a book on René Magritte and she turned it so I could see the picture she was looking at. The picture was of a man. I think that it was Magritte himself, or at least I assumed he probably was. He was wearing a hat and in front of the man's face was a white bird. I thought briefly of the birds on the lake twelve miles north of the farmhouse, and the joy of watching hundreds of them moving on the shore, the impact on my eyes every time I rode out that way. This was different. This picture was simpler, clean cut, easy to view, yet what did it mean?

'It looks more like a dream of a bird than a real bird. Is he painting something he dreamed?' I asked, fearing scorn, but nonetheless wanting to be involved, wanting a conversation. Needing one, really. I had only spoken to my horse all day, as Kulu wasn't much of a conversationalist.

'Sort of,' she said. 'He isn't painting from a dream, but it is about dreams in a way, about illusion and reality.'

'It makes you think, doesn't it?' I said. I took the book from her and studied the picture.

'Turn the page,' she said. I did, and there was a picture of a man painting a bird, the same bird, or one very similar.

'What do you make of it?' she asked. 'What does it make you think?'

I didn't know if she knew the answer or if she wanted my input. 'Well,' I said, 'the thing about it is that we see the artist right there in the picture. So he can't be painting what he was actually looking at. He couldn't see himself. So he's painting something other than what he is looking at. He's painting the truth of the situation, not just what he can see of it.'

'Yes, that's interesting. But then, he still hasn't really got at the truth of it.'

'How do you mean?'

'A picture of a bird wouldn't be the truth because it misses out the painter there himself. So he paints a picture of a man painting a bird. But now what there really is, is a man painting a picture of a man painting a picture of a bird, so he would need to paint that.'

'And so on and so on, forever,' I said, understanding something that struck me as incomprehensibly profound.

'Yes. I suppose no painting can ever quite capture the truth.'

'Well, you can't draw a picture with yourself in it that captures everything, but you could paint somebody else. Then you would get the real truth. Couldn't you?'

'But if you are there to do the painting, it needs to have you in it as well. If you had a roomful of painters, each of them trying to paint the whole room, each would capture the others but fail to capture himself.'

'It's fascinating, isn't it? They would sort of spiral on and on forever, getting closer each time but never getting to the end.'

'If you could paint that, then you would have the truth.'

'So why put one painter in the picture? Why not a picture of a man painting a picture, which is of a man painting a picture?'

'I don't know. I suppose the point, if a painting really has a point, is that once you put the painter in at all, you can never finish. Just leave him out and make do with painting what you see. Don't try and capture the real truth. All you can paint is your own perception. That is as near to the truth as we can get. We can understand each other but not ourselves. I think that makes sense. If Freud is right about the mind, then it is quite true that somebody else can get to the truth about us much better than we can.'

I was starting to get confused. Horace would have known what to say. He would have explained it all to me. He would have understood.

But then it came to me. 'Maybe that is why the bird he is painting is a dove. It represents his mind, free from his body. It can understand the truth, even though he could never depict it. His body is stuck under his bowler hat, like it can't get to the heights his mind can. We can understand truth, we just can't physically draw it.'

We both looked at it. It was an explanation, of sorts anyway.

'What does the book say?' I asked.

'It doesn't explain it properly,' she replied. 'It talks about reality and illusion.' She looked around suddenly, as though seeing her surroundings for the first time.

'A bit like here,' she said cryptically.

It was the only real conversation I can remember us having.

The walls of that room were lined floor to ceiling with books. There were three very old rattan chairs, each with cushions and thin rugs on them, and the whole room looked battered. But that just added to it. It had character, as if it had absorbed all the wisdom of the hundreds of books it housed. Life in that room moved at a different pace to the rest of the world I knew.

I liked the smell of the books; I liked the way the light came into the room. I can still hear the slow swirling of the ceiling fan and the almost imperceptible squeak that it made. My mother had become so used to it that she couldn't hear it any more. It was just like what she said about the painting, about illusion and reality. We see each other's, but seldom our own.

Who knows what my mother saw as she looked at me. Did she see something that she didn't like?

I looked at her and I saw a tall, slender-boned woman dressed in a cotton skirt and a long-sleeved blouse with a book on her lap. But what was she really? I could define her, woman, wife, mother, and yet, of course, there was so much more to her. She was the complicated sum of all her experiences, the joys and tragedies, the successes and failures of her life. And the truth was, I knew very little about her.

I suspected I never would. Maybe she could see me with more clarity than I could her. It's funny, but it was that conversation that made me decide to study Fine Arts when I got to university.

Now, it might sound like I was imprisoned there, on that farm. In some ways I was, I suppose. Certainly that last year dragged so slowly I started to feel I wanted to get away. Nothing was the same without Horace there with me. It was still my home, and I loved it, but I felt frustrated, I think. Yes, frustrated.

'Will you be ready for your university entrance exams?' my mother asked suddenly.

She was actually referring to my final year school exams, which I would be sitting in town. The very fact that she did not know what they were called did not surprise me, although it was surprising that she was asking me a question. I was taken aback. It was very rare for her to ask me anything at all.

I nodded.

'It will be quiet here when you are gone,' she said, in a matter-of-fact way.

I wondered briefly then how her relationship and mine would evolve after I left. I did not doubt that I would be back. It was where Horace and I came from; it was the place we loved more than anywhere else in the world. Of course, we had been nowhere else, but I knew that no matter what life held in store for me, my roots were there, buried beneath the surface of Kenyan soil, be it moist or baked hard, and that no picture I ever saw in life would mean the same to me as that of the sun setting behind the tree on the hill.

We had not seen Horace since he left the previous September. He wrote every week, one letter to our parents and another letter for me. His letters to them were brief and they asked me once what he wrote to me. I knew what his letters to them said because I read them when they were not around. They were mainly about his studying, college life and his rooms in Trinity. There was nothing really personal in them. His letters to me were different. He told me about how he looked forward to me being there the following year, things we would do together and the friends he wanted to introduce me to. His letters gave me hope and opened up the possibilities of another life, even though it was still beyond my imagination.

Horace and I looked alike. Our skin, which would have been fair had we lived in another climate, had become used to the sun, and we both had the same tanned appearance. I still have it a bit. It's strange, like somehow you can be changed genetically if you live somewhere for long enough. We both developed this fair hair, bleached by the sun. Horace wrote that his hair had darkened a bit since living in Dublin, but not by much, and that his skin had not changed at all. I looked forward so much to his return. It was the expectation of that homecoming that kept me going through those months, an expectation, as it turned out, not to be fulfilled.

I had known loss before, the death of a pony, the death of dogs that were my pets, and the death of Kulu's two-year-old daughter. Those deaths had grieved me desperately even though I knew, or perhaps had learned, that they were just another part of life. But what was about to happen changed everything.

It was the end of June when Horace was due home.

I had recently learned to drive, and because my father was too busy, it ended up that I drove my mother to the airport. It was the longest trip I had made, being over four hours each way, and it started out on a good note. My mother was excited. We both were. It was not often we went to Nairobi. We drove in an amicable silence most of the way. We stopped once to stretch our legs and then continued on. The suspension in the jeep was not great, which I had not realised before that journey.

I became nervous when the traffic built up about twenty minutes before reaching the airport. Most of my driving thus far had been either across country or on track roads with the occasional trip into town, and I was uneasy at so much bustle on the road.

The jeep was heavy and I was tiring. I could feel my mother becoming slightly agitated, and that made me even more nervous. I suggested to her that she take over the driving but she shook her head.

'You must get used to this.'

I nearly asked why but I didn't, as it would sound rude and I didn't want to do anything to damage the truce that appeared to have evolved between us over the previous months.

'Your father and I are giving Horace the money for a car for when you both are in Dublin,' she suddenly volunteered.

This was wonderful news. It had never occurred to me that we might have wheels in Dublin, and I could see why she thought I should get used to busy traffic.

I smiled at her. 'That's really nice,' I said.

'Concentrate on the road.'

I could see her hand clenched as she clutched the door handle. It didn't help me knowing she was that scared of my driving, but then she said the most conciliatory thing I'd ever heard her say to me.

'It's not you. I mean, it's not your driving. It's just that I'm not used to the traffic.'

I realised then that she might even have been glad that I was the one who was driving, and for some reason that increased my confidence and I got us safely into the airport and found a parking place. I was occupied with what she had just said. *'It's not you.'* I wondered if there was more to that comment than was immediately apparent within the context of my driving. I wondered then for one fleeting moment if it meant an exoneration of some kind, though I did not know from what I was being exonerated.

It was another hot day. It was just coming up to the start of our winter. The nights could be quite cold, but I remember that day as being very sunny, probably one of the last days of summer. We were both excited as we waited for the arrival of Horace's plane. It really did seem like just another day, though a special one because Horace was coming home, and there was no warning of what was about to happen. My mother even clutched my arm as the arrival of the flight was announced. We looked at each other in a mixture of excitement and pleasure. A shared moment.

The doors opened as the passengers began coming through with their bags. Through the glass, I saw Horace with his case and he saw us. I'm sure of that. His face lit up and I said to our mother, 'There. There he is.'

Behind him, several African men appeared and they all came through the glass doors at more or less the same time. I saw Horace look back to see who was pushing him. Then I recognised our President, and it was one of his bodyguards who had held out his arm to hold back the passengers and let the President through. I did not think it was likely he had come in on Horace's plane. They must have just arrived at the same time.

Horace stopped and so did time. Everything stood still.

I can still see the clock above the glass doors. The time is frozen at 12.20. Horace is dressed in casual trousers with a shirt open at the neck, a jacket over one arm, his bag held in the other hand. The men are behind him. The President is dressed in a dark suit with a white shirt and tie and the bodyguards are in long, multicoloured ethnic clothing. One is wearing a hat. They are full of their own importance. Then suddenly, somewhere just behind me someone shouted, and I turned. I turned back to see what was happening, and looked forward again as I tried to understand what the sounds were. I knew the sound of gunshot well, but not like this, with screaming and hysteria as people dropped to the floor or ran in all directions.

The President was hit and so was one of the bodyguards.

But it was Horace who died.

He died there, butchered on the dusty white floor of an African airport, and it was his blood that formed the red pool around the men.

At first we could not get through to him, but I think, I am almost sure, that he was still alive when my mother cradled his head and I held his hand. I am almost sure I saw something in his eyes before the light went out.

We buried him beneath the tree on the little hill beyond the farm where the horizon meets the sky. And that is my image of Kenya, of where I was born. Horace sleeping forever near a skyline where at sunset a tree connects the earth and the sky like a black etching in a sea of changing colours.

Six

'That's awful,' Conti said. 'Unimaginably awful.'

I had never told anyone all of that before. I had told Fred some of it, and he may have guessed other bits. He had wheedled little bits of it from me, but I think he realised I was not comfortable talking about it. I had not been able to tell him about the gunfire and the screaming and the blood. Now, maybe because time had passed, it came out easier, and I think, too, it was a sign of my affection for Conti that I told her at all. And once I had started, I just had not been able to stop.

'I'm sorry,' Conti added.

I shrugged. 'A bit different to your upbringing, I should think,' I said.

'Very.' I could see that Conti was struggling to know how to react. Maybe that was why I had never told the whole story before, because of how it might make other people feel. It is difficult enough to handle one's own emotions without having to handle someone else's; I mean, when their emotion is based on what you have told them. Grief is such a deep, personal thing.

She touched my arm. 'You know, I really am very sorry.'

I did not know what to say. I needed us to move on. I really did not want to dwell in this moment of her regret for me and my embarrassment. I feared it would appear that I had told her so that I could get her sympathy.

'I don't usually tell anybody this. In fact, I never tell anybody this,' Conti said, 'but my mother didn't die when I was born.'

I remembered the conversation we had the first day we met.

'It's what I tell people because I don't want them to know the truth.'

'You don't have to tell me if you don't want to,' I said.

'But I do want to. I want . . . I want to share something in exchange with you. The truth is that my father came here when the war ended, he and Alessia. I think he was the only one of his family left by then. He was in his thirties, but by the time he met someone and fell in love he was already nearly forty, or just forty, I don't know exactly. It was quite a while later. Anyway, this girl he met, she was really young and he loved her desperately. With passion. Those are the words he used. And he married her and had me. She disappeared as soon as I was born. I don't think she even came home with me from the hospital. As far as I can make out she just abandoned me,' Conti laughed.

I could not work out if Conti found this funny. It was hard to see how she could.

'Why do you think she left?' I asked.

'I don't know. Babbo said that she was just too young. I think he was devastated at the time, but he put all his love into me. I've had a great time. I wasn't missing anything, really. I mean, it's not like I knew her. And at the end of the day, if she didn't want to know me, why would I want her? I have probably been better off without her.'

I wondered about this. In my own relationship with my mother, there had been, and continued to be, an endless sense of hurt and rejection, but for all of that I was still glad I knew my mother. There had been good times as well as bad, and I had some memories that I conjured up from time to time; Luther knocking on my mother's window, or my mother sitting in her deckchair in the shade, sometimes preparing vegetables or fruit, sometimes just sitting with a book and a cold drink in a tall glass. But it was more than that, I now realised. It was the fact that I knew my mother that gave me a sense of my own past, my own place in the big scheme of things.

'Have you ever thought of looking for her?' I asked tentatively.

Conti shook her head. 'No, I feel angry with her. She abandoned me and she abandoned Babbo. If she wanted to find us she could have done so easily enough. I can't imagine it would have been all that hard to trace the name dei Fiori.'

'Well, no,' I agreed. 'I don't know too many people called dei Fiori.'

'And I was photographed a lot when I was growing up,' Conti continued, as if long since reconciled to this fact. 'I was in magazines and things everywhere. She could hardly have missed them all. If she had any interest in me, or Babbo, she could have found us if she wanted to. I don't care where she is now. Best that she doesn't try and make contact with us now, we are happy as we are, without her.'

'Isn't that a sad story?' I said to Fred over dinner that evening. I had puzzled over it. I could not help but feel that Conti's mother must have followed her daughter's growth and progress, although at a distance. But then I thought about my own mother and how contact between us had dissolved. The only real reminders were the two Christmas cards I had received since I had left. I feared that these too would peter out in due course.

'Aren't people strange?' I persisted.

'Nowt as queer as folk,' he replied. Catching the serious look on my face, he added, 'They all seem very happy as they are, next door, I mean. Maybe things worked out for the best.'

Sometimes Fred would joke with me and I didn't always realise when he was joking. This was probably because of my own upbringing, which did not feature much in the way of teasing, and after Horace died I don't remember any laughter at all.

'They do seem happy, don't they?' I said.

'You have to be very careful going looking for a long-lost relative. Who knows what you are going to find.'

He was probably right. If you are happy with what you have,

you should be careful not to spoil that. I sometimes wondered why Fred had fallen in love with me, and whether he was happy with what he had got. I dearly hoped so. I knew that I was damaged goods, though maybe 'damaged' was too strong or too explicit a word. But I knew that I lacked a lot of things, and one of them was worldly wisdom.

'How did you meet Fred?' Conti asked me. It was some time later and we were sitting in her back garden. The cherry blossoms were falling from the trees, and Lorina was now old enough to gather them in a basket.

'He was the second person I met in Trinity. The first was my roommate, Daisy, and she introduced us. He asked me to play tennis with him.'

'And you did?'

'Yes,' I said.

'Part of me is surprised that you did.'

'Really?' I was surprised that she would say this. 'Why?'

'Well, don't take this wrong, but, well, you aren't the most out-going person in the world, are you?'

It was entirely true and I knew it, but even so I felt a bit surprised that my introverted tendencies were so transparently obvious, and I was surprised that Conti would cheerfully blurt it out.

'You're right,' I said. 'It was an effort. But, everything was an effort back then. I don't think I had a clue how to live. I didn't know the basic things that other people always seem to know. I think it was all those years when I was by myself with just Horace. I know that all that stuff just comes naturally to people, but it is something you learn how to do. Only I never really did.'

'Well, you must have made a lot of new friends going to university though.'

'It was very different. I mean, you can imagine. One minute I knew a dozen or so people in the world, and the next I was in the middle of a big city.'

'What about all the tennis friends?'

'There were only a couple I really knew. It's a funny thing, actually. I knew all of the faces at our tournaments, and I soon recognised everybody, but I wouldn't say I knew any of them. I just knew what their serve was like, and things like that.'

'It must have been a culture shock, moving to Dublin.'

'Yes. I think it may have been exciting, but I was almost too withdrawn to realise that. Even with all the new people around me, I mostly preferred my own company. I met Daisy and Fred and in some way part of the void was filled. They were great at meeting people and making friends and I just drifted along with them. I missed my brother so much. I must have been very withdrawn. Nothing seemed quite real to me without him there to share it with. I remember how I felt so cold all of a sudden. I wasn't used to gas fires and things like that. I was eighteen the first time I knew what it was like to feel real cold. I had no idea it could be like that. Of course, the nights are cold in Kenya. When the sun goes down the temperature drops, but it is not this biting chill that freezes the bones. Looking back now, and it's not that long ago, although a lot has happened in the meantime, I don't know what I would have done if I hadn't met Fred.'

It was a time I chose not to think of any more. If asked for a word to describe that period of my life, I would have said 'numb'. I had been completely and utterly frozen. When the clock stopped at twelve-twenty for Horace, it had also stopped for me.

And that was how Fred had found me. He called me his African ice maiden. I didn't say much at all. My outward appearance of health and agility covered a disconnected, frozen interior. I think it was that internal silence that attracted him. He did not see me as cold, just as shy and quiet. He used the term 'ice maiden' jokingly. It was some time before I told him that my brother had died, though I was unable to tell him what had actually happened. That night he held me with all the tenderness he possessed. He saw now that what he had taken as calmness in me was in fact a cover for a deep-rooted fragility. He wanted to love me and for me to feel his love. He needed me to know that I was not alone. I think he had already realised the harshness of my home life. He told me once that he admired my strength, but I don't think it was strength at all. I told him that I was a human being living in a state of shock. He said that he wanted to remove that shock and to be the person who would let me come alive again. I asked for nothing and indeed I expected nothing, but in so many ways he gave me everything.

'Did you ever go back? To Kenya, I mean?' Conti asked.

'No. Not yet. I suppose I hoped they might come to me, but they didn't. We send cards at Christmas.'

'Birthdays?'

I shook my head. 'My mother could never remember the date of my birthday. It was Horace who always reminded her. Birthdays ceased as soon as I left.'

'So you haven't seen them for a couple of years?'

I shook my head. 'That's right. Not since I left.'

'I think you're very brave,' Conti said. 'It isn't fair what has happened to you. You are so very brave.'

I didn't feel at all brave. It was nice to think that Conti admired some quality in me, but I knew that it was not bravery. It was simply that I had no other choice.

My mother stands at the foot of the hill. Her face appears carved from stone. My father climbs the hill with the other men carrying the coffin. I walk a little way and then I look back. My mother is standing there and her face is suddenly etched with the grief we all feel. I walk back to her. There will be time later for me to stand or sit on that hill where Horace and I spent our childhood. Now I return and stand beside my mother. I reach for her hand. It is a gesture of love, or maybe of understanding, or maybe just the acknowledgment that we are in the same place experiencing the same thing.

My mother does not let me take her hand. Even now, she is incapable of realising that I need her. Her head never moves, her eyes are distant, far away, in some other place. I drop my hand and look back at the hill. I had driven her to that airport that awful day. I feel a sense of responsibility.

I want my mother to touch me. I want her to know that we are sharing the same pain. And yet she cannot do it. I feel guilt. The sun is beginning to burst in the west, shattering golds and reds and yellows breaking the sky. In the distance, far away, even the jungle seems silent.

Beneath me, the earth, always teeming with life, appears to have died.

Conti had been indulged in every imaginable way, raised with all of Babbo's love and money. By the time she had married Joe, she had travelled widely for a young woman of the seventies. She had been to Paris and New York, Moscow and Madrid, and she brought into her marriage very different attributes to those I brought to mine, and yet there we were, living side by side in our separate homes, each household functioning in entirely different ways. I saw her as a wonderful combination of mixed cultures, Italian and Irish, warm and funny, glamorous and sophisticated.

'I'm glad we're neighbours,' I said to her.

'Me too. I usually get on better with men than with women.'

Conti sometimes threw out odd comments like that, comments that both encouraged and tantalised me. I warmed to any titbit of affection or admiration that came my way.

We smiled at each other as Lorina carried a little basket of blossoms over to us.

It was one of those blissfully peaceful summer afternoons. Joe was working in Dublin on some case or other and Fred was reporting on a tennis tournament for a radio show. He had recently started doing a little radio and television sports coverage. It was not the most dependable of work, often involving being called in at the last minute, but he always made himself available in the hope that it would become more permanent.

Meanwhile, because of his absences at the weekends, I was spending more and more time with Conti. I felt a kind of glow that she sought out my company. It was lonely when Fred was away at the weekends, and even when he was at home he was increasingly engrossed in sport, be it on the television, the radio or in the newspapers.

There was a strange similarity to the past, lying in the garden with Conti. It reminded me of lying under the tree with Horace, even though the conversations bore no resemblance, none whatsoever. Horace and I used to bring water in a bottle in a knapsack with us. Conti and I drank martinis.

That afternoon, Babbo and Alessia had disappeared off together on what the Count referred to as 'an errand'.

'The mind boggles,' was Conti's reaction to this as I giggled.

'Do you know the saying, "beware of an old man in a hurry"?' I asked.

'Indeed I do, Helena, and that was a supremely suspicious old man in a hurry,' Conti said.

An air of secrecy had surrounded this 'errand' for some days. Conti wondered whether he was going to get some gift for her or Lorina, as he sometimes did.

'Lucky you,' I said.

'Or maybe lucky Lorina,' Conti replied. 'Who knows?'

We spent that afternoon lounging in the garden. I read a book to Lorina and Conti and I chatted, taking it in turns to doze in the sun. She went inside a while later to make more cocktails and she brought them out on a tray. We sat there peacefully in their small orchard, sipping our drinks, becoming pleasantly light-headed and discussing the correct constituents of the perfect cocktail versus the perfect martini, while in truth I didn't even know the difference.

Our reverie was interrupted by the sound of a loud, oily type of engine on the road outside.

'I wonder what that can be,' Conti said, dragging herself upright. The sound seemed very close.

I looked around expectantly as the noise got louder before it died away.

'Maybe we should take a look,' Conti said with lazy curiosity but nonetheless settling back in her chair.

At this point the Count and Alessia appeared, wearing crash helmets. The Count was dressed in leathers.

Despite his new attire, or perhaps because of it, there was a lively spring in his step and he beamed happily at us from inside the helmet.

'What . . . ? What . . . ?' Conti said, trying to form a question that she could not frame.

The Count removed his crash helmet with a flourish.

'Oh my God,' said Conti to me, smothering a giggle but also slightly shocked. 'It's Biggles' dad.'

I could not control my laughter. This was unfortunate because I had just consumed the last of my champagne cocktail, which was now threatening to emerge from my nose. Conti was too concerned with her father to notice. It was the first time I had ever seen her not totally in control.

'Come,' said the Count, 'I show you.'

Beneath the house in the right-hand section of the double garage where Joe usually parked his car was a motorbike with a sidecar.

'Nice, eh?' said the Count proudly.

That was not precisely what Joe said when he came home shortly afterwards and nearly drove into it.

Conti tried reasoning with him. 'He's an old man,' she said.

'I know,' Joe said in a combination of dismay and disbelief. 'He is an old man. That's the whole point. We had such trouble getting him to stop driving, but in fact he would probably be safer in a car.'

'It's given him a new lease of life,' Conti argued.

'Wonderful, just wonderful. Well, he's not to take Lorina out in it . . . no, Conti, for God's sake, we can't even let him go out on it. If he has an accident, we are accountable. No responsible adult would let a man of that age out on a motorbike.'

'He is an adult,' said Conti. 'He told me he was an adult quite firmly and can decide for himself what he wants to do. I don't see what we can do to stop him, really. And he's so pleased with himself.'

'I can't imagine what right-minded person would sell that to an old man who is so feeble he can hardly walk.'

'Well, wait until you see him now. He's more upright than he's been in ages. He and Alessia are in their element. I've never seen him as animated and enthusiastic about anything; well, not in years anyway.'

'What possessed him?' Joe wondered aloud.

The Count, in fact, had been looking through the few old photographs he had brought with him from Italy and had come across one of himself with Mussolini, bringing back memories of distant times, when happiness seemed to have been connected with his motorbike. In fact, Joe felt quite alarmed when he looked at the picture and it was clear that Mussolini and the Count were very fond of each other, with the two laughing together on a balcony that he thought he recognised.

'Is good picture, no?' the Count said when he saw Joe peering at it. 'Benito and I . . . happy days.'

It was all Joe could do to dissuade him from framing it with pride and displaying it in the dining room.

The Count's only regret was that the shop was unable to sell him old-fashioned goggles and furthermore insisted that he bought a helmet.

'I am like spaceman,' he said, looking at himself in the mirror.

Joe, realising there was little he could do against Conti's opposition and the Count's enthusiasm, withdrew.

Privately he was amused at the image of the Count and the cook, but he kept that amusement to himself. He was, however, adamant that Lorina should not be taken out in the sidecar.

'I don't know what to do,' Conti said to me. 'Babbo and Alessia want to take the bike out during the day, and Joe is adamant that Lorina can't go with them, and I'm out at work . . .'

'Maybe you could convince your father only to go out at the weekends when you're around,' I suggested.

'Helena, I love him dearly, but I don't quite trust him. I'm afraid he will agree to whatever I say but then do his own thing. I'm thinking of getting a nanny or a housekeeper. Someone I can rely on.'

I said nothing. Each to their own, I thought. I had not changed my views on who would raise my child. If and when I had one, I was going to give it all the love and attention a child needed and I would raise it myself, not have someone else do it during daylight hours, leaving me with a sleeping baby at the end of the day. I knew, though, that such an approach simply would not suit Conti. If it did then she would already be doing that. Conti did not mind that Lorina's first words had been in Italian, lovingly taught to her by the Count and Alessia. Even now, though, Lorina still had not spoken in English. She toddled along on her little legs with her huge dark eyes, calling for Babbo.

Conti went ahead and employed someone to come in during the day and she and Joe had an argument over it. He told me about it in a moment of pure frustration.

'I tried to stop her,' he said, 'but she pointed out that I was not prepared to cut short my working hours, so why should she? I can see the logic in that, but I can't cut short my hours, and she can. She only does a few hours a day anyway. And it's an unnecessary expense, but she pointed out that she was paying for it. By which she means the Count. She says that I'm not out of pocket, which is true, but as someone who was brought up with a mother who worked all the hours of the day and the evening too, I think children need their mother around.'

Of course I agreed with him, but I could also see that Conti could not bear to be at home all the time.

'Children are happy if their parents are happy,' I said to him. I thought of my upbringing, and I had been happy in most ways, but if my mother had been a happier person I am sure I would have been too. 'It will make your life easier,' I continued. 'Conti will be happier and the household will run more smoothly.'

These were facts, and anyway I felt loyalty to Conti and if I said anything else I would have been letting her down. She needed my support. One of the main appeals of having a housekeeper would be that she could do the things Alessia ought to have been doing. A cook in her seventies had her limitations, and the situation of late had turned into one where Conti was helping to take care of Alessia rather than the other way around.

'Plus Conti gets a real kick out of her work,' I went on. That was true, in a fashion. She had recently appeared on the front of a new catalogue leaning against a portmanteau with a seductive look on her beautiful face. The same picture was used for advertising in a number of newspapers and magazines. She loved the limelight and was revelling in it.

'I know,' Joe said. 'You're right.'

Much of his time was spent arguing in court, where his skills were used to the full. At home, he needed respite from that vicious competitive environment, and so he seldom took issue with things. In court, he needed to win. At home, he just wanted Conti happy. To him, that was winning, and it did not matter what she got away with in the meantime. Thus, they both 'won' in most things. And it was possible, just possible, that as the mother, she actually did know what was best for Lorina. Of course, if somebody in court had been foolish enough to suggest such a thing he would have verbally levered them round all four walls of that courtroom and back again. Now, though, he found himself pretending that Conti was right. On the rare occasions when something was important enough for Joe to want to contest Conti, she had a way of missing the point, or bringing up something irrelevant, or just playing her trump card of being upset and hurt, to which there really was no answer.

Seven

I finished my degree. It took two more years and then I was done. My time in Trinity was wonderful, but I often had the feeling that I did not get as much from it as other students did. I enjoyed studying, but at the end of the day, when my peers were heading to the Buttery or to pubs in town, I made my way to the station and went home to my husband. But I had no regrets about being married.

On the contrary, I had the feeling that I had been privileged to have met Fred so quickly after my arrival in Dublin, but because I was married I missed out on flirtations and boyfriends, parties and one-night stands. 'Missed out' is probably the wrong term. I had found love so quickly and I was glad, but I felt on the outside of things as various matings and break-ups took place.

There was talk in the department of my staying on after my degree, and I considered it briefly, but in the meantime one of the art galleries in the city centre offered me a junior position and I took it. My allowance from home had stopped as soon as I had finished studying, and Fred and I needed the money. He was freelancing now, and some weeks he was inundated with work and at other times he was at a loose end. Our mortgage was not high by other people's standards, thanks to the money Fred's godfather had left him, but it was difficult to make ends meet and my salary would ease that problem.

I found the discipline of a normal job quite rewarding. Instead of organising my own time, I went to work and came home at regular hours.

The dress code was smart, and when I fretted over having to get new clothes, Conti gave me some of her things that she no longer wore. The quality of her cast-offs were a far cry from the cast-offs I had had as a child. Horace's hand-me-down shorts and T-shirts were always the worse for wear by the time I got them. Conti's discarded suits were beautifully tailored in the best of fabrics and still looked completely new.

'I can't,' I said when she showed them to me.

'I won't be wearing them again,' she said. 'They're going out. I need more space in my wardrobes and you might as well have them.'

Put like that, I couldn't resist. They were beautiful and she seemed to take so much pleasure in pairing them with different blouses and shirts that she no longer wanted.

She was so generous. I almost cried when I took them.

'I can never repay you,' I said.

'Our friendship,' she said. 'That's repayment.'

That sounds like it was one-sided, as though I gave her friendship and she gave me clothes, but it wasn't like that. The friendship was mutual. I really loved her company. She made me laugh. I had no idea back then what, if anything, she got from me.

She took me to a dressmaker who made the suits slightly smaller, as I was thinner than Conti. They came back to me a week later and I hung them lovingly in my wardrobe with my few other items. I thought of Conti's bulging closets and for some reason it made me feel very humble. I decided not to tell Fred that she had given me her clothes, as I did not want him to be upset or annoyed and I had the feeling he might be. He liked her just as I did, and I know he enjoyed Joe's company, and I did not want him to feel diminished by her generosity. I would have liked to have asked Conti to keep it our secret, but it seemed to me that this would be colluding behind Fred's back, so I said nothing other than to thank her repeatedly. She admired the suits on me and I basked in their loveliness.

Some time later, the gallery was putting on its first exhibition since I had joined the small staff. We were putting together a compilation of African paintings. There was one of a sunset and somehow I was photographed looking at it. I was startled when Fred showed me the picture in the newspaper. The caption read, 'Hauntingly beautiful'.

'I didn't even know I was being photographed,' I said. 'The picture is beautiful. I detract from it.'

'The caption refers to you, silly,' Fred said. He sounded proud. 'I'm going to contact the paper today and get a copy of it. It's absolutely lovely.'

The phone rang. It was Jackson and Marjorie and they both wanted to speak to me. 'It's the most beautiful picture of the most beautiful daughter-in-law,' Marjorie said.

I didn't see myself the way she did. I wasn't beautiful. If someone was looking for beauty, it was Conti they should look at, not me.

After they hung up, I said to Fred, 'I'm not beautiful.' I wasn't fishing for a compliment; I just did not understand. 'I'm just a person who found adulthood. An accident.'

'No,' Fred said, 'You're no accident. You are more like a butterfly that emerged from a chrysalis. A beautiful butterfly.'

It was strange, the self-esteem that I got from that single photo and the kind comments.

Conti, however, was not quite so complimentary about the photograph.

'It's not particularly good,' she said. 'Quite grainy, in fact.'

'I know what you mean,' I said.

'You should smile more,' she continued. 'You look a bit grim in this picture. It's very sombre. You really could make more of yourself.'

I knew she did not mean this unkindly. She was right. I was too serious, but the picture of the sunset was really lovely. And I did dress sombrely, but all I had were her lovely suits and my own rather worn dresses and jeans.

Conti knew how to dress. She always wore lots of jewellery, nice accessories, very high heels and the sheerest of stockings. Her little black numbers were low to expose as much of her perfect cleavage as possible. Her hair was often pushed back behind one ear to show an expensive earring or to elongate her neck. Some women just have that skill, and Conti was one of them.

'Maybe we should go shopping together some time,' she said. 'We could get you some new clothes. I could help you choose. It would be fun.'

I thanked her. I knew she meant well, but in my heart I knew I could not wear such low-cut tops or skirts with slits up the sides. I did not have Conti's self-confidence and I feared that a shopping trip with her would just underline that fact. I also feared what it would cost. Conti spent her money on Grafton Street, usually in Brown Thomas, and anything she saw that caught her eye she bought without a second thought.

During the week following the opening of the exhibition, two things happened. The first was the arrival of an artist who wanted me to pose for him. He had seen the photograph in the paper and he wanted to capture the look on my face on canvas.

I found that funny. 'You'll have to make do with the photograph,' I said with a smile. 'I could not pose. I wouldn't know how.'

'It's simple,' he said. 'I just want you to sit while I paint your face. That is all.'

'No, really, I couldn't.'

'Well, I'm going to leave you my phone number,' he said. 'You might change your mind. I really would love to paint you.'

He was preparing for an exhibition of portraits for the following year. He had been asked to produce six. Five he had. He wanted another one and he tried to convince me to sit for him.

He left his contact number, having asked my colleagues to encourage me to phone.

The second surprising event was that numerous people came to the exhibition and recognised me. Some actually said they became interested because of the photograph. One man brought me a lily. He said he had not been sure from the article if I actually worked in the gallery or if I had been a visitor, but that if I had not been there when he came, he was going to leave the lily in front of the painting of the African sunset.

I brought the lily home and put it in water. I had this warm feeling inside, an encouraging feeling. The idea that anyone would come to the gallery because of me was very reassuring. In my heart I knew it was because of the paintings, but there was a nice sensation attached to the whole business.

'We'll have to have you photographed more often when we're opening a new exhibition,' the gallery director told me.

I smiled, unsure if he was being serious or not. In some way my self-esteem improved during that week. I would have liked to have told Conti about the artist who wanted to paint me, but I knew that she had not been particularly pleased with my photo in the paper.

It was human nature. After all, she was used to being in newspapers and magazines, and she may have felt it was her right in some way. I didn't see it as jealousy, more that she saw me as having stepped on her turf, and she was my friend and I did not want to upset her.

Living with a little confidence was a lot better than living with none. Being married and being loved by Fred had given me a boost in that regard. Now I had had another bit of a lift and I did not want to do anything that would diminish this. People probably had weeks like that all the time, but I did not, and I wanted to enjoy it just as it was. I loved the fact that my parents-in-law had phoned and praised me. I was proud of the fact that the gallery director had come and spoken to me. It was as if I suddenly mattered.

I wondered if love and praise and admiration had always been there and I just had not known how to identify it. I probably spent too much time thinking about all of this, but it was all new.

I remembered the Count when he appeared with his motorbike in his leathers and how he had almost bounded around the corner into the garden with a spring in his step like I had never seen before. I was like that.

I felt happy. It's pathetic that something like a tiny bit of praise could make me feel like that, but it did. I felt reassured and comfortable with myself, and maybe because I was more relaxed than I had been during those long, slow years since my brother's murder, I finally became pregnant.

'Father, where do we get our names?'

Horace and I are sitting up in our beds, him reading a book, and me just being. I can see him through the open door in the room across the passage. Father has come in to say good night. He does that every evening. Sometimes he is very quick and I know he has work he wishes to continue, and sometimes he dawdles in the doorway before going to join Mother. Most of his days are spent reading and working in his study. He oversees the running of the farm from a remote distance, which seems both to suit him and to work well. Lately he has been working on a new set of mathematical schoolbooks, having received a new contract from a publisher to write or compile appropriate work for various school levels.

'What names?'

'Mine and Horace's.'

I am delaying the light being switched off. I like when he tells me things.

'Well, Horace was named after a writer. He was a Roman poet.'

'And me, Father? Who was Helena?'

'That's another story. Time to sleep, Helena. Goodnight now.'

And the light was gone.

My home was a sanctuary. I loved it. I liked the warm feeling of security it gave me when I came up the lane returning from work. It was a haven, a shelter from the outside world. I kept it immaculately clean and tidy. Our bookshelves grew over time and I dusted the books once a week with a feather duster that slipped lightly over the tops as I moved quickly around the room. The kitchen was a haven and I kept its surfaces empty and spotless. Our bedroom was a quiet place, a place where we slept and made love, our clothes neatly put away or deposited in the lidded laundry basked. Fred had a habit of abandoning his shoes around the house. I did not ask him not to, but instead waited until he was not looking and then brought them to the bedroom and placed them in his wardrobe.

When I found I was pregnant, I was disbelieving. I looked around our home and thought of what was happening, that I was going to bring life to earth, to create a human being, and to have the responsibility for that life as long as I lived. It seemed to me to be the most momentous event imaginable. My world changed.

Everything seemed more vibrant and more colourful than it had before, as if somehow the volume level of my life had been turned up.

Fred was overjoyed. He wanted me to rest, to put my feet up, to keep the baby safe.

'I'm fine,' I said to him. 'I don't need to rest. Honestly, I've never felt better.'

He and I had now been together for five years. We had become so accustomed to each other, so at ease with each other that habit and routine had taken over. But now he reverted to the way he had been in the early days and months of our marriage. He fussed over me, bringing me tea in bed, putting out the rubbish, rubbing my feet when we lay on the sofa in the evening and whispering to me how much he loved me. It was like everything was being enhanced, the two of us together pitted against the world.

And yet, I felt anxious. I was slow in admitting it to myself, partly because I could not properly explain what it was I feared. It was to do with the routine of my life, my life as I knew it, being irreversibly disturbed just at the point where I seemed to have become at ease with it. It was also to do with the enormity of the responsibility of what we were embarking upon. My mind was full of questions: what would happen if there were complications during the pregnancy? What if something went wrong or if our child was ill? What if he or she didn't have a happy life? These were not intrusive fears, more like shadows that hovered on the edges of my consciousness.

Fear is a consuming emotion. I had known it after Horace died and I had come alone to Dublin. In a way I had to learn how to fit into this western world where everything was new to me, and now, when I looked back, I could see that my childhood, which was all I had known, had become part of something that was gone. It belonged in the past and the life that had been my norm had been replaced by my life with Fred.

And now this life with Fred was going to be irreversibly changed and I could not imagine what it would be like. I was filled with hope and happiness, but there was anxiety there too, anxiety that gnawed away at me.

Buried in the midst of these thoughts was my memory of Tuesday.

Tuesday was a little girl, the baby daughter of Kulu and the housemaid.

Why she had been named Tuesday was never clear to me, as she had been born on a Sunday, although, as it happened, she died on a Tuesday. Memories of her now haunted me. In the scheme of things, her death had happened and time had moved on. I had only been seven years old when she died, but now, as an adult, I thought about her and I saw things differently. I wondered if maybe I had been protected from the true meaning of Tuesday's death, of the real loss, of the pain of adults who perhaps had gone out of their way to hide as much as possible from Horace and me. Aspects of one's memories become hazy with time. I could not remember if Horace and I had ever talked about Tuesday and her death with any real emotion.

It was I who told Horace.

'Tuesday is dead.' I said it in much the same way as he had once said, 'Florence died.' Florence was a bat of which he was particularly fond. I had never been able to distinguish Florence from any of the other bats that gathered beneath the eaves, and I remembered having no strong feelings about Florence's demise other than worrying that it might upset Horace and ruin our day.

When Tuesday died I did not know what her death was going to mean. She had been too little for me to play with as a friend. She lived with her mother and Kulu and her brother at the back of the house.

My own mother gave me no guidance. Whatever burial took place happened while Horace and I were elsewhere. There was a sense that life had come and gone and that no mark had been made on the earth by the passing of tiny Tuesday. But I felt such terrible guilt. I think Horace did too.

Kulu went away for a while. He disappeared three weeks later and did not return for a month, and when he reappeared, life resumed much as before. Kulu never said anything to Horace or to me about Tuesday.

In truth, if I felt loss at that time, it was to do with Kulu's absence, not with Tuesday's death.

Now, as an adult, I realised that it was the unknown and the not knowing in life that were so frightening. I vowed to make things clearer for my unborn baby, to show it more in life, to teach it, to guide it, to give it love and security and a foundation for the future that would be more stable than my own. Yet even as I had these thoughts, I had the feeling I was being unfair. My home life had been stable. All that had really been missing was the knowledge that my mother loved me, and so I vowed to love this unborn child inside me.

I was in Conti's bedroom when I told her about the pregnancy. She had invited me over, insistent that I should borrow some of her gaudier pieces of jewellery, and we were looking through various velvet-inlaid boxes.

'I rather like the simple things,' I said, picking up a silver chain with a tiny silver cross on it. 'My mother has one of these, just like it. It's pretty.'

'Far too plain,' Conti said, taking it from me and pushing it to the bottom of the box. 'Babbo gave it to me when I was little. It belonged to my mother.'

I wished I had not admired it.

'Look, try this,' Conti continued, picking out a necklace of large coloured stones. She held it around my neck and we stood in front of the mirror.

'Not really my style,' I said gently. 'Conti . . .'

'Yes? Why not? What's wrong with it? It will suit you. Go on, live a little.'

'No, it's not that. I want to tell you something . . .'

'Hmm?' Conti asked disinterestedly as she rooted further in the box and then took out another one.

'Conti, I'm pregnant.'

Conti almost dropped the box. 'You're what? Really? I don't believe it.' She laughed and shook her head. 'So am I.'

'What? Really?' I echoed. 'Oh, that's wonderful.'

I could hardly take it in. We would go through these months together. 'When are you due? Oh, this is so exciting. We'll do this together.'

Conti laughed. 'What a coincidence,' she said. She sounded almost casual about it. 'Try this,' she said, taking out a sapphire blue necklace with diamantes interlinking the precious stones.

'That's beautiful,' I said. 'You have so many lovely necklaces and bracelets.'

'Babbo,' Conti said. 'Poor old Joe, he never knows what to buy me. Babbo always gets there first.'

'Are you scared?'

'Scared of what?' Conti asked, puzzled.

'The pregnancy, everything to do with it . . . '

'Well, I'm not delighted, if that's what you are asking.' Conti slumped onto the bed, the jewellery momentarily abandoned. 'I suppose I always thought I'd have lots of children, but I'm not particularly maternal, if you see what I mean. And then, after we had Lorina, and God knows a baby is an awful bloody tie, you can't do anything. Anyway, this one is an accident. Just bad luck.'

'Bad luck? Conti, don't say that. Even if it is an accident, it will be wonderful.'

At the time I fleetingly thought that what she said was not a safe thing to utter. Inside me, even though I was only a few months pregnant, I could feel life. It was like the unfurling of a bud, the parched, cracked earth in the dry season suddenly feeling moisture and a seed unleashing its shoot to break through the hard soil. I felt alive.

I was afraid, but I was also ecstatic. It was as if, unknown to me, this was what I had been waiting for my whole life.

Conti was insistent that we went to the same obstetrician. We made our appointments for the same day and travelled there and back together. We went for a scan at the same time, trying to surpass each other in the amount of water we had to drink before the examination, with me, for once, outdoing Conti.

Then Conti was called back for another scan almost immediately. It was a possibility that had terrified me throughout, but which had never occurred to Conti before that phone call.

'We need to check something,' she was told.

'But you said everything was all right. I thought everything was fine.'

'I'll go with you,' I said. Joe was busy in court. 'It will be all right, I promise. We'll go through this together.' The gravity of the mutual reassurances had changed, and now I was the one doing all the reassuring.

I sat with Conti and held her hand while the scan was taking place.

The rhythmic, gentle thump of a heartbeat could be heard, with something like a small echo behind it.

'Does that sound all right?' Conti said, looking at the screen.

'Just one moment, Mrs Martin. I'm going to get someone to look at this.'

We were left together as the radiologist went in search of a doctor.

'For God's sake, don't leave me, Helena.' Conti looked and sounded scared.

'It's going to be fine,' I reassured her. 'It's definitely going to be fine. I won't leave you.'

I was looking at the screen but could not work out what I was seeing. It looked like whatever was there had five limbs. I wondered if that meant it was a boy. Neither Conti nor I had asked the gender of our babies at the previous scan, having agreed we did not want to know.

Conti had said that if she had to have another baby, she would like to have a boy. I did not tell her that I wanted a boy too. I feared that I might not know how to love a girl. I had not yet put this into words, neither aloud nor in my mind, but it was a fear that was slowly evolving into some sort of clarity. I felt I had learned from my mother the skills and affection that could be directed to a boy. But a girl? I doubted myself. I knew that if I told Fred this, he would dismiss it as nonsense.

But for me, the fear was real enough. It was an acknowledgment that was slowly coming to the fore. Watching Conti bringing up Lorina with a distinct lack of maternal care had reinforced my fears. She had been raised with no mother and it seemed to me that she had never bonded with Lorina. It was not that she did not love Lorina; I'm sure she did, but she gave her little attention.

A doctor arrived, and more gel was smeared on Conti's stomach as she held my hand. I could feel her grip tighten. I could feel her fear almost as a tangible entity in the room, and I sat there hardly able to breathe as the doctor watched the screen.

'You're right,' he said to the radiologist. 'Well, Mrs Martin, how do you feel about having twins?'

'Twins?' Her relief was palpable.

'Oh, Conti,' I said. 'Oh, that's wonderful.'

'Is it?' Conti said. 'It's certainly a relief that that's what this is all about. I thought there was something wrong.'

'Well…' There was a pause, and in that pause I could sense that something was amiss. They were identical twins sharing one placenta, but one twin's heart was not beating as regularly or as strongly as the other. That was the faint echo we were hearing.

'What does it mean?' Conti asked.

'It's too early to say. We'll be monitoring you more than usual. You must not worry, it won't help. There is no reason to think this pregnancy won't go full term, and as I said, you'll be monitored. If there is any change we will see it immediately. You will get full support.'

'No need to worry . . . ' Conti grimaced on the way home. There was no stopping for tea or juice that day.

'It's really strange,' she continued. 'I don't remember feeling like this when I was pregnant with Lorina. But now I feel protective, I think that's the word. I want what's inside me to be safe. I feel afraid.'

I held her hand.

'You probably did feel the same with Lorina; you just don't remember it so clearly. It's going to be fine. They said there was no need to worry. We'll get through this together.'

I had never been in this role before. I was not just a friend, but the stronger one, the one providing support. In my heart I feared that something would happen to one or other of Conti's twins, or worse still, to both, and I knew that I could not rejoice in my own situation because of that.

My personal fears diminished in some way. They did not disappear, but they had less meaning. My pregnancy was normal. I would live with it, and however afraid I might feel, I knew it was nothing to what Conti was enduring. We continued home in silence with me driving.

Joe was adamant that Conti should give up work, just as she was adamant she should not. She compromised by going in three days a week, but found that she could not keep that up for long. She was tired, distracted and somewhat frayed.

'I can't imagine feeling normal again,' she said to me.

'You will,' I reassured her with more confidence than I actually felt.

As our pregnancies progressed, I began to feel as if I had never been any other way. I could not imagine what it was going to be like not carrying this baby. I wanted to write and tell my mother, but feared the silence that would follow and knew that that would hurt more than anything, so I did not put myself in the position of getting no response.

Fred's delight was ongoing, which was reflected in his

cheerfulness. He felt fulfilled in some way by having me pregnant, in the knowledge that he was going to be a father. He brought me flowers at least once a week, presenting them to me with a gentle kiss.

'You are so loving to me,' I said.

'Was I not always?' he asked, puzzled.

'You were. I just meant that we seem closer.'

'You seem happier,' he said to me. 'It makes it easier to show my love.'

'But I've always been happy with you,' I said.

'It's not that you didn't seem happy with me,' he pondered. 'It's more that you had this underlying sadness. I had tried to understand your sadness, and I think I did understand it. But it seems gone now, and I love that.'

Jackson and Marjorie were thrilled for us.

'I don't believe either of us sees ourselves as old enough to be grandparents,' Jackson said. 'Though having said that, I must admit I don't think we are young enough to be Freyn's parents.'

'Does that mean they are happy for us?' I asked Fred when he repeated this conversation.

'They're delighted,' he reassured me, 'and they both said you will make a wonderful mother.'

I smiled ruefully. I knew and understood my fears now. Over the weeks, they had come to make sense to me. There was nothing I could do about them. They would wait and only time would tell if I would have to confront them.

The seasons passed and reluctantly I handed in my notice at work. It was difficult to give up the job, which I loved, but the reluctance was reduced by the fact that I was about to start this new job as a mother. I was surprised at how vigilant and nervous Fred was about my pregnancy, especially as his mother had played tennis right up to the day she gave birth to both him and Freyn, but then, as Conti said, maybe that was why he was so nervous.

'We've decided to go for yellow,' I said. 'It's neutral.'

Conti and I were out shopping for baby clothes and were discussing the colours of the babies' bedrooms.

'We're going to have one room painted in pink and the other in blue,' Conti said.

Their house was so much larger than ours, with a seemingly endless variety of bedrooms, despite the Count being ensconced upstairs in one of them and Alessia in the basement.

'If the babies are girls, we'll put them in the pink room, and if boys we'll put them in the blue one and Lorina can move to the pink one and we'll do her room up as the guest room,' Conti said.

I knew that Conti had known Lorina's gender before her birth, but now it was as if she were taking the lead from me. When I spoke of the surprise element of a baby's gender and how I did not want to know in advance, Conti followed my approach. 'It's one of the few real surprises a human being can have,' she had said.

We continued to browse through the store, and I began to look at cots and cribs. I was not entirely prepared for the price tags I saw on some of them, and wondered what sort of designer accessories they could possibly amount to. Fred and I had inherited Freyn's cot and various baby items and I had no intention of replacing them, but nonetheless I looked at the items with interest.

'Helena?' Conti seemed shaken. Her voice was not the smooth, polished dulcet voice that I was so used to, but had turned into a vulnerable, wavering voice. 'I'm afraid of preparing for two babies, in case . . . you know . . . in case . . .'

Conti already owned one of everything from the time when Lorina was small. Now, she did not know whether she would need a second set. I felt I had been insensitive even though this shopping trip had been Conti's suggestion.

I had never seen or heard her like this before. The confidence she normally exuded from every pore suddenly deserted her when we spoke about the forthcoming births. She was fine most of the rest of the time. It was really only when our conversations drifted into babyhood and all that went with it that she appeared uncertain and she allowed me to see the chink in her usually smoothly polished armour.

'What do you think? Should I buy another one? A second cot?'

How could I possibly answer a question like that? To say no suggested that I thought the second twin was not going to make it, contrasting somewhat with the confidence I was trying to convey. But to say a confident yes brought its own risks. The thought of having two of everything, being ready for two babies, and then having to put away a cot that was not needed would be horrible. I struggled to formulate a response.

'Please,' Conti persisted. 'What do you think?'

'What does Joe say?'

'Oh, Joe. He's too busy for this kind of thing. Don't get me wrong, he's thrilled we're having a baby – babies – but he sees this as woman stuff, I think.'

This was not quite true, but Joe had learned from Conti's pregnancy with Lorina that she did not require his input, at least not over and above what was biologically essential. He was treating her with caution. She seemed to him to be totally different.

In the past, when she was pregnant with Lorina, he recalled her saying to friends and colleagues, 'Of course we know the baby's sex. It was the first thing I asked.' Now she wanted to know nothing about the babies. It was as if she were trying to distance herself from what was happening.

'It's at times like this . . . ' I stopped myself. I had been about to say that it was at times like this it would be nice to have a mother around. It was something I had been repeatedly thinking, but it would not be the most tactful thing to say to Conti, whose mother had simply left her.

It was like treading on eggshells. I did not know what to say. I wanted to comfort her, but I felt I did not have the skills. I was always tactful with her, but now it was very difficult to get it right.

'What were you going to say?' Conti asked.

'Oh, I don't know. It's at times like this that you need your friends. You have to think positively. You are in good hands, Conti. Everything is going to be all right. They know what they're doing. And I'm here with you.'

Eight

The week before I stopped working, the artist who had asked me to sit for him approached me again. He did it via the director of the gallery, who encouraged me to do the sitting.

I did not tell anyone because I wanted to surprise Fred, and because I rather feared Conti's discouragement. Every day I travelled to the artist and we sat and talked for a while before he began working.

His name was Simon Petersen, a tall, lanky man of Norwegian descent. He had come to Dublin in his twenties to study, and now called it home, just visiting Norway occasionally. He described to me a small town that glistened in the snow and ice on the streets. He told me of coloured roofs that emerged as the snow melted.

'A far cry from Kenya,' I said with a smile, 'and a far cry from Ireland.'

'I'm only describing the winter, though. The summer has its own joys. When you mentioned Kenya just now, a look came on your face. That is the look I want. So, when I'm painting, I need you to think of Kenya; yes, just like that. It's the look in the photo that I originally saw, when you were looking at the painting of the sunset. You are to think of that.'

He placed me near the window with the light coming in and my face slightly turned. It was not an uncomfortable pose, though I did tire after a while and found it hard to sit so rigidly straight.

Two children are lying on the ground under an umbrella tree. One is Horace. One is me.

'Aren't animals clever, the things they can do?'

'They often aren't, it's all about instinct. About behaviour.'

'How do you mean?'

'I read a great example the other day. There's a funny kind of insect called a Sphex wasp. He makes a burrow in the ground—'

'Like my anthill?'

'I think so, only it isn't quite so big. When he has made his burrow, he cleans it out carefully, and then he goes hunting aboveground for prey.'

'What does he eat?'

'Crickets and things like that.'

'Eugh. Not very nice.'

'They are very nice if you are a Sphex wasp. Delicious. After he has found a cricket, he stings it to paralyse it, so it can't move and get away. Then he drags it to his burrow. But then he does something funny. He leaves his cricket behind while he goes inside to check that his home is still safe and then he reaches out and drags his prey inside to eat it.'

'Or maybe to save it for later, like a treat?'

'He seems very clever, doesn't he? The way he checks that nothing nasty has got into his burrow while he was away? But he really isn't clever at all.'

'Why not?'

'Because they did these experiments on Sphex wasps. You wait for him to sting something and bring it to his burrow, but then, when he goes inside to see if the place is as he left it, you move his cricket.'

'Poor waspy fellow.'

'He comes out of his burrow to find his cricket gone. Do you know what he does? He goes to find his cricket, and then he drags it back to his burrow. But then he doesn't just drag it in there, he likes to check again that the burrow is as he left it. While he's checking you move the cricket again, he comes out again, finds it again, drags it back to his burrow again, you move it again . . . He just never figures out to just drag the cricket in there without checking it first. He will never take the cricket straight into his burrow, even if you only move it a little distance away.'

'But why doesn't he just decide to take the chance that nothing nasty has crawled into his wasp hole? He must get hungry.'

'He never decides anything. He just keeps doing what his programming tells him to do. Never learns anything, never remembers anything, never weighs things up. Eventually he dies of starvation.'

'But Horace, that's so sad.'

'It's just nature; it's just how things are. Mr Wasp isn't really like us; he is just stuck with his programming. But we can decide things, learn things, remember things. We don't just follow our natures.'

'Do we have a programme?'

'I don't know. If we do, it is a much more complicated one than his. Animals are changing, evolving, but they are doing it very slowly. It takes thousands of years, Helena, just to get a little bit bigger or a little bit faster. But we seem to be changing much faster than them. It's our language, our way of thinking about things.'

'But the wasp tries so hard. It isn't fair.'

'Yes, but he never learns anything. Maybe by the time people live on lots of different planets and are flying around in spaceships, maybe by then he will figure out to just pull his cricket into the burrow.'

I laughed. 'I hope so. Now, show me how giraffes walk, Horace . . .'

'Let's take a break,' Simon said to me. 'What were you thinking about?' he asked as he made tea.

'I don't think I was really thinking about anything.'

'Well, where were you in your head?'

'I was under a tree on a hill behind the farm, in Kenya. I grew up there. Under the tree, I mean. At least, I grew up more under the tree than on the farm. My brother told me stories there.'

I was smiling as I said this. It would make no sense to anyone else, but it did to me.

'I had a horse called Tiger. He was lovely.'

'Not a very African name,' Simon said wryly.

'No,' I laughed. 'I'm not sure how he was named. My brother probably. He chose names for my pets. He loved animals. He knew so much. He read every book on wildlife he could lay his hands on. And when we were a bit older he subscribed to some scientific journals on nature. He used to tell me stories. It's funny, actually, because the stories he told me were mostly not to do with African animals. They were random things that interested him. When I was very young I thought these animals all lived in Kenya and I used to watch out for them.'

'Were you allowed to leave the farm by yourselves?'

'No. One of the men who worked the farm always accompanied us. His name was Kulu. He used to come with us and would sit somewhere in the vicinity and leave us to read or talk. He came with us until Horace was old enough to use a rifle. After that we were allowed out by ourselves.'

Time . . . the things we do with it, and the things we shouldn't do. It is long ago. Kulu is busy and Horace wants to go out on the horses. We are forbidden to leave the farm alone. Kulu has to be with us. Horace is eight and I am seven.

'We'll go to the tree and back,' Horace says.

We already have the horses out when Kulu says he cannot come for a couple of hours. Horace checks. There is nobody around.

'We'll be out and back and no one will miss us,' Horace says to me.

I am not sure we should, but like a sheep, I follow Horace. I would have followed him to the ends of the earth. Silently we take the horses out the back. We circle the farm and head for the umbrella tree.

'They might see us,' Horace says, looking back over his shoulder to our home, now in the distance.

'Let's go back,' I suggest uneasily.

'We'll go the other way,' he says, turning his horse.

Tiger and I turn with him. I feel a mixture of reluctance and excitement. We are not allowed to go that way, not ever. There grasses get longer before thinning out, and the trees get denser and denser, until they are so thick there is no light among them.

'Just to the trees,' I say.

'Come on,' he calls.

We canter through the grass until it thins and now the brush and scrub are closer, sporadically scattered in front of us, thicker and deeper behind. The trees ahead are like in a fairy tale, dark and frightening and hiding things that children should not encounter.

We never get that far though.

Suddenly Horace's horse rears up on its hind legs and then comes to a standstill.

I pull up beside him, wondering what has happened. We both look in amazement. There on the ground is a small spotted cat. A leopard cub. Horace is down off his horse in seconds and has the cub in his arms.

'Oh, you are so beautiful, aren't you,' he says as he strokes the tiny head.

The cub moves in his arms. It is very small. I wonder how

it has got there. He passes it to me to hold while he remounts his horse. Its fur is soft and its ears pointed. Its eyes are blue. They stare at me. Then Horace takes it back from me and we ride home.

'Where is your brother now? Are you still as close?' Simon asked.

I shook my head. 'May I have some more milk in my tea please?' I asked.

He went to the kitchen and fetched it. 'Say when,' he said as he slowly poured a little more into my cup.

'That's fine. Thank you.'

He sat back down, watching me.

'He died,' I said suddenly. There was a long silence. 'He just happened to be in the wrong place at the wrong time,' I added.

'I'm so sorry. What happened to him?'

'He just happened to be coming through a door at the same moment as our President. Somebody tried to kill the President that day. They killed Horace.'

'By mistake?'

'Mistake?' I thought about the word. 'It was just random what happened to him. He was in the wrong place at the wrong time. That's all there is to it.'

'Sometimes I think we want there to be a reason for everything, even when there isn't one. We want things to make sense.'

'Yes, I know what you mean. I wanted there to be a reason why. But there was no reason. It just happened.'

'We tend to interpret things into patterns,' Simon said. 'Our minds are always looking for the pattern, even if there isn't one. I suppose what we see as strange and unlikely coincidences are really only normal things happening. There is no real reason behind any of it.'

'We do look for explanations. I wanted an explanation for why Horace had to step through those doors at the moment he did, that moment when the President came through and the assassin was ready. He could have been anywhere else in that line of people and he would have lived. If one person had pushed in front of him, he would have lived. If his bag was at a different place on the baggage carousel, he would have lived. If the President's plane was one minute earlier or later, he would have lived. If the thing that drives steps up to planes took a few more seconds getting there, he would have lived. Things had to be exactly and precisely the way they were that day for my brother to get killed. And there is no explanation, none. Things happened to be that way, and then he was dead.'

'It's awful,' Simon said.

'It's bad luck. You can see yourself as being lucky and then something like that happens, and you think you have no luck. Or that there is no such thing as luck . . . ' I hesitated.

'Go on, please. I'm interested.'

'I don't really think there is such a thing; luck, I mean. That some people have and some people don't. I mean, obviously if you are born into awful poverty and are missing your legs you have been unlucky. But unlucky just describes in short the awful situation you are in. You aren't in the situation because you are unlucky; you are unlucky because you're in the situation, if you follow me.'

'I think I do'

'The bad luck isn't the reason for the awful situation; the awful situation is the reason for the bad luck. And so luck sort of follows the event, it doesn't determine anything. It is a way of describing things, it doesn't make anything happen. It's a sort of explanation, an explanation that doesn't explain anything.'

'Wow. What did you study?' Simon asked suddenly.

'I studied Italian and Fine Arts. I think I wanted to be an auctioneer, but I don't have the personality. I'm shy. And I don't have any real desire to do something about it, about my shyness I mean. I'm not the kind of person to change things, to move mountains, to shake up the world. I'm just me.'

'Don't say that. I think you are fascinating. It's great painting you because you are so unique.'

'No, I'm not. I'm not putting myself down, it's just that I know I'm nothing special. I know people who are special. My brother was truly special; he was unique, not me. My friend Conti is special too; she's strong and charismatic. She knows what she wants and she gets it. She has that bold determination that I haven't got.'

'And would you like to be like that? To be like her?'

'A bit of me wants to say yes, but the truth is no. I am me. I wouldn't be comfortable being like her. In order to be like her I would have to be harder, tougher, more ruthless, I suppose. And while I admire her character and for being the way she is, I actually would not want to be like that. I suppose I would not know how to live like that.'

Now it was Simon who smiled. 'I'm glad. I wouldn't be painting you if you were. I don't know this Conti, but I'm quite sure that what I see in your face, I would not find in hers.'

'Oh, no, don't say that. She's beautiful. I think she would be a wonderful subject for you to paint.' He shook his head. 'No, really,' I continued. 'She has wonderful bones, clear skin, bright eyes. She's stunning.'

'You can try and sell her to me all you want,' Simon said, 'but it's you I'm painting, and I've no interest in painting this Conti. Now, let's get back to work. Have you finished your tea?'

I nodded and went to tidy away the cups on a tray. 'Why did you want to know what I studied?'

'I wondered if you studied philosophy or something like that'.

'I don't think I have the brains for that.'

'Oh, I think you do. You're a thinker.'

'Not really. Well, sometimes I am, but it's just that I've thought a lot about luck. You got me on my pet subject.'

For the rest of that day, I sat there quietly as Simon painted.

Nine

Back home, Conti was undergoing a change that was not to her liking. She was aware that she did not feel as she usually did. Her confidence, her charisma, her charm, all the characteristics she most liked in herself, seemed long gone. She tried in vain to carry on in her usual fashion but was slowly beginning to admit defeat.

Joe was, as ever, busy with work. The Count and Alessia had their new preoccupation and were gone every day up into the Dublin or Wicklow mountains. As Joe had said, they were less likely to kill anybody on their motorcycle out there than in the city. The housekeeper looked after everything at home and Conti found herself just sitting around, reading magazines, lying on the couch, passing time and worrying.

She was continually tired, but she would have liked to be doing something. This stagnation was not through choice, it was down to her feeling that something was wrong with her. The maternal instincts which she so obviously lacked before now kicked in with a vengeance, and she feared for what would happen to the babies she was carrying. Both she and they seemed irredeemably fragile. Something now mattered to Conti more than Conti herself did, and it was something she could do nothing to protect.

One healthy twin. One weak one.

Her thoughts dwelled on the weaker twin she was carrying. She did not like weakness. In fact, strange as it may sound, she was almost afraid of it. She saw weakness as failure. That one of her twins was weak reflected, or so she thought, some flaw in herself. These thoughts and fears were new to her. Like many of the most effective people, she was not given to prolonged introspection. She had no time for it. She was Conti dei Fiori before and Conti Martin now. She had made the transition from one situation to the other simply by bringing everything and everyone she knew with her. But now everything was different.

She was different.

For the first time in many years, she wondered about her mother.

She had not lied to me, although even in her moment of honesty she had not told me the whole truth. She had, though, told me more of the truth than she had ever told anybody, including Joe. He had believed her when she said that her mother had died in childbirth. Why would he not? He loved her. As far as he was concerned, what Conti said had to be true, or at least treated as if it were. She had told Babbo never to tell him, that it was easier for her if Joe believed her mother was dead.

She did not worry about having told me the almost-truth. She knew it would go no further, or at least not further than Fred, which did not worry her. She felt she knew Fred's type. He was secure, self-confident, from a comfortable background and generally more like her than either Joe or me. She correctly suspected that I would have told Fred in order to have something to share with him.

Until now, she had seen me as being weak, but it was a weakness that suited her. Having a friend like me gave her someone to whom she could show off. Conti would never have admitted this to herself, but deep down she knew it to be true. If asked, she would have described herself as being a good friend, a confidante, someone dependable from whom I could learn, even though her self-indulgence was often at my expense.

I was her first real female friend and she liked having my confidence. Other friends in the past had mostly been attracted to her because of her wealth and the aura of confidence and success that she carried. Just as I was infatuated with her, there was something in me to which she was attracted, perhaps my naivety and my lack of worldliness. She did not have to pretend with me, as I always seemed impressed with what she had to say and what she did. She knew I had never had any friends in the past, other than my brief encounter with Daisy, and in some way I think she felt that I was lucky to have her. And I was. Her generosity and her sense of fun surpassed her few flaws, which I readily overlooked. I was aware of them and I avoided them where I could.

Of late, Conti's relationship with me had changed markedly. As both our pregnancies progressed, for the first time she acknowledged that she found something in me that she envied. It did not seem fair to her that my pregnancy could be so easy and so straightforward while hers seemed riddled with uncertainty. She could hardly bear to bring herself to think of the babies growing inside her, one strong, one weak, one growing and thriving, the other struggling. Conti had never before felt as useless as she now felt, and the feeling worsened every day.

There was no one to whom she could talk and offload her fears, and trust that what she said would not be repeated; no one other than me. And I listened. I tried reassuring her, but the effects of this reassurance were short lived. Before long, Conti would feel tired again, tired and frustrated. It was like nothing she had ever dealt with before. She now felt a sense of injustice. That she had already given birth to a healthy child did not give her any comfort. She told me one day that her interest in Lorina had always been minimal.

'I don't know why I care now. I mean, with Lorina, well, sure, there was a sense of expectation when I was pregnant. But I always assumed it would be all right. And it was. But now, I don't know.'

'Oh, Conti, of course these feelings are normal. There was no reason to worry with Lorina.' Even as I said this, I was not sure that I meant it. I too was concerned about the baby I was carrying, but knew, or at least felt, that I had less to fear. I diminished these concerns because they seemed unwarranted in light of the turmoil through which Conti was going.

'I know I'm not very maternal. I don't have to be,' Conti said, not for the first time, trying to convince herself. 'But I feel scared. I don't want to lose the baby.'

I did not ask her if she feared that if she lost one twin she might well lose the other. I suspected this thought had not occurred to Conti and I did not want to open a Pandora's box that would leave my friend in a worse position, if that were possible.

'Conti, look, I don't know but I sort of feel that as long as they have not actually confined you to bed in a hospital, it must be all right.'

'They're talking now about a caesarean section.'

'Well, that makes sense. You have to trust them. The very fact that they are making plans like that means that they think you will carry through to term. It's going to be all right. I'm sure it is.'

'Where do you go every day when you go out?' Conti asked suddenly.

'What?' I was startled.

'I see you leaving. Where are you going?'

'Oh, that. Well . . . '

'No, tell me. Please. I'm stuck at home and I'd love to know. Any gossip is welcome.'

'It's a surprise,' I said sheepishly. 'This artist asked me if he could paint me months ago, but I was too busy, and now I have time on my hands. I know, I know. Don't laugh.'

'No, don't tell me. You're letting him paint you. God, the pregnant Mona Lisa!' She burst out laughing.

'Oh, Conti, don't laugh. It's only my face. It's for some exhibition; nothing important. I haven't told Fred. It's nothing really. I didn't tell him because I thought it would be a surprise for him. Simon, the artist, is nearly finished. Only a few more sittings. He says he'll be ready in time. It opens next month.' As I said it, I knew that I wanted Fred to be both surprised and pleased.

Simon claimed to be ecstatic about the way the portrait was progressing. The afternoons I spent with him were precious. They had given me a sense of fulfilment and a time to think. We talked about things that were important, or at least, important to me. I felt stronger than I had felt in years. There was a sense that I was a person; not a shadow, not a younger sister, not an unwanted daughter, not a wife, but a person who had some worth. I had no new beliefs in how I looked. I was sure I was still the same girl who rode her horse and gazed at a distant horizon, but there was something more to me now, as if I were growing into my personality and becoming at ease with it.

Simon had listened to me. He listened to me in a way that Fred rarely did. This was no indictment of Fred, it was just the way our relationship functioned. Love, sympathy, empathy, support, kindness; these were the ingredients of our marriage. I had been adrift when I met Fred. That feeling of aimlessness had, to some extent, diminished over the years but it receded completely when I was with Simon.

At first it puzzled me, but then I realised that the conversations I had with Simon in some way mirrored those with Horace. Their intensity and their depth were similar.

It made me look at my relationship with Fred in a slightly different light, as though trying to clarify it. If there was loneliness in my marriage, it now seemed intensified. I would hardly admit to myself that I felt lonely, but when I was with Simon there was a feeling of something stronger, something new in me, more like a real person.

Simon claimed that I was a wonderful subject to paint, and this boosted my self-esteem, which I always found so precarious. If I looked at myself through his eyes, I became more interesting. Perhaps that is too strong. I think that maybe I became less uninteresting.

I knew that Fred loved me just as I was. He had married me knowing that I was introverted and quiet and he had never demanded more of me. But the afternoons with Simon opened up something else, and while I had fears about the actual birth of my baby, and fears that it might be a girl, I also felt the emergence of an inner strength hitherto untapped. I sometimes felt that I should be having these conversations with Fred, but the pattern with him was such that I was the listener, not the talker, and so I talked to Simon.

'It's actually going to be shown? In a gallery?' Conti asked.

'Oh, only some small place,' I said. I really wished that I had not told her. 'Won't you be too embarrassed to go to see it?'

I had not thought of that. 'Well, no. Not really. I mean, it's not me. It's something that Simon has painted. I'm going for him, he asked me to. It's his work. Not anything to do with me.'

'God, I'd be too embarrassed to see a painting of myself on a wall.'

'I don't think I see it like that,' I said. It was a puzzling comment, seeing as Conti must have had at least a dozen photographs of herself in her home. 'It's just a reflection of what he sees. It's nothing to do with me, really. And anyway, there will be loads of other paintings; this one isn't special, it won't even be noticed. There are other paintings by him and by other artists as well. I think each painter will exhibit six portraits, or maybe six pictures, I'm not sure. In Simon's case he has painted portraits. Mine isn't anything special.'

I tried to play the whole thing down, as I could not bear the look on Conti's face. Conti looked sulky and at the same time slightly like a cat.

That I, in my smooth, problem-free pregnancy, should be having such luck and such attention added to Conti's sense of the unfairness of life. Jealousy is a human failing and the person who suffers from it is consumed. I felt that playing down my bit of good fortune and diminishing myself would help her. The pattern of our friendship let that happen and I didn't question it, but I knew to steer well clear of such a thing happening again.

What Conti needed was something to occupy her mind, but she did not read books and there was a limit to the pleasure she could get from her glossy magazines.

Later she told me that she went to Babbo's room that night. He was listening to Verdi.

'Babbo?'

'*Cara, si,* what is on your mind?'

'Babbo, I was wondering about Mamma . . .'

'Ah, what you wonder?'

'I was wondering why she left me.'

'She no leave you. I leave her. Why you ask?'

He was moving his hands in rhythm with the music.

Conti stood there, startled. He had never said this before. But then, she hadn't asked. It had been years and years since she had brought up her mother.

'*Si.* I leave her. Why you want to know? You better with me.'

'What do you mean?'

'What you mean, what I mean?'

'I mean – what do you mean you left her?'

'Ah, is long ago. I do the right thing. I always do the right thing by you.'

'Babbo, please, I don't know what you mean. I know you always did the right thing by me. I know that. But what are you talking about? What do you mean when you say you left her? You said that she left us. You said she left me in the hospital.'

'Ah. *Bene.* I do the right thing by my little Contessa.'

'Babbo, what are you saying?'

He would be drawn no further. He turned the music up and now pretended to be holding a conductor's baton. 'Listen,' he said. 'There is more in music than in anything else in the world.'

'Babbo, please.'

But there was nothing more. She had the feeling he had not intended to tell her, that he had just let it slip.

She thought of telling Joe but feared his reaction. She did not want to expose this development to anyone. She could not imagine what it meant. She tried sounding out Alessia.

'Alessia, do you remember when I was born?'

'*Sì.*'

'Where was it?'

'Eh?'

'Where was I born?'

'Your passport – it say, no?'

But now she didn't trust her passport. She remembered Babbo once saying that any document could be bought for a price, including a passport. She didn't trust anything.

And so she niggled at me, trying to undermine me about the portrait, and about anything else she could think of, in fact. I could feel her frustration and I let her away with it. I should not have done that but I did because I loved her. Love is very blind.

We need our mothers. I learned this as a young girl, when I felt rejected by mine. I craved my mother's love then, and when I didn't get it, I learned. Unlike the Sphex wasp, I learned. I wanted to be a good mother. I believed that that was all that I could do.

I sometimes wondered if Horace had lived, if somehow he had survived that afternoon, what would have happened. Would my growing older with him beside me as a brother have given me something that would have made me stronger, more sure of myself? I do not know. I only know that at 12.20 that terrible day when time stopped, I was cut adrift. But being pregnant gave me a sense of being. I was going to be needed when my baby was born, and I was going to give my baby everything I could. I read every baby book in the library in the hope that I would find what I would need to know and what to do. I had seen bonding, second hand, admittedly, but I kept telling myself that I would be able to put this second-hand knowledge into use somehow.

But still, I wanted my mother now in a way I had not known since I had left, and listening to Conti, I could not help feeling that she needed her mother too. Of course, I could not say or even suggest this. Conti was Conti. She pretended and covered up and even though I knew this and I could see it, I still could not digest it. It was as if I didn't really believe it. I didn't really know anyone else and so thought that she was perfect. But who is perfect? What is perfection? Yes, I saw her flaws. How could I not? But I forgave her. I admired her and I loved her.

I loved Fred. I knew he wasn't perfect, but he was perfect for me, and I hoped I was perfect for him. I looked at my marriage during those days of the painting. I wondered at it and why it worked, but it did work. That was the truth of it. We compromise sometimes in our relationships; we must. No two people are perfectly balanced. You have to work at it to make it successful. I realised that, and that was good.

Fred too was growing into a new phase in his life. He was growing into fatherhood, excited at the prospect, and just as I reassured him, he reassured me. He was glad to have a wife who was not like his mother. I liked my mother-in-law, and while I knew that Fred loved his mother, I also knew that she left him feeling short in some indeterminable way. Marjorie's success on the tennis court, the trophies that adorned her home, her strength and her prowess were hard to live up to. It was true that Fred did not aspire to his mother's specific success, but it was also true that he did not feel he had achieved what she would have liked for him. She often said things like, 'Oh Fred, you should be playing tennis, not writing about it,' or 'I had such hopes for you on the tennis court.' He never reacted to these comments, but I knew that they must have hurt. The fact that she loved me always pleased him. On some level he was aware that my simple nature was such that his mother could not fail to love me. His mother was always on the move, busy with the next moment rather than the present one.

I, on the other hand, enjoyed simple things. I enjoyed the smell of the barbecue, the leaves falling from the autumn trees and the buds unfurling in spring. I liked reading, gardening and cooking. I pored over cookbooks and I took to spending more and more time in the garden, despite the coldness of the winter. I wrapped up warmly and planned a herb bed and a flowerbed, trees that I would plant and where I would place them. Horace would have said I was preparing my nest.

'We need to take a break, you're thinking about something else.'

Simon's voice interrupted my thoughts. I tried to think about nothing. That calm, timeless nothing, where just a tree stood on a hill.

'I'm going to finish this without you. We're done,' Simon said suddenly after gazing at me for a moment.

'I'm sorry. Have I messed things up? My thoughts sort of wander sometimes. It isn't easy to keep the same expression.'

'Not at all, you've been great. I realise that I haven't really needed you for the last day or so. I've got what I wanted. I think I just liked you coming here. It's the artist's need for diversion.' He smiled, and was obviously pleased with his painting as he stood back to look at it.

'Really, it's fine,' he continued. 'If I keep on adding to it, I might go and mess it up. This is just the way I want it. And believe me, I don't always feel like that about a painting.'

'Can I see?'

'No. You can see it at the exhibition. I only have a little to do to it. The frame is on order. It's going to be fine.'

'I don't know what I'll do without these sittings,' I said. 'I have got used to coming here. I shouldn't have given up work so early, but Fred wanted me to. I think it was a mistake. I still have a month to wait.'

'You wouldn't have been able to come here and continue work, not while pregnant. It would have been too much for you. So I'm glad you gave up work early, even if you aren't. I would have been one picture short.'

I nodded. I knew that what I had got from these days had been very different from what Simon had got.

'You know,' Simon said thoughtfully, 'I have really enjoyed this time, painting you. I think it's reflected in the painting that I enjoyed doing it. It has been enlightening.'

'How nice,' I said. 'I do hope we can stay in touch, and all that.' I felt awkward. I so enjoyed his company. I had very few friends and felt I had no idea how to make them, but with Simon I had found it easy. It had come naturally.

'Yes, I'd like that. We really should keep in contact. It's so easy to lose touch with people.'

And now I smiled. It was what I had felt but did not think he had too. I thought he had just seen it as his work and I was there to assist him by sitting silently with my mind thousands of miles away.

'Maybe sometime I could paint you again? I'd like that. You've been such a good model. I'd paint you with a different expression maybe, smiling like you are now.'

He took my phone number and address before I left. Going home, I wondered how friendships began. Were they just random encounters where you hit it off with somebody, where you just clicked? It had been that way with Daisy and then with Conti, and now it was that way with Simon too. They had been my first real friends, except, of course, for Horace. Horace and I were just thrown together by the accident of birth. As for Fred, he gave me endless love and affection, and more than that, he was simply a wonderful companion, and our relationship always

133

seemed easy and natural; yes, there were compromises, but it seemed to move along under its own momentum.

'There is a theory,' Horace says. 'It is to do with separation. It claims that everybody is within six degrees of separation from everybody else.'

'What does that mean, Horace?'

'Person one knows person two, two knows three, three knows four, four knows five, and five knows six, and in this fashion every two people are connected through one of these cosmic chains of acquaintance. But only a few people know that it has been tested.'

'How could that be? How could you test that?'

'A famous psychologist tried to test the theory. He chose arbitrary pairs of people, completely at random. The first was given a letter and told to send it on in the direction of somebody else, a person he didn't know and had never met. An American college student might recognise the name of the intended recipient as being Indian, and so pass the letter on to his Indian friend. The friend then passes it to his parents in India. They then know somebody whose parents live in the right area . . . Fairly often, the letter would arrive at its intended recipient within six moves. Sometimes it didn't, but then, the theory is that the two people are connected via a chain of no more than six people, not that they can figure out the shortest chain. It would only take one person to send the letter on to the second best person, and the whole thing breaks down.

'Even fewer people know that out of hundreds of letters that were sent in this way, a large number of the successful ones turned out to have gone via the same small group of people. It all depended on groups.

'Some people have tightly knit social groups. If you could

get the letter to anybody in the group, it would then reach its destination in one move. But nobody in any of those groups would be likely to appear in a number of chains. A very few people, though, appeared in lots of different groups, at the points where the lines of connection between people intersect and overlap. Often, they would be very well-travelled people who had friends and relations all over the world. And often they would be Renaissance-style men who divide their time between dozens of different hobbies and interests, thus cultivating connections in many different groups. These few people are the key links in the chains connecting us all. Their names came up again and again in all efforts to test the theory.'

I try to suppress a yawn.

'Are you paying attention?' Horace asks.

'Of course I am. I just prefer hearing about animals.'

'We are animals,' Horace says. 'This is about us. Our connections. Our links.'

'How could we ever be linked to anyone? Maybe through Luther we're connected to a brilliant herd of elephants,' I suggest.

'Oh, Helena. Humans are interesting too.'

I thought of Horace under the umbrella tree and I thought of how, when my parents were gone, I would be the only person who remembered him. He had no other links to reality at all. I was his only connection to anybody or to anything. But as I thought about that, I wondered if it was the truth. I liked the idea that somehow we were connected to other people, that the distance between people was illusory.

I thought of the people I knew and I wondered if, in some way, I could be one of the people in the links to which Horace had referred. I had a mother from Italy, I was raised in Kenya, studied in Ireland, my first friend, Daisy, was connected to people in the American Embassy, and I married a man with an American mother. Conti, living next door, was the daughter of a man who had been a trusted friend of Mussolini. I could link myself to people in power without realising it. I was sure our Kenyan President would remember our name because Horace had died in his place.

I found the thought fascinating; the links we have without realising it. Fred and me, Conti and me, Simon and me . . . and therefore Fred, Conti and Simon were all linked.

I tried talking to Conti about randomness, connection and luck, but with little success.

'You're raving,' Conti said unhelpfully. 'It's your hormones.'

Conti believed in God and saw His hand at work in most things, which prevented any deeper conversation about this topic. Her Roman Catholic education in an expensive Irish convent induced her to believe that there was a God and that He loved her.

I did not believe in God. There had been no God in my upbringing. I had read about God as a child and my mother had said, 'He is an idea in some people's minds, but he does not exist.'

'But some people believe in Him,' Horace says.

'I used to believe in Him,' our mother replies. 'I was brought up to believe in a God, merciful, decent, and on my side. He does not exist.'

We try asking our father.

'I don't know,' he replies. 'I have no firm views on the matter.'

'Mother says there is no such thing.'

'I know,' he says. 'She is so very sure of it. I can't argue with such certainty.'

'But why is she so sure?'

'Who knows?' he replies.

'Horace?'

The ground is hard and dry and dusty. The sun lights up our world, a vast ball moving across the sky. Its light is our life.

'Yes?' Horace is reading.

'Do you think the sun is God?'

He looks up at the sky, shielding the light with his hand.

'It's our god,' he replies. 'It's our concept of god. Yes, it will do. As long as it shines, there is life.'

'But the rain? Don't we need the rain too?'

'Sun and rain,' he says thoughtfully.

I am pleased that I have given him food for thought.

The time passed slowly. It was not that I was specifically waiting for the exhibition or indeed for the forthcoming birth. It was more that I was missing the afternoons spent with Simon. It made me wonder again about my lack of friends. It was true that I had got on well with colleagues at the gallery and had enjoyed lunching with different ones on different days, but I felt that they were not real friendships. I saw a failing in myself to be able to relate easily to other people. I could do the superficial stuff quite well, but I tired of it easily. A fifty-minute lunch was as long as I wanted to spend in someone else's company, other than with Fred or Conti. And now I felt that with Simon. I had the feeling that my whole life might be like that – a long series of short conversations. It gave me a sense of failure.

'Conti?'

We were in Conti's room and both of us were lying on her bed, on our backs. My hands were on my stomach. Conti's were by her side.

'Mmm.'

'Do you feel interested when people talk about things, like the weather and their work, things like that?'

'How do you mean?'

'I don't know. I suppose when people talk trivia, how do you keep your interest going?'

As I asked the question, I suddenly realised that a lot of what Conti said was trivial and I hoped my friend would not realise that she could be included in the generality of the question.

'When people tell you things, those are things of interest to them. I suppose that's what sustains the conversation,' Conti said.

'But do you never want to yawn? Or to . . . I don't know. I just get so fed up with little things.'

'I don't really know. I suppose most things that seem important are pretty trivial in the grand scheme of things, aren't they? But then, what's trivia to one person is important to another. You know, like if someone's dog is ill or something.'

I knew this was true. I also knew that Conti dealt, to a large extent, in trivia, and yet I found Conti exciting. I saw myself as dull, but I was safe within myself because I was used to myself.

I felt very muddled, torn between the knowledge that dullness in other people bored me, and the awareness that I was dull. I had no notions of grandeur, only too aware that I was one small person on a very large planet, as individual as one animal within the context of its own life, but with no more individuality than that single animal had when running with its herd. I realised that I was about to emulate my mother. I would stay at home and care for my baby, sustain myself with reading, and that that could well be the sum total of my life. Conti seemed to aspire to more. I did not know if I aspired to anything other than to be the mother I was about to become.

'I can't wait to have these babies and to get my life back,' Conti said suddenly.

'Your life back?'

'Partying, meeting people, having fun. I hate this state.' Conti's voice was rancorous. 'It's so tedious, and yet . . .'

'Go on.' I was both curious and concerned.

'I don't know. I miss people. Oh, I know, I go along with Joe to various events and stand like a hugely pregnant woman beside him for ten minutes before I have to sit down, but that's not what I meant. I have the feeling that my life won't be the same.'

'Of course it won't be the same. I mean, in a good way. Our lives will be different, fuller, more complete.'

I know my voice was hopeful. I hated hearing Conti sounding close to despair. I needed my friend's usual happier outlook. I needed her optimism.

'Helena, can I tell you something?'

'Of course you can.' I was expecting Conti to talk again of her fears about the unborn twins.

'I've been trying to trace my mother.'

I did not know how to react to this. 'Oh,' I said with interest.

'But I'm not able to.'

It was then she told me about her conversation with Babbo, how he had briefly admitted that he had left her mother, not the other way around. She told me how she contacted the hospital that her birth certificate stated as her place of birth and how there were no records of her there at all.

'I feel so upset,' Conti said. 'I've always despised my mother for abandoning me. I've never felt any interest in her whatsoever, but now it's different. I keep wondering did she wake up one morning and find that I was gone, and how that must have made her feel.'

'There must be a way of tracing her,' I said.

'I don't know what it is. And anyway, couldn't she have found me if she really wanted to? And Helena, you must not tell anyone, not even Fred. I haven't told Joe.'

'Why haven't you told Joe? You should.'

'I don't want to. I don't feel like it,' Conti said. 'It's enough being pregnant and not knowing what is going to happen with my twins. It makes me feel weak enough without admitting what Babbo has done. Joe doesn't even know that my mother is alive. I told him she was dead, so I can hardly tell him now that not only is she alive, but that she didn't abandon me, that Babbo abandoned her.'

I was shocked, both because Conti had lied to Joe about her mother's very existence and also at the idea of Babbo having just removed Conti from her mother. No matter what rights he felt he had as a parent, nothing, in my mind, could justify that.

I realised, of course, that I had told Conti much more about my life in Kenya, and in more detail, than I had ever told Fred, but I told myself that it was different. It was not that I had kept anything secret from Fred, it was simply that I had told him the rudiments rather than the depth. When I first met him I had been too close to Horace's death and I could not express myself.

I tried prevailing upon Conti to tell Joe but I gave up, as it was clear that Conti regretted telling even me. It seemed such a terrible mess and it made me see my own life in a clearer context.

Because of that conversation with Conti, I decided to contact my own mother after the baby was born. I felt I owed her that, that it was the least I could do. And what was the worst that could happen? That my mother would not respond? I wondered how my father would take the news of a grandchild. I could not imagine. Would either of them feel pleased? Or might they feel it was an irritant? Or would they just ignore me? I sometimes thought back to that day when I was driving my mother to meet Horace and she said, 'It's not you.' As I remembered other things from the past, I knew that those words were laced with meaning, as an apple might be laced with cyanide. Perhaps that is too strong, but I sensed there was something profound behind her words that I could not quite grasp.

Yes, I would write when the baby was born. I could be no worse off. At least I had a mother to write to, unlike Conti.

The invitation to the opening of the exhibition arrived and I decided to surprise Fred. I planned that we would have an early dinner in town in some place near the gallery, and then we would happen to wander past the gallery and I would suggest we take a look inside. I do not remember if I shared this plan with Conti, but the evening before the opening, Conti rang and suggested we all go out to dinner together.

It was Fred who answered the phone. I could hear him in the kitchen.

'Hang on, Conti, while I check with Helena.'

He came in to where I was lying like a gigantic beetle on its back on the sofa.

'Conti is suggesting we have dinner tomorrow evening.'

'Oh,' I said as I saw my plans evaporate. 'I was going to ask you to have dinner out with me, just the two of us,' I said.

'Well, we can do that another night. If you're up to going out to dinner, let's meet up with Conti and Joe,' Fred said.

'But – '

'It will do you good,' Fred said. 'You need to be getting out more.'

'Where does she want to eat?' I asked.

Fred mentioned a place that had recently opened in our village, a good twenty miles from the city, just about as far from the gallery as possible.

'It would be nice to meet with them,' I said simply because I could see that that was what he wanted. 'But let's make it somewhere in Dublin, as I have to go in tomorrow, and by the time I get home I know I will be too tired to go out again.' This was a valiant effort on my part to move the venue closer to the gallery and still keep my little secret.

'Conti says she'll bring the car, so that's not an issue,' Fred replied. 'I said I'd call her back, so what do you think?'

'Ask Joe and Conti to join us, I've already booked a table,' I said with unaccustomed determination. 'I'll phone back and ask for a table for four. It's early though, six o'clock.'

Fred went and called Conti back and when he returned he said that they would be delighted to join them but did it have to be so early?

'Oh, Fred, it does have to be so early,' I said. 'I have a surprise for you.'

Dinner had become a familiar routine between the four of us. We would have the Martins in and the Count came too, or Joe and Conti would invite us out to a restaurant. The arrangement suited both parties. I had once said to Fred, 'Darling, do you think we appear mean by not taking them out to dinner and just inviting them here?'

'Possibly,' he said, 'but we don't have their money and it seems stupid to try to live up to their expectations. Anyway, you're a brilliant cook and they like coming here and so does the Count.'

We had dinner in town and Conti was in good form. Everything was fine until we left the restaurant. I was beginning to worry about the exhibition and what they would all make of my portrait. As we approached the gallery, which was on the way back to the car, I said we had to go in and Conti procrastinated.

'I'm so tired,' she said.

'Please,' I said to her. 'We have to go in. We simply must. Ten minutes only,' I said, giving Fred an urgent glance.

'We can find you somewhere to sit,' Fred said to Conti. He looked slightly puzzled but he had read my urgency. 'I promised Helena we would drop by.'

'Oh,' Conti said. 'Oh, I see. Is that tonight? Helena, you secretive thing, why on earth didn't you say?'

'Conti, if you're not up to it, we don't have to go.' I could feel myself backing down.

'Of course we have to go in,' Conti said. 'The thought of seeing you on the wall is enough to perk me up.'

The place was full of artists, reporters and guests, all of whom were enthusiastically quaffing champagne whilst enthusing at length about matters artistic. There was a buzz of excitement and glamour with people whirling past and talking a bit too loudly. I felt distinctly out of place and looked around for Simon.

'Where do we go?' Conti asked.

I felt lost and had no idea where we should go. Fortunately Simon appeared, pushing through the throng and reaching down to kiss me on the cheek.

'Helena, you're late. Photographs have been taken of my other subjects but not of you.' He gestured for me to follow.

'Simon, you have to meet my husband, Fred, and my friends, Conti and Joe Martin,' I said.

'Hello, hello,' Simon said shaking hands all around. 'Now you must all come. I'll show you my section and then I'll see if I can still find a photographer. Helena must be photographed.'

I did not see why. I felt as far removed as was possible from what was going on, conspicuous and out of place.

Simon led us past the mass of people, nodding and greeting his way through.

'Slow down,' Conti said. 'Some of us are pregnant.'

'Sorry, sorry, Helena,' Simon said, taking my arm.

'I meant me,' Conti said, bristling.

Simon looked at her. 'Why, so you are,' he said with a laugh. 'But come along anyway. We can't have you giving birth here in the main hall.'

I cringed, as I knew that Conti would be really furious by now.

The portrait had pride of position on an end wall, perfectly lit, and I stood in front of it in surprise. I had had no real idea what to expect, but I hadn't been expecting this.

'Wow,' Conti said. 'You posed naked.'

The portrait took in all of my head and hair with the light streaming through it, and finished just at my shoulders. My

143

shoulders were bare, which was presumably what Conti meant.

'I wasn't naked, Conti, I was wearing a wide-necked top,' I said. 'It was pushed down at the shoulders.'

'What do you think?' Simon asked, apparently oblivious to what had just been said.

'It's wonderful,' Fred said. 'Truly wonderful.'

'It's beautiful,' Joe said. 'I don't know anything about art, but I know this is a great painting.'

I smiled at Simon. 'Well done,' I said.

'But were you naked?' Conti persisted.

'Of course not,' I said. 'I was seven months pregnant.'

Fred slipped his arm around my shoulder. 'I love it,' he said. 'Thank you, Simon. You've captured her just as she is.'

As I stood staring at the portrait in front of me, I noticed that Simon had added things to the painting that I did not remember being in the room. There was a white bird behind my shoulder, perhaps on the mantelpiece. It was not particularly clear in the painting, but it was there. I remembered the conversation with my mother: 'We can see each other, but rarely ourselves.' I wondered what they all saw.

Later I asked Fred about it, but he had not noticed the bird. He had seen only me.

Ten

'The cuckoo lays its egg in another bird's nest and flies away, leaving another bird to hatch and rear its young. The chick is born and it pushes out the other bird's eggs.'

'That's so mean, Horace.'

'That's life, Helena. The antelope gives birth and then hides its young in the tall grass, rejoins the herd and visits it regularly to feed it until it is strong enough to follow her.'

'Why does it hide its baby?'

'Because of predators. Maybe lions or leopards – they would want to eat it. Each mother is doing its best for its young.'

It rained incessantly for the next couple of weeks and then suddenly it stopped and spring had arrived. The bluebells flowered around the tall trees and the sun shone through the buds on their branches, surrounding our house with a sense of renewal and warmth.

I woke at about two in the morning. I lay still on the bed, feeling the contractions, and remembering how I had been told to wait until they were closer together and regular. It was quiet in the house, and despite the fears I had been having I now felt excitement surge through me, knowing that my world was about to change forever and that these were the last hours of my life as I knew it. A new life, with me as a mother, was about to commence.

The pains were not as bad as I had been led to believe, so I drifted in and out of a doze until it was nearly seven o'clock, when Fred, rising to go to work, leaned over to kiss me.

'Fred,' I whispered, 'they've started.'

'What have?'

'The contractions.'

Fred was off the bed and into his clothes in a matter of moments.

'How far apart are they? When did they begin?'

'I think you better phone the hospital,' I said suddenly. 'Say we're on our way.'

I could hardly get out of the bed. In the way that hours can sometimes be added to a clock in the blink of a sleepy eye, my baby had somehow managed to sneak up on me. One moment it all seemed far away, the next my contractions were less than a minute apart. It was not at all what I had expected.

Fred raced downstairs with my bag, which was already long since packed in anticipation of this moment. He threw the bag into his car and came back upstairs to get me.

'Fred, I'm not sure about this,' I said as we began our ungainly descent into the basement and through to the garage.

'It's all right,' Fred replied. 'I'm here.'

I could actually hear the pounding of his heart as he held me close, and his tone rather suggested that he was every bit as terrified as I suddenly was, despite his efforts to sound reassuring and confident. One way or another, we made it through the games room and into the laundry room. I began to gasp.

'I'm not going to make it to the hospital,' I said.

An alarmed Fred looked around in horror at the bleakness of the laundry room.

'Are you sure?' he asked, hoping for divine intervention.

I fell to my knees and started panting for breath.

Fred lifted me and made a quick decision. 'Fifteen-love,' he said suddenly, reverting to the tennis scores as a way of comforting himself, and he carried me back to the games room. The table tennis table, a present from his mother, with a net across its centre and its rickety legs, did not look sturdy enough to hold my weight, so the billiard table it had to be.

It was a half-size table that Jackson had bought for us at an auction the previous year. His father was of the opinion that the price was ridiculously low. Be that as it may, we could not have afforded it. To give Fred his due, I know that he loved that table, but he did not hesitate in lifting me on to it, pushing the scattered balls aside as he did so. 'I'll phone for an ambulance. Hold on. I'll be right back.'

And there, on the billiard table a few minutes later, as an ambulance sirened its way to our leafy suburb and with Fred holding my hand and reminding me to breathe, while unable to breathe himself, our baby son emerged into his father's loving hands. It would be touching to say that he potted a ball upon his entrance, but that would not be the truth. The truth was that I ruined a perfectly good billiard table.

I had no idea that human birth could be so quick. Neither had the ambulance men, who came in through the open garage doors and found us huddled on the billiard table.

'How undignified,' I said when I was able to speak.

'Fifteen-all,' Fred said to the surprised men.

I knew that he was giving me points for my breathing, which I had kept under control. I had thought about Horace during those final moments of the birth and how he would have been fascinated, not just by the gory details, but by the fact that there was no holding the baby back. He was born regardless of surroundings or circumstances. He could not wait for me to hide in the long grass or to be driven to the hospital. I held him against me and gazed in amazement and wonderment. I had a son.

Later, as I lay in the hospital bed, a doctor came in to check me over. She was young, with her hair tied back, and I realised at the same moment as she did that we knew each other.

'We meet again,' she said as memories of her samples with the bacon on top in Daisy's fridge came to my mind.

'Hello, Doctor,' I said. I had no recollection of her real name, or if I had ever known it. I was disturbed to find she was now loose in a hospital, and even more startled to have her pummelling my stomach.

'You've done a great job,' she said to Fred, who stood there, beaming proudly.

When Doctor left, Fred sat beside me holding my hand. 'I'm not sure what great job she meant,' he said ruefully. 'I didn't do anything except put you on the billiard table.'

'I couldn't have done it without you,' I said to him.

I was kept in the hospital for three days despite my best efforts to be released. 'You've been through a traumatic time,' Doctor responded to my objections. 'It's not everyone who gives birth alone at home,' she said.

'But my baby is all right?' I said, suddenly concerned.

'Just perfect,' she said. 'And you are too. Make the most of it; rest up and let us look after you. You'll be coping alone soon enough.' It was interesting to see how Doctor had managed to grow up. She even looked clean and I could understand what she was saying.

I could not wait to get home, but it was nice being looked after and reassuring to be shown how to feed and change and bathe my baby.

'What are you going to call him?' the nurse asked as she fussed around me and Doctor.

'Once upon a time, there was a little girl named Helena. She had blonde hair and blue eyes.'

I lie in my bed listening to my father. I am eight years old. This is a new story. He never tells stories about me. This is exciting. I don't want to go to sleep and I am afraid he will stop if I blink my eyes.

'She had a sister . . . ' Does he not mean to say brother? I listen carefully. Surely he means an older brother? Sometimes he is distracted and doesn't pay proper attention. Maybe he means brother. He must have. I have no sister.

'She was not just a sister, but she was in fact a twin. Two little girls. One named Helena, one named Carolina.'

That is my mother's name. My mother is Carolina. What does he mean?

'They were living in a city in a time of war.'

'Which war?' Horace calls in from his room across the hall.

'The Second World War,' he replies.

Silence from Horace's room. I hope his question has not interrupted my father's flow of words.

'There they were,' my father eventually continues when it is clear no more questions are coming from Horace's room, 'two little girls, Carolina and Helena. And one night, when they were in bed, the sirens started and they did what they always did. They got up quickly and ran with their mother down the stairs and to the shelter in the garden. Some nights they slept in the shelter, but that night they didn't. That night they had been sleeping at home in their own beds. But the planes that were coming to bomb them came faster than they thought. They were on top of them and the shelter was bombed before they reached it. There were many people out on the streets and in the pushing and shoving to get to another shelter Carolina let go of Helena's hand and she lost her sister in the crowd.'

He is silent now.

'What happened, Father?' I ask hopefully.

'Carolina never saw Helena again.'

'And their mother?'

'Their mother was killed in the bomb.'

'But what happened to Helena?'

149

'I think she too died that night. They just never found her. Carolina hunted for her. She searched everywhere. She stayed alone in the bombed-out apartment. She waited in case Helena ever found her way home. But she never saw her again.'

'What happened to Carolina?'

'Some time later she was rescued – found in the basement of the apartment block, hungry and frightened, but waiting, always waiting for her lost sister.'

I listen. I hate the thought of my mother as a frightened child hiding in a ruined building hoping that her mother and her sister would return. I had never imagined that one of my parents could be frightened, and the thought makes me feel queasy.

'She grew up and then I met her and we married. It's a happily ever after story,' my father says, patting my hand and standing up abruptly.

It does not sound very happy to me, though. I think of my mother sitting with her books. I think of her waiting all those years for Helena to reappear. It is a sad story. I don't like it. My mother never holds my hand, not once. I think of her holding her twin sister's hand, and then letting it go, forever.

My father leans down and kisses me on my forehead.

'And so we called you Helena.'

Names. It was so difficult to find the right one. Fred and I looked at our baby in his little glass bed in the hospital. Fred reached in and lifted him out and passed him to me and we sat there gazing at our little boy.

'I think I'd like to name him Lionel,' I said.

Fred nodded. 'A great name,' he said.

'Could we call him Lionel Horace?' I asked tentatively. It seemed selfish to me that I would choose both his names.

'Lionel Horace Wolff,' Fred said. 'I think that is a wonderful name for him.'

Three days later, Fred drove Lionel and me home. The traffic, the streets, the noise seemed so busy and loud and I felt slightly dazed until we were out of the city, and then I had a feeling of calmness as we headed south.

'The oddest thing happened,' Fred said, sounding puzzled. 'When I went to settle the account, there was no charge.'

'Because I didn't give birth in the hospital?' I asked.

'I didn't really understand,' Fred said. 'I had already given them our insurance number and I know that some of the account was being paid by the insurance company, but I thought the bill would be more than that.'

'That is odd,' I said. 'What did they say?'

'They said the account had been settled.'

'They'll catch up with us later,' I said. 'We'll probably get some awful bill in the post in a few days' time.' Fred agreed.

At home, Lionel's room became a cocoon of love and warmth. I sat for hours just watching him sleeping, waiting for him to waken so that I could look into his eyes. His tiny hand clasped around my finger and the emotion I felt was stronger than anything I had experienced before. His skin was soft. He lay in my arms. This was love.

My parents-in-law had the billiard table re-covered as a gift to their grandson.

>*Dear Father, dear Mother,*
>*Fred and I have a son. You have a grandson . . .*

I was careful to include Fred as much as possible in this letter to my parents. If they did not reply, I thought, it would be a rejection not only of me, but of Fred and Lionel too. I knew this line of thought was illogical, but it was the best I could do to protect myself.

*We have christened him Lionel Horace, and al-
though I know every parent must think this of their
child, he is without any doubt the most beautiful baby
we have ever seen.*

Did my mother think that when I was born? Did all mothers?
Had my mother felt hope back then? And had I done something
to dissipate that optimism or let her down somehow? I did not
know. I could only wonder.

I knew that every parent considers their own child to be
considerably above average in the grand scheme of things, and
that half of them simply had to be mistaken. I had heard the usual
parental patter from colleagues at work, from Conti and from
Marjorie – walking already, talking already, reading and writing
already – as if each of these accomplishments were a minor
miracle achieved only a by a select few gifted children. I found all
this cant very tiresome and repetitive, and wondered at how these
mothers reconciled their belief in the extraordinary potential of
their own offspring with the evident fact that the world is full to
bursting with average and unremarkable people. What parent has
ever thought, let alone said, 'Oh, well, little so-and-so is a friendly
little fellow, but he is a bit thick?'

Perhaps the total inability to muster up the slightest bit of
objectivity as to the merits of one's own offspring is essential to
the evolution of the species. If parents could see their children as
others see them, well, what then? It would be the death knell of
the human species. That's what Horace would have said. Of
course I, too, now a parent, found myself thinking those very
things I had scorned.

His face is so perfect and he is so incredibly good . . .

Fred said that Lionel looked like me, but I did not want to put that in the letter in case it made my mother less interested, if indeed she would be interested at all.

He looks so like Horace . . .

I wrote the letter, but I did not post it for a long time.

Two weeks later, Conti's twins were born. She was told they were identical twins, although they didn't look the same. One was strong, one was very weak. One wailed with gusto, the other barely whimpered. Alice lay in her mother's arms as Edith was taken away immediately. Alice fed enthusiastically at Conti's enlarged and perfect breasts while Edith, in intensive care, was prepared for her first heart operation.

I forced myself to leave Lionel with Fred while I went to visit Conti in hospital, although Fred was thrilled to have Lionel to himself for once.

'Oh, she's lovely, Conti. She's so lovely,' I said, putting flowers on the table and looking into the baby cot on wheels beside the bed.

'Yes,' Conti said, looking at the baby Alice. 'You're perfect, aren't you?'

'How is Edith? What's happening with her?'

'I still haven't held her. She's so tiny and so helpless. It's not just her heart, she has something wrong with her back.'

'Her back?'

'It's twisted and too short . . .'

I could feel Conti's despair and her frustration at being unable to do anything. I held Alice in my arms and wondered at how different Conti's baby was to my own. There was a different feel, a different smell and the baby lay differently in my arms to Lionel. I had often wondered how animals all seemed to be able to identify their own partner or their own offspring, even where it seems impossible that they could. One way or another, though, they always found a way. Horace had told me that.

Alice cried out, and I realised that the sound was completely different to Lionel crying. I smiled as I held Conti's baby, now safe in the knowledge that I would know and identify my own anywhere, through sight and through sound.

'It's all such a struggle,' Conti said, exhausted.

It was so unlike Conti. I could tell she was in pain. My friend had changed over the previous months, but I had imagined that the old Conti whom I knew and loved would have bounced back. The Conti I now saw was far from being bouncy and I missed her, missed the way she used to be, and missed the way we were together.

But nothing was that simple. I knew that. It would take time. And in time, I trusted, Conti would be her normal self again, that gregarious and funny person upon whose head no hair would begin to dare to even think of being out of place.

I realised that I, too, had changed. All I really wanted was to get back home and be with Lionel. It wasn't that I did not care – I was sorry for Conti, desperately sorry – but I could see there was simply nothing I could do to help her.

'If there's anything I can do to help,' I said, placing Alice back in her cot.

Conti nodded. My flowers seemed so useless, pointless really. I picked them up and brought them over to the basin. 'I did not know what to bring you,' I said.

'Coming to see me is better than anything,' Conti said. I had the feeling she was biting back tears. 'I didn't even get in to visit you when you were in here,' she said. 'I'm sorry.'

'Don't be silly,' I said. 'You were nine months pregnant. Anyway, I didn't even manage to get myself in here in time.'

She laughed then. 'I know,' she said. 'Anyway, that's why I picked up the bill for you,' she added.

'What?'

'It was my gift to you,' she said. 'I know I've been difficult, moody even, and you've always been so nice.'

She had paid the account; I couldn't believe it. 'Conti, I had not realised. They never said.'

'I told them not to,' she said to me. 'Come and sit beside me.'

I did not know how I was going to tell Fred or what he would say.

It became clear over the next few months that Alice was being sidelined in Conti's efforts to attend to both of her twins. When both babies needed her attention, as they often did, Conti would see to Edith first. Increasingly I found myself looking after Alice's needs, and would often change her or feed her a bottle while Lionel slept.

I was glad that I had not had twins. It was all I could do to look after Lionel. It was all Conti could do to look after Edith, and, in the middle of it, Alice got as much, if not more, attention from me as she did from Conti.

Facial similarities between the twins became more apparent, but as Alice grew bigger and healthier with the passage of time, Edith seemed correspondingly smaller and weaker. The differences between the two became clearer and clearer, differences that were underlined more mercilessly with every passing day.

The days and months passed. When the babies were one year old, Edith had a second heart operation.

Although the Martins now employed a full-time nanny, she was away on holiday when Edith suddenly took a turn for the worse, and so Alice stayed with us. We tried putting Alice's cot in the spare room at first, so that neither child would disturb the other, but, after two days of running around between them, I found it easier to have them both in the same room.

Alice was more demanding than Lionel, and although I loved

her, it was with relief that I passed her back to the Martins when Conti returned home with Edith and the nanny came back from her holidays.

'I don't know how to thank you,' Joe said when he came to collect Alice and her things. 'I feel I should have kept her with us over the last few weeks, but Babbo and Cook, they just aren't up to it. You can imagine . . . '

I could well imagine. It was asking a lot to expect a pair of octogenarians to entertain a seven-year-old while looking after a one-year-old baby. The pair of them could hardly look after themselves, and it was remarkable how they were able to take care of Lorina, getting her to school on time and collecting her.

'I don't mind, it's no trouble. I'm just glad Edith is all right.'

'Conti thinks we need a second nanny as well as the house-keeper. I really don't know how we're going to manage.'

'Any time I can help, just let me know.'

'You're very kind, Helena. I don't know what we'd do without you. Maybe Conti is right about us needing a second nanny. We can't go on imposing on you like this. It's been on my mind lately and this latest operation, well, we really must do something about it.'

'I'm sure it would take some of the pressure off you too.'

'It's Conti. Between us, Helena, she isn't managing too well. It has just been too much stress for her.'

And for you, I thought. Joe seemed to have aged visibly over the last year, and I doubted that Conti provided a great deal of emotional support.

'Anyway, thanks again.' And with that, he was off.

I wondered how Lorina was coping with the addition of her new sisters to the family. Any new sibling meant that the existing one became less important in their parents' eyes. Where once you were at the centre of their world, you were now forced to share that position, at best. The existing one was forever stuck with the

156

knowledge that they alone were not enough, but how much worse where they were comprehensively outshone by their new brother or sister? And the best way to outshine a sibling is to be unwell. The slightest bleat of discontent would then be seen as incomprehensibly selfish. Everybody felt sorry for the sick child, but who would really feel sorry for the one left behind? Nobody. And Lorina had not only been ousted as the baby in the Martin house, but had been ousted by twins, one of whom was sick and who demanded all of their parents' time and attention.

It was difficult to warm to Lorina, though, even before the birth of her sisters. There was something about her that made me feel slightly uneasy. Lorina's eyes did not meet the person she was addressing. She had no interest in the twins and she spent as much of her time as possible with Babbo. After all, the old Count loved nothing more than to devote his time to her.

He had been forced to relinquish his motor scooter following an encounter with the law, after which Joe, who represented him in court, said he was very lucky not to have been imprisoned. To try to speed away from the police had shown a serious error of judgement on Babbo's part and the judge said he had no choice but to remove the offender from the streets once and for all.

Babbo tried playing deaf in the court, but to no avail. He then tried to encourage Alessia to drive the bike, but she had no understanding of balance, and even though the sidecar kept the bike firmly upright and stable, she nonetheless could not sit upright on the bike for more than thirty seconds.

'Dio,' Babbo exclaimed in disgust. 'You manage to stay upright when you cooking, and even when you in sidecar. Why you no stay up when you on bike?'

Regardless of his cajoling, teasing and fury, Alessia could not manage it, and the bike was sold.

Eleven

Lionel grew. A sturdy baby, he developed into a stoic toddler, a happy little fellow who followed me around with love in his eyes. I marvelled at how he listened to me right from the moment he was born. Lying in his cot, his eyes followed me around the room. As he grew he would lift his arms to me when I came into his room and would nuzzle into me and hug me when I lifted him. My heart swelled with love all the time. I did not know there could be such an emotion. It was overpowering.

> *Dear Helena,*
> *I cannot tell you the joy your mother and I felt, and still feel, on hearing your wonderful news. The photograph you sent is on our mantelpiece, and we love looking at it. We like the name you chose for your son, our grandson, and hope that you will bring him and Fred to meet us. I would like to visit you, but your mother would find it easier if you came here. You know how she does not like to leave home.*
> *With love,*
> *Your Father*

I read this letter a hundred times before Fred came home that evening.

'Look,' I said, thrusting the letter at him excitedly.

'That's wonderful'.

'I'm so happy. They seem so pleased.'

He hugged me. He knew that, more than anything, I was simply relieved that my parents had replied to my letter.

'I'm pleased for you, but I really can't take the time off at the moment. And even if I could, we can't afford it. Is there really no chance they would come here?'

'I don't know. My father never takes time off, and my mother dislikes leaving the farm, even to go into town. I don't know. I don't think it's likely. She really doesn't like to leave home.'

'We'll see what happens. You should write to them again, let them know you'd like them to visit.'

'But you'd like them to visit too?'

'Of course I would.'

I could not imagine them coming. They rarely travelled anywhere. The only time I remembered my father ever leaving my mother and the farm was when he and Horace once went north on horseback. We had once spent a week in Mombasa as a family when I was little, but my mother had pined for home and the holiday had been cut short.

My ability to open myself to rejection never failed to amaze me. That one letter had made me happy and I should have left it at that, but I could not and I did not. Instead I wrote to them again, telling them how thrilled I would be if they could visit, if they could just find a way.

Months passed before I heard back from my father, saying my mother was not well. She was not ill as such, just not well enough to travel at the moment. I read between the lines and I knew that he wanted to come but that it was my mother stalling. It hurt. It hurt so much that I had to bite back the tears as I put the letter away.

I knew not to expect them; I suppose I had known it from the previous letter, but that old feeling of rejection returned. I tried brushing it off, but it was difficult. All those feelings from childhood returned, the sense of not being enough. Horace had been accepted and I had not. I felt that my parents would have travelled halfway around the world to visit him if he were alive.

I thought now, as I had done before, how much better for everyone it would have been if I had died and not Horace, if somehow I had got between that bullet and my brother. It was an unpleasant way of thinking because it got me nowhere, indulging in images of them weeping over me. I would have been forever perfect, a person to be spoken about only in hushed tones.

Putting Lionel down in his cot, I vowed that I would never make him feel as I had. I wanted to stand between him and an uncaring world. I had read how Zeus had given his daughter, Athena, his magical shield, the aegis. Nobody messed with Athena after that. As well as being a magic shield, with the head of Medusa nailed to the middle of it, it reminded people who her father was: mess with me and you mess with Zeus. But I had no magic shield to give. If my father could not protect me from cruelty and neglect, how on earth could I protect anybody from anything? That knowledge was suddenly quite terrifying. Horace had died, and Lionel seemed so very vulnerable.

I felt like I was going mad and that I could not handle anything. It was really to do with tiredness, too many disturbed nights and my hormones all over the place. I needed to talk but had no one to talk too.

Somehow I could not load any of this on to Fred. It seemed unfair to put it on his shoulders. Years earlier we had talked, really talked, about things that mattered, but now I was afraid of disturbing the equilibrium we had reached. I did not want him to feel like he had let me down in some way. We were strapped for cash living on his salary alone and I felt he would feel responsible because we did not have the money to visit my parents. At that moment I did not want to see them anyway. I still had not told him that Conti had picked up the hospital bill. I could not bring myself to tell him. I was afraid he would feel that I had somehow managed to put us into this position where Conti felt it was perfectly all right to pay our bills.

I wished I were more like an animal. Animals do not fret and worry about things. They just are. I would have been better off if I could just simply be, without having been condemned to think about everything, over and over, until my sense of reality began to slip away.

One of the good things at this time was the incredible love I saw that Fred had for Lionel. Coming home from work, the first thing he did was to go to Lionel and hold him. He would sit for hours whispering to him, which filled my heart with joy. I wanted to talk with him, but I did not seem to have the energy.

Nor could I talk to Conti. It would not have been fair. I knew that my problems, enormous as they seemed to me, were really nothing compared to what she was going through. To moan to Conti about my mother's lack of care for me would have been like rubbing salt in her wounds, and on top of her attempts to find her mother she had the added difficulty of caring for Edith, which was obviously taking its toll. To try to talk to her would have been nothing short of insensitive.

Then out of the blue, Simon telephoned. He had sent flowers when Lionel was born but I had not heard from him since. Lionel was now thirteen months old. I suppose I thought that he had gone out of my life just as Daisy had done. Despite our promises to keep in contact, my letters to Daisy and hers to me had trickled out within two years of her leaving Trinity and returning to the States. Simon said he would be in Wicklow the following day and asked if he might drop in.

I was excited at the prospect of his visit. I wanted to show him Lionel and I needed company. He arrived in the early afternoon, bringing a bottle of wine and a large teddy bear.

'I'm a typical man,' he said, handing me the gifts. 'I didn't have a clue what to bring you as a present. I don't know how big babies are or what kind of clothes to buy for them. Hopefully one of these will entertain Lionel and you will enjoy the other.'

'They're great,' I said. 'You didn't have to bring anything, it's just nice to see you. Shall I open this? Will you have a glass of wine?'

'No, you keep it for when Fred comes in and you have time to unwind. A cup of coffee would be perfect.'

I brought him to Lionel's room and Lionel, who had been having a nap, woke with a yawn and smiled happily. Simon was enchanted.

'He likes me,' he said.

I was about to say that he was one of those babies who smiled at pretty much everybody, but decided not to. Lifting him from his cot, I handed him to Simon and Lionel reached up and stroked his hair.

'What a darling,' Simon said.

As I put on coffee in the kitchen, he asked, 'Have your parents visited you?'

'No, they haven't.' How had Simon managed to ask just this question, as if he had homed in on it somehow, like he could see right through me? Was I that transparent? That was probably why he had wanted to paint me – because he really saw me, saw me for what I was and for whom I was, whatever that might be. I took Lionel from him.

I had the sensation that I was going to cry. I put Lionel in his playpen, but my sudden silence brought Simon around to me and he looked into my face. 'No contact?' he asked.

'It's not that,' I said, brushing away the tears that now would not stop forming in my eyes.

'I wrote to them and they wrote back; at least, my father wrote. And I should be pleased enough that I got a response.'

'But . . . ?'

'Well, he said he would like to come to visit . . .'

I reached into a drawer and pulled out my father's letters. I passed the first one to him.

'It's a nice letter,' he said.

'Yes, but the next one said they definitely wouldn't come. That my mother isn't up to the journey.'

I passed him the second letter, and he read it thoughtfully.

'I think it says that they can't come right now. They do want to come, only they can't right now,' he said. 'I know that I don't know the nuances in your parents' letters, and that you maybe can read things into this that I can't, but on the surface it looks to me that they do want to come and that they are pleased and excited about Lionel.'

I nodded. 'I know. I keep telling myself that. But I'm just so disappointed. I had this feeling after the first letter that maybe I had broken through some barrier and reached them.'

'Helena, I think you have. I mean, they obviously care about you. Who knows what is happening that they can't jump on a plane right now? It doesn't matter. What counts is that they do care. You remember telling me how they sometimes sent you a Christmas card, sometimes not? Well, at least you're talking now. It's got to be better than it was. Try not to be too disappointed. If nothing else, you've made a start. And I'm sure they'd love to get more pictures of this little chap.' He nodded his head towards Lionel, who was playing with his bear. 'Let them know how he's doing. Just tell them little things, anything; I'm sure they will love to hear it. And even if you don't get the response you want, take it slowly. Keep up the contact.'

'You know, I think you're right,' I said, going back to pour the coffee. 'I have nothing to lose. A bit like when I wrote and told them about Lionel, I was scared I'd hear nothing, but the truth is I expected to hear nothing so anything that came back was positive. I will keep sending them pictures.'

'Have you thought of visiting them?'

'Money is too tight just now, and Fred is too busy. It's just not the right time.'

I did not want to tell him that money was always too tight and that I could not imagine us ever having enough to make that particular trip.

'Then remember, your parents are coping with you not going to them just as you are dealing with them not coming to you. Keep writing. It will work out. Someone bought your painting, you know,' he added.

'Really?'

'Just the other day. It's in London now.'

'Who bought the painting of me?'

'I don't know. It was done through some dealer and I'll get paid quite a lot of money once the London exhibition is over and the painting is actually sold. I think it's going abroad somewhere.'

'I'm glad for you,' I said. 'It's strange to think of a picture of me on the wall in somebody's house somewhere with people looking at it. It's different to thinking of it being in a gallery.'

'You said I could paint you again,' Simon said. 'May I take you up on that?'

I nodded. 'But wouldn't you prefer to paint a new subject?'

'No. I worked well with you and I would like to try it again, perhaps in a different context. I have to think about it, but I wanted to check that it would be all right.'

'But Lionel . . . I don't leave him with anyone. I don't like to.'

'You could bring him with you. We could try it. I know little chaps don't like to sit still and can be an awful distraction, but it's worth the try. And if it's too difficult, well, we'll find some other time.'

'Let's leave it for a bit, if you don't mind,' I said. 'I know it's not the right time now. When Lionel is older.'

When he left I felt inordinately sad. I knew I would not see him for a while, but he said he would phone. It had been the first proper conversation I had had with anyone in quite some time.

I felt a pang of guilt when Fred came home looking tired and

164

we ate dinner and I tried to express interest in his work. I felt very small and insignificant. I puzzled over it as I poured him a glass of Simon's wine.

I knew that I had what I wanted, full-time motherhood and the role of a supportive wife, but I missed outside conversation, knowing what other people were doing and thinking. This might seem a contradiction to the frustration I used to feel when at work, and trivia was discussed over coffee or lunch. I then realised that my conversations with Simon were probably the closest I had come to the conversations with Horace. It was not that Fred was not a good conversationalist; he was. But most of what he talked about now was to do with sport. I sometimes felt that we did not talk about what really mattered. We skirted issues. We avoided depth.

Somehow it had become our way, as if it was understood that some things shouldn't be discussed. A large dose of mutual blindness and forgetfulness by now seemed essential to our married life, and I wished it was not that way. Nothing could be said or done without the presence of that thick, cumulative, suffocating layer of mutual understanding that meant that nothing really meant what it literally meant any more. Nothing could be said without being understood as meaning something else entirely.

There was no real lack of honesty in our relationship, but there was a lack of real meaning, and once that is gone, it is very hard to retrieve. For all our mutual kindness and supportiveness, for all the love that was between us, there was now only limited communication. With Simon I had spoken of my feelings, my fears and hopes and worries. I never spoke of those with Fred. It was understood that I did not want to, which was my own fault due to my skirting around the issue so many times before. The problem now was that I had no idea how to begin such conversations with him. I wanted to remove the build-up that had accumulated over the years so we could just be the people we once were.

That evening, I felt that I had betrayed him in some way by talking so freely with Simon.

I tried telling Fred about my day. 'Simon Peterson came over to see Lionel,' I said, and even as I said it, I knew it was not the complete truth. Simon had come over to see me. Without even meaning it, I had managed to start off with a lie. How had this happened?

'Did he?' Fred said. 'That's nice. My mother phoned. We have this weekend free. I don't have to work, so she suggested we come over for a couple of days, play a bit of tennis and that.'

'Oh, what did you say?'

'I said yes, of course. It will be nice to get away.'

I would have preferred to have stayed home and have a few days alone with just Fred and Lionel, but I did not like to say so. I felt that Fred would see it as a rejection of his parents' plans, which indeed it would be. So I agreed. It was easier. But I knew what the weekend would be like. It was an unbroken pattern. It would all revolve around sport; results, trophies, dates, games, memories of specific matches, and of course the prize-winning Mullingar heifers. I would feel left out if I did not make the effort. I wanted to make the effort to be part of it, but sometimes it seemed so trivial.

'What are you thinking, Horace?'

He's turning the pages of a magazine, flicking back and forth. Something is on his mind.

'I'm wondering what makes us different from animals. If anything does.'

'We're cleverer?'

I watch him as he puts the magazine down.

'Yes. We're cleverer and we can talk. Communication helps our progress. Animals sort of learn how to do things, you know, from their parents. And there are other things they are born able to do. But they never learn anything much beyond that.'

'Why not?'

'I don't know. Their brains don't work like ours do. They haven't got concepts like we have.'

'I don't understand.'

'Neither do I, but I wish I did.'

'Animals can play, though, can't they?'

'I know what you mean. But it's all about instinct, about rituals. Maybe that's what people do as well. We have rituals too. But we have a lot else as well. Animals are always busy doing the same things, they're always concerned with eating and mating. Everything revolves around that. That's what survival means for them. Getting enough food, protecting themselves from attack and finding a mate.'

'Not Luther, though.' We look down the hill and Luther is standing there, watching us.

'No, not Luther.'

'I wonder if that is because of his life with us or because elephants are different to Sphex wasps or leopards?' I ask.

'Elephants are different, but then, all species are different to each other and yet carry similarities,' Horace says. 'In many ways, elephants are like us. They remember like we do. They grieve, you know, when one of their own dies. They stay for a week or longer beside the dead elephant. If they come across an elephant's skeleton, they caress its jawbone just like they would if the elephant were alive. They visit their dead.'

It occurred to me then as we sat in front of the television that maybe, just maybe, if I had not met Fred when I had, that I could have met someone else. Had I just been receptive to love and friendship and it happened to have been Fred whom I had met? It seemed a callous thought because I loved this man who was now dozing beside me on the sofa, and I could not imagine my life without him. But I was aware of the randomness of it all. If Daisy had not been on my corridor, and if she had not known Fred, would I even have met him?

It was another evening and we were sitting with Joe and Conti on the deck that Conti had built in imitation of ours, and the sunlight was slowly fading. It was a warm summer evening and the gnats and midges filled the air. Conti had lit citronella candles to keep them at bay. I was reminded of my own parents, and evenings sitting on the veranda, candles glowing on the table, the air still and silent.

The memory came to me with an element of surprise. Horace and I had come back from our ride early, before sunset, and we had left the horses in the stable at the back. Coming around the house, I saw my father with a glass of something long and cold beside him as he sat reading. In the chair opposite, with her back to the protective rail, my mother was sitting shelling nuts, and beside the basket of nuts on the table was a small tray with bread broken into pieces on it.

Luther is behind our mother, behind the wooden rail, with his trunk resting on her shoulder. Every so often the tip of his trunk touches her face and then stretches out pointedly at the tray, and she feeds him a chunk of bread.

'You're home early,' our father says.

'Get yourselves a drink,' our mother says, 'and bring it out and join us.'

Luther watches us with his unblinking eyes. Sometimes he looks like he is smiling.

'We're waiting for the fireflies,' our father says, looking back at his book.

It is a new evening ritual. He would come and join our mother and read for a little while she sits contentedly in her chair with Luther like a guard dog or a guardian angel at her shoulder.

'I'll go and close the gates,' Horace says. 'Helena, will you get me a drink and I'll be right back.'

Usually there is someone there to close the gates, but not that evening. I glance back as I go indoors, and I see Horace walking across the dry, dusty land in the direction of the gates. Luther leaves our mother's side and follows him, lumbering along with his tail whisking in the air. A few minutes later, when I return with two glasses of ice and lemonade, both our parents are on their feet and Horace is shouting.

'Luther! Luther!'

They have reached the gates just as the light starts to spiral outwards as it begins the last phase of its journey downwards in the sky before night falls, and Horace and Luther have stood for a moment looking westwards. And then, as Horace begins to close one of the gates, Luther, who has never shown any interest in what was outside the farm, other than occasionally accompanying us to the umbrella tree, suddenly steps forwards and walks out through the gates, setting off in the direction of the sunset.

'Luther!' Horace is calling as he starts to run after him.

'Let him go,' my father yells, running across the yard. 'Come back, Horace. It's getting dark. Come back at once.'

Horace is distraught. He berates himself, explaining that he had not closed the gates when we got back because he wanted to continue galloping and had been enjoying himself too much.

'Don't blame yourself,' my father says, taking his arm and leading him back towards the farmhouse. 'If Luther wants to leave, there is nothing we can do about it. He's free. Free to stay and free to go.'

'But why? Why did he suddenly decide to leave?'

'Maybe it was just the right time. Maybe it was the look of the sunset and he was just ready.'

'Will he come back?' I ask.

My mother shakes her head. 'We didn't care for him enough . . .'

'No.' My father stands with his back to us, staring out into the ever-quickening darkness. 'That isn't true, Carolina. No one could have looked after him better than you. Luther will come back if he wants to. He knows where we are. And we did care for him. He's alive only because of us. There is no blame here.'

My mother does not look like she believes him. My father strikes a match and lights the candles on the table and we sit in silence with my mother's hand resting on her shoulder where Luther's trunk had been.

'The deck is great,' Fred said. 'They did a really good job of it.'

Conti nodded. 'I've wanted it ever since I saw yours, years ago now. I'm glad we finally got around to it.'

'It makes ours look old,' Fred said with a laugh. 'Next thing, we're going to have to get ours updated and modernised.'

'Don't do that,' Joe said. 'If you do, as soon as Conti sees it, she'll want ours done again.'

We all laughed, including Conti. 'I'm going in to get another bottle of wine,' she said. 'I wanted a refrigerator out here on the deck, but Joe wouldn't hear of it.'

Joe shrugged. There might have been a slight tension, but it was unclear, and Conti got up and went inside.

'How are things with Edith?' Fred asked.

Joe shook his head. 'Not great. But you probably know that,' he said, looking at me.

'I don't really,' I said. 'Conti doesn't say much.'

'The prognosis is bad,' Joe said. 'They say there will be one operation after another over the next few years. It sounds more like we're buying her time than actually giving her quality of life.'

He looked down at his glass and I could see the grief in his face.

'It's bad enough that she can't speak. But now on top of that, they say she'll never walk.'

'Some animals ignore the weakest one. Knowing they can't save it, they won't waste their energy on it. Some even eat the runt in a litter, or abandon it and leave with the stronger babies. The weaker one can't keep up and it gets left behind.'

'Is that what happened to Mother's sister?'

'No, that's not what I meant. I meant babies. I think Mother's sister was about eight or nine when she got left behind in the bombing. That's not the same thing. That's not nature taking its course, that's war. That's different.'

'I wouldn't like to be left behind.'

'Don't worry. I won't leave you behind.'

But he did.

The pattern of our lives had changed. The men continued to work hard and we women brooded over our young. Over the years, Joe, Conti, Fred and I usually had dinner together one evening each month. Once the children were about five years old, we abandoned these dinners and replaced them with Sunday lunches with the children.

From an early age, Lionel showed an interest in animals. This probably was not that surprising, as I read him animal tales and told him the stories I remembered from my childhood. He had a pet rabbit called Mr White which he adored. He trained Mr White to jump over sticks of spaghetti that he slotted into his Lego bricks. The corridor looked like a mini gymkhana and Mr

White scurried down the passageway, leaping over the jumps with Lionel encouraging him enthusiastically from the sidelines and rewarding him with carrot sticks and an endless supply of hugs.

From time to time over the years, Freyn came to stay with us if Jackson and Marjorie were going to Wimbledon or the French Open. Freyn was a really lovely child, gentle and caring, and very loving to his nephew, Lionel. Lionel, for his part, adored this uncle who was a mere six years older than him. Marjorie had been so careful about nutrition and health both for herself and for Fred while he was growing up, but for some reason Freyn missed out on that care and she allowed him fast food, takeaways and ready-made meals. The result was that Freyn was very overweight for a child of his age. It was puzzling that she did not see the connection and often bemoaned his appetite, his weight and the difficulty of buying clothes to fit him. When he came to us I tried my best to get him to eat as we did, and being such an agreeable child he ate what I gave him, but he always seemed hungry, and no amount of fruit seemed to satisfy him.

We had a swing in the garden that Fred had made from rope and a tyre. Lionel swung on it, climbed the ropes and hung upside down, shouting in glee. Freyn, on the other hand, sat and cuddled Mr White or asked if he could help me in the kitchen.

Fred and Freyn liked each other but they did not talk as siblings. The age difference was such that Fred's relationship with him was somewhat removed. Fred was more like a benevolent uncle with him than a brother.

Lionel, Alice and Edith were close, with Lionel and Alice going to school together, and Alice and Edith communicating by some form of osmosis.

'Alice is my best friend,' I once heard Lionel saying to Jackson and Marjorie. 'We sit beside each other in school and we play together. But when Alice is at home in her own house, then Edith is her best friend.'

He was perfectly happy with this arrangement. I watched them through the kitchen window; he and Alice were playing on the grass while Edith sat silently in her wheelchair. They included her in their chatter and her eyes went from one face to the other. Edith was so tiny in her wheelchair, often too ill to come out and join them. Today she had been feeling better.

'It's funny how we learn to accept things,' Conti said, stirring sugar into her coffee.

I was not sure what she meant and I came away from the window and sat opposite her.

'Eight years ago,' she continued, 'if someone had told me that the highlight of my day would be sitting drinking coffee with you, I would have told them to dream on.'

I grinned. I knew she did not mean that like it sounded.

She looked up just in time to see my smile and she looked puzzled for a moment. 'I didn't mean that I don't like drinking coffee with you,' she said.

'I know,' I reassured her.

'It's just that I did not imagine that all of this would happen and that I would learn to live with it and take pleasure in the fact that today Edith is sitting out in the garden.'

'We adapt. We get used to things that we would have seen as being impossible,' I said.

'I wish. . .' she said, but she did not finish the sentence, nor did I ask her what she wished. Looking through the window, there was only one wish she could have had, and that was for Edith to have a normal life. We learn to take pleasure in little things that once would not have interested us.

'If you could have any one thing, Helena, what would it be?'

Horace back, alive and well? My mother paying me loving attention? My childhood, with all its faults and all its happiness? It was a good question and, while I wanted those things more than anything, I realised that I would trade nothing for Lionel. In my own way I was happy sitting at that table drinking coffee with Conti, knowing that my son was safe and happy and well.

'I don't know,' I said. 'How about you?'

'I want my old life back,' she said.

'We can't go back. Part of living is accepting that.' I said it as much to her as I did to myself.

'Don't be so smug,' she said, irritated.

'I'm sorry,' I said. 'Your question made me think of the things I've lost and how I see things now. I did not mean to sound smug.'

'God, I'm sorry,' she said. 'I didn't mean you're smug. I know you're not. I didn't mean to snap like that.'

'It's all right,' I said to her. 'I meant that sitting here with you at this table is as good as this moment can be. Maybe that is smug, maybe you're right.'

'No, I'm not right,' she said. 'I'm frustrated and I took it out on you. Forgive me.'

That was Conti. She lashed out when she could not handle things, but she really had a heart of gold. I knew she was selfish, but life had made her like that. It did not mean that she was not intrinsically kind and good. All the maternal love that Lorina had missed out on was now directed at little Edith. Conti, for all her money and her father's love, was dealing with things that most people don't have to deal with, and because of her upbringing she did not realise that; given the lot that she had to live with, she had it better than most would have. She had a cook, a housekeeper, a nanny and a structure of support, but she did not see that. All she saw was what she did not have.

I wanted to tell her that it could be a lot worse, but I did not. Despite all my understanding, the word 'smug' had hurt. I wanted to remind her that this conversation had started by her saying that she was taking pleasure in drinking coffee with me knowing that Edith, for once, was sitting out in the garden, that this was as good as it could be right now.

While I knew I was haunted by the past, I no longer hankered to have it back. Of course, it was different for Conti. Her past was so charmed in many ways, so full of freedom and fun, and now she found herself diminished by circumstance.

My past had seemed charmed to me, but for some reason I had a better handle on acceptance.

Twelve

Behind the houses, beyond the meadow was a small river. I took Lionel and Alice there for picnics over the various summers as they grew up. They played in the grass or sat on the riverbank on summer days, trailing their feet in the clear water. When they were little I worried one might slip out of my sight, and while it was fun with both of them, I preferred when it was just Lionel and me. Later, as they grew older, that changed; it became more entertaining with them both. I enjoyed their interaction and they played in the water while I lay on the rug and read.

'Mum, what's that?' Lionel was staring at the water with his mouth open.

'Oh, Lionel, Alice, look. It's a beaver.' Not just one beaver, but several, and they were busily building a dam.

'What are they doing?'

'They're building a dam. They're blocking part of the river.' I was as excited as the children. 'I can't believe it. I read how some beavers were being introduced into rivers in Scotland. They must have brought them here too. How wonderful. Look how they do it.'

They were damming the river at its narrowest point, working tirelessly with their twigs and mud.

'Why are they doing it?'

'Helena, do you know what this is?'

I look over Horace's shoulder to see the picture of a wet but furry looking animal in water. He has a nice face with little pointed teeth. Like a pudgy rat who had just got out of the shower.

'What is it?'

'It's a beaver. They build dams to block up rivers and streams. Would you believe that it is because of beaver dams that wetlands are created? The American Indians thought that beavers were sacred because they did so much to help other aspects of nature.'

'Why do they build dams?'

'The interesting thing is that they have no choice. That's what a beaver does. It builds a dam. It's what nature tells it to do. These beavers are damming a river, but the truth is they would build a dam anywhere they could. If you have a speaker with the sound of running water coming out of it, beavers will cover the speaker in mud. They just hate the sound of running water.'

'I don't understand. What does that mean? What are you saying?'

'Well, it might look in the wild that the beaver is being really clever, building this dam, making a lodge beside it – a lodge is his home – ensuring he has food, but all the time he is just doing something that nature is forcing him to do. It's more like an instinct than a choice or thought. They hear water, they build dams.'

'They're making a home, Lionel. Come sit and watch them and I'll tell you what they are doing. They have a plan, like a blueprint in their brain.'

'What's a blueprint?'

'It's ... don't worry about the word blueprint. They are going to do what nature intends them to do. It's their instinct to survive. They will build this dam, and we can come and watch them every day. Beside the dam, hidden behind branches and twigs, will be their home. It's called a lodge. And in the lodge they will have baby beavers. The babies are called kits. They never overfill their lodge. They will just have enough kits and no more, just enough to care for and to make sure their family will continue. If something bad happens, if they are threatened in some way, they will have more kits. They will make sure they continue.'

Lionel and Alice sat side by side and listened to me while watching the working beavers.

'But what happens when the babies grow up and want to have babies of their own? Will the lodge get too full?'

'No. When the babies are two years old, they will leave and make their own dams and their own lodges and fill those lodges themselves.'

'Aren't they very clever to know how to do that?'

I could hear my own voice in Lionel. There was the same wonder and curiosity I had felt as a child.

It suddenly occurred to me that I had mislaid that sense of wonder for myself and I had no idea when that had happened. It was there now, but it was to do with Lionel. My whole existence was related to him. What joy I felt was in watching him and seeing the world through his eyes. It satisfied me, but it also puzzled me.

I kept thinking about Conti wanting back her old life while I had no real interest other than in the present. All I wanted was to be with Lionel, talking to him and listening to him and guiding him.

We picnicked down at the river and I wished Conti would bring Edith down to join us, but of course it was not that simple. The grass in the field connecting the houses to the river was too long and it was awkward to carry Edith for any distance. She now had an electric wheelchair and her little fingers learned quickly how to move it, but it would get caught in the long grass.

Lionel and Alice included her in everything that was possible. They were a strange threesome. Lionel read and read and told the twins the things that interested him. Alice asked questions, Edith watched and silently listened. Her gaunt little face was a pale, sad echo of her healthy sister. They sat holding hands, a strange telepathy between them that was reflected in the questions Alice asked. Some of the questions were her own, though some, I felt, were Edith's coming to her through the touching of their hands.

'But why does the bird of paradise do that? What word did you say?' Alice asked.

'A lek?' Lionel replied. 'That's a male bird of paradise. He will fight the other males to get a mate. It's in his nature. He will build a nest for the mate and attract her in by a show of strength and beauty.' He was sitting on the sofa, Alice and Edith beside him, and suddenly it is not his voice I hear, but Horace's.

'All birds of paradise have ten primary feathers and twelve tail feathers.'

'Horace.' I can hardly speak.

The bark of the tree is hard against my back. I have pulled back into it in an effort to hide.

'What is it?' Horace says, glancing up at me.

I nod my head in the direction of the south-west, beyond the farm. 'Horace,' I whisper.

He gets to his feet and reaches for the rifle.

'They won't touch us,' he says.

'I'm afraid,' I whisper.

The baboons are coming, jaunting along across the open brush. Every year they make this journey. It's all right when we are inside the farm and I can bravely look out over the gates or the fence.

'It's all right,' Horace says. 'As long as we do nothing they will ignore us.'

I think of trying to climb the tree, but the branches, such as they are, are very high up.

They are getting closer and I know they have seen us, though they pretend they don't. They walk and walk, like a family of vagrants. Then the biggest one, the one who marked me when I was just a tiny girl, stops and looks at me. The fur is high around his neck. I can see his huge canine teeth. They all stop now.

I can hardly breathe.

'Horace,' I whisper, 'don't let him take me.'

Horace has the rifle half-cocked. 'If I shoot, they will attack,' he says.

It is like a standoff. I'm pressed against the tree. The male's glittering eyes are fixed on me.

Then, from the distance, there is the sound of trumpeting and Luther is coming at a good pace through the farm gates.

They turn as one and look at Luther, who is coming fast towards us, and then, without further ado, they continue on their journey past the tree in the direction of the forest.

My knees buckle and I am sitting on the ground. Horace stands and watches them as Luther comes and positions himself at the foot of the hill.

'I think they are just curious,' Horace suggests.

I am not so sure, but I agree that we won't tell our parents, as it might inhibit our activities.

Conti had got rid of the nanny and replaced her with a nurse, both to assist with Edith and also to help the Count, who had aged suddenly. He slept more often than not, and while he still moved quite spryly, he often appeared not to know where he was.

On a late summer day when Lionel, Alice and Edith were twelve years old, the Count settled himself in the orchard next door. Edith was sitting in her wheelchair opposite her grandfather, where she had been strategically placed so that the nurse could see them both from the house. Edith watched as her grandfather's head slumped forwards onto his chest and she wondered if she should wake him. She knew that if she slept like that, she would have a pain in her neck later. Alice came and joined her, sitting cross-legged on the grass at her twin sister's feet.

'It's very hot,' Alice said to her. 'Do you want me to push you farther into the shade?'

Edith shook her head. 'As soon as the sun reaches Babbo, I should wake him,' Alice continued. 'He'll cook in this heat.'

Edith nodded. She still had never spoken, even though the doctors said there was no clear reason for it. Lionel said it was as if talking were too big an effort for her. She observed and listened and Alice did the talking for them both.

'Lionel is coming over in a while and we can play cards or Scrabble,' Alice said. 'We'll go inside then. It will be more comfortable.'

Again Edith nodded. She was looking at the Count now. It had occurred to her that his breathing must be very shallow, a bit like her own breathing, and that was why his chest wasn't moving. It struck her as odd because when her breathing was that shallow she usually made a noise when inhaling. And the Count was making no noise.

Alice followed her eyes and saw she was looking strangely at the Count. She sat more upright and looked again. Then she got up and went over to her grandfather and she put her hand gently on his.

'Babbo,' she said, 'maybe you should wake up now.' But as she said it, she felt a sense of panic. She tried again, a little louder. 'Babbo? Babbo?'

Lionel appeared around the side of the house.

'There you are,' he called. He was dressed in shorts and a T-shirt and he was smiling happily. 'Mum made ice cream, and she said you must both come over. I'll push you, Edith.' He stopped as he saw Alice's face peering at the Count. 'Alice?' he said.

Alice looked at him and then back at the Count.

'Lionel,' she said, trying to keep her voice steady, 'will you

181

bring Edith inside and I'll join you in a minute?' He heard something in her voice and he moved forwards to do what she had asked. Her voice did not sound like that of a little girl; it was suddenly more grown up. He knew something was terribly wrong and that she wanted Edith out of the situation. They both always went out of their way to protect Edith, but Edith had heard it too. She tried to pull herself from the chair but was not strong enough. She made a moaning sound. Alice looked in panic at Lionel.

To steady herself, she reached out to hold on to one of the low branches of the plum tree under which the Count had dozed off, but this movement was enough to stir the tree and it rained plums down on the old man. He did not stir. The three children stared at him in ever-increasing shock, as it was now apparent something was very wrong.

'I'll get Mum,' Lionel said. He would have liked to have brought Alice and Edith with him, but neither seemed to hear him, so he came running home.

'Babbo, he dead,' he announced to me, his pattern of speech and his accent momentarily resembling the expired Count.

'What?' I said, not quite following.

'Dead. Gone. Dead.' He often spoke like a dictionary and it usually amused me. This time it was as if the words were stuck in his mouth and he couldn't get them to flow freely.

'Are you sure?' I asked as we ran up the laneway and into the Martins' drive.

'He didn't move, even when all the plums fell on him,' Lionel explained matter-of-factly. I had not quite followed where the plums fitted into the story even though Lionel was, as ever, succinct. But the Count was dead and both his lap and the ground around him were showered with plums.

Alice and Edith spent that night with us. It was the first time Edith had spent the night away from home other than in hospital, but Joe had seized on it when I suggested it.

'Thank you,' he said. 'You're the only person I trust her with, and I think we need to get both girls out of the house while Conti is like this.'

Conti was completely distraught and the nurse was now caring for her.

We went back to our house and I fed the children and got them ready for bed. After I had checked on Alice and Edith, I hovered on the landing. I wanted to go to Lionel, but I needed to be sure the twins were settling. Through the half-open door, I could see Edith looking at Alice beseechingly.

'You want to know where we go when we die,' Alice said.

Lionel said she could always read her sister's thoughts, especially as they mostly resembled her own.

'Mum says you go to heaven,' Alice replied. 'You know that.'

Edith stared at her again.

'Yes, but what is heaven? Well, I don't really know. A kind of storage place for the dead people, I suppose,' Alice said.

Edith was still looking at her and I felt that she was thinking that when she died, Babbo would be there waiting for her. Personally I did not find this a particularly reassuring thought, but maybe Alice thought that it was offering Edith some solace, so she said nothing for a moment.

'We'll be together always,' she tried, reaching a hand across from her bed to Edith's. The curtains were open and there was a little light in the room, just enough to see each other's faces but no more. Edith seemed to know the hand was there and she took it. They clutched each other's fingers.

Edith nodded. Both knew they were just offering the other what the other wanted. Both knew that it was not going to be like that. Despite all the similarities and all the luxury given to them, they knew there was nothing similar in their lives. They viewed time differently. There was no jealousy or resentment on

Edith's part. She loved her sister just as Alice loved her, but Edith's life was second hand. There was a terrible immediacy to her ill health and her weak heart, but her 'real life', as she saw it, was seen and lived by Alice. She lived off Alice's stories of her days' adventures, of the things that Lionel told her, of how she was doing at school. She remembered every single thing that Alice said and she lived her life through Alice's experiences.

She stared at Alice.

'You want to know if Babbo was in pain?' Alice asked. 'No. I know he wasn't. Dad said that he just went to sleep. I think that must be a nice way to die.'

It was nice for the Count, I thought, but not for the rest of them. Joe had been so good with them when he came racing home from work, whereas Conti had only been able to cry. And Alessia had wailed. She had howled out her grief to the garden and the fields and the sky and then gone indoors and sobbed uncontrollably until she collapsed on a sofa and fell asleep.

'Mum?' Lionel called.

I went into his room, picking up his clothes from the floor and depositing them in his laundry basket with a smile. I liked the fact that he was just like Horace, who had never found the laundry basket in all our childhood.

'Mum, where has Babbo gone?'

'He's gone to be buried,' I replied, closing his cupboard door.

'No, I mean, where is the real he gone?'

'The real he?'

'You know, the person he. The talking he. The one who listened to music and tried to speak English but preferred Italian.'

'Ah, I see,' I said. 'His soul, or his spirit, you mean. The real he – it's a nice way of putting it. I think he is somewhere that he wants to be. Somewhere that he was happy.'

'Like under the plum tree?' Lionel asked.

I wasn't sure how to answer. I didn't want Lionel to start

finding the plum tree haunted or saying something that would frighten Edith and Alice, but he had gone back to his book and did not appear to be expecting an answer. But I thought of what he said, of the Count dying peacefully beneath the plum tree. I thought of Horace at peace beneath the umbrella tree.

Conti reacted to the news of her father's death with fury. From appearing distraught like Alessia was, it soon transpired that there was real anger mixed with her grief. The anger was to do with the fact that the Count had died without ever revealing who her mother was. Her tears were an outpouring of anguish.

'I always thought he would tell me. I thought he had to tell me. I could not imagine he would die without telling me,' she said, rifling through his room, looking in drawers and cupboards in the hope of unearthing something. Joe, in the doorway, was trying to stop her. I hovered uncertainly outside.

'Tell you what?'

'About my mother. Where she is.'

'You told me your mother was dead.'

'Well, she wasn't. He left her. He took me and he left her.'

Joe watched her. If, for a moment, he thought she was making this up, he realised almost immediately that she was telling the truth and that she was desperately upset by it. Whatever annoyance he might be feeling at discovering she had lied to him, he put aside. He was a pragmatic man and he could see he was dealing with pure emotion and it was not the right time to pursue his own feelings.

'If there is anything to be found,' he said, 'it's more likely you will uncover it by being systematic.'

But Conti was emptying drawers of underclothes onto the floor and kicking them out of the way when nothing was found hidden among them.

'I don't want my mother anyway,' she said. 'I just want to know who she was and why he left her.'

'I want you to tell me what you're talking about,' Joe said as he tried to pick up the tossed clothing. She told him then about the conversation she had had with Babbo when she was pregnant with the twins.

'Why did you never tell me this before?' he asked in surprise.

'There was no point. What could you do?'

'Well, for one thing I could have asked Babbo while he was still alive.'

'If he wouldn't tell me, why on earth would he tell you?' she snapped.

Joe knew how upset she was and there seemed little point in telling her that he was upset too – upset that the Count had died, upset for her and for the children, but upset too that she had kept this secret for all those years. It implied a secrecy that he had not expected from her.

I slipped away back to the children and left them to it.

At this point Alessia, who was not much younger than the ancient Count, having wept profoundly for a week, found a new lease of life and decided to return to Italy.

'But shouldn't we encourage her to stay here?' Joe said to Conti when Alessia's plans had unfolded.

'If she wants to go back to Italy, why not?' Conti could see that life would be a lot easier if Alessia were gone. Alessia staying would sooner or later mean that more nursing care would be needed, this time for her.

'But we owe her,' Joe said thoughtfully. 'I mean, this has been her home. Or rather, you are her home. She's always been with you.'

'But she wants to go. We should let her.'

'I'm not happy about this,' Joe said. 'She's elderly. The world she knew over there won't be the same. She has no idea what it's going to be like.'

'She has relatives, I think,' Conti said. 'Look, if she wants to go, we can hardly stop her.'

'Well, I'm going to talk to her before she goes,' Joe said.

'Talk to her?'

'Ask her about your mother.'

'She won't tell you. She wouldn't tell me. I asked her a while ago.'

Joe, however, had advocacy skills that Conti did not.

'Alessia,' he said. He was down in the kitchen, which was her domain. He had poured them each a glass of wine. She was sitting in her large white apron on a hard chair at the table. He sat opposite her. 'Conti has told me that you want to return to Italy.'

'*Sì,*' said the cook.

'Well, before you go – and you are only to go if you're sure that's what you want – I would so like to hear the story of how you and the Count left Italy. It's part of history and I would like to know it in case the girls ever ask.'

'Is nothing to tell,' she said carefully.

'Then tell me about the war. Tell me how you and Babbo left.'

'It was coming to an end. Our Mussolini was in trouble and the Count, he say we must leave. He had papers for us and we went north to the mountains. It was long ago. I only remember the snow. Nothing more.'

'Had you seen the snow before?'

'No. I only saw the sun.'

'How long did you stay in the mountains?'

'Too long. Two years it was. In . . . how do you say . . . in a hunting house.'

'A hunting house? Ah, I see. A hunting lodge.'

'The Count, he was a good man, no matter what they say. But he say we cannot go back. Our place was gone. He asked friends and they say his home destroyed, his art taken.'

'That must have been very difficult. Very sad,' Joe said, refilling their glasses.

'*Si.* Very sad.'

'And did he get married?' Joe asked.

Alessia thought for a little while, then shook her head.

'Never?'

'No.'

'And Conti?'

'*La bella* Contessa,' Alessia said with a smile.

'Yes, *la bella* Contessa,' Joe continued. 'Where was she born?'

'In the village.'

'The village near the hunting lodge?'

'Ah yes. In hospital nearby.'

There is a laboratory in a building. In this particular room there are two desks and on either side of the room there is a tank. In one tank there are fish, in the other there is an octopus. One morning the scientists come in and all the fish are gone. There is no trace of them. Nothing. Not a fish. The tank is empty. The scientists are puzzled. They refill the tank with more fish and get on with their work. The day ends. They turn off the lights and leave. The following morning they arrive at work and the fish tank is empty again. They accuse each other.

'Is this a joke?'

'Did you take the fish?'

'Maybe it's the lads next door.'

'If it's a joke, it's a very stupid one.'

That night they lock the door when they leave, but when they return in the morning the fish tank is empty again and the door is still locked.

'Is it the caretaker who is doing this?' They ask him carefully, not wanting to insult him but feeling he has to be the perpetrator. But he denies it.

'Maybe it's the cleaners,' someone suggests.

The cleaners come in at seven in the morning.

'But we locked the door.'

'Well, they have keys.'

'We can hardly accuse them.'

The cleaners are contacted and asked if they noticed what was in the room.

'An octopus,' they replied.

'And fish?'

'No, no fish. Just an octopus.'

'I know,' says one of the scientists. 'We'll leave a movie camera running. We'll stay as late as possible and turn it on before we leave. It will run for four hours. Maybe we can find out that way what's going on here.'

One of them stays until nearly midnight and the camera, positioned in a corner of the room, is turned on when he leaves and locks up.

The following morning they arrive all together and unlock the door. Once again, the fish tank is empty.

They reset the reel on the camera and run the film. They cannot believe what they see. About fifteen minutes into the film, the octopus pushes up the lid on his tank, climbs out the side and down onto the floor. He splatters his away across the lab and up the side of the fish tank. He lifts the lid and devours the contents, one by slippery one, and then returns across the floor to his own tank. He climbs back in and with one long tendril he reaches up and pulls the lid down neatly on top of the tank and settles down for the rest of the night.

Horace tells me that story. He says, 'They thought the fish were in no danger.'

'But they were. Oh, the poor fish.'

'The point isn't "the poor fish", Helena. The point is sometimes things look like they cannot happen. It was a possibility no one considered.'

189

And so they moved to a village in the mountains and Alessia shopped in the local market. They lived quietly. The Count was waiting for a good time to move them abroad. He did not want to go back to his home town.

'Our lifestyle was gone,' said Alessia, her English vocabulary improving with each glass of red wine. 'The Count, he say there could be reper...' She struggled to find the word.

'Repercussions?' Joe suggested.

'Yes, repercussions, and we must start a new life as soon as he can arrange it. I want to go back to our old home, but I also want to stay with him. I live in his family all my life. So did my parents.'

'Yes, of course,' Joe said reassuringly. 'I can understand that. He was your family. I can see that.'

'The village, it had refugees in it. Some orphans from the war, they were living there. The Count, he met a girl. Very young. Too young,' Alessia said, grimacing. 'The Count, he is sure this is love. I think he hopes to bring her with us. But I not so sure. She very young.'

'What year is this?' Joe asked.

'It year Conti born. It is 1956.'

'And he married this girl?'

'No. He no marry her. She have baby and then we leave.'

'And she stayed behind?'

'Si. We just leave with the baby.'

'You didn't tell her you were going?'

'I do not know what the Count tell her. She have baby and we leave.'

Joe considered the facts. The Count had left Italy in a rush and could not go back. He settled in a village where he appeared to have hidden for nearly ten years, including the time hiding in the hunting lodge. It smacked at best of repercussions, at worst of war crimes, with the Count running and covering his tracks, and Joe knew it.

And then there was the further event of the baby being born and the Count and the cook absconding with it. And then he thought of something else that had bothered him a few months earlier.

Lorina had written an essay on fascism in Europe and he had seen it lying on her desk and had read it. It had struck him at the time as being one of the most vitriolic excuses for fascism that he had ever heard and he had wondered where she had got her ideas. He had tried talking to her, but she had clammed up when she realised he was displeased. He knew he had not handled her correctly, but at the time he had been truly dismayed at what she had written.

It now occurred to him that her ideas might well have come from her grandfather. Joe had never doubted that Babbo was ruthless and self-centred, but he had not taken it one step further in his mind. Because he loved Conti he forgave the old man everything, but now he was forced to look at him in a new light.

'And Conti's mother . . . ?'

'Young girl.'

'What happened to her?'

'Nothing. I don't know. Maybe she still live there.'

'But he took her baby and didn't tell her?'

'Well, she know when she find baby gone,' Alessia said.

It was unbelievable, so coldly calculating and cruel. In fact, it bordered on being evil. Joe wanted to shake her. Whatever about the Count behaving in this fashion, he could not believe that a woman would not have tried to stop him.

'Did you not think perhaps Conti should have been with her mother?' he asked, trying to keep his voice warm and friendly.

'Count, he say Conti better with him. Young girl have no money. No good education. Count, he had lots. He want his daughter to have the best. Young girl uneducated. No family. Poor. The Count, he like tradition.'

Joe could not imagine what he was going to tell Conti.

'Do you remember the name of the village?' he asked suddenly.

Alessia only remembered it was in the north.

'And the name of the girl?'

Alessia remembered that all right. Her name was Elena. She did not know her surname.

So they paid Alessia's fare and Joe told her that she was welcome to come back if she wanted to.

Joe came to me that evening. Fred was late home and Joe came in, pale and shaking. I was in the kitchen when he appeared.

'Helena, can we talk?'

'Of course,' I said.

'Do you have a drink?' He looked around.

I was surprised. I had not seen this Joe before.

'Yes,' I said, asking him to follow me into the living room. I gestured to the drinks and he helped himself liberally to a brandy.

He told me then about the conversation with Alessia. I listened in silence.

'What do you make of that?' he said.

'About her going back to Italy?'

'No, about Conti's mother and the Count's treatment of her.'

I should have put it together then, but I did not. The coincidences involved were too great, even for me, who believed in coincidence. But I just did not see this link in our stories.

'It's a shocking story,' I said to Joe. 'Have you told Conti?'

'No,' he said sharply. 'I need to digest all of this. When we first met, Conti told me her mother was dead, and I believed her. Now I'm wondering what else she lied about.'

'Joe, I don't think it was a real lie. I think it was more that she couldn't accept the truth as given to her by her father. He had said her mother had abandoned her. That must have been a terrible thing to live with.'

'But she told you and she didn't tell me.'

'All I can say is that it was not meant to hurt you, but rather to protect her. And she told me because I told her something bad that had happened to me and we were comforting each other.'

'I have no idea how to handle any of this. Alessia is leaving, Conti is irate with her father, the twins are upset, and I have no idea at all how to cope.'

'I think you're doing pretty well,' I said. And he was, considering what had happened and unfolded.

He got up and poured another brandy. 'It's so calm in here,' he said suddenly, looking around as if taking in his surroundings for the first time. It was calm, certainly by the standards of what was happening next door. Lionel was in bed reading. The twins were asleep. Fred's dinner was slowly overcooking in the oven. The house was quiet. Joe downed his brandy, and somehow, through all of this, Lorina was forgotten.

Thirteen

Of all the people who had suffered loss in the Martin household that week, it was Lorina who was the most affected. She watched through the window as Alessia left. The two people with whom she had had the most contact had gone within a week of each other. She was eighteen now, awkward and sullen. Although she left Edith alone, she went out of her way to tease Alice. If she wept, she did it quietly in her own room.

Conti took herself off to town for a shopping trip. 'Retail therapy,' she said to me. 'If I don't get out of that house, I'll scream.'

I did not point out that she had screamed; so loudly, in fact, that we had been able to hear her next door.

It was mid morning and I was cleaning the kitchen when there was a tentative knock on the door.

'Hello.' Alice's little face appeared. 'May I come in?'

'You can always come in, Alice.' I glanced at the child. Her face looked slightly grimy, as though she had been crying and had wiped her eyes with dirty hands. 'Is everything all right?' I asked, concerned.

'Yes, it's fine,' Alice replied with a small smile. 'Is Lionel around?'

'He's in his room. We're going to go down to the river. We were just getting ready and then he was going to call for you.'

'May I go to his room?'

'Yes, of course. Are you sure everything is all right? I mean . . .' I hesitated. I didn't want to intrude. Alice was the kind of child who clammed up if she was asked anything she did not want to answer. Alice stood there, looking uneasy.

'Come, let me wipe your face,' I said. I did not blame Conti for needing personal time, but I hoped she had not knowingly left Alice like this. I carefully washed Alice's face, only too aware that Alice was trying to suppress further tears.

'Do you want to tell me?' I said gently.

Alice shook her head. 'Lionel,' she said.

I nodded and let the child go. Lionel would tell me when he was ready, and then maybe I could help.

I could hear Alice's footsteps going down the hallway and Lionel's bedroom door opening. A few moments later, both of them came running down the corridor.

'Mum, Alice and I are going on down to the river,' he said as they went out through the kitchen.

'Lionel, wait, I'm coming with you. I'll just be a moment.'

'No, don't come. We'll be back shortly.' And they were gone, the door banging closed behind them.

I was understandably puzzled, and I went into the living room and watched as they came around the side of the house and down the outside steps into the back garden. They ran across the grass and out the back gate. I could see them in the long grass in the meadow, two colourful moving creatures as they raced across the field until they disappeared. I did not know if I should follow them. I wanted to give Lionel the space he implied he needed, and yet I felt I ought to go after them. Back in the kitchen, I put drinks and sandwiches in a bag, and then, locking the door, I followed them.

I found them at the river. Alice was hunched up on the ground and Lionel was pulling branches to the edge of the bank. He broke off twigs and laid everything out on the edge. At first I could not see what was wrong or understand what he was doing, and then, slowly, I took in that the dam was broken and the river was flowing through where it had been so painstakingly blocked by the beavers.

'What happened?' I asked. I would have assumed it had been some accident or freak of nature, or indeed the simple strength of the water's current, if Alice had not arrived crying at the house and the two children had then left so abruptly.

'The beavers worked so hard,' he said.

'They'll rebuild it,' I reassured him. 'Come and sit beside me. You've helped them by lining up the sticks, now let them handle things.'

Lionel came and joined me and Alice. I took a napkin from the picnic bag and wiped the tears that were pouring down Alice's cheeks.

'It's all right, Alice,' I said gently. 'They will rebuild it if they think it's the right place for it.'

'It's not all right,' Lionel said crossly. 'It isn't all right, is it, Alice?'

'It's not Alice's fault,' I said evenly. There was tension here like I had never seen between the children before.

'If you don't tell her, I will,' Lionel said, standing in front of us with his back to us. I was suddenly reminded of my father. It was extraordinary. Lionel's stance was just like my parent's.

'It is my fault,' Alice said. 'I told Lorina about the lodge and the dam.'

'Lorina? What does she have to do with it?'

'She's a bitch,' Lionel interjected, swivelling around with fury in his face.

'Lionel, please. Language,' I said, now bewildered.

'Lorina did this,' Alice said quietly with an air of resignation. 'I should never have told her.'

'Lorina did this? Broke the dam? Why on earth . . . ?' I was staggered.

'Because she is a mean, cruel bitch,' Lionel said.

'Lionel, please don't use language like that. If she did do this, it's appalling,' I said.

'Oh, she did it all right. She can't bear the idea of any animal having a nice home.'

196

'How do you know she did it?' I asked.

'She told me,' Alice said.

'Why did you tell her about it?' Lionel said.

'I didn't really. She overheard me talking to Edith. I was telling Edith all about it,' Alice said. 'I was hoping that maybe Edith could come here with us and I thought if I told her, maybe she'd feel strong enough to come here. And Lorina was outside the door, listening. I saw her too late.'

'I'm going to kill her,' Lionel said with fury in his voice.

'What would that achieve?' I asked him. I too was angry, but I was suppressing it as I tried to handle Lionel and Alice. 'Alice, don't cry. This is not your fault.'

'If I kill her, it would mean she couldn't do it again,' Lionel said.

'She won't do it again,' I said. 'I'll see to that.'

'No, you can't,' Lionel said. 'She'll take it out on Alice. I'll kill her and that will solve things.'

'Lionel, be reasonable. Killing someone solves nothing. It makes things worse. It's how wars are started. Intelligent people find a rational way of solving a problem. Taking the law into your own hands fixes nothing.'

'But the beavers will fix their dam and then she'll do it again.'

'I'll talk to her,' I said.

'It will make it worse. She'll blame Alice. She blames Alice for everything.'

'I'll talk to Conti,' I reassured him. 'I'll be careful, don't worry. But this won't happen again. I promise you.'

I did not know if it was a promise I could keep, but I was certainly going to try.

'Mama?'

My mother does not look up. She is reading.

'Mama?'

'Hmmm.'

'Did you have a sister?'

Now she looks up. She stares at me, startled, and then she nods.

'What happened to her, Mama?'

'She died,' my mother says.

'How did she die, Mama?' I wanted to tell her that I was sorry. I wanted to say I could not imagine anything worse in my life than losing Horace.

'I let go of her hand,' my mother says slowly, as though thinking about it. 'We could hear the planes coming and we were running. We were holding hands. Tightly. Never to let go.' She rests her cheek in her hand and she closes her eyes.

'We were twins, you see. We were born together, we lived together. I thought one day we would die together. The sky was dark and we could hear the planes getting closer over the sound of the sirens.'

The bombs started dropping relentlessly. Two children running with their mother and with others. It was bedlam as they raced for the shelter. In the push and shove they separated and one little girl was left alone, looking backwards and forwards. her eyes following the disappearing crowd, uncertain whether to go after them or to wait and to be found by her sister and her mother. The buildings around seemed to explode and the child could no longer go forward as explosion after explosion broke the road and ripped the buildings apart, sending bricks and mortar, iron girders and glass in all directions. Rooted to the spot as the gulf between her and safety widened until it disappeared in the rubble and dust, she finally found her legs could move again, and she went back, back the way they had come.

The streets were no longer recognisable. She found a

place she thought was her home. The entrance was gone but there was sufficient space to slip through down to the basement. They would come back and find her. They would know she would find her way home.

My mother never held my hand. I now know why. If she is not holding it, she cannot let it go.

I lean over to her and I kiss her cheek. As I turn away, I can taste salt on my lips.

Conti's reaction was not what I expected. She had become far more volatile than she had been in the past, and if anything, I feared she would go over the top and attack Lorina. I chose my words carefully.

'What am I supposed to do about it?' Conti said.

'I thought you might speak to her,' I said.

'If you want to speak to her you can, but quite honestly I've more to worry about than some beavers in a river.'

'I didn't want to interfere,' I said.

Conti shrugged. She clearly had no interest in Lionel or Alice's problems. 'Beavers in a river! For God's sake, Helena, who bloody cares?'

'Alice cares, and so does Lionel. And believe it or not, so do I,' I said through gritted teeth. I felt really annoyed and I wanted to shout at her, but I knew it would get me nowhere. I still cared about her as my friend and as a person who was going through her own problems. I wanted to say that if Conti was even a halfway caring mother, she would care too. No parent would condone their daughter being so destructive if they were thinking clearly. But I also knew there was no point in pursuing this with her and that I was going to have to talk to Lorina quickly before she went and repeated her performance at the river. I was sorry now that I had not spoken to Joe instead, but it had never occurred to me to do so. It would have felt like going behind

Conti's back, and I knew that Conti would have liked that even less.

'How's Edith?' I asked.

'Edith?' Conti seemed surprised. 'She's the same. Nothing new there. We're going for a check-up tomorrow.'

'A regular check-up?' I wondered if something had occurred.

'Yes, nothing special. The usual.'

'I'll take Alice tomorrow for the day,' I said.

Conti's irritation with me seemed to the fore. 'Lorina can care for her,' she said. 'That child spends much too much time in your place.'

I said nothing. I could see I was going to be at the receiving end of Conti's frustration regardless of what I did or said.

Lorina was skulking around on the steps when I left.

'Hi Lorina,' I said.

Lorina nodded a vague acknowledgment of my presence.

'If you're not doing anything,' I said, 'why don't you come over and have some coffee with me?'

'Why? When?'

'Now, and for no particular reason. I thought it might be nice. Your mother is busy and I could do with some company.'

Lorina, looking suspicious and mumbling something about her mother always being busy, stood up and dusted down the seat of her shorts.

'Okay,' she said.

In the kitchen I put on the coffee maker. 'Perhaps it's too warm for coffee. I always like it at this time of the day, but maybe you would prefer some juice?'

'No, I'd like coffee,' Lorina replied. 'Babbo always had coffee at this time too.'

'Come and sit,' I said as Lorina hovered beside the sink. 'A biscuit?'

Lorina shook her head. 'I'm trying to lose weight,' she said tentatively.

'Good for you,' I responded.

'It's very difficult when every meal is full of carbohydrates,' Lorina said, suddenly becoming more open. 'There's nothing like an Italian family for pasta, pasta, pasta.'

I smiled inwardly. I knew she was grossly exaggerating. Conti was a fish fanatic and loved salads and seeds.

'Only half an Italian family,' I corrected her.

'That doesn't seem to matter in our house,' Lorina said. 'We're more Italian than not. Dad likes Italian food, and Mum does too. She never puts on weight no matter what she eats.'

'Fred has to be careful with his intake,' I said. 'I never put on weight, but I'm still always counting the calories. Some people are just like that, and there's nothing you can do about it.'

'Except eat less,' Lorina said.

Glancing at her as I poured the coffee, I saw something in the girl's face that I hadn't seen before. Maybe it was a reflection of rejection, or maybe just of sadness. It was difficult to be sure. I always thought of Lorina as glowering and sulky, but there was something else there now. It suddenly occurred to me that she had no one with whom to talk. She appeared to have no friends. She had spent all her time with Babbo, and now both he and Cook were gone.

'You know, Lorina, if you're lonely, I'd love some company. Lionel is often busy, either with friends or with Alice, and I spend a lot of time alone. I have to be here during the holidays, so I don't get out much. I love having someone to talk to while I'm drinking a coffee.'

'Oh.' It wasn't much of a response, but it was better than nothing. 'Mum is either not at home or else she's fussing over Edith.'

I nodded. 'Yes, it's difficult for your mother.'

'It's difficult for the rest of us,' Lorina said bitterly. 'At least Alice has Lionel to play with.'

And you have no one, I thought. Now I felt sorry for her.

'Lorina, look, I really mean it about you coming in here for coffee, any time. Any time at all. I only ask one thing from you. Leave the beavers alone. They are very special to Lionel and Alice, and actually they are very special to me too. I spent my childhood with animals, in a fairly wild place, and I love them and can't bear any harm to come to them.'

Lorina looked out the window. She didn't say anything, but at least she was not denying what she had done.

I took a deep breath and continued. 'When I was a child, we had an elephant that lived with us.'

'An elephant?' Now Lorina's voice was surprised. 'Really?'

'Yes, really. His name was Luther, and he was a wonderful animal. He had been found as a baby by my mother. Usually if a mother elephant dies, the rest of the herd take in her baby and rear it as their own, but sometimes if the herd is in difficulties – a lack of water, not enough food, something like that – they have to reject an orphan because they know that they simply can't carry the burden. Anyway, that's what happened to Luther. Or so my mother said. And I think she was probably right. And so, Luther lived with us.

'My mother has this story that one day when I was very little, maybe about two or three, she came out of the house and I was sitting in the yard and Luther was there standing in front of me. I don't remember this at all, but I've always liked hearing about it. Anyway, she got a fright because he was so big, even when he was a baby; he and I were about the same age, you see. And there he was, standing in front of me, and for a moment she thought he was going to do something to me, like put his foot on my head, and she was afraid to move in case she startled him. I don't know if you know this, but elephants cover themselves in dust. It protects them from the heat. Well, Luther had picked up a cloud of dust off the ground. The earth was sort of red and soft in the yard, and he churned up this dust. He was already covered in it himself, and now he shook it all over me.'

'Wow. Why did he do that?'

'My mother claimed it was because I wasn't wearing my sun hat and that Luther knew I should be in the shade.'

'That's great,' Lorina said. 'I like that.' She was smiling now.

'Do you know, you have a lovely smile, Lorina.'

Lorina smiled again. 'What happened to Luther?' she asked.

'He grew up. And one day when my brother Horace and I came home, Luther walked out the gates of the place we lived. He just walked off into the sunset.'

'Just like that?'

'At the time, it was just like that. We thought he was gone forever. My father said he would come back, but my mother didn't think so. She was terribly sad.'

'Were you sad?'

'Yes, desperately. We were so used to him. He was part of the family. Horace and I wanted our parents to leave the gates open so he could come back, but they wouldn't.' I laughed now as the memories of that time returned.

'Why are you laughing?'

'I'm laughing because they should have left the gates open. They should have known. Luther had already knocked down one of the walls of the place he slept. When he got too big for it, he simply knocked down the wall and walked into his stable that way. My parents had been about to build him a new place, or have the old one enlarged; I don't remember which. But anyway, he just walked through the old door and the wall went with it. They should have known from that what he would do. Then, a few weeks after he disappeared, my mother woke one morning to find him tapping on her window. And of course he had come back. And he had walked straight through the gates, knocking them off their hinges.'

'Did he stay?'

'No. We reckoned he had found somewhere else to live and he would come and go when he wanted. And one day he didn't come back. I think he found a place to live that was more suitable, hopefully with other elephants. My father said he had undoubtedly found a herd that had accepted him. But we didn't mind now. We felt he was safe and well. He was a really great animal. I think of him out there sometimes. I think he is happy.' I did not add that I had seen him once more, one more time that was etched in my heart.

'I love that story. I think it's great,' Lorina said. 'I'm going to do that some day.'

'Do what?' I was startled.

'Just go off into the sunset.'

'I think you'd be terribly missed.'

'I doubt it,' Lorina said bitterly.

'Oh Lorina, you are wrong,' I said. 'For starters, I'd miss you. I'm looking forward to more coffees like this one. And even if you can't see it at the moment, believe me, your parents would miss you.'

And they would. They would be fearful for her and would want her safe return. They would want to know what she was doing and how and why. Even if they did not show the love Lorina needed, they did love her. I knew that. I knew that events and life had made them as they were. But regardless, they loved Lorina.

> *Dear Father, dear Mother,*
> *I'm enclosing photographs of Lionel. Some are of him with Fred and me, and some with a friend. We are all well. Lionel is doing very well in school, excellent marks and a good student. He's happy and he's healthy.*
>
> *I don't think I ever told you about the river behind our house. It's less than a quarter of a mile away across*

a field and through some trees. And there in the river
a family of beavers have set up a lodge and a dam. I
think they too are thriving. For some reason they
made me think of Luther. Have you seen him? He
was so much a part of our childhood and our family
life. I was telling someone about him earlier today
and I just wondered if he had ever come back again to
visit.

I promise I will write more often. I do hope you
are both well.
With love,
Helena

Lionel reported no backlash from Lorina.

'What did you say to her?' he asked over dinner the following evening.

'Nothing really,' I said. 'We just talked. I think that all she wanted was to talk. I think she has a difficult time at home. Alice has you and that's a big support for her. But Lorina has no one, and it must be very hard. Conti is so preoccupied with Edith. It's tough when you have no one to talk to.'

'You have Dad to talk to,' Lionel said.

'I wasn't talking about me. I meant Lorina.'

'I know,' he said, 'but I meant if you had no one to talk to, you can always talk to Dad, or to me.'

'I know that,' I said, giving him a hug.

Dear Helena,
Your mother and I are both well and were very
pleased with the photographs. Lionel looks so grown
up. It's difficult to think that he is still so young. And
at the same time it is impossible to believe that so
many years have passed. We both think he has a look

of Horace about him and that is very comforting.
Who is the girl in the photo with him?

Luther did not return. Your mother makes sure
the barrels are always full of water just in case he does
reappear so he will have something to drink. It would
be comforting if he returned, and maybe he yet will.

Your mother joins me in sending you our love, and
our love to Lionel too.
Your Father

Just as my parents waited for Luther's return to the farm, I waited for Simon Peterson to telephone. I knew that I should not. I knew from the last contact that there was something between us, but I did not really know what it was. The best I can do is describe it as a kind of bond. We could talk easily with each other and I liked that.

After his visit when Lionel was a baby, he had sent me a postcard from Bergen in Norway, a picture of a cable car above the village, and a message that said, 'I will return.'

I had kept it for two weeks and then, because I was keeping it a secret from Fred, I knew that I was doing something that was leaving me feeling uncomfortable and I tore it up and threw it away. It was not an easy thing to do.

A few years later, when Lionel was about seven, Simon posted him a catapult and a model glider, which Lionel painstakingly stuck together and promptly lost in the long grass in the meadow.

And then, some months after the Count died, Simon phoned.

'Helena, long time. May I come and visit?'

'Simon, I was thinking about you the other day. I haven't heard from you in ages. Of course come over. Lunch tomorrow?'

'What can I bring you?'

'Not a thing. Just yourself.'

'What does Lionel like?'

'He's a reader,' I replied.

Simon arrived with a bottle of wine and he brought Lionel a pile of books: novels, non-fiction and a book of records and dates. Lionel was delighted and retired to his room to devour them.

'So how are you, Helena?' Simon said as he sat beside me in the kitchen.

'I'm fine. We're all well.'

'And what are you doing with yourself?'

'Nothing, really. Being a mother and wife.'

'And are you happy?'

'Yes. It's like an interlude in life, I think. I sometimes wonder what I'll do when Lionel grows up and doesn't need me around. I toy between the idea of going back to work in a gallery or maybe going back to study. But I haven't decided. Plenty of time.'

Simon nodded. 'It's nice that you feel there's plenty of time. I don't feel that. If I'm not working, not being productive, not with something to occupy my mind, I feel stultified. And yet here you are, the epitome of peace and calm in this idyllic place.'

'Sometimes I feel time heavy on my hands,' I admitted. 'When Lionel is at school, the days are very quiet. Sometimes I feel like I'm wasting time. Maybe that isn't what I mean. Passing time? But then holidays come and I'm glad I'm here and not trying to organise someone to look after him. Not that he needs much looking after, I know, it's just that I like to be here. He still needs me as a full-time mother.'

'He's very lucky,' Simon said.

'On the one hand, yes he is,' I said. 'On the other hand, we have to do without things because we're only bringing in one salary. Sometimes I think it would be easier for all of us if I were earning too. It's tough on Fred.'

'Is it? I would have thought it was very nice for Fred. You look after the home and care for both him and Lionel. Sure, maybe you do have to do without some things, but it looks like your life is nice. You're not materialistic. It seems to me to be a very nice set-up.'

'I usually see it that way,' I said. 'But sometimes I look at my friend, Conti, and she has everything. No, that's not true; I meant she has everything that money can buy.'

'And is she happier than you?'

'No, not at all. But then, one of her children is very ill, so how could she be?'

'But if her child wasn't ill, do you think she would be happier than you?'

'I don't know. Possibly not. She likes things; nice things. Things you can buy. I like those things too, but they aren't of great importance to me. I don't have the need to keep updating or upgrading our possessions. I think she does. And I think that must be difficult. At least, to have that need would be difficult for me.'

'You radiate contentment, Helena. I think that is what I like about you.'

'Yes, I'm content. I'll never set the world alight. I'm happy living quietly. Maybe that's not so bad.'

As I said it, I wondered if it was true. Was it enough to live quietly? But then, there would be time later, time to do other things. For now, the important things were raising Lionel and the security and love within our home. Our house was quiet, just as it had always been. I liked that. I enjoyed going over to Conti's, where something always seemed to be happening, where voices were loud and conversations spilled over each other. But it was always pleasant to come back home to the peace of our own place.

Lionel once said our house was very quiet. I had worried if it was a criticism, but even when Alice or one of his school friends came over, it was still quiet. After a while I realised that he liked people who were quiet. He chose friends who were like him, thinkers, readers, gentle people. He enjoyed going to the Martins, but he also liked coming home.

Lionel displayed many of Horace's traits and it puzzled me how that could happen. He hung on his father's every word and loved talking to him when Fred was around. He was like Horace in that respect and it reminded me of him when he sat at the dinner table and said things like, 'Dad, how can we be sure the world is round?'

He read continually and I wondered if he read so much because he learned it from me; but while I liked reading about art and keeping abreast of what was happening in the world of exhibitions and galleries, as well as reading fiction, Lionel liked facts. The pile of books on the desk in his room attested to this. He perused dictionaries and encyclopaedias with the same dedication as Horace had once done. And just as Horace shared his knowledge with me, Lionel shared his with Alice, and Alice, in turn, with Edith.

Mr White, his rabbit, had died some time earlier, and since then we had become a regular menagerie. There were the Greens, which were three identical stick insects, although Lionel claimed to know the difference. He worshipped them, spending hours lying on the floor watching them. He had a fish tank with a variety of guppies and tetras. There was a feral cat that hovered around the back garden to be fed, and a family of foxes in the meadow that lay in full view of the house, basking in the sun or cavorting in the evening.

'I wish we had an elephant,' Lionel said regularly.

'Sorry darling,' I said each time.

That summer, Lionel came in one day and said he had had a word with the farmer who owned the field behind the house. I had to suppress my smile at his imitation of adulthood, but at the same time I was impressed at what he had done.

While our house was much smaller than the Martins', we had a gate into the meadow that led to the river, while the Martins did not. This gate gave us access to the field and the farmer had never objected to our going across it to the river. The height of the grasses varied from season to season and the farmer cleared the field sporadically. Now Lionel had approached him.

'I asked him if I could keep a track mowed across the field regardless of the season.'

'And what did he say?' I wondered why Lionel had done this. He had never mentioned having a problem with the length of the grass in the field; quite the opposite, in fact. I knew that he and Alice loved running through it and hiding from each other.

'He said yes. As long as I keep it in a straight line between our gate and the trees, I can keep the grass short.'

'And did he ask why?'

'Yes, he did. It's why he agreed, I think. I explained to him that Alice and I couldn't push Edith's chair through the long grass. We want to bring her to the river. She wants to see the beavers and their dam. They've rebuilt it, you know.' Lionel was pleased with himself.

I was incredibly proud of him. He was so decent and caring. His friendship with Alice was such that he would do anything for her. And making Edith happy, or at least giving her some happiness, was of profound importance to Alice. Lionel seemed so understanding of Alice's link to Edith. It was a link that I knew must be fraught with pain. Alice had thrived as a baby, done all the things that babies do at just the right textbook time, while Edith had wilted at every landmark.

Sometimes I wondered what would happen next door. For every step forward that Edith took, she seemed to take at least one step back. Every operation Edith underwent was both preceded and followed by some hope, but always ended with the situation staying virtually the same or worsening. Sometimes I thought about what Joe had once said when he referred to buying Edith time, quantity not quality. I worried for them all and I worried for Lionel.

'That's lovely,' I said. 'Does Edith know what you've done?'

'Not yet. I haven't told Alice yet. I'll go over later and tell her. Oh,' he suddenly looked concerned. 'Do you think Conti will have a problem in letting Edith come with us?'

'I shouldn't think so,' I said. 'In fact, I imagine she'll be delighted. It would be lovely for Edith. Her trips out are rare enough and are usually to a hospital or a doctor's surgery.'

At an early age, Edith's school attendance had become so sporadic that a tutor had been found and she was taught at home. This made me think of my own odd upbringing, but there had been more sense to mine than there was to Edith's.

There was an effort to give Edith some semblance of normality, but this was counterbalanced by her illness. It was a hopeless, relentless situation. She could read and write, but the tutor had finally given up and sought employment elsewhere as she was constantly being cancelled at the last minute because of Edith's health, which fluctuated from one day to the next.

Fourteen

'I shouldn't have damaged the beavers' dam.' Lorina was back in our kitchen drinking coffee. She came out with this sentence with no preamble.

'Why did you do it?' I asked, slightly surprised but with polite interest, while not expecting any kind of coherent answer.

'I don't know exactly. I think I didn't see why they should be able to make a home for themselves and have a normal beaver life,' Lorina said with a wry smile.

'I think I understand,' I said gently.

'I wish I hadn't done it.'

'They've fixed it, you know. They remade it, both the dam and the lodge. They say that what doesn't kill us makes us stronger.'

'Next door . . . at home, I mean . . . it's awful.'

I said nothing. I really felt sorry for Lorina. All the negative thoughts I had harboured against her had evaporated. If it was difficult to watch what was going on from the outside, it was nothing to what it must be like living there.

'I wish we were like other people.'

'Lorina, most children growing up feel like that. At least I think they do.'

'Did you?'

'In some ways I did. I didn't really know anyone else. We lived in a remote place and contact with the outside world was limited. I think it was something that suited my father and my mother too. So my brother Horace and I didn't know any other life to envy. We read a lot, and if I envied anything it was the lives of the people in the books I was reading.'

'But you had a lovely life. All that freedom, and Luther, your elephant.'

'Everything looks different from the outside, you know. We learn things in our childhood, and some of those things are useful when you grow up and some are not. I think my brother and I were probably quite lonely, but we didn't know any better. But when I grew up I found it very difficult to relate to people and to make friends. I had never learned how to do that as a child.'

'And do you think I have?' Lorina looked at me, puzzled. 'I don't know how to make friends. I have no friends. Babbo was my friend, and that was it.'

'But at school?'

'I don't get on with them. They're so juvenile.'

'You know, Lorina, it's possible they're not so juvenile, but that you are just more mature, or you expect something more adult because of your friendship with your grandfather.'

Lorina nodded. 'Either way, I can't relate to them and so I've no friends.' Suddenly she shook her head. 'Do you know anyone who died? Close to you, I mean.'

I nodded. 'My brother died when we were in our teens.'

'Oh, I see. I didn't know. I . . . I don't know what to say.'

'That's all right. There isn't anything you can say. I was your age when he died.'

'Was that awful?'

'Yes. It was unbearable. But there isn't anything you can do when something like that happens.'

'It isn't fair,' Lorina said.

'No, it's not fair.'

'It isn't fair that Edith is going to die. Sometimes I think we're all sitting around waiting for her to die, to not return from some operation, or just to not wake up, and there isn't anything we can do. It's like sitting watching someone on death row, although I suppose even then they have a better chance with some last-minute appeal.'

This was not what I was expecting. I was not prepared for

any of this. I looked at Lorina, who was now staring down at her hands.

'And there's no appeal for Edith? Oh, Lorina. Now I don't know what to say. All I can come up with is that life, no matter how feeble, is precious, and we should make the most of it. Live it to the full.'

'It's the waiting,' Lorina said. 'I don't mean for Edith to die. I mean to grow up and escape from it all.'

'But we don't escape from things,' I said. 'Most things come with us. That's why it's important, when you're in a situation, to try to do your best, to live up to your potential, to be kind. That way, it's some kind of comfort later.'

'I don't know what you mean.'

'I mean that when my brother Horace died, while I grieved for him, and in fact I still grieve for him because I miss him desperately, I know that even if I could put the clock back, there is really nothing I would do differently. He and I were always kind to each other. And there is nothing I regret about the time we had together.'

'I don't know what you've been saying to Lorina,' Joe said to me that weekend, 'but you're a very good influence on her.'

'What makes you think that?' I asked, surprised.

'She's a changed girl,' Joe said. 'She's kinder, more patient, more giving. I don't know, it's difficult to define. And when I asked her about it, instead of going into a sulk – and believe me, in the past if I asked her anything that is what would have happened – now she said it was because she talked to you.'

I did not know what to say. It was both amazing and gratifying that I could have had any influence over anyone, let alone Lorina.

'Anyway, thank you, Helena. I've been worried about her. She's difficult, awkward, unfriendly, I suppose, and now there has been this incredible change. And I, for one, am grateful.'

'You know,' I said tentatively, 'and forgive me if I'm intruding, I think it's very difficult for Lorina. It's difficult for you all, I know that, but you all have outlets of one sort or another. I'm not sure that Lorina does.'

'I should be giving her more time,' Joe said with a grimace. 'But it's not easy. My work, you know . . .'

'I know.'

And I did know. I knew it from my own parents, knew how they let their own work and interests absorb them.

Time passed. The years seemed to blur into each other. Looking back, I sometimes saw those years like photographs and sometimes like videos. The time of babyhood and the early years of Lionel's childhood slipped into each other. I enjoyed each moment of them, watching my son growing and learning. Each achievement was a milestone. He crawled, he stood, he walked, he fed himself, he went to school.

I had pined when school began, but learned to fill the waiting hours with housework and reading. Unless it was winter, I spent long hours in the garden, weeding, tidying, tending the flowerbeds. My love abounded. Fred was supportive, a hard worker, a loving husband and father. It was he who helped Lionel with his mathematics, I who helped him with his reading in those early years. I would have been more than capable of giving him whatever help he needed with figures, having learned solidly at my father's knee, but I knew it was important for Fred to have good contact with Lionel and for Lionel to admire him and look up to him. I wanted everything to be right, to leave nothing to chance, to take nothing for granted and to give everything that I could.

In the Martin household, it had been Babbo who had helped Lorina with her schoolwork. No one in particular helped Alice. She picked things up and passed them to Edith. They got by.

Suddenly, Lionel was fifteen and I did not know how that had happened.

He came into the kitchen, the laces of his trainers undone, a sleepy look on his face, his thick fair hair uncombed, his T-shirt deliberately torn.

'Good morning, darling,' I said, looking up from the journal I was reading.

He mumbled a greeting and went to get juice from the fridge.

'What are you reading?' he asked.

'Do you know there is only one living survivor of the Crimean War?'

'What's a Crimean War?'

'It was a war that took place a long, long time ago. Once upon a time there was a tortoise – Timothy, it was named. It was found on board a ship during the Crimean War.'

'When was that, Horace?'

'A long time ago. Now don't interrupt, I'm trying to tell you. Timothy was found in 1854 and was probably already at least ten years old when he was found. Only he wasn't a he. Later they discovered she was a she, but she had already been named by then. Timothy was found on a ship and became the ship's mascot.'

'Whew. I was afraid you were going to say something bad happened to him.'

'No, nothing bad happened to him. Just life. He lived on the ship during the war, and when the war was over, he went on to serve in other wars.'

'I wonder what happened to his family.'

'Well, I don't know. No one ever will. There are some things you just never find out. So Timothy served out his time in the Navy. And then he retired to dry land, and the Earl of Devon took him in to live out his life on his estate. And there he lived, and people came and went, and lived their lives and died. And Timothy lived on, and on and on.'

'Where is he now?'

'He's still living on their estate. It says that during the Second World War he – well, she I suppose – had been living in the wisteria flowerbeds, but now dug a little shelter under the steps to the house and hid there during the Blitz.'

'What a clever little tortoise, to hide and to stay safe.'

'Hmmm,' Horace said, his eyes busily scanning the page ahead. 'Underneath his belly, etched into his shell are the words, *Where have I fallen? What have I done?* This was the family motto.'

'What happened to him?'

'Nothing. He's still living there – safely. Growing old.'

'I'm reading a story,' I said slowly. 'A long time ago, my brother told me about a tortoise called Timothy.'

'Tell me,' Lionel said as he filled a bowl with cereal.

I told him the story Horace had told me. 'I've just read that he died. They think he was about one hundred and sixty-five years old,' I added.

'Amazing,' Lionel said. 'You should write down all the stories Horace told you.'

'It's odd to think of all the wars he lived through, the things he saw.'

'If tortoises could speak?' Lionel said.

'Yes, something like that.'

'You really should write down those stories,' Lionel said again. 'I've always loved hearing them. Alice likes them too. And Edith.'

I thought about that. It was interesting that Horace's voice in some way lived on. I had had no idea that Lionel repeated them. Maybe he was right and I would write them down sometime.

I thought again about getting a job. In my heart I knew that I should be doing something, finding some way of fulfilling myself. It was not that I did not feel fulfilled, it was more that I felt that I was not contributing in a more meaningful way. I saw an advertisement for yoga classes in the local hall, and I said to Fred that I was thinking of going.

He looked up at me from his newspaper and nodded. 'Whatever you like,' he said.

'Fred, I really do want to know what you think,' I said to him.

He put the paper down. 'Do you? Do you really want to know what I think?'

I thought he was going to say something more and I did not reply for a minute until I realised that he was just looking at me, waiting.

'Yes,' I said, slightly puzzled.

'Helena, we don't talk, not any more, and I sometimes wonder if we ever did.'

'What do you mean?' I asked.

'I have no idea what you're thinking most of the time. I have no idea if you're happy or sad. Don't get me wrong, you're a great mother and the house runs perfectly and I know that I'm lucky, especially when I look at other people and their problems. But are we happy?'

I looked at his kind, handsome face and did not know how to answer.

'I thought we talked,' I said carefully.

'We talk about Lionel and the house and my work, but we never talk about us, about what we are thinking or feeling, about hopes and plans. Not like we once did.'

I was glad of that last phrase, because until he said it I had the feeling that he meant we had shared nothing. The awful thing was, he was right and I had known it for a long time.

I felt slightly horrified. He sat there looking at me for a long moment, and then he said, 'Yes, take up yoga. I think it will suit you,' and he returned to his paper.

'Fred, please,' I said. 'I want us to talk, to communicate. I want to...' To what? To break through the silence of years? To love him like I once had? To feel passion and joy?

'To what?' he said. He didn't look up this time.

'To talk,' I said feebly.

'Do you know how to talk?' he said.

'That's horrible,' I said. 'What do you mean?'

'Oh, I know you talk to Conti. I know you know how to fill time, how you're a good listener. I know you're a good person, but I want you. I want to communicate with you. I want to know what is going on in your head. I want more. I often have the feeling with you that your inner life is greater than the life we lead, and that I don't feature in it,' he said. 'I feel that I have let you down in some way that I don't even understand. I think back to our early days together, when my heart pounded. And do you know something, Helena? It still pounds. It pounds when I come home and I see you standing in the kitchen and I want to hug you, but I feel that you've put a barrier between me and your heart. And I don't know why.'

I was appalled. I wanted to walk away from this conversation, but it was too big. I knew that I had to say something or do something to let him know that I understood, and that I was capable of changing.

I needed to think, but all I could think of was the female bull-frog who leaves when she has laid her eggs, and how I had not done that. I had never even thought of such a thing. I had stayed and loved my mate and my baby and the years had passed and I had somehow got it all wrong. Looking at Fred's sad eyes as he gazed at me, I wanted to break through the barrier. And I did not know how.

'I love you,' I said.

'I know you do.'

'But . . . '

'Then talk to me.'

'You once called me your ice maiden. I thought it was all right to be me.'

'You don't get it, do you?'

'I want to get it,' I said. 'I need to get it.'

'You are my ice maiden, but I need access to you, access like you used to give me. Remember how we talked? Remember lying awake all night, just talking? I need that. I want it. I know you didn't tell me everything. I know that you told Conti more about your childhood than you ever told me. And that's all right. I know that at different times we talk differently, and I know you were very close to what had happened when we talked. But later, I would have liked you to tell me about the dust, and you and Horace, and the umbrella tree. I want to know if that's all still there inside you or if it has been replaced. I need to know if we are going to survive.'

It was like an ultimatum. I had no idea how to start or what to say. I had no idea if I could open up again like I once had with Conti. I had no idea if I wanted to, but it was clear that if I wanted to maintain my marriage, I was going to have to do something.

'I have to leave for work,' Fred said. 'I'll see you later.' He got up and gathered various pieces of paper and notes off the table.

'Maybe we could go out tonight,' I said tentatively.

'Yes,' he said. 'Let's do that.'

I wanted to tell him that I loved him, but I had the feeling that the phrase had little meaning. Yes, I loved him, but it had been said so often that I was not sure if the words carried depth.

I bumped into Conti in the village. 'I'm on my way into town,' she said. She seemed pleased with herself or with the day. 'I'm just doing the shopping before I go in case I'm running late.'

I wanted to ask her if she had talked to Fred about me, as I was puzzled that he knew I had talked so freely to her, but at the same time I knew that it did not matter. Either she had told Joe and he had said something to Fred, or maybe she had. It was irrelevant, because what Fred had said was right and I knew I had to do something about it. It was my problem and there was no point in blaming someone else.

'I'm going to join a yoga class,' I said. 'Interested?'

'Hmm, when is it?'

'Thursday mornings, just once a week.'

'Count me in,' she said. 'It will limber us up and make us more supple. I've always fancied being able to sit with my ankles at the back of my neck.'

I laughed. It was not quite the image I had of what I wanted from yoga.

'I'm also going to go to a word processing class,' I added.

'You can leave me out of that one. I can type and I have no interest in the world of technology and computers,' Conti said.

'You look great,' I said. She did. She was wearing a cream linen suit and had a red silk scarf around her head. She had recently bought a silver Mercedes, open-topped with a red leather interior. We came out of the shop and stood beside her car. She popped her sunglasses down on her nose and grinned at me.

'Thanks,' she said.

'Going anywhere nice?' I asked.

'Just shopping,' she said. She sounded slightly vague and I had the feeling she was looking at me suspiciously from behind her glasses. I had meant nothing by the question other than mere conversation. 'Pursuing the endless question of interior décor,' she added as she hopped into the car.

Conti had little interest in the running of the house. As long as it was clean and operating smoothly, she was satisfied. She liked it looking its best and ensured the children were kept to their bedrooms or the playrooms, of which there were several. The hall, living room and dining room still resembled a lavish Italian home with a richness of brocade and gilt, the walls enlivened by paintings and tapestries.

At one point she contemplated ripping it all out and updating it to a clean and streamlined modernity with white walls and a minimalist approach to furnishings. She went as far as consulting an interior decorator, but after two meetings changed her mind. Removing the old Italian world from the house would be like removing the last vestiges of Babbo. She suspected that Joe might like the place revamped, but she could not bring herself to do it.

She took to going up to Dublin a couple of days a week with nothing more in mind than having coffee with old friends or colleagues from her catalogue days, combined with some personal shopping and grooming. The world she had created at home seemed confined and small in a way that gave her little fulfilment. The life she had had prior to the Count's death had depended to a large extent on her father and how important she was to him. He had given her self-esteem and worth. The value she placed on herself had been through his eyes and how she was reflected in them. She needed something to replace that.

She grinned at me and waved as she took off, and I had the feeling that she was up to something. Normally I would have felt some curiosity, but that day I felt none. I was so engrossed in my own worries about the conversation I had had had with Fred and the conversation that lay ahead.

I wanted to fix things with Fred, not just to get through the moment but also because I knew that he was right, and that for us to work, I needed to do something. But the problem was that I could not see what was expected of me. Of course I remembered that I had felt guilty and uncomfortable because I could talk so freely with Simon, and maybe also with Conti. It did not seem that unreasonable that we talk to different people about different things. The more you know someone, the more difficult it is to speak completely freely because everything you say can be laced with things that have gone before. Sometimes that is good, because shared jokes or comforting can be done with a simple reference to something else, but once you have actually stopped talking with meaning, it is very difficult to go back and find a way to do it.

Having dinner with Fred that evening made me feel like I was in a minefield. We were very polite with each other as we perused the menu and Fred chose the wine.

'White?' he asked, looking up at me.

'Yes, please,' I said.

I wanted him to open the conversation, but he didn't. He seemed to be waiting. The wine came and he tasted it and nodded. And still he waited.

'I don't know where to start,' I said. 'Nothing has changed in my feelings for you, but you're right in that we don't talk, not really. I will take responsibility for that. It's not that I don't want to talk, it's more that I sometimes don't know what to say. I don't want to disturb the peace and equilibrium between us – not that I have anything to say that would disturb it . . . ' I trailed off. I had made it sound different to the way it was.

'Joe told me that you had told Conti how your brother had died,' he said. 'Do you know that you never told me that? Somehow I had picked up the idea he had been killed in a car crash. I have no idea where I got that from, and I was shocked to find out what had happened.'

'Oh, no,' I said. 'Please understand, I wasn't keeping that truth from you. At the time, when you and I were talking, I couldn't put it into words and I knew I was being vague, but I didn't want to cry or to open the wound. And it was such a wound back then; I didn't want to lay that on you for you to have to comfort me. I wanted us to have this wonderful clean start together where the ghosts of the past couldn't intrude.'

'I understand that,' he said, 'I really do. It was just that it came as a shock ten or twelve years later when I heard it, and I felt excluded and maybe even belittled in my ignorance.'

'I am so sorry,' I said. I felt really upset. I, who had found it strange that Conti had hidden her mother's existence from Joe, had managed to hide something so intrinsic to my history from the man I loved.

'Your life is laced with silence,' Fred continued. 'Do you remember you told me years ago that you had not yet told your parents we were going to get married? Can you imagine how that made me feel? Of course, I understood later that your relationship with them is a very particular one, just like my relationship with mine is, but at least I told you how mine functioned and about my feelings of letting my mother down by not pursuing a tennis career. With you I had no idea what the problem was. And do you know something? I still don't.'

We stand at the foot of the hill beneath the tree. The men are carrying my brother's coffin up the hill. The sun is setting. My mother will not touch my hand nor take it in hers. Her face is carved in stone. The world has come to an end. I can imagine no tomorrows. Luther lumbers towards us. He moves his head slowly from side to side and his trunk swings. He caresses my mother with his trunk. He touches me gently. His eyes are heavy.

Later, as we walk back towards the farm, I turn to look at the tree, and Luther is there beneath it, standing on the hill, and he is churning up the dust and piling more on the place where Horace is buried.

We leave the gates open, but Luther does not come home. He stays beneath the umbrella tree for six days.

224

'My mother lost her twin sister during the war,' I said. 'In some way it affected her relationship with me. It still affects me. I feel that if one of us had to die, it would have been better if it had been me and not Horace.'

Fred reached his hand across the table and took mine in his.

'We don't deal with death very well,' he said. 'No one tells us how to. I'm glad you are alive and with me. I'm glad you've told me what you just did. I think it's awful that you would feel like that, but I am glad that I know.'

He did not berate me for not having let him into my fears and memories earlier. He seemed to feel that to seize this moment was the best thing to do. He was right, but I wondered if I would have had that magnanimity had the positions been reversed.

'Horace was at Trinity the year before I arrived. I had been excited about coming to Dublin and was so looking forward to having him there for my undergraduate years. When I came alone, I think I was in a state of shock. I had suggested to my parents that maybe it could be postponed by a year, as I wanted to be with them, but they were adamant that the plans should be adhered to. All I wanted was to stay with them. I needed them. But they did not need me.'

I cannot say that that dinner with Fred was a big success on the culinary front as neither of us was able to eat. By the time we left the restaurant, I had given him access to every hurt and every bit of grief that I knew, not just the past, but things to do with the present too. I told him about Conti's gifts of discarded clothing and how she paid for Lionel's birth. I told him of my feelings of inadequacy with Lionel nearly grown up and how I worried about time. I felt exhausted and I think I felt afraid too. I felt as though I had exposed a part of myself, like lifting a stone and   seeing a thousand creatures run amok and fearing that he would step on one of them and the wound inflicted by that would be worse than the wounds already there. But he was Fred, and of course he did not do that.

'Horace, if animals behave to a blueprint, what does that mean?'

'It means they behave according to their natures. When the elephant comes upon a dead elephant, he will grieve. He will scatter dust on it and will hover by it for a long time and will keep returning. It's in his nature. The bowerbird lays out blue items to attract a mate. He will search endlessly for those blue jewels. It's in his nature. The beaver will always block the sound of water. It's in his nature.'

'But what about us, Horace? What do we do?'

'We too are true to our natures. We will defend ourselves, protect those we love, find shelter and food. It's in our nature.'

'What if we have a different nature?'

'What do you mean?'

'There are people who are bad, aren't there? People who do bad things. Kill each other and hurt each other. Why do they do that?'

'They see it as a form of survival. It's in their nature.'

We sat in the car, holding each other, Fred and I, and I was reminded of that day nearly twenty years earlier, coming back from his parents' house, when he had pulled the car in to the side of the road because he could not wait until we got back to Trinity.

'I love you,' he said.

'I love you,' I said. For some reason, this time, the words carried no fatigue within them. They were real.

Fifteen

I saw less of Conti. We met once a week for our yoga classes, the weeks that she remembered to come. She was stunningly supple and thrived on the praise she received at the class. For my part I enjoyed it because it meant that after those classes we had lunch together and she was in good form.

I look back now and I can clearly see that I pandered to her. It was a definite flaw in my character, along with my other flaws, but I did not see this particular flaw clearly yet.

'Come and have lunch on Sunday,' Conti said.

It had been quite some time since we had done that, and while I would have liked to for the sake of harmony, we had already made plans for Sunday.

'Sorry,' I said, 'we can't. Freyn is home from university and he and Jackson and Marjorie are coming for the weekend.'

'Bring them too,' Conti said, 'and I won't take no for an answer.'

Over the years, the Martins had met Fred's family at least once or twice a year, and while they were by now fairly well acquainted, there was always a slow start to these meetings, which I found to be a strain. It was both kind and generous of Conti to invite them over when they were visiting, but I always had a sense of discomfort. I felt, correctly, that the reserve came from my in-laws, and in particular from Marjorie. My father-in-law always took his lead from his wife, and so the initial strain had a strange echo to it. It was Joe, Fred and me who carried the momentum, as Conti appeared either unconcerned or oblivious to it.

Every time it happened, I wished that the dinner or barbecue was not taking place. I found the warm-up period excruciatingly slow and slightly embarrassing. It was as if Conti was not aware that she was somehow irking someone.

So that Sunday afternoon we went to the Martins', where their long rustic table was set beside the orchard, overflowing with salads, meats, breads and oils.

Like Freyn, Lorina had just finished her second year in university and was home for the holidays. She was studying in Manchester and had flown home the previous day.

Jackson and Marjorie were now in their seventies and their eccentricities were becoming more pronounced. Jackson was complaining about an influx onto his land of some Hereford cattle, which he claimed had terrorised his Mullingar heifers and he had called the police. He felt he had not been taken seriously by the *gardaí* and suspected that the cattle belonged to one of them. He had applied for a gun licence.

'To what end?' Joe asked, puzzled.

'If a dog terrorises your sheep, you're allowed to shoot it,' Jackson said.

I glanced at Fred, who looked like he had not followed the logic. I nudged him under the table. It struck me as being the kind of comment that should be cleared up quickly, or we could end up visiting Jackson behind bars.

'I'm not sure I follow,' Joe said. 'You're not suggesting you would shoot the Herefords, are you?'

'I most certainly am,' Jackson said.

Fred now looked suitably horrified as it dawned on him what his father meant. He looked at Freyn, who simply raised his eyes to heaven.

'Don't worry,' Marjorie said, seeing the look exchanged between her sons. 'He had to apply to the local police station for the licence. They won't give him one, seeing as the cattle undoubtedly belong to one of them.'

'A legal route might be a more sound way,' Joe said, glancing at me. Jackson mumbled something about gun laws being made to suit criminals.

I got up to go into the house to help with the drinks and Marjorie made to come with me, but sank back into her chair with an irritated moan.

'Hip problems,' she said. 'Ignore me. I'll be fine in a minute.'

'I imagine that has curtailed your tennis,' Joe said politely.

'Not a bit of it,' Jackson said. 'You're fine on the court, aren't you, dear?'

I didn't hear her answer.

I had just come out of the house carrying glasses and I could not help but think how the scene set before me looked like something from an advertisement for Italy. The slightest breeze made the heat bearable and Conti's colourful parasols gave the table adequate shade. The trees were heavy with unripened plums and the only absentee was Babbo. I wondered if Conti still found that difficult.

Freyn was now twenty-one and seriously overweight. He was sitting at the far end of the table with Lorina on one side of him and Lionel on the other.

'This is very pleasant,' Marjorie said as Conti seated herself at the table, having checked that Edith was comfortable and giving her daughter a kiss.

'And how is work?' Jackson asked Joe.

'Very busy,' he replied.

'Like sport, crime is something that doesn't go out of fashion,' Fred interjected with a laugh.

'Just as well,' Conti said somewhat enthusiastically. 'In a sense we live off its proceeds.'

'No,' Joe replied firmly. 'We live off the proceeds of keeping law and order.'

'Well, in reality, we live off the inheritance from Babbo,' Conti rejoined. It was not said sharply, just factually.

It was an odd thing to say, and not completely true. It was as if Conti were diminishing Joe in some snide way, and yet she seemed oblivious to any slight she might have inflicted. She nonchalantly reached for the carafe of wine and topped up her wine glass before offering it around in a somewhat distracted way with a distant smile on her face.

'Don't you love these days of summer?' she then said, raising her glass.

I had the oddest feeling that she was toasting something. There was something about the way she lifted her glass and seemed to hold it up to the table or to the sky.

'The best part of these days,' Lionel said to his uncle Freyn, 'is swimming in the river. It doesn't matter how hot it is, the river is always cold.' Conversation at either end of the table split it in two, as the children warmed up and took Freyn into their corner.

Glancing down the length of the table, I noticed changes in Lorina. She was no longer the silent, sulking girl of her childhood summers. Instead she was looking almost peaceful. Her eyebrows were plucked and her face seemed lighter. And was that a tint of lipstick on her full lips? I smiled at her and she grinned back at me. She really had changed. She had grown up a lot since leaving for university.

I was aware that Lionel was tall for a boy of his age, but he was like a different species to Freyn, who was now really a young man. Freyn had always been big as a baby and a child, but now he was truly enormous. There was something kindly about him. He was a well-meaning young man, I thought, introspective and intelligent but not given to saying much. I knew he was loved dearly by my parents-in-law, but there was something about him that set him apart. It was apparent now at the other end of the table.

He was always very serious, with an odd intensity about him. His seriousness reminded me of my mother-in-law, but that aspect of Marjorie's temperament was directed towards tennis. It was why she was so good at it. Nothing had got in her way during her career. With Freyn, it was not quite so easy to determine what it was that preoccupied him. He just looked like he was thinking about something, but it was unclear what.

Alice, Lionel and Edith looked so young and innocent by comparison with Freyn and Lorina. Lorina was now laughing and I thought how like a flower she was, how she had blossomed this last year, how agreeable she had become. She smiled, almost beguilingly, at Freyn. He was looking at her quite intently but was managing to give the impression of being relaxed. He did not have his parents' ease, but he covered it well. He was like Fred in that respect. He had a sort of inbuilt charm.

From having felt uncomfortable earlier about the party, I started to relax. Conti continued to be detached. She was participating, but in a remote way. Her laughter seemed slightly louder and higher than usual, her involvement a little withdrawn, as though she were not quite with us. Watching her smile and seeing a light in her eyes that had not been apparent for some time, and the casual way she pushed back of a lock of hair, I suddenly thought that she had someone new in her life.

The thought shocked me and I missed Marjorie asking me something about Lionel going to back to school.

'I'm sorry,' I said, pulling myself back to the present. 'I wasn't paying attention, Marjorie. I was so taken with how Freyn has changed, how they all have, in fact.'

'Spare me from teenagers,' Marjorie replied with a laugh. 'At least you're not quite at that stage with Lionel. But it will come. Fred went through it. Freyn has just come out the other side.'

'How do you mean?' I asked. Lionel was already fifteen, well and truly a teenager.

'Oh, a stage comes when nothing you do is right. You have to wade through it. Good support from Fred will help you, believe me.'

We were still talking like that when I became aware that something had happened. I looked down the table, and Freyn was half-standing with a look on his face that I did not recognise. Lorina had stopped eating and was staring open mouthed back towards the house. One by one, the three other children stopped talking. Lionel dropped his knife on his plate and it clattered there for a moment before falling from the table to the ground.

Slowly I turned my head, as indeed all the adults were doing, and I looked behind me.

I had a strange feeling that this had happened before.

From the side of the house, two men had appeared. Both were wearing balaclavas. Both were carrying guns. One looked like a shotgun. The other gun was smaller, more compact. I took these things in as in a dream. This could not be happening. Such things did not happen twice in one's life.

But it was happening.

Joe and Fred were both standing now.

'Don't move,' the first man said, the one with the smaller weapon. He gestured with the gun that they should sit back down. 'We're not going to hurt you. Not this time. And you,' he said, pointing the gun down the table towards the children, but looking at Joe. 'You are not going to hurt me, now are you?'

'Who are you?' Joe said. His voice was tight but his hands were loose on the table. 'What do you want?'

'I've told you. Now remember it.'

And with that, they were gone. Back around the side of the house as if they had never been there.

Fred was moving forward now.

'Call the police,' he said to Joe. 'Who were they?'

'I don't know,' Joe replied. 'I . . . I don't know.' His eyes had narrowed and he was standing too. 'Stay here,' he said and he raced around the side of the house.

Fred followed him. Lionel and Freyn made to run after them.

'It's all right,' I heard myself saying. 'It's all right.' I did not know to whom I was saying it. Perhaps to the children to reassure them. Perhaps to myself. Alice's face was completely white and Edith was gasping slightly.

It was Jackson who stopped Lionel and Freyn.

'Stay here,' he said to his son and grandson, his voice firm and strong. He had his hand on Marjorie's shoulder now, as if both reassuring and protecting.

'Yes, everyone stay here,' Conti said, sitting back down and pouring the wine. 'The men will deal with it. There's nothing we can do. They're gone.'

My mind had gone back to the airport in the few minutes it had taken for all of this to happen. There is nothing you can do when the trigger is pulled. If you are in the wrong place. If your name is on that bullet, and it was Horace's name all those years earlier, there is nothing except for the silence afterwards, and the grief. But we had survived the incident; all of us. That strange feeling of déjà vu that I had felt when they first appeared was gone. But I could remember it. Clearly. It had nothing to do with what had happened that hot day in the airport. It was different. It was like time standing still and being repeated.

'They're gone. There's nothing to be worried about,' Conti repeated.

I wondered if Conti was drunk.

'I have to say, you must lead a very exciting life if you find nothing to worry about in what just happened,' Marjorie said. Her voice, although icy, was shaking slightly.

Conti shrugged. 'Nothing happened,' she said.

I exchanged glances with both my parents-in-law. Both were looking as surprised as I was.

Fred and Joe came back to the garden. Joe was unsure if he wanted to phone the police.

'You have to,' Fred said.

'I think you must,' Jackson agreed.

'But nothing actually happened,' Joe said.

'They were threatening not just you, but also the children. You simply have to call the police.'

'Who were they?' Conti asked.

'I have no idea,' Joe said.

'We can identify them,' Lionel said. 'In an identity parade. Like you see on television.'

'Yes,' Alice agreed enthusiastically. 'We saw them clearly.'

'They were wearing balaclavas,' Joe said. 'I want the children kept out of this. I will call the police. You're right, I'm not thinking clearly. But I don't want the children involved.' He went and put an arm around Edith and kissed the top of her head. 'I'm sorry, all of you. Not quite what you expect at the average barbecue.'

'Much more exciting,' Lionel said.

I wanted to hug him. He was so enthusiastic about things and appeared completely unfazed by the events. Freyn was the same.

'Did you see them out the front, Fred?' he asked.

'No, they were gone. A motorbike. We just saw it disappear at the end of the lane.'

'You should have taken the car and gone after them.'

'Now Freyn,' Marjorie said, 'I think Fred and Joe were absolutely right not to go after them.'

'The police . . . you need to phone them now.'

Fred took the children next door to our house to get them out of the way. He had his arm around Lionel's shoulder as they left and Lionel looked back at me and raised his thumb supportively. I would have liked to have been the one to go with them, but I took pleasure in seeing Fred and Lionel interacting like that.

The police came and took statements.

'Did you recognise either of them?'

'No, neither. Two thugs. That's about it.'

Of course inquiries were made into Joe's work. It was agreed that somehow the men must be related to one of the cases in which he was involved, but there was no way we could identify who they were, not having seen their faces. We spent hours turning pages and trying to pick out the intruders, but to no avail. It was impossible, not having seen their faces.

We all agreed on various aspects, like the height of the men, their clothing, the fact they were probably from Northern Ireland. But most of Joe's cases at that time were connected with drug prosecutions in Dublin and a precise link couldn't be made with any particular case.

'And you've definitely not seen them in court?'

'I don't know. I honestly can't tell you. I feel I should know, that I should remember or make some link, but I don't.'

There were no leads.

Joe returned to work, but he was uneasy. The previous year he had been offered a position in a law firm that dealt mainly in white-collar crime. This of course had happened in the past, but the previous year he had considered it for the first time, but had then turned it down. At one point he had harboured political ambitions, but the reality was that he did not have the time. It had long been clear to him that his lack of background did not help although marrying money had. But the problems at home – Conti's lack of motivation since the Count's death, Lorina's general behaviour and Edith's ill health – all put a burden and a drain on him. Now, he reassessed the situation with his customary clarity, and having done that, he contacted the firm and asked if the offer might still be there.

'They've offered me the position again,' he told Conti that night.

'Oh? And what are you going to do?' she asked.

'I'm taking the job and I've cleared my desk. I've passed all my cases to colleagues, and I'm taking a long holiday. I'll start in the firm in six weeks' time.'

'Why? And without even discussing it with me?'

'I discussed it with other barristers this morning. Everyone agrees that I must do what is right for my family, and this is right for our family, Conti. I don't want such a thing to happen again. I don't know which case that event in the garden related to, but this way I get a clean start. A new company with a different type of crime. Just as dirty in its own way, but without the threat attached to it. We'll go on holiday now, take a few weeks off. I've been meaning to do that for a while. We'll go away, the five of us.'

'A holiday?' Conti seemed almost horrified.

'What's wrong with that? Lorina won't want to come away with us for much longer. She's almost grown up. And we've had to postpone real holidays in the past because of Edith's health, but she's been having a good summer. I think a holiday is just what we need, all of us. And it will get us away from here and from whatever was going on last Sunday.'

It made sense. It was difficult for Conti to argue against, although the last thing she wanted was to go on holiday.

I was right in sensing that Conti had found someone to fill her days. She had indeed met a man on one of her forays up to town, a man who, because he was not her husband, made time for her and her alone.

It was something she had missed and now she had found it. Joe had always been sidelined by Conti. He learned early in their relationship that she needed time with Babbo, and he eased back, which suited him. It meant he could give all the hours he needed to his work and that he need not feel guilty about being late.

By the time Babbo died, Conti and he had long settled into a routine. They actually expected very little from each other. He earned a good living so she and his family could live well. She kept the place impeccable, usually by paying other people to do it, and was there when he needed her on his arm or when he felt like playing families.

Now that she wanted more, she had no idea how to ask it from Joe. He was as he had always been and she did not even realise that she needed to break through the barriers she had erected a long time earlier.

So a couple of times a week she had lunch and sex with a man in the city. There was little about him that mattered to her. If it had not been this man, it would have been another one. After the initial flirtation they kept their lunches short or even skipped them altogether, meeting instead in a hotel of his choosing. He was attentive in bed and simply gave Conti the distraction she needed.

'Of course, I'm not doing anything wrong,' she said to me. 'Doing something wrong would be getting involved with someone. I'm not involved.'

I was feeling uncomfortable. There was nothing in this that I wanted to hear.

'Stop looking at me like that, Helena. Everyone does it. It spices up their marriage.'

'You mean you and Joe are happier because of it?'

'No. Yes. Something like that. I make fewer demands on him. I'm happier, therefore he is too.'

There was something about it that I didn't like. It didn't make sense. Conti could clearly justify to herself what she was doing, but it was outside anything that I could understand.

'Everyone does it,' Conti said again.

But I saw it as betrayal. I knew I could not bear it if Fred had done that to me. I would have no idea what I would do if it happened, and I said as much.

'Fred is probably already having an affair,' Conti said blithely.

'Please don't say that,' I replied. 'He wouldn't. Our marriage isn't like that.'

'Neither is mine, but it's what people do. It's how we survive marriage.'

'Why are you telling me this?' I asked.

I did not want to know about it. It undermined everything that I saw as being safe. I did not really view life as being safe at all, but what I had and how I lived were safe and I did not like that feeling of these things being eroded. And knowing what Conti was doing was eroding my feelings of security.

'I'm telling you because Joe is insisting we go away on a holiday, kids and all, and I don't want to go.'

'Maybe a holiday is just what you need,' I said.

'Don't be ridiculous,' Conti said. 'Holidays with children are worse than life at home. All you do is pack up what you've got and take it with you and live in confined circumstances in a hotel or somewhere, whereas you could have a much better time at home, with more space, things you are used to . . .'

It was not how I viewed holidays. Even the weekends spent with my parents-in-law and Freyn were precious in their own way. There was the time in the car driving there with Lionel and the three of us, Lionel, Fred and myself, stopping for a pub lunch somewhere on the way. I saw all of that as being special, watching Fred and Lionel chat while away from home, away from the little things that entrap us, noticing how Lionel's tastes changed over the years, small things maybe, but big for me.

I tried telling this to Conti, but even as I said it I knew that my circumstances were so different. I was not travelling with three daughters, one in a wheelchair with desperately limited mobility.

'Oh, Helena, you live such a small life. You should get out more. Who could possibly get excited about a journey in a car?'

But there was not the money for us to have holidays, not holidays like the Martins could have if and when they chose. We had gone twice to England when Fred was reporting over there and Lionel and I had enjoyed every exciting second of those trips. We had the occasional week in the west of Ireland and I loved every moment of that time too. I felt put down by Conti's comment, but there was nothing I could do about it. And the truth was, I did get excited about a trip in the car with Fred and Lionel, and I knew that if I got pleasure from something like that, it did no harm.

Yes, I should have been more irked with Conti then, but I wasn't. I valued her friendship, enjoyed her confidences and I liked laughing with her. And her life was not easy. As she had once said, money can buy you everything, but it cannot fix certain things. And aspects of her life were difficult. I knew that, and so I forgave her all the little put-downs; I knew she did not mean to hurt me. She was my friend.

I told Conti then that Fred and I had been through a bad time earlier in the year but we had talked through it and we were stronger for that. Conti was momentarily interested.

'You never said,' she said reproachfully.

'It was difficult enough talking to Fred about it,' I said. 'It was all I could do to open up to him. It wouldn't have been helpful to offload it onto someone else.'

'Not even me?'

I wanted to say, 'Especially not you.' In light of what Conti had now told me, I could see that her advice would have been to go and have an affair and that would fix everything. It would have fixed nothing.

In our new way of sharing things, I told Fred about the conversation I had had with Conti.

I felt belittled by Conti's observations on my life and in some way I feared that maybe she was right. She was so much more worldly-wise than I.

'Did you ever think of having an affair?' Fred asked me.

'No, of course not,' I replied. 'Anyway, I don't know anyone I would have an affair with.' The minute I said it, I felt uncomfortable. It was not the whole truth; there had been Simon. It had never come to that, of course, but it had been there on the edge of our friendship. I remembered how I had enjoyed talking with him, and I remembered too the way he had looked at me, in a specific way. But then, he was an artist. He looked at everything in a specific way – people, light, inanimate objects, everything.

I wanted this conversation with Fred to move on and away, back to a safer place. I saw no point in telling him about any of the conversations I had had with Simon. I felt they would hammer home the silence between us that had lasted for so many years. I instinctively knew that Simon valued my friendship and would not step across the boundaries beyond a little flirtation. I knew that I had let him access the bad parts of my life in such a way that he knew the value I put on loyalty and security, and that I would do nothing to disturb my relationship with either Fred or Lionel.

'Did you ever think of having an affair?' I asked Fred.

I did not want to know the answer. I did not want to ask the question, but it was the only thing I could think of saying to move us from the place in my head.

He shook his head. 'No,' he said. 'Tell me, why did Conti want you to know all of this?'

'I think she just wanted to rant a bit about being forced to go away on holiday when she didn't feel like it.'

'Where are they going?'

'Somewhere in the Caribbean. St Lucia and I think Tobago, maybe. Three long weeks. And she's dreading it!'

'Some people! They don't know when they're lucky. Though I suppose right now she doesn't feel lucky, does she? All she wants is to be here with her lover and instead she has to go away. . . '

'And play happy families; that's what she calls it.'

'Yes. If it's not what she wants, then it isn't very satisfactory,' Fred agreed. 'Somehow I don't think she should have told you,' he continued thoughtfully.

'Oh? Why not?'

'Well, it's difficult to say. You're so . . . innocent. My mother once said to me that Conti was like a form of contamination. She's careless,' he said. 'We don't tell people things we know they can't handle.' I did not know he and Marjorie had talked about that, and I remembered Marjorie warning me long ago the first time she met Conti.

'Of course I can handle it,' I said. 'It's what happens in life, out there.' I gestured vaguely towards the window and outside. 'Just because I wouldn't behave like Conti doesn't mean that I can't know about it.'

He smiled at me. 'I offended you,' he said. 'I didn't mean to. Of course you can handle it, but I don't think you should have to.'

'She said that in the real world, that's what everyone does,' I grimaced.

'Of course it isn't,' he said. 'There are people who don't betray their partners. People like you and me. For us, betrayal is something we just don't do.'

'Betray,' I said. 'Yes, that's the word. I couldn't see what it was. I think I saw it as a form of selfishness.'

'It's that too,' he said to me.

'You know, when the gunmen were there,' I said, 'I had this weird feeling of déjà vu. I really felt like it had happened before.'

'Your brother?' he asked.

'Well, yes and no. I suppose it was because of what happened to Horace. I feel silly saying this, because nothing really happened, and you all seemed to get over it; I mean, you sort of handled it. Yes, everyone was shocked and I think the children were excited afterwards rather than disturbed. But I was disturbed. When the gun was pointing at us, and I don't think it was even pointing at me, but I felt like I was looking down the barrel of it and everything was moving very fast and I was caught in some way . . .' I paused.

'Please, tell me.'

'It was as if I was seeing something. Something important, but only important to me. Like time stopping or else moving so quickly. I know that's a contradiction. But it happened very fast and yet I thought a thousand things during those seconds.'

'What did you think?'

'I thought . . . I thought there is only so much time. This is it. This moment. And all my love for you and for Lionel was in my mind. And I thought, I won't see Lionel growing up, and I wanted to see him growing up. I want to always be there for him, and yet you can't always have what you want. I thought of Horace too. I could feel him, as though he were there at that moment. And I could feel the heat of Kenya. It's so different to here. It smells and tastes different, and I had it in all my senses, the timelessness of it, the unending, relentless depth of it . . . '

'Thank God we talk,' Fred said. He put his arm around me and I rested my head on his chest and felt safe within that moment.

'Don't change, Helena,' he said. 'Stay as you are.'

But I had changed. I was already changing. Something had changed me or had changed in my overall perception that Sunday afternoon. Time seemed to gallop from that moment. From the slow passing of years that blended into each other as Lionel was growing up, now it moved too quickly. Every time I looked, he seemed to have changed. He was growing fast. He no longer wanted me to put my arms around him. He still gave me the odd kiss, but he was withdrawing from me and from Fred, becoming his own person, I suppose. But it was happening so fast, just like everything else was.

Sixteen

I was sitting on the deck shelling peas. It was a lovely long summer day with a clear blue sky and the fields almost shimmering in the heat. Lionel came out and stood beside me. He took a handful of the peas and put them in his mouth.

For a moment I saw my mother sitting on the veranda in her old rattan chair, a sun hat on her head, stoning mangoes into a bowl, a small, sharp knife hooked into her hand. Luther was behind her, his trunk resting on her shoulder, occasionally nuzzling the nape of her neck. I remember coming over and crouching by the bowl of mangoes on the ground and reaching in and taking a piece.

'Don't,' my mother said. 'They take so long to do.' But they were nicer like that, straight from the bowl in the mid-afternoon. Horace had picked them that morning.

'I would serve them whole,' I said. 'I would just put them in their skins on the table and let us peel and stone them ourselves.'

My mother had laughed. 'Stop, Helena. You'll spoil your appetite.'

Spoil my appetite? I was eating the mangoes that were going to be served, so in what way was I spoiling my appetite? I stopped though. There was not much point in arguing with my mother.

Now, I smiled at Lionel. 'They're nicest raw, aren't they?' I said.

He nodded and took another handful and sat beside me. I knew he was missing Alice, away on holiday in the Caribbean.

'Remember I asked if you would write down the animal stories?' he said.

'Yes,' I replied.

'Did you?'

'Not yet. I will. One of these days I will write them down for you.'

'When I finish school,' Lionel said, 'I'm going to study zoology.'

It was years since I heard how he was going to drive a train and be a fireman. I sat there, slightly startled, because that was what Horace had been studying.

'Why zoology?' I asked.

'Is it a bad choice?' he asked. He sounded slightly defensive.

'Not at all,' I said. 'I think it's a great choice. I just hadn't seen it coming.'

'I want to go and work in Kenya,' he said. 'That's where you're from, isn't it? I want to work there on a game reserve.'

I could see it. It was so strange as it unfolded before my eyes. Lionel would go back to Kenya. Back? It would be the first time for him, and he would find a home there. I would return there to visit him. Maybe Fred would agree to our retiring there one day in the distant future. Maybe I would sit beneath the tree and watch the sun go down again. Lionel would live and work with animals. In some way, history would be repeated. I looked ahead for the first time and I saw a vision that filled me with joy. I smiled in delight at Lionel. 'I like it,' I said. 'I think it would suit you.'

'Do you think you and Dad would come too?' he asked.

I imagined our house on the market. We would sell it and we would move. Fred would love it. He would love the life there, enjoy the peace. He could still work as he did now, if he wanted. Or maybe he would give that up. He would have the choice. The world of technology, of computers and the internet, would give him freedom. We would build a place on my parents' farm. Maybe we could work on the farm. My father was getting old. Maybe I would sit with my mother in the evening, watching for the fireflies and peeling mangoes . . .

I knew not to push it. It had to be Lionel's dream too and the fact that it had come from him was wonderfully exciting.

We sat there on the deck and I went on shelling peas and he talked about career guidance in school and how he had got brochures from different universities, and the past and the future seemed to mould in a way that was full of optimism.

But time was ticking, and I did not really hear it.

Far away in the Caribbean, under a blue sky on a silken sandy beach, Conti was stretched out on a sun bed, half dozing and half watching the sea. Palm trees grew in clusters in a curve around the tiny bay, and a few hopeful windsurfers stood on their boards on the water, waiting for a gust of breeze to move them. Alice and Edith were lying on the sand and Lorina was sitting cross-legged beside them. It was one aspect of the holiday that Conti had not expected. She had imagined there would be the usual bickering between Lorina and the twins, and it was both a relief and a surprise that this was not happening.

In the sea, Joe raised a hand and waved to her. It occurred to her that he might be beckoning her, so she closed her eyes and let the heat overwhelm her as she half slept and half consciously dreamed.

They were lazy days. The complex at which they were staying indulged them in every way. They had two luxurious chalets, and Conti's initial assumption that Lorina would sleep in their chalet came to nothing, as the three girls seemed happy to be together. As she had not even imagined this development, she had not bothered to think what she would do with regards to making love with Joe. It would have been easier if Lorina had been with them. It would have reduced the opportunity for intimacy, which she now realised she simply did not want. If she had thought about it at all, she had imagined it would be easy just to have sex with him to keep him happy, but when confronted with this she found it rather more difficult that she had thought.

'Of course I'm sleeping with Alice and Edith,' Lorina said. 'You and Dad need time together, and it will be more fun for us, won't it, Alice?' she said.

Alice nodded and exchanged glances with Edith, but it was soon clear that the changes that had taken place in Lorina were a real and positive development. Lorina appeared content being with her sisters, keen to engage them and to be involved with them. In the sea, she was happy to tow Edith on a lilo in the shallow water, and in the evenings it was she who organised them and went down to dinner ahead of their parents. The days drifted by with the occasional trip around the island, either in a rented car or on a catamaran.

'I think this holiday has done us all a lot of good,' Joe said.

It was the second last evening and dinner was over. The girls had retired to their chalet and he and Conti were sitting in the bar, having a last drink before bed.

Conti nodded. She felt relaxed and comfortable in herself, which she realised she had not felt in a long time. She knew that Joe had done his best both for her and for the girls and she felt a pang of guilt. She could hear in his voice that he was looking for reassurance.

'It's been a good break,' she said.

'It takes both of us, you know,' he commented.

'What does?'

'To make an effort. To compromise. To make it work.'

'To make what work?' He glanced at her face. He was unsure if she was deliberately toying with him and did not know what she was thinking.

'What do you mean?' she asked.

'To make a marriage work, it takes both of us. That's what I mean. It was different when your father was alive. I, possibly incorrectly, tried to give you as much space as you wanted, as I knew it was difficult to have three generations living in the one house. But now, well, I would like us to try a bit harder.'

'I try hard all the time.'

'I know you do, but I meant that we need to make time for each other. We need to take time out, just the two of us – the odd weekend, short trips, whatever – just so that we have personal time. I do love you, you know.'

She did not answer at first. She thought about what he had said. And she was not sure that she loved him. She was not sure that she had ever loved anyone. She sensed this might be an important thing to be aware of, but she dismissed it because it did not suit her to spend time thinking about it.

'I love you too,' she said, patting his hand.

'Do you?' he asked. He looked at her closely now. She was looking radiant, with her tanned skin glowing, enhanced by a low-cut, white summer frock.

She had an odd sensation of inadequacy as he looked at her. She had always been aware that he was more moral than she. It was not that she did anything that she would see as being particularly immoral, but there was the feeling that maybe she did not live up to his standards.

'We don't talk enough,' he said to her.

'Of course we do. We talk all the time.'

'That's not what I meant. I was talking about other things, not what the children are doing or about Edith's health or those things that we fill each other in on. I meant other things. Like, are you happy?'

'Of course I'm happy. How could I not be happy? We have everything. Well, most things.'

They were both silent, deep within their own thoughts. Conti was thinking of Edith and of the cruelty of her situation, and the hopelessness of it, and how the only way to deal with it was to see Anthony, her lover. He gave her respite.

Joe said, 'I've got something to tell you. Perhaps I should get us another drink?'

Conti nodded, wondering what was coming.

'I think I may have traced your mother,' he said to her.

She looked at him in amazement. 'You what?'

'You remember I told you I had that conversation with Alessia before she left? Well, I've had people looking since then.'

'All this time, you've been looking? I had no idea. I've tried not to think about any of it. Elena – you said Alessia said she was called Elena?'

'Well, that's what Alessia said. That was the only link I had. And eventually she was found.'

Conti was trying to digest this. She had given up any hope of ever finding out who her mother was.

'Is she . . . ?' She was afraid to ask, afraid of both the question and of either answer.

'Yes, she's alive. It's not all good news though,' Joe said gently. 'If we have found the right person, well . . . she's in a sanatorium in the north of Italy.'

'She's alive.' Conti couldn't take this in. 'My mother is alive?'

'Yes, but unfortunately she's unstable. I think that might be the best way to describe her.'

'Unstable? Mentally?'

'Yes. More like a child than an adult. Living in the past, in a dream world. Well, that's how it was described to me.'

'How long have you known about her?'

'I only heard a few days before we came away. I didn't say anything until I was sure, as sure as I can be. I heard for certain on the day we left and I decided it would be better for you if I kept it until the end of the holiday. I know this is a lot to take in, and I imagine it must be difficult to . . . ' he searched for a word. 'To comprehend.'

'Do you know why she's mad?'

'I didn't say mad, Conti, I said unstable. Maybe mad is

the right word, I don't know. But it's harsh, a harsh word, more difficult to deal with.'

'I can't take this in,' Conti said. She drank deeply from her glass and her hand was slightly shaking as she put the glass down on the table. 'I think I would like another one,' she said.

Joe gestured for a refill and then turned back to her. 'I can't imagine what this must be like for you,' he said. 'Let me tell you what I've found out.'

In a room with bars on the windows, an elderly lady paced the floor. Sometimes she stopped and wrung her hands as though in grief or in pain. She had long since stopped talking. Only little scraps of her life were known either to her or to anyone else. Snippets, all of which were filled with anguish. A file, which had been put together about her, began in the last year of the war. She, just a little girl, had been found in a shelter, terrified, crouched on the ground, sobbing uncontrollably. At first she could not speak, and then she gave her name. Lena. She said she was looking for someone, but she could not remember the name. She could not remember her own surname. They reckoned she was about nine years old. She was in shock. In her sleep, she cried out for her mother, but when she was awake, it was as if there were shutters closed in her mind. She could remember nothing.

She was taken to an orphanage where she shared a room with other shocked and frightened children. At some point a photograph was taken of her, her little face staring vacantly at the camera. But afterwards, when they showed her the photo as it was being glued into her file, she looked at it and her eyes opened wide. For the first time she showed signs of something happening in her mind. 'Lina,' she said, staring at it.

'No, it's a picture of you, Lena,' she was told.

She shook her head. 'It's Lina,' she said.

'What is your name?' the doctor asked her.

'Lena.'

'And this picture, who is in it?'

'Lina.'

In her absence, they discussed the possibility of her personality having split, until a young nurse timidly suggested that maybe Lena had a sister and that she thought it was her sister in the picture.

'A sister?'

'Why not? Perhaps a twin. It would explain why she thinks it isn't herself.'

And so they tried again with Lena.

Sometimes it was as if they might make some kind of breakthrough, but they could never be certain if she was really remembering or if she was just trying to be obliging. She was gentle and sweet-natured and it was difficult to discern what was really going on. And there was so little time and so many children, lost or orphaned, frightened and bewildered. They put together as much information as they could on each child in the hope that they would be claimed by someone, somewhere. And indeed, many were.

But many were not.

Lena was moved to another orphanage, where she stayed until she was fifteen, when work was found for her in a nearby village.

'What kind of work, Joe?'

'As a cleaner, a domestic help in someone's home. She worked hard, apparently. There were no complaints. But in the summer of that year she met a man, an Italian who had moved to the village.'

'Babbo?'

Joe nodded.

'And she had me?'

Again Joe nodded. 'The hospital records show that Lena X gave birth to a girl. The baby was registered as Carolina dei Fiori.'

She held the tiny baby in her arms. Her soft fair hair fell on the baby's cheek and it stirred in her arms. She clutched it close to her chest, feeling its light breath on her bowed face. This was the first thing she could remember holding that was actually hers. The name Carolina came to her. Lina. Yes, it was short for Carolina. Carolina … A memory stirred. It was faint, too vague to hold on to, a wraith of recollection haunting some dark forgotten recess in her mind. Carolina.

If you looked in the mirror, there were two of them. She remembered that now, for the first time. And Lena, like Lina, was not the full name. It was something else. There was another sound in front of it. Yes, she was sure she had been called Lena. If she thought very hard she could remember being called: 'Lena, Lena.' But that wasn't her real name. Elena? She wondered. She could not be sure. She told the Count, 'I think my real name is Elena.'

He nodded as he held the baby.

'May we call her Carolina?'

'Yes,' he said.

And when she woke later, the baby, her baby, her little Carolina, was gone.

And she could not find her. There was no one to help her. No one understood the enormity of what had happened. Carolina was gone, just like the other Carolina, the child in her memory, the image of herself. All was gone. Forever.

Conti listened to Joe's story as she drank. He brought her back to their room; she stumbled in the dark as he guided her up the path. He tried holding her in his arms in their bed, but the night was hot and she pulled away, drunkenly falling from the bed   before vomiting on the floor and weeping for all the things she had lost but had known nothing about.

'I would have been better not knowing,' she said to Joe. 'What use is a deranged mother to me now?'

'Oh, Conti.' He tried wiping her face and lifting her from the floor. 'We can talk about this tomorrow. You can't think clearly

251

when you're in this state. Come, come,' he tried to soothe her with soft words, getting her back into the bed before cleaning up the mess.

'I don't want my mother now. Not this mother. Not like this. It's not my fault. Why should I have to deal with any of this?'

'Not now, Conti. Leave it for now.' He was regretting letting her have so much to drink, even though he knew he could not have stopped her. If Conti wanted something, she got it, and he knew it. The problem here was that she had got something she did not want, and would now shy away from it. He would talk about it with her when she had slept and had recovered.

Outside the window in the dark, Lorina sat on a chair beneath her parents' window and wondered what they were talking about. She knew only that Conti's mother was dead. That was what she had been told. But what she had now heard clearly opened another avenue. And it also made her think about Babbo.

She had loved him. He had been the rock in her childhood. He doted on her, and even when he had been forbidden to take her out on his motorcycle and sidecar, he had of course ignored these instructions and waited until her parents were not around.

She was aware back then of the difficulty it had created for her, as she had to deny being on the bike and pretend she had been doing other things at that time. Now she realised that it had been unfair of him to put her in that position. So much of her childhood had been spent lying to her own parents, and now that seemed to her to be very wrong. No adult should compromise a child like that.

She also knew from her conversations with me that perhaps Babbo had not been that good for her. She had loved him with all her heart and his death had devastated her, but she had become aware that the time she had spent with him had in some way alienated her from her peers and probably also from her parents.

Sitting in the dark outside her parents' window, she felt angry.

This anger was directed mainly at Conti. In a sense, Conti had left her to be raised by her grandfather, and from the little she could make out through the open window, it now appeared that this same grandfather had actually stolen Conti as a baby. What kind of parenting was involved in any of this?

She stubbed out her cigarette on the paving and got to her feet. She felt wretched and wished she were back at home so that she could talk to me. She would have liked to have talked to her father, but she did not know how.

Back in her room, she checked on the sleeping twins. Alice had pushed their beds together and they were asleep holding hands. The moon shone in on them, and despite her anger, she found herself smiling. They really were very nice, she thought, and none of what had happened was their fault.

Conti woke with the hangover from hell. There was a dull, relentless throbbing in her head, a vile taste in her mouth, her tongue felt furry and swollen, and a wave of nausea washed over her.

Then she remembered. Slowly but surely, Joe's words of the previous evening returned.

It was not fair, she thought. Just when she was recovering from Babbo's death, just when Edith seemed marginally less unwell, just when she had found herself a lover, Joe had to find out her mother was still alive.

What was she supposed to do? Go and visit this madwoman in a padded cell?

She wanted to obliterate the story. She did not want it anywhere in her mind. It was not her fault, Babbo had done this. He had taken her from this woman, and he must have had a reason. He had always done what was best for her.

Maybe he saw that she was crazy and didn't want his daughter to be raised by her. Maybe . . . maybe what? She did not know. She knew he was self-centred, but as she had always been a part of that centre, it had not disturbed her. His love had been directed towards her. He had taken pride in her beauty and had encouraged her to be like him. She did not know how else to be.

And just like he had behaved in the past, she now wanted to do the same. She would close the door on this information Joe had presented to her. She did not need this in her life. She cursed Joe for telling her. She had been better off not knowing.

Joe, of course, would not see it like that. She knew he would be expecting something from her. He could not really want her to visit this woman or to have anything to do with her. Could he?

It transpired that Joe was unsure what he wanted or expected of her. He seemed to be waiting for something from her, and she had no idea what it was. They spent the last day on the beach, sunbathing and swimming. Conti had the feeling that Lorina was looking at her in an odd way. 'Are you all right, Lorina?' she asked her.

'Yes,' Lorina said and turned away.

'Home this evening,' Conti said, trying to sound cheerful. All she could think was what an awful end it was to the holiday.

She had dreaded the whole idea of the holiday, and yet she had enjoyed it. There had been a simplicity to the days that had been fulfilling in ways she had not expected. And the girls had been so well behaved. There had been no fighting between Lorina and Alice, and even Edith had appeared to be in less discomfort, the smile on her face less pinched, less fraught with underlying pain.

Lorina nodded.

'Are you sure you're all right?' Conti said.

'I'm sure,' Lorina said, getting to her feet and walking down to the water's edge.

Conti picked up her magazine and rolled over onto her stomach to read. After reading a couple of pages, she realised she had absorbed none of the content and had to return to the beginning of it. And returning to the contents page made her think about the opening chapter of her life.

For a moment, she imagined Joe taking Lorina away at birth and never seeing her child again. She sat up abruptly. The idea was appalling. She had always acknowledged her lack of maternal feelings towards Lorina, but nonetheless she knew that if such a thing had happened, she would probably never have recovered.

She looked up to see Joe emerging from the water. He looked tanned and healthy as he came up the beach and she found herself needing him, glad that he had chosen that moment to return.

He came and sat on the sand beside her.

'That poor woman,' Conti said.

He glanced around, as though unsure to whom she was referring, and then returning to her, he touched her hand.

'Yes,' he said.

'Do you think . . . ' Conti began slowly and with a rare moment of insight, 'Do you think it's possible that I have no really strong maternal feelings, not like Helena anyway, because I had no mother growing up?'

'You're a good mother,' Joe said.

'I'm not really, you know,' she said somewhat wryly.

'You have been a good mother to our girls,' he said.

'I meant the question,' she said. 'I really meant it. Do you think that is a possibility?'

'I don't think it matters. I love you. I married you. We have three daughters we love. That is as good as it gets for us.'

'Is it?'

'This isn't like you, Conti,' he said. 'You never have self-doubt. You should not have doubt now. You've done nothing wrong. Whatever has happened is not your fault.'

'I know that, but I don't see what I'm supposed to do now.'

'You don't have to do anything. You can sit on this for a while and give yourself time to absorb it. It's a shock. It has to be.' That was true. 'It's an enormous thing to have happened,' Joe continued. 'In its own way, it's as big as losing a parent.'

'I just never expected to find her,' Conti said. 'I feel that I'm supposed to be happy, but I don't feel happy.'

'What do you feel?' he asked.

'I don't know. Shock maybe.' Or disgust, she thought, but she did not want to say that to Joe.

She had always assumed that her mother was wealthy. It had seemed to her most likely that she was some society woman who had not wanted to be tied down by a child. Even later, when Babbo had told her that he had taken his baby and left the mother, she still had not understood what that might mean. It did not seem likely that her mother was some poor orphan. And it was horrible that Babbo might have used her and then just abandoned her. Decent people were not supposed to behave like that, and she had always assumed that she came from decent stock.

'What's up with Mum and Dad?' Alice asked Lorina.

'How do you mean?'

'I've never seen them talk as much. Maybe it's because they've found time,' Alice wondered.

'Maybe,' Lorina said. 'Or maybe not . . . '

'Go on,' Alice prompted her.

'I overheard something last night,' Lorina said slowly. 'Mum's mother is still alive.'

All three girls looked up the beach, surprise registering on Alice and Edith's faces.

'She doesn't look particularly happy,' Alice said thoughtfully.

'I don't think she is,' Lorina said. 'I think . . . I don't know.'

'Can we talk to her about it?' Alice asked. She looked at Edith. Her sister's placid little face expressed nothing.

'No. I think it would be best just to know this and not to say anything,' Lorina replied. She was uncertain if she had been right in telling her sisters, but she had needed to tell someone. She thought now that she might be sorry for passing on this bit of information. 'Don't say anything. If I hear anything else I'll tell you, but I think we should leave it for now. She does seem upset, and we don't want to add to that.'

Seventeen

The Martins were gone a week when the phone rang and I answered it. I had been making a picnic lunch, as Lionel and I were planning on climbing the Sugar Loaf, which was something we did most years.

'Hello?' I said, glancing at the table and remembering I had to pack drinks.

'Helena?'

The accent . . . the voice . . . I could hardly breathe.

'Yes?' I said almost tentatively.

'It's your father.'

'Father?' My voice faltered, almost in disbelief. The sound of his voice, his accent, his intonation were embedded in my mind, but I did not know that I would so easily recognise them. But it was he. There was no doubt about it.

'Father,' I repeated.

And then suddenly there was a pang of fear. Why was he phoning? Had something happened?

'Everything is all right,' he reassured me, as though realising what I must be thinking. 'Your mother is fine. I am here in Dublin. I flew in this morning and I am hoping to visit you.'

'Today?' I could hardly believe this. All these years with so little contact, and now suddenly he was here, less than two hours away.

'If it would suit you? I took the chance that you would be at home. Foolish, perhaps, but I came on a whim. I wanted to see you.'

'Of course, of course. May I come and collect you?'

'It would be quicker if I just take a train. Perhaps you would meet me at the station? I've taken a bus to the city centre and I appear to be close to a railway line.'

'Of course I will.'

Having told him where I would meet him, I put the phone down. Standing in the hall, I caught sight of myself in the mirror. My face was pale despite my summer tan. I could hardly believe it. For a moment, I wondered if I could have imagined the phone call. All those years and no word from him other than the occasional letter, and now a phone call, and he was here. I swallowed hard. There was a lump in my throat. I did not know if it was excitement, expectation or maybe fear. Why had he come, with no forewarning? Just a phone call: 'I am here.'

He looked the same. Any fears I might have had about recognising him disappeared in that instant as he stepped from the train. He was dressed in stone-coloured trousers and shirt, with a shabby jacket that I thought I might have remembered from the past. Perhaps he was a little stooped, but that was the only immediate difference. Getting closer, I could see his hair had thinned, but only a little. The lines on his face were etched more deeply. He seemed more tanned than I recalled, but that was probably because I was now more used to pale skin. His smile, however, was the same. The silence of his face was the same. His eyes looked deeply into mine.

He held my hand as he kissed my forehead.

'It's been too long,' he said.

I nodded. 'I'm sorry,' I said lamely. I knew the words were inadequate, but there were no words to rewind the years and to touch on what had happened, on Horace's death, on the terrible silence in the house afterwards, on the guilt I had felt because it had been Horace and not me.

And what did I mean by that? I did not even know. It was a thought I'd had before but dismissed as meaningless, but it was there again now. I knew, as I had known back then, that it would have been easier for them if it had been me who had been killed, not Horace. My mother's favourite.

'Lionel?' my father asked.

'He's outside in the car, waiting. Fred is at work. He'll be home later.'

'Good.'

I had not realised how foreign my father's voice was. I had grown up so used to it, and to its intonation, that I knew nothing else. Yes, I had been aware growing up that there were differing voices in our neighbours, accents hinting at different backgrounds, different countries, but until now I had not clearly heard the sounds from my own home.

Lionel had been full of curiosity in the car on the way to the station. 'How come this grandfather has suddenly turned up?'

'I told you before, Lionel, he and your grandmother live in Kenya. It's where I was raised.'

'But why have we never visited him, or why hasn't he visited us before now?'

'There was never the time or the money. We wrote. He always sent you his love, his and your grandmother's. I told you that before.'

'I know.' Lionel was silent as he contemplated this. 'What's he like?'

'He's a good person. He was a good father. I think you and he will get on well.' I wasn't sure if this was true or not, but it seemed like the right thing to say.

'What will we talk about?'

'Oh, Lionel, I don't know. Don't worry.'

Now, when they met, Lionel was suitably agreeable to his new-found grandfather, asking him what he should call him while shaking his hand with enthusiasm.

'You choose what name you would like to call me,' my father said. 'There are so many possibilities. In Italy I would be Nonno.

Your grandmother is Italian. She would be Nonna. Here, perhaps Grandfather?'

'I have a grandfather,' Lionel said. 'I mean,' he hastened to add in case it had sounded rude, 'I mean that I call my father's father, Grandfather. Perhaps I could call you Grandpa.'

Later, Lionel said to me, 'You never told me my grandmother is Italian.'

'I never thought to say it,' I said. 'I don't think of her as being Italian. I've only known her in our home in Kenya. I think of them, like me, as being from there.'

'Grandpa,' Lionel said, 'why do you live in Kenya if you're really Irish?'

'I'm not really Irish, although my father was. My family had a farm in Kenya and I was brought up there,' my father said. 'We spoke English growing up, and when the war was over and I was old enough, I came to Dublin to study. And after that I went to Rome, and there I met your grandmother, Carolina.'

Lionel nodded. Previous generations were of little interest to him. He was missing Alice's company. His new grandfather seemed nice enough, but there was something stilted in the afternoon. He had the feeling he would prefer to be somewhere else.

'I might go and read?' he half-asked, half-suggested to me.

'Of course,' I said. 'I'll call you for dinner.'

When he was gone and my father was settled with a coffee and sitting on the deck, I came and sat beside him.

I wanted to ask why he had come. What had happened that he had suddenly made this move?

He was watching me carefully. 'We miss you,' he suddenly said. 'You do know that, don't you?'

I nodded. I did know it. It had come as a slow realisation. I had once realised it when talking to Lorina, and in a different way I had realised it while talking to Lionel a few days earlier. I missed them too. I missed home.

'Why have you never come back?' he asked.

'I felt . . . I don't know.' Anything would sound lame. 'I missed you too. I missed everything . . . Horace . . . you know.'

'Yes. I know. But life goes on. We learn to pick up the pieces, even if we can never see how we ever will. But we do.'

'Do we?'

'To some extent, yes, we do. Look at you.'

I wanted to say with irony, yes, look at me, I've never recovered, I never moved beyond that day, and then I realised this simply wasn't true. I might still hover on that terrible event from long ago, but I had in fact become another person.

'You moved away, went to college, married and had a child. You did survive. And I'm proud of you for that.'

'You and Mama? Did you pick up the pieces?' I asked.

He looked down the garden thoughtfully. 'We do what we can,' he replied tentatively. 'We have both known loss before. My parents. Your mother's parents, her sister . . . it isn't easy. It's never easy. In one sense, loss in war is explainable. It is not that you handle it any better, it is more that it happens and is less unexpected because of that. Your mother . . . '

'She didn't handle losing her sister.'

'No, she didn't. But she was a child. She carried guilt. She shouldn't have, but she did. She blamed herself for letting go of her sister's hand. Afterwards she hid in the basement of their home. She was there for days, no food and no water, but I don't think she even noticed that. She was waiting, both for her mother and her sister. And of course neither ever returned. And when there is no body, no one to bury and to grieve for in a burial place, it is more difficult, I think. Horace dying . . . well, what can I say? The old cliché, we should not have to bury our children. It is they who should bury us. But at least we had him to bury.'

I could not remember him ever speaking so openly to me before. I knew that he and my mother had had a close relationship. I somehow thought, or maybe hoped, that their mutual support had helped them cope with Horace's death. I had never been able to see it from their angle, only from my own. I did remember trying to connect with my mother after Horace had died. I remembered my mother moving further and further away from me. I had no real memory of my father after the shooting.

'Did they find the bodies? Of her mother I mean, and of her sister?'

'No, nothing was found. The Allies arrived shortly afterwards and there was a mass exodus from the city. Your mother was carried along in crowds of people. She was lucky, although I don't think she has ever seen it like that.'

He was silent. We both sat with our own thoughts. I could imagine my mother, younger than Lionel, so much younger, alone and frightened and fleeing. It was the most horrible thought. I pushed it away. I had seen pictures from that period of history, showing poverty, destruction, fear, and my poor mother had been part of that.

'Her father?' I asked tentatively.

'He was a soldier. He was killed early on in the war.'

'I . . .' I began.

'Yes?' he said. 'Tell me. Please, don't go quiet on me now.'

It was difficult. Exposing my own wounds would sound like I was laying blame, but if I did not speak, there could be no honesty. I tried again.

'I sometimes feel that it might have been easier for you and Mama if I had been the one shot that day in the airport.'

He looked at me with a mixture of horror and sadness, and then he reached across from his chair and put his hand on my arm.

'Helena, my dear Helena. No. That is all I can say. No.'

'No?'

'No, it would not have been easier. You and Horace are – were

263

– our children. We loved you both. We still do. One of you dying was devastating. Either one of you.'

'But Mama?'

'Your mother loved you both. She just didn't know how to show that love to you in the same way as she showed it to Horace. Her love for you was mixed with fear. You were the link to Lena, Helena, her lost sister. You were named after her. When she looked at you, I think there was some female link, something that made it harder.'

I remembered my fear when I was carrying Lionel, that if he were born a girl that I might not have known how to bond with him. That was what had happened with my mother, only in her case, that fear was even more real because it was based on loss. It might not completely make sense, but I could see it, even if only for an instant.

I remembered Horace once calling me Lena when I was little, and our mother saying, 'No, no, she is Helena. That is what we named her, we will not shorten it.'

'She wanted me to go away to school,' I said, remembering.

'It wasn't that simple,' my father said. 'She wanted you to be safe, and she feared that if she was caring for you she wouldn't fulfil the task. And for whatever reason she didn't feel that fear in raising Horace, and yet the awful irony is that she could not save him. There are some things we cannot change. Events we cannot avert . . .'

'The bullet we can't avoid,' I said with a shiver.

'That's right. Your mother came to understand that better after Horace died and after you left. She spoke about it sometimes . . . how she now saw that there was nothing she could have done to save her sister, just as there was nothing she could have done to save Horace. Things happen, sometimes terrible things, and it comes down to being in the wrong place at the wrong time, and that, she now realises, is what happened. None of this affects her love for you.'

264

'I felt hurt and rejected,' I said. I feared I might sound childish, but my father did not take it that way.

He said simply, 'I know. I really think we should have tried to stop you moving away. Delayed it maybe, for a year or more, so that we could try to function as a family.'

I nodded. What could I say? I would have liked their love then, but I had felt nothing. There was that terrible feeling that my death would have had less impact. It was how my mother must have felt when she lost her family.

'I should tell you that it was my idea that you should still leave. Your mother wanted you to stay. She said that you needed to be with us, but I felt that your best chance of recovery was to stick to the plan. I feared that if you stayed, you would never leave and I wanted you to have a life of your own.'

'Mama wanted me to stay?'

'Yes, and now I think she was right. Sometimes we only get one chance to get things right, and I think I got that one wrong.'

It did not matter that they had made me leave. It mattered that my mother had wanted me to stay.

'Why did your brother Horace die?' Lionel asked me later.

'Were you listening?'

'Not really. I could hear your voices coming from the deck to my bedroom window.'

'It's all right,' I said. 'It doesn't matter. I just wondered. Horace, well, Horace died because, as your grandfather said, he really was in the wrong place at the wrong time. It's as simple as that. As awfully simple as that. I used to wonder the same thing. I railed at the unfairness of it, but life isn't fair. Things happen. And Horace's plane happened to arrive slightly early. Or the other plane did I don't know. Maybe both arrived on time. Normally the passengers would have been held back to let dignitaries through.'

'Dignitaries?'

'There was the President, his bodyguards, an entourage. Maybe someone made a mistake. I don't know. You hear of catastrophes every other day, and the truth is that sometimes it comes down to good or bad luck, call it what you will. There is a terrible randomness about life. That's what I think. It was good luck for the President. Supposing Horace had missed his plane, or supposing the gunman had better aim. So many possibilities, but the wrong things happened that day. And the wrong person, our darling Horace, just happened to be in the wrong place at that precise moment.'

All the tiny ratchets in the wheel of life slipped into particular positions that day. And it was unlucky for Horace, and for those who loved him. I could see that. It seemed very clear to me now.

'I'm sorry,' Lionel said.

I kissed him. 'As your grandfather says, life goes on.'

'It's not fair.'

'I know. But then, life isn't fair. Life goes on, and we must do with it what we can.'

'Do you think you did what you could?'

I was not sure that I had done everything I could. I looked around at our house, the home that I had allowed myself to be drawn into and to assist in making, the nest that I had built, the child I had carried, the husband I loved. It was the best I had been able to do. Maybe that was not so bad.

I listen at windows. Long ago. I listen outside doors, and crouch beneath sills. I listen to Tuesday crying in the days before she died. It is at the end of the dry season. My father has taken Horace with him up country. Tuesday's mother has said only the doctor from her tribe can help. He lives two days away. My father has brought our doctor from the town, but Tuesday's mother refuses him. My mother says that they must do what Kulu's family thinks best. My father leaves with Horace.

266

Tuesday cries on and off most of the day. Then in the late afternoon there is silence. I creep away and I get my book and lie on a rug on the veranda. Luther comes into view. He stands in the middle of the yard. The dust rises and settles around his feet as he stands still. I glance at him and then go back to my book.

And then the noise begins. It is like a roar that rises in an almighty wave around me. I have never heard anything like it before. Startled, I jump to my feet. It's Luther. He is trumpeting at full pitch. The sound shatters the stillness of the day. In the distance, storm clouds loom.

And then he stops.

People have coming running from various places and they stand as I do in a mixture of amazement and fear. Then suddenly there begins a wailing, the loud, shrill cry of Tuesday's mother.

Tuesday has died.

I never find out if Luther's cry heralds her death or if it is a response to it.

Or indeed, either way, how he knows.

The rains come later, and my father says, 'It's more likely he knew the rains were coming and it was that to which he was reacting.'

Fred came home early. I had phoned him to say my father had suddenly turned up.

'Are you all right?' he asked me as he came through the kitchen door.

'Yes,' I said, turning to him and putting my arms around him.

'Why has he come?' he asked.

'I think he just wanted to see me. Come inside, you must meet him now.'

'I don't know how I'm supposed to react,' Fred said.

I could understand his misgivings. My parents had not come to our wedding; there had been no acknowledgment of the marriage. He had never heard anything from them in all these years. I could see that he might be feeling annoyance or distrust, but true to character, he pushed those feelings aside and, taking my hand, went through to the living room with me, where my father was looking at photograph albums, all the pictures of Lionel growing up and his different achievements.

He got to his feet. 'Fred,' he said.

'I'm delighted to meet you, sir,' Fred said, putting out his hand.

The men shook hands, eyeing each other both with care and curiosity.

'It's good to meet you at last,' my father said.

It worked well. Fred was welcoming, and my father, normally reticent and given to silence, talked more openly than I had ever heard him talking before. There was a gulf, the gulf of silent years, but everyone seemed determined not to waste this time, this visit, and these precious days.

I lay in bed that night with the window open and the curtains slightly apart. Fred had kissed me before he fell asleep.

'He's a nice man, your father,' he said.

I nodded in the dark. Yes, he was a nice man. And that was reassuring. His love was reassuring. These were things I would carry from these days.

My father had left my mother with difficulty. It had seemed to him that it was high time for this visit. I imagined him packing a bag and with the enormity of the trip he was about to undertake hovering in front of him, telling my mother that he was about to go away and leave her. It would have been a first in their marriage. They never left each other. I would ask him about that. I closed my eyes.

My mother was sitting on the veranda, sun hat on her head, shelling peanuts. Luther was standing behind her. When the nuts were shelled, she would pulverise them to make peanut butter. Luther's trunk nuzzled her neck. He was hoping for a piece of bread. She took a piece from her apron pocket and held it out. He reached for it. He looked like he was smiling. A feeling of warmth filled me and I stirred in my sleep. I knew I was dreaming. There was love there, even if I did not feel it was directed towards me, it was there and it encompassed me.

I woke to find Fred making love to me. But it was not like his normal gentle caressing; it was passionate, almost to the point of violence. He pinned me down on the bed and entered me forcefully while his tongue penetrated my mouth. He kissed me as he had never kissed me before. He thrust deeply and I wound my legs around him.

When he was finished, he withdrew slowly, and in the moonlight, I could see he was staring at me.

'I love you,' he said.

I wanted to ask him why he had never loved me like that before, what it was that had changed, why he had taken me like that.

He lay back on the pillows and smiled. 'I love you,' he repeated.

And I knew he meant it.

'Father, was it not difficult leaving Mama for these few days?' I asked.

He agreed it was. 'It is the first time I have ever left her,' he said. 'I promised her when I married her that I would never leave her. It was a promise I gladly made and I have adhered to it. I have never wanted to leave her. She and I carved out a life for ourselves in Kenya. Things were difficult there after the civil war, but we stuck with it. It is our place. It is where we put down roots as a partnership. My roots were already there, but your mother needed roots. She needed a place to call home, a place where she would be safe and where she could have a family. I gave her that.'

'And leaving her now, to visit me?'

'She agreed I should come. She didn't want to leave to come too. She wants you to visit her. In a sense, I am the emissary. Do not misunderstand – I wanted to visit you. I have wanted to for years, but always hoped you would come to us. The mountain and Mohammed,' he said somewhat vaguely, with a wave of his hand.

'I'm glad you came,' I said.

'I am too. Don't put things off,' he said. 'If you have things you want to do in your life, do them. Don't put things off thinking there is always tomorrow.'

I remembered then that sensation of time moving very quickly, so unlike when Horace died, when time had stood still, and when it restarted it was at a crawl; a slow, dull moving through endless days.

There were days I had enjoyed, taken just as they were, loving Lionel, loving Fred, accepting everything. I thought again how time was galloping past. Looking back, it seemed like only yesterday that Lionel was just a baby and then a toddler. And now, here he was across the table, pouring coffee. And my father, he had been in his prime when I left home; he was now an old man. How had this happened? It seemed my life was filled with pockets, and those pockets were filled with events, but the seams that contained them had split and the contents spilled over from one section into the next.

It was the following day and Fred was at work.

The phone rang, and I jumped. I had been so absorbed in my thoughts that for a minute I did not recognise the sound.

Lionel got up and answered it. 'Yes,' I heard him saying, 'hold on and I'll fetch her. Mum?'

I got up slowly and went to the phone, eyebrows raised, asking Lionel who it was. He shrugged and passed me the handset. 'Hello?' I said.

'Helena, Simon here. May I visit?'

I invited him over, explaining that my father was there but that it would be nice for Simon to meet him.

He came in the early afternoon, complete with his usual bottle of wine, a book for Lionel and flowers for me.

'This is Simon Petersen,' I said to my father.

When I introduced them, I had the feeling they had met before.

'Petersen,' my father said. 'Yes, yes, I see.'

The men shook hands.

'Simon is an artist,' I explained.

'I know. This is a pleasure.'

There was something in their greeting and in the way my father said this that took me by surprise.

'Do you two know each other?' I asked.

'No,' Simon said. 'I just know of your father through you.'

'And I've heard of Simon,' my father said.

'Oh?' I was surprised. I could not imagine how or why my father would have heard of him.

'You've forgotten your mother's fondness for books on art and catalogues. She came across Simon's name some years ago. I happen to remember it.'

He did not say, 'My child, when your mother saw the portrait of you in an art magazine, she had to have it.' He did not tell me that the portrait hung in the farmhouse above the mantelpiece with all the photos of Lionel lovingly lined up below it. I had no idea. But I wish he had told me that they had bought that painting and hung it in their room. What can I say? It would have vindicated everything. It would have told me there and then the place I had in their lives.

'Oh,' I had not thought of this. I had forgotten my mother's reading and the direction it had taken before I had moved away. I had forgotten that we had talked about her books and that we had grown closer in that last year before I left. Of course my mother must have missed that.

She must have started sharing her reading with my father. It was strange to think about. Of course she would have gone on reading, even though nothing could ever be the same. What else would she have done to fill the hours?

We drank tea and then Lionel asked if we would like to visit the beaver lodge with him. My father seemed delighted and enthusiastically got to his feet.

'Are you sure, Papa?' I asked. I was aware he must be tired. The journey he had made was long and he was going back in only two days' time.

'Quite sure,' he said.

We walked across the field together, with me pulling back, as I wanted to see Lionel walking ahead with my father. I wanted this image to hold in my mind and to contemplate later. Simon walked slowly beside me. He smiled at me.

'You seem . . .' he searched for a word. 'I don't know. Happier?'

I smiled back at him. 'I feel . . . joyous, joyous that my father has come here. That all doors are open. I don't know if I'm explaining that properly, but I feel that something significant has happened.'

Yes, I felt joy. That was the word. And I knew I had never felt it before, not like this. Not since I was a child. I felt alive.

'Your son is growing into a fine young man,' my father said. 'Fulfilling promise.'

'It's great that you came to visit,' Fred said. 'It's so good that you've met Lionel. I'm sorry my parents couldn't come down. I would have liked them to meet you. They would have liked it too.'

'Maybe I should have given you notice I was coming. But I decided so suddenly. Perhaps it wasn't the right way to do it.'

'Perhaps it was,' I said. I was clearing plates from the table.

'These days have been wonderful, seeing you and seeing that you are well. You meeting Lionel, and Fred too. And hearing about my mother . . .'

He nodded. 'Life isn't always easy,' he said. 'It's not obvious. We think things are a certain way, and they are not.'

'He's quite an obscure man,' Fred said to me in the privacy of our bedroom later.

'But you like him?'

'Yes, I like him. He's an interesting contradiction, the mathematician for whom all things make sense, for whom logic is overriding and far reaching, and the man who has survived wars and has had to deal with the consequences of an accident. In some ways, he and your mother have seen more than most. And they survived.'

'What else could they do?'

'Oh, Helena. You're so stoical. You don't even see that many people would have caved in.'

'But it felt like I was caving in.'

'Well, you didn't. And that's why I love you.'

'You loved me last night,' I said tentatively.

'I did. With a passion,' he laughed. 'It felt like you were a different person, someone I could finally see clearly.'

'A different person? You mean you weren't making love to me?' I was startled.

'No, I didn't mean it that way. I was making love to you, but I saw you more clearly. I've always felt the need to be gentle with you, as though you're fragile. I feared I could hurt you in some way; I don't necessarily mean physically. But you're not fragile. Or at least, not as fragile as I had thought. You are strong, like your father.'

I liked what Fred had said. I had only ever seen myself as someone weak and inconsequential, but he was seeing something else. And I liked what he was seeing.

At the airport the next day, as I leaned up to kiss my father goodbye, he put a hand on my cheek.

'Papa, I never asked you how you heard that day when Horace was killed. How did you find out?'

'I was in the study,' he said thoughtfully. 'I was on page sixty-eight of the sixth book in the textbooks I was writing. I had reread the previous chapter and I was calculating the difficulty of the problem I had set. I can see it all so clearly. And then suddenly, there was this noise. I jumped. It was so unexpected. I came outside and Luther was standing in the front yard and he was trumpeting. I remember feeling my blood running cold. I suddenly knew it was the noise you and your mother had described all those years earlier when Tuesday had died. Then Luther dropped his trunk and it dangled down between his legs and I knew something terrible had happened. Kulu came running. He stood there for a moment looking at me, then at the sky and then at Luther.'

I stood there, shocked. 'What happened next?' I asked.

'Kulu said, "It's Horace, sir. It's Horace."'

'Did you believe him?'

My father nodded. 'I don't know why, but I did. I don't know how he or Luther knew, but they did. And I knew in that instant that there was nothing I could do.'

He kissed me on the forehead. 'I love what you have grown into,' he said. 'Be strong and stay true to yourself. And don't put things off. Come and visit me and your mother. Give her another chance. We need you. She does not have your strength. She still lives in the past no matter how she might try to live now. She still believes her sister is alive somewhere in the world, looking for her. She lives with dreams; don't be like that. Live now. Visit us. Do the things you want to do.'

'Have you tried to find her sister?'

'Of course I did, long ago, but the town was wiped out. The

few survivors escaped with your mother. There was no one left.'

I kissed my father goodbye, and watched as he went through Security. He turned and waved, and long after he had disappeared, I stood there with one hand in the air.

In a sanatorium in northern Italy, up in the hills, an old woman paces the floor, wringing her hands. 'Lina, Lina,' she murmurs. 'Can't you hear me?'

In a farmhouse in Kenya, a woman carries a bowl of mangoes out to the veranda. She sits down to pit and peel them while searching the horizon. Her head is raised and she gazes in the direction of the west, where a single umbrella tree stands on a hill.

Eighteen

The house seemed quieter again when my father left. I found myself walking into a room and hoping that he might still be there. I missed him.

'The termites build their nests. The outer shell is hard. It can be as hard as concrete. The inner walls are parchment thin, made from chewed-up wood. They build their nests in trees or underground, or in some places, out in the open. The ones in the open are strange skyscraper-looking buildings that can stand up to six metres tall.'

'How tall is six metres, Horace?'

'Taller than a giraffe.'

'Horace, why are they shaped like that?' The pictures show elliptical-shaped structures.

'The termites build them at an angle so that the sun only hits the narrowest parts. It keeps the nest cool.'

I nod as he turns the page.

'Inside there is a queen and all the workers, and they build and build. Each nest is different inside, but there's a strange thing here. Wait a moment...' I wait impatiently, but I know to say nothing or he will not explain it to me. 'Yes, I see. How odd. . . '

'What is it, Horace?'

'It seems that each side of each nest is exactly the same in structure as the other side of the nest. If the scientists put a thin wall right down the centre of the nest that is being built, so that the workers are separated from each other, they will still build exactly the same design on either side of the wall.'

'Maybe the queen termite tells them how to do it.'

'No, the queen is stuck in one half. She can't communicate with the other half. And yet they build exactly the same way, as if they have a blueprint in their minds, born with it or conveyed to them as soon as they are born. How can this be?'

I wait. I do not understand. It is as though the termites in one nest had exactly the same minds, with an inbuilt pattern. That's what Horace is saying.

'Well, how does it happen?' I ask.

'I don't know,' he says. 'No one knows. It just happens. They know what the others are thinking. They do the same thing.'

'Are they all part of one whole thing?' I ask, thinking hard.

'Yes. I think that's the answer.'

I am so pleased. I do not always understand.

'Like they are one big brain, and each termite is just a little bit of it?' I ask to make sure I am getting it.

'Yes.'

Now I am not sure if he is pleased I understand.

'But what happens if one dies?'

'Probably it's like our own brain – if a cell dies, other bits compensate, I suppose,' he replies.

The Martins returned from the Caribbean. St Lucia had lived up to everyone's expectations, or so the initial reports indicated as relayed through Lionel.

'They had a great time,' he said.

'Edith?'

He nodded. 'She did too.'

He had become more reticent in what he passed on to me. From always spilling everything out to me, he now was reluctant, sometimes just giving the bare bones of an answer, sometimes shrugging. Fred had said this was normal, but to me, it was not. I had not encountered it before in my narrow upbringing, where Horace and I had relied on each other for friendship and company.

Now Lionel's life seemed to be separating from us. He was keeping his own counsel, becoming more detached. He used to share his thoughts with me, ask me questions about little things as well as big. Now he was withdrawing.

He and Alice sat by the river and listened to the flow of the current and, little by little, Alice told him about her grandmother, lost and now found. He told her about his grandfather and the surprise visit. No links were made, and because he did not tell me, no links could be made. The pockets of information were intact in themselves, but isolated. Nothing overlapped.

'You look wonderful,' I said to Conti. I had dropped in on her because there had been no sign of her since their return.

'Do I?' Conti brushed her hair back. 'My tan is good,' she said, eyeing her brown legs and stretching out her arms.

'Yes, it's great,' I said. 'Was it fun?'

'Oh, it could have been worse,' Conti said nonchalantly.

I wanted to ask about the absent lover, but it did not seem appropriate to bring it up.

'Did you and Joe get on all right?'

Conti nodded. 'Yes, that was fine. The children enjoyed themselves. Edith loved it. The sea did her good. The sea was fabulous, though the path down to it from where we were staying was steep. Joe carried her. She is no weight, really, so that was good. We did a couple of day trips and we just lazed the rest of the time. It suited us as a family,' Conti said.

'That's great. I'm pleased for you.' I wondered if this meant that the affair was over, and if Conti would settle down again. It was positive to hear Conti talking about her family.

'He's been in touch,' Conti continued.

'Who?'

'Anthony. We were no sooner back than he was on the phone.'

Anthony. It was the first time Conti had given her lover a name. It made him more real for me, and that unnerved me. As long as he was nameless, I felt I had been able to keep him at arm's length. But now he was there, a named entity, someone who might destroy the Martins' marriage if Conti was not careful.

'Were you pleased to hear from him?'

'Not really. I wanted time to get over the holiday and to think about things.'

That sounded good, as though Conti might have seen that it was not the best idea.

'What did he want?'

'What do you think?' Conti said with some bitterness in her voice. 'He wants to see me.'

'Conti, listen, you don't have to see him. You don't have to do something you don't want to do.'

'Don't I?'

'Of course you don't. You don't need to see him ever again if you choose.'

'I'm afraid it's not that simple,' Conti said.

I had the feeling Conti wanted to tell me something, but she started and stopped and I waited, wondering.

'We got home,' she began. 'I felt jetlagged and sort of disoriented. Joe was in fine form, clearly refreshed from the holiday and fussing over me in an odd way. We had sort of connected better on the holiday than I thought we might. Certainly better than I had expected. Joe went off to work.'

She told me bits of what happened on the holiday, but she did not tell me that she had got blind drunk and out of control, the first time she had done such a thing since they had been together and that Joe understood her distress and was gentle and kind to her, waiting for her to open up to him.

She told me he had no sooner left the day after they returned than the phone rang. Still in bed, half-dozing, she reached out and picked it up.

'Hello?' she said.

'You're back at last.' Anthony's voice sounded strong and determined down the line.

She pulled herself up in the bed. She was totally unprepared for his call. When she had last seen him, she had said she would make contact on her return.

At that time, it was exactly what she had intended to do. But now, things were different. She felt it was all she could do to cope with home, Joe and the children. She needed more time before pursuing her relationship with Anthony, if indeed that was what she wanted to do. All the excitement she had felt in his company had somehow evaporated in the previous few weeks. The flight home had exhausted her. She felt drained.

'Anthony, hello. I can't talk right now.'

'Joe has left for work,' he said. 'Why can't you talk?'

She wondered how he knew that Joe had left, and then she assumed that she must have told him before the holiday that Joe was starting his new job that morning.

'The children . . . things have happened. I'm . . . it's not a good time.'

'I'll call you later,' he said. 'I thought we could meet this afternoon.'

'I can't.'

'Now, now,' Anthony said chidingly, 'I won't take no for an answer.'

'I really can't meet you today,' she said. 'We're only just back. I'll call you in a day or two. Please don't call here. It's awkward. One of the girls might answer.'

She was not used to not getting her own way. She did not like his tone or the words he was using. They were too forceful. They did not reflect the way their affair was run, and she could not imagine why he thought she would respond positively to being addressed like that.

'Tomorrow lunchtime then,' he said. 'The usual place.'

She thought of the hotel where they usually met and she suddenly found the whole idea somewhat seedy. Whatever thrill had been there was gone now.

'Be there,' he continued.

'I can't,' she said again. 'This is not a good time. I'll call you when it is.'

'I'll see you tomorrow,' he said and he hung up.

She felt distinctly uncomfortable when she replaced the receiver. There had been the hint of a threat in his voice. She did not know what to do. She decided not to turn up, but even as she made the decision, she had the feeling that the affair was not going to end just like that.

And she was right. He rang the following afternoon and Alice answered. He asked to speak to her mother.

When Conti took the phone from Alice, she instinctively knew who it was before saying a word. She thought of hanging up, but knew he would call again. He no longer appeared to be accepting the boundaries, boundaries she thought they had both created and by which they would both abide.

'Hello,' she said. She was aware of Alice hovering in the doorway.

'I won't ask where you are,' Anthony said, 'because that's clear.'

She gestured to Alice to leave, but still Alice remained, a concerned look on her face as she gazed at her mother.

'Who is it?' Alice mouthed.

'I'm on the phone,' Conti said, grimacing at her daughter.

'Whoever you're talking to, get rid of them. I want to talk to you,' Anthony said.

'I'm sorry, I can't talk now,' Conti replied.

'I suggest you get yourself into a place where you can talk to me.'

'This isn't a good time,' Conti continued. 'I'll call you back when I can.' She hung up.

'Who was that?' Alice asked.

'Oh, someone to do with the phone bill,' Conti said, trying to sound vague.

'Why couldn't you talk to him?'

'I don't know where the bills are. I need to look them up and see what he was talking about.'

Alice shrugged. The phone rang again as she went out the door.

'Hello,' Conti said, eyeing the door and listening to Alice's departing footsteps.

'Don't hang up on me again,' Anthony said.

Conti decided to pretend Alice was still in the room. 'I haven't had the chance to look up the paperwork,' she said cryptically.

'I want to see you. Tomorrow, same time. Be there.' Now he hung up.

Conti stood there, unsure what to do. It was five minutes later when I appeared at the door.

'Helena, would you do me a favour?'

'Of course I will.' I was, as ever, eager to please.

'I can't get rid of this man and I don't want to meet him, and for some reason he won't take no for an answer. Would you come with me tomorrow?'

'Go with you? What good would that do?'

'If you're there when I walk into the hotel, you could greet me and insist I spend the afternoon with you.'

'Conti, I'll do it, but I can't see it working. If he's being as adamant as you say, he's not going to just disappear because I turn

282

up. Either he'll insist on meeting you again, or . . . '

'I don't know how to get rid of him.'

'That doesn't sound like you. You said he was married too. He can't put this kind of pressure on you. It's unfair. Anyone can see that.'

'I don't know. I'm suddenly wondering if he is in fact married. He said he was and I believed him, but I know nothing about him.'

'Does he know anything about you?'

Conti suddenly remembered the early morning call the previous day, when he had referred to Joe by name. She had thought at the time that it was odd that Anthony knew Joe had left for work, but it was not that. It was odd that he knew Joe's name. She had been discreet all along, giving no information other than her own name, just enjoying some time with this man and the relief it had given her. She was sure she had said nothing other than that she was married and had children. She had given him no more information than that. It was all private, just as her affair had been.

The feeling of unease increased.

'What is it?' I asked, seeing the discomfort and lack of composure on my friend's face. There was clearly something wrong.

'I'm not sure. It's just a feeling. He said something yesterday and I don't know where he got the information from. I never referred to Joe by name, I'm sure of it.'

'And?'

'He said something about Joe. He said "Joe has left for work by now", something like that, and at the time I thought it was odd, but then I thought it made sense one way or another, and now I'm not so sure. I'm as sure as I can be that I never gave him Joe's name.'

'Look, if I can help by going there, I will, but I don't think it's going to get rid of him. You can only do that by telling him it's over.'

'What if he threatens to tell Joe?'

'Do you think he might?' I was now feeling really concerned.

'I don't know. He was sort of menacing on the phone. I feel there's an agenda, but I don't know what it is. I thought we were just having a summer fling, something that either of us could take or leave.'

'Do you think he wants you to leave Joe? That he wants you for himself?' I asked.

'I don't know. I can't imagine why he would. I have three children. No one is going to want to take me on with three children. Not that I want to be taken on. I'm a happily married woman,' Conti said.

The whole thing did not add up to a happily married woman, I thought. Happiness did not appear to play any role in any of this. I saw Conti's relationship as duplicitous, as a betrayal of the man she purported to love. I couldn't imagine how Conti might see the whole picture, but a happily married woman was not part of it.

'What am I going to do?' Conti said.

'I think you're going to have to meet him. If you can't get rid of him on the phone, you're going to have to turn up and tell him where to go.'

'I need this like a hole in the head,' Conti said, shaking her head in frustration.

'Has something else happened?' I asked. 'Is Edith really all right?' I wondered if that was the problem, because clearly Conti was preoccupied and I had the feeling it was not just to do with this Anthony.

Conti shrugged and shook her head. 'Edith's okay. It's just stuff,' she said vaguely. She could not bring herself to put it into words.

Having always seen herself as being somehow better or above other people, she now felt a sense of diminishment, of being less than the person she perceived herself to be. But it was worse than that. It was not just that she was brought to the level of other people, but somehow she had sunk lower. That her mother was some poor demented woman, with no background to speak of other than as a domestic servant in post-war Italy, was simply unbearable.

She had never felt empathy for other people, and now could feel nothing for this lost woman. Her thoughts circled around and around as she tried to understand. In her mind, she railed against Babbo, cursing him for the lies he had fed her, for the ignominious situation in which she now found herself.

One of the things she had liked about me, and about her friendship with me, was that she knew she was better than me. This was a fundamental fact to her, and I knew it. This attitude might have turned away other friendships in the past, but with me it had never come to that. I always appeared to accept the status quo, to enjoy her company and to look up to her. That she should be less than me, as she saw it, was something she could not bear. And so she said and did nothing.

Looking at her, I knew there was something wrong, something more than Anthony and his persistence.

'If I can do anything,' I said hesitantly, 'you know I will do it. Just tell me.'

What could anyone do?

Conti spent the afternoon and evening trying to work this out. She now cursed the day she had met Anthony. She had been coming out of a department store and he was walking down the street. They had quite literally bumped into each other. It had been quite a bump and she had almost fallen and had dropped some of her bags. He picked them up for her, still apologising, and then had asked if he could buy her a drink or a coffee or even a bite to eat. And she, in that moment before heading back to the car, had suddenly thought how she could put off the moment of going home. And she had thought, why not?

It had all seemed so easy, an obvious thing to do. He was attractive and attentive, and at the time it was exactly what she needed.

Now? Well now it was exactly what she did not need.

She could not risk him phoning when Joe was there. And if she did bring me along with her, she realised that what I said was right – it would not actually fix things. No, she would just have to go and meet him and spell it out to him. Either the affair was over, or it was on hold, but either way she simply could not deal with him right now. Yes, she would meet him. She really had no choice.

Joe came home from work that evening to find Conti sitting on the sofa with a martini in hand and a bowl of olives beside her. She was picking up one olive at a time with a cocktail stick, dipping it in the martini, and then eating it.

'Hello,' he said, putting his head around the door. 'Fix me one of those too, would you? I'm just going to change. Tough day,' he added.

She wanted to say, 'Tough? You don't know what tough is. I've had the tough day.' But of course she did not. She did not dare say anything. She got up and went to the kitchen to fix him a drink and to top up her own. She would deal with Anthony tomorrow.

Coming back into the room, he sat down in one of the large armchairs. 'Where are the girls?'

'Over with Lionel,' she said, handing him his glass.

'All well?' he asked.

'Yes, fine. Edith has perked up, I suppose. She's looking better anyway. The holiday did her good.'

'Good,' he nodded. He looked preoccupied.

'What's up?' she asked.

'Nothing much. Teething problems. I suppose it comes with all new jobs.' He had come home the previous day in good spirits.

The day had been spent getting used to the new offices, meeting colleagues, sitting in on meetings and making notes. It had been much as he had expected and he had felt uplifted by the prospect of new challenges.

'Anything in particular?' she asked vaguely. She was not really interested and also knew from experience that he was not inclined to talk about work at home. He tried to keep them separate.

'I suppose I've been dealing with drug crime for so long that I had just got used to a particular way of doing things and seeing things, prosecution being my forte. New firm, new beginnings and with that comes new ideas. It all takes time. In its own way, white-collar crime is no different. The clientele are, but the lack of morality is just the same. The knowledge that what I do can release someone onto the street, someone who should really be behind bars . . .'

'Well, that's the way it's always been. You knew that when you decided to study law,' Conti said pragmatically.

'I know, but it doesn't always make it easy. Not when you see someone in the flesh, or read the file and you know that his, or indeed her, release can have catastrophic consequences for other people. It's why I liked what I was doing before.'

Conti nodded. She guessed he was thinking about the gunmen in the garden. 'Any particular problem?' she asked.

'Not really. Well, maybe. It's an odd one, though. Before I came to this firm, I had a case coming up, a young drug dealer. Standard stuff. Now he's come looking for a new defence lawyer and they're giving it to me.'

'Can't you say no? I thought the whole idea of the new job was that you would be giving advice rather than appearing in court.'

'It appears he asked for me, and I have no real reason to say no.'

'So what's the problem?'

'It's not a problem *per se,* it's just that I left my regular role as a barrister because of what happened at the barbecue, and I thought that by doing that I would leave everything that might be connected to those gunmen. Now, this is the first case in the new firm, and I've already read the other side of it,' he shrugged. 'I would be given it to read anyway, but it was odd, already being so well acquainted with it. I suppose it's interesting, looking at it from the defence point of view and trying to work out if there is any defence whatsoever. His father came in with him today. Nasty bit of goods, the pair of them. He asked about you.'

'About me? Who did? What?' Conti felt the hairs on the back of her neck stand up.

'Not specifically, don't worry,' Joe half-laughed. 'The father wanted to know if I was married and had children. He said then I would know how he felt, he and his wife. He said they would do anything to protect their son and that I must get him off.'

'Oh.' Conti did not know what to say. She wanted to ask questions, but couldn't think of anything that would not sound unnatural. She had a feeling, a horrible, sick feeling, that she was going to recognise the name.

'Where are they from?' she asked.

'Belfast,' he said, 'but they live in Dublin. Why?'

'I just wondered.'

'I'm going to get another one of these,' he said. 'Then I'll be back to normal.'

'Is this a slippery slope?' Conti laughed. 'Needing two martinis to recover from the day?' She tried to sound light-hearted, but her heart was sinking by the minute.

'Well, join me on my slippery slope,' he replied. 'Let me refill yours at the same time.'

She handed him her glass and tried to get her mind to settle down and to think about what he had said. Was it a coincidence? Northern Irish? Of course it was. It had to be. She did not actually know that Anthony was from Belfast. Yes, he had a Northern-Irish accent, but so what? Lots of people did. He could be from somewhere else in the North.

'Why isn't he in custody?' she asked.

'He should be. In fact, he would be if I had been here, but he got bail while we were away. I don't think I would have let that happen.'

The following morning, Conti came to see me before leaving for town.

'But if it is the same person,' I said reasonably, having listened to her story, 'then he is married and you have as much of a hold over him as he has over you.'

'I didn't think of that.'

'What's his name?'

'Joe didn't say and I didn't want to ask.'

'I meant Anthony's surname.'

'Oh. Brown, he said. It might not be his real name, though.'

'Anthony Brown? It sounds innocuous enough.'

'It now sounds like it might not be a real name. I'm becoming a conspiracy theorist,' she added with irritation.

I went to pour us coffee and she pulled my newspaper across the table and took a look at it.

'Oh my God,' she said.

'What?' I turned back.

Her face was ashen beneath her tan. 'Oh God, Helena,' she said.

I looked at the paper I had been reading, trying to work out what had attracted her attention.

'That's him,' she said, stabbing at the photo on the open page.

'That's Tony McEntee and his son,' I said. 'Not wanting to prejudge innocence or guilt, of course, but they sound downright dangerous.'

'That's him,' she said again.

I sat down and looked at the picture. 'Are you sure?' I asked.

'Of course I'm sure,' she said. 'We've screwed often enough for me to recognise his face.'

The headline said: 'Still out on bail.'

I was really shocked. 'He's a drug baron, Conti! His son is up on some charge, a serious one, and there has been an ongoing report in the paper about the fact that he managed to get bail. Conti, you can't go and meet him. He's dangerous, seriously dangerous. You don't know what he might do. You need to think,' I said. 'You have to work out how to handle him. I really don't think you should go and meet him.'

'Helena, I have to. He'll tell Joe if I don't go and meet him.'

'What if you tell Joe first?'

'I can't. Joe would never understand. Ever.'

'But . . . ' I grimaced. 'Didn't you tell me with a great deal of confidence that everyone had affairs? You implied that Joe did too. You even implied that Fred had.'

'I'm sorry,' Conti said. It wasn't contrite, more dismissive. 'I shouldn't have said that. I only said it to justify what I was doing. Some people have affairs. I know that Joe would not be able to handle it. I have too much to lose. I can't tell him.'

I looked at her, wondering if she knew how much she had disturbed me by suggesting Fred was having an affair. But Conti was clearly too preoccupied with her present predicament and I did not want to upset her further.

'I don't know how to advise you,' I said. 'I'm sorry.'

'I better get going,' Conti said. 'I'm going to be late.'

'Come here afterwards. It will give you time to recover before going home.' I did not add that I wanted to know how things went, but I did. I suddenly remembered that afternoon in the garden when the two men with guns had appeared, and I wondered if there was any link. Conti got up to leave.

'Be careful,' I said. I was afraid to mention what I had been thinking, and I could not think fast enough to work out if Conti would be better off knowing my fear or not.

Conti sighed. She went into the hall and looked at herself in the mirror, patting her hair. 'Do I look all right?' she asked.

'Yes,' I said numbly. I could not help feeling that how Conti looked was the least of her problems.

'See you later,' I said as she went out the door.

'See you later.' 'See you soon.' These are the things we say to people as they leave us, and we never imagine they might not actually happen. We assume that we will see them again, and again and again.

But as I said 'See you later' to Conti as she went out the door, a bit of me was not sure that I would. I had this sense of something terrible impending, and the only thing I could think of was that it was to do with her meeting Anthony. I wondered when the court case was due to start. I tried to remember what I had read in the papers, but I couldn't. I went back and reread the article, but it said nothing about dates. I felt there must be some leeway because Joe had only just been given the case. He would be given time to prepare. It must be coming up though, maybe in the next few weeks.

Precious weeks, precious time flowing like sand through my hands. Lionel in his room reading or out with Alice. Lorina now back in Manchester. Freyn had finished college by now and was doing an internship at a daily paper. Marjorie and Jackson were at home, probably playing tennis, and if not playing, then talking about it. My parents were in Kenya waiting for me to visit.

I was going to talk to Fred. I was going to suggest I got part-time work and it would help finance the trip.

I thought of my parents with love now, and with forgiveness. For the first time, I saw that I needed to forgive them, even if

I was not sure what it was I had to forgive. It did not seem to me that they had done anything so terribly wrong. They were what they were, and they were good people. Yes, my mother showed me little love, but how could she have done otherwise? She lived with fear. I felt that somehow I had learned from that, even though I had not understood it. But surely, I had learned to embrace life more than she.

How blind we are. How like our parents we become and we do not see it.

Nineteen

The wind blew. It lifted the leaves on the trees and I saw them hugging tightly to the branches. Autumn was nearly in, and the wind, which had had warmth in it over the previous few days, now carried a chill. The leaves were giving way, drying out as if they were tired of holding on, and they fell in cascades of colour to the ground. Their golds and reds, yellows and ochres twisting like coloured paper as they were torn away and blown down the garden.

I took down the net curtains to wash them, and as I held their thin, light folds in my arms and carried them through to the washing machine, I was aware that I had done this twice a year for as long as I had been there. Each year, I had climbed up a ladder and lifted these same curtains from their hooks, and when they were washed, I had brought them back and hung them up while they were still damp, carefully easing them back into place and leaving the windows open to allow them to dry. I looked at them now, and I saw that they had aged. I did not know when this had   happened and why I had not noticed it before. What had I done? And oh, so much more horrifyingly what had I not done? There is time, I reassured myself. There is still time. Time for what?

For all the things I had put off.

'Papa,' Horace says over supper that night. Our father looks up. 'I have a new pet.'

'Really?' My mother says, suddenly interested. She was forking her food slowly around her plate and had appeared more withdrawn than usual.

I'm feeling nervous. I'm not sure how Horace is going to explain the arrival of this little kitten.

He gets up and fetches it, bringing it back in his arms.

My parents' eyes widen.

'Where did you get that?' my father says, getting up and coming around the table.

'I found it,' he says lamely. 'I rescued it,' he adds.

'That has to go back,' my father says as he takes it from Horace. 'We can't keep that here.'

'Why not? It's mine. I found it. It's my kitten.' Horace is determined.

'Horace, it's a leopard cub,' my father says. 'Where did you find it?'

Horace is silent.

'Helena, where did you find it?' my father asks me.

I don't know what to say.

'I'm not going to shout,' my father says, knowing that's what I fear most. 'Just tell me.'

'We just found it,' Horace says quickly to protect me. 'It was lying on the ground.'

'Horace,' my father says, 'don't you know what it is? It's a leopard,' he repeats as if he has not already said this and as if we do not know. 'Leopards don't change their spots,' he says. 'Do you know what that means, son? It means exactly what it says. This little cub will grow up and be a leopard. You can't domesticate it. It will always be what it was born to be. A predator, dangerous – beautiful, yes, but dangerous.'

'But Luther lives with us,' I says timidly.

'Luther is an elephant and he chose to come with us.'

This is not exactly the truth, but Luther does live quite happily with us. I don't see why the same can't happen with this cub. After all, Mother had rescued Luther; Horace has only learned this from her.

My father looks out into the night. 'We can't bring it back now,' he says thoughtfully. 'But tomorrow morning, first thing,

294

as soon as the sun is up, you and I are bringing that back to exactly where you found it.'

Horace looks sulky but he does not say anything.

My father calls Kulu in and asks him to keep the cub for the night. 'No point in you bonding with it,' he says to Horace. 'Kulu will look after it. And you and I are getting up at dawn.'

He and my mother exchange looks. 'I didn't know there were leopards this close,' he said. 'They haven't been seen in this vicinity in years as far as I can remember.'

My mother nods.

'But what if it can't find its family?' Horace says.

'Well, that will be your fault,' my father says. 'You should have left it where it was. Tell me you didn't go into the bush.'

'No, it was before we got there.'

My mother shivers. 'Its mother could have been close,' she says.

'I suspect she was,' my father comments. 'She may have been moving her cubs and was coming back for this one. I think you are quite lucky you didn't meet her, Horace.'

We are sent to bed.

Looking out my window before climbing into bed, I see the moon, sickle-shaped and white, close to the earth. I think I see something moving in the dark, two yellow eyes gleaming in the night, but when I blink, there is nothing.

In the night, the leopard's mother comes. She comes through a window in Kulu's place to retrieve her cub. She attacks Tuesday, who is sleeping in the room with the open window. She mauls her on the way to finding her cub.

And Tuesday dies because of Horace and me and the cub.

I waited for Conti's car to return. I was half-waiting at the window, going back and forwards to the kitchen, tidying and cleaning. The net curtains were hanging again in their windows. The afternoon had dragged. Seconds moved slowly into minutes, the hands on the clock appearing to hardly move.

I was worried. The longer Conti took, the more worried I was becoming. I hoped Conti would come straight over, but instead Joe's car drove up the laneway and swung into their drive and I knew I would not hear from Conti until the following day. I busied myself preparing dinner. Sometime later, I heard Conti's car returning and I breathed a sigh of relief. At least she was home.

'Sorry I'm late,' Conti called, coming through her door.

'Where have you been?' Joe asked her, pouring her a drink.

'Oh, shopping, Helena and me. The traffic, you know,' she said vaguely.

'Not to worry, you're here now,' he said. 'How was your day?'

'Fine, busy, you know.'

'Good, good.' He was preoccupied.

'And you?'

'Good news,' he said. 'I've turned down that case I was telling you about.'

'What?' She was startled.

'I didn't like doing it, as you know. Turning it down, I mean. But I didn't want it, and I decided I would just tell them. I don't think there was any connection with that incident in our garden at the barbecue, but in case there was . . . well, I told the other partners about it and they agreed it wasn't worth the risk. So I'm free of it.'

Conti was shocked. She didn't know what to. She tried reassuring herself that it would be all right, but she couldn't see how it actually could be.

'Helena, I've tried, but I can't talk him back into taking the case,' she said.

It was the following day and she and I were talking while

Lionel and Alice were at school.

'Anthony said Joe had to take the case. That's what this has all been about,' she explained. I was having a problem following everything.

'Please start again,' I said. 'I don't understand.'

'Anthony wants me to put pressure on Joe to take the case.'

'Why?'

'Because he says, rightly, that Joe is the most likely person to get his son off. But Joe is adamant that he won't do it. I don't know what to do. Anthony says I have until Friday to make sure that he does, or he's going to tell Joe about my relationship with him.'

'But...' I tried to digest this. 'But telling Joe isn't going to make Joe take the case.'

'No, but he says if his family is going to fall apart because of this, then so is Joe's.'

'Supposing you tell Joe first? Supposing you just tell him what has happened?' I suggested.

'I can't. Joe will leave me.'

I couldn't help thinking that if Conti wanted her marriage to stay intact, she shouldn't have gone down this path, but it wasn't a particularly helpful thing to say, so I kept quiet.

'Helena, what am I going to do? I can't get Joe to take it. He got out of it yesterday morning and is adamant that he won't take it back on. He got a bit irritated with me for pushing him, and he never gets irritated with me.'

I could see that Conti was really upset, but I could not think of what to say. Platitudes like 'it will be all right' seemed fairly useless. It was not going to be all right.

'The worst that can happen,' I said slowly, 'is that Anthony will tell Joe. That's the worst, isn't it?'

Conti nodded. It was not the worst, but she couldn't think what to do. She didn't want to share Anthony's other threat with me. It was too frightening. She couldn't say that after telling Joe, Anthony said that even if Joe forgave her, he, Anthony, would see that someone in her family would die to make up for losing his son to prison. 'One way or another, Joe will take this case,' he said. 'You see to it.'

She felt depths of despair. It was like when Babbo had died and she had not been able to see anything in any context. Her grief over his death had been mingled with her anger over his hiding her mother's life from her. Now she was torn between her worry over Anthony's threats and the knowledge that her mother was alive and poor and mad. She couldn't handle any of it.

She wanted to lash out, and she saw me as being so content and self-satisfied, sitting there in her kitchen.

'Everything is all right for you,' she said. 'You've got it all.'

'Conti, of course I haven't,' I said gently. 'No one has. It might look like that on the outside to people, but it isn't like that on the inside.'

'Well, what's wrong in your life?' Conti said. I ignored the nastiness in her voice. I thought she was actually asking me a question and that she really wanted to know.

'While you were away,' I said, 'my father came to visit. It churned up everything from the past. Things with my mother, the sense of loss I had as a child . . . '

'What's wrong with your mother?' Conti said, picking up the sugar spoon and ladling sugar into her coffee.

'It's not important,' I said. 'It is to her, of course, and so to me, but in the grand scale of things in life, it's not. But when she was a child she lost her twin sister, and because of this she has always had a problem with me.'

'Why?' Conti said uninterestedly.

'It's one of those things that isn't cut and dried,' I said. 'They named me after her twin, Helena. She was called Lena. My mother is Carolina; her name was shortened to Lina. Lena and

Lina . . . and my mother has never really recovered from her sister's death. And for some reason, a reason I sort of understand, but it's complicated, she had a problem relating to me. She had no problem relating to my brother, but a problem with me. . . '

Conti, who had only been half listening, was now trying to keep her hand from shaking. The spoon rattled as she replaced it in the bowl.

'Where was this?' she asked.

'What?' I was now lost in my own thoughts.

'Where did she lose her sister? And when?'

'I don't know, somewhere in Italy, during the war. I don't know exactly where.'

Conti listened in amazement. Could this be? Could such a coincidence occur? Could my mother be her mother's sister? I had just said my mother's name was Carolina. That was Conti's real name. Had she been named after my mother? It was too much. It couldn't be. And then she remembered a conversation she'd had with me. It was during the time I was having my portrait painted and I had come back talking about randomness and coincidence, and how I believed that all of life was a series of coincidences, some good, and some bad.

'What was the name of that artist friend of yours?' she asked. 'Do you remember? You told me about some conversation you had with him about coincidences.'

'Simon Peterson,' I said. 'Yes, I remember that conversation. He said he did not believe in randomness. He believed that everything is connected. He said that people don't see those connections, but they are there.'

I thought Conti was thinking about Anthony and his threats. I did not realise what was going on in her head as bits of things started to fall into place. She was sitting there staring at me as though she had never looked at me before. I did not realise that she had suddenly discovered we were cousins. Conti accepted me as the woman next door, a sort of confidante, someone to whom she could show off while knowing that she was superior to me by birth, by wealth, by position in life.

'Where is your mother now?' she asked me.

'You know. She lives in Kenya,' I said. 'With my father on the farm where I grew up.'

Conti's mind was in turmoil. The idea that my mother lived in comfort on a farm, with my father, while her own mother was in a mental home somewhere in Italy, abandoned by her husband when Conti was born . . . no, it wouldn't do. She couldn't bear it. She had always thought she was better than me, luckier, happier and more fulfilled. She had always thought she had everything and that was the way it should be.

How could I sit there worrying that my mother didn't love me enough? How ridiculous this was in her eyes. At least I'd had a mother and a home life, and now that seemed enviable. And there I was with Fred and Lionel and everything just right in my life.

'I have to go,' Conti said, getting to her feet. 'I've to take Edith to have her eyes tested.'

'Oh no, is she all right?' I asked, and even as I said it I knew that it was a stupid question. Edith was never going to be all right.

Conti shrugged. It was too much trouble to even begin to knock me down to size.

'What are you going to do about Anthony and Joe?' I asked.

'I don't know. I need to think,' Conti said. She wanted out and away from me, I could see that.

She kept looking at my face, and I did not realise, of course, that she was seeing it as a reflection of her own. She had always been aware that she and I looked somewhat alike, with similar hair and the same shaped face, but she had always liked the fact that she was fuller than me, more voluptuous both in her figure and, as she saw it, in her very existence. That supposition suddenly seemed to falter, and indeed to alter.

The coincidence in names and in the stories of our respective mothers was too much to be just that, a coincidence. It was real, and Conti knew it.

Conti didn't want to see her life as mine, suburban wife, nice home, loving husband; she wanted more. She wanted to retain the rather grand image she had always had of herself; daughter of an Italian count, happy, fulfilled, with her own sense of importance. She wanted to hold on to the romantic notions she had of her own life, but they were falling apart around her. Nothing was real; everything seemed based on some sham. She did not see that the very flaws that were in her father were recreated in her. His snobbery, his belief in himself and his selfishness were all part of her. The love he had given her, his indulgence in her, his pride in both himself and her had made her what she was. She needed to hold onto those things. Without them, she felt she would be nothing.

'By the way,' she added, going out the door, 'you're my alibi for yesterday. Joe was pushing to know where I had been. If he asks you, we were out shopping together.' And she was gone.

That rankled. Maybe I should not have let it, but I did. Joe had always been kind to me and to Fred. He and Fred still had the occasional drink together and caught up on each other's lives. I found the idea of being used as an alibi for Conti's deceit quite unpleasant. It irked me that she hadn't even asked me, but just given it to me as a *fait accompli*. She was gone before I could say anything.

I toyed with the idea of telling Fred, of filling him in on the connection between her affair and Joe's client, but it all seemed so contaminated with something vile that I postponed telling him.

I told myself that I would tell her that she could not use me as an alibi. I had conversations in my head in which I stood up to her and said that if she did not tell Joe what was really going on, I would. She was not going to drag me into her sordid little affair. I was so brave when I wasn't actually in her company. I could see her clearly when I was away from her, but I had always lacked guts when she was there.

Joe refused to take the case despite Conti's pleas. During that long week she nearly told him what had happened.

'Joe?' she said one evening towards the end of the week. They were in the dining room and the girls had gone to bed.

'Yes?' He sipped his wine. His mind was elsewhere.

'Have you ever done anything you really regretted?'

Joe reflected for a moment. 'I suppose that sometimes we make decisions that in hindsight were not the best, but on the whole I usually feel that if I make the decision with as much thought as possible, I can't really regret it. After all, I will have made it on the facts as known to me. Why do you ask?'

'No reason, I was just wondering.' Conti did not know how to proceed. It seemed a chance to come clean, to tell him what had happened and to have him take over the situation and to decide what to do. But she couldn't bear the idea of everything falling apart.

She met Anthony again that Friday in an effort to postpone things and to convince him that she was doing her best to coerce Joe into taking the case again.

'What did he say?' I asked when Conti returned.

'No dice. Those were his exact words.'

'Is there anything I can do?' I asked.

'There is nothing anyone can do.' Conti sat there, crestfallen. 'My only hope is that his wretched son will get off.'

'How was it left?'

'He said he'd be in touch.'

Nothing happened. It was as if everything was on hold. How and why, Conti did not know. I stopped asking her if there had been any developments. I suppose I thought or maybe just hoped that the problem had gone away, and I suppose I was so irritated at being used as an alibi that I pulled back and let her get on with things.

I had other preoccupations. Lionel filled a lot of my thoughts. He was brusque both with me and with Fred. I knew it was normal, normal in that that was what other parents said happened – children withdrawing, being more involved in their own thoughts and activities – and I hoped it was typical. It seemed so sad to me, all the precious time Lionel and I had had together, and he now seemed to avoid me. If I went to give him a kiss, he pulled away.

'Aw, Mum,' was what he said.

So I pulled back to give him space.

'There are consequences to all actions,' my father is addressing Horace.

'We didn't mean any harm,' Horace is saying.

I'm by the window. I don't know if my father knows I'm there. I think I have blended into the wall.

'There is no "we" in this, Horace,' my father says. 'Helena does what you say. You say "jump" and she jumps. You say "let's take the horses to the trees", and she obeys. She never stands up to you.' He is silent now.

So is Horace.

There are tears running down my cheeks.

'We . . . I didn't know. I didn't think . . . ' Horace tries. I know he can hardly speak, he is so distraught.

'I know,' my father now says. 'What has happened is terrible. Tuesday is as important to her parents as you are to us. Her death is devastating for them.'

'I don't know what to do,' Horace says.

'There is nothing you can do now,' my father says. 'It is done and we will live with it.'

He leaves the room and Horace kneels on the floor. I can barely see him through my tears. I curl up in a ball beneath the window ledge.

My mother comes in and she takes Horace's hand and pulls him to the sofa, where she sits with her arms around him.

'Life goes on,' she says to him. 'I know you had no idea such a thing could happen.'

'Father...'

'Your father is devastated that he did not prevent this. He knows he should have got rid of the cub immediately. He blames himself.'

'But I did it. I brought the cub here.'

'Horace, listen to me,' my mother says. 'In my heart, I know I would have done the same thing you did. What you saw as an act of kindness turned out to have terrible consequences. But it was not deliberate, and we will live with this as a family.'

'How can I ever be forgiven?' Horace asks her.

'You must forgive yourself,' she says. 'It is the only way forward.'

That winter was quiet. There was ice and bitter sleet and it seemed colder than previous years. Inside, our homes our lives continued. I took a job as a proofreader. It was work I enjoyed, although I found it difficult to read and enjoy anything I was not actually working on as I became more and more aware of looking at structure in other books rather than just enjoying the content.

My yoga classes continued and Conti turned up the odd time. I enjoyed the classes, and liked the woman who gave them.

During that time, Fred and I talked a lot about Lionel, with Fred reassuring me that it was perfectly normal to be a truculent, selfish teenager.

'But why?' I asked. 'Neither Horace nor I were like that, I'm sure of it.'

'I have no idea,' Fred said. 'I just know that I was, my friends were and we both saw it in Freyn.'

'I never saw it in Freyn,' I said. 'Yes, Marjorie used to say she had problems with him, but he was never rude or grumpy with us.'

'But that's the norm,' Fred said patiently. 'They behave fine outside but take it out on us at home. Honestly, it's normal.'

'But why didn't I experience that growing up?' I asked, puzzled.

'I have no idea,' Fred repeated. 'Maybe because of your isolated upbringing and you didn't get to see other teenagers so you had no one to emulate? I really don't know. I do know, though, that you're worrying too much about it.'

He was right. It just seemed to me to be a terrible waste of time and I hated the changes in Lionel. I also knew from other parents that whatever belligerence Lionel was directing towards us, it could have been a lot worse. 'Aw Mum' was the height of his rudeness, but it saddened me.

Come early spring, Lionel started talking about Kenya again. He told me that my father, who now wrote regularly to him, had said that when he was older and had his degree, maybe Lionel would like to base himself on the farm. My father also wrote to me and included a bank draft so that we could come and visit.

I was thrilled. I had almost saved the money to get us there anyway and I had this feeling that everything was coming together.

It was weeks later, on a Saturday morning in the papers, that I read in the death notices that my yoga teacher had died suddenly. In the same paper, I read how the son of Tony McEntee was caught at an airport trying to flee the country. His bail was rescinded and he was now behind bars. I wondered if Conti knew.

Fred had gone to work for the day, promising that he would spend Sunday with Lionel and me. There was a memorial service the following day in our local church for the yoga teacher, who had been 'a pillar of the community', as it was put in the paper. We would all be going, Fred and I because I had liked the woman, the Martins because it was what should be done. I would see Conti then if not before.

I was not sure if I should bring Tony McEntee's son's arrest to Conti's attention, because there was little Conti could do. I thought about it on and off during the day. It wouldn't go away, and in the end I decided I would tell Fred. I could not hold it inside me for much longer; the knowledge that the Martins were in danger was too real and too frightening. I kept telling myself that nothing would happen, but I still had a feeling of impending doom.

But it was late when Fred came in that Saturday night, and he wanted to talk about the sport on which he had been commentating and how he had gone to the pub afterwards with a group. The time wasn't right to begin to tell him of my unease.

It was later still when Lionel returned from a party. I got up out of bed when I heard the door.

'Is that you, Lionel?' I whispered down the hall.

'Yes, Mum.' I heard the sound of the refrigerator door opening and I knew he was lifting out the milk. I hesitated in the corridor, wanting to go and talk to him, yet knowing that he might brush me aside.

'Good night,' I whispered.

'Night,' he said, and I heard the fridge door slamming shut.

Teenagers, I thought as I went back to bed. My mother-in-law was right. They were difficult years. I paused at the window, gently pulling aside the curtain so I could look out at the clear night sky.

Fred stirred in the bed, and looking back, I could see his face clearly as the moonlight lit it. I smiled at him as he turned over, and then I got back into bed.

Next door, Conti, who had begun to read the newspapers

with an avidity not surprising under the circumstances, had spent that day fretting over the article, wanting to ask Joe about it, and then changing her mind over and over.

The following day, they had to go to the church service for the yoga teacher. She could not sleep. Every time she tried to get her thoughts into some kind of order, they dissolved into disarray as Tony McEntee's voice entered her mind.

At one point she got up and checked on Alice and Edith. Both were asleep, Edith curled in a sad, twisted position, and Alice facing her. She had the feeling Alice was not asleep. She and Lionel had been out at a party and had come home late, sharing a taxi and just inside the agreed curfew.

They would go to the service and pray for this woman or whatever they were supposed to do, and then they would come home and she would tell him everything. And then it would be all right. Somehow he would make it all right. Joe would bring her to Italy to meet her mother and then take her away again. She would tell him about Anthony Brown and the Tony McEntee connection and he would understand and still love her. Everything seemed more precious, more immediate, more important than she had realised.

She was tired. She turned again in the bed, and she could feel Joe pulling the covers back over himself. She grimaced. She had not meant to disturb him. Let him sleep. Tomorrow he would deal with everything. And no matter what happened, it would have to be better than today.

As sleep started to come, she suddenly wondered what Alice had actually been up to, and she was wide awake again. She began to wonder if something was going on between her and Lionel, and the more she thought about it, the more she puzzled that it had not already occurred to her. She had just seen them as best friends, nothing more, but now the uncomfortable thought came to her that maybe they were more than that. They were related and they did not know it. Suppose they were somehow involved with each other? The idea was awful. What would she do? She had to make sure that nothing happened between them. But how could she do that without telling Alice?

She had a sleepless night.

Twenty

'Lionel?' I called to him through his closed bedroom door. There was no answer. I opened the door a fraction. 'Lionel?' I repeated.

'Aw Mum,' he mumbled.

I closed the door quietly. What was the point in getting him up to go to the service? He didn't even know the woman. He might as well sleep. He had been late going to bed and he needed his sleep. He stirred a little, and then rolled over and went back to sleep. So I said nothing, just very quietly pulled the door shut.

Fred and I sat in the kitchen and had toast and coffee before leaving.

'We should get him up and make him come with us,' Fred said, getting up and going to look out the window.

'Why?' I asked as I put sugar in his coffee.

'Well, my parents would have made me get up.'

It didn't seem a particularly good reason to me. 'He's tired. Let him sleep,' I said.

And so Lionel slept and we got in the car and went to the church.

Next door, Conti was shooing Alice down the stairs. Alice was pale and rather sick looking. 'Are you all right?' Joe asked her as he carried Edith down to the hall.

'Just tired,' Alice said. 'Do I have to go?'

'You're up now,' Joe said. 'You can go back to bed when you get home if you're still tired.'

Edith and Alice looked at each other. Neither flickered an eyelid, but each knew what the other was feeling and thinking.

Alice felt the pain in Edith's back. Edith knew that Alice was feeling really sick and that her head hurt. Edith could feel it.

Oh, God, Conti thought, remembering how she had

promised herself that she would tell Joe everything. She wondered why things sometimes seemed easier in the middle of the night than during the day. She didn't know how to handle any of this. She would wait until they got back from church. Who knows, maybe she would receive some divine inspiration in the church.

The service was short, followed by coffee and cake and what the vicar called a 'yoga moment'. We never found out what the yoga moment was, as Alice, who was getting paler and paler, suddenly said she was going to throw up.

People were milling around, talking about the weather and the service as Joe took Alice outside.

'Were you drinking last night?' he asked as he hurried her away from the church hall. She didn't get to reply. Instead, she doubled over and vomited against the wall at the side.

'I'd better see if Alice is all right,' Conti said to Fred and me. 'Will you look after Edith until I get back?'

'Of course,' I said, reaching for the wheelchair. 'We'll get you some cake,' I said to Edith as Conti walked out of the church. Fred went and got a plate for Edith and filled it with a slice of chocolate cake and various iced biscuits.

She smiled up at him as he passed it to her.

I smiled at him too, and he gripped my elbow. I glanced at my watch. It said 12.20.

There was something wrong. I could feel it. I looked around at people gathering near the food. I could hear kind words being said about the yoga teacher, but something caught me and I couldn't place it.

'Fred,' I said, 'could we go outside? Please take me outside. Edith . . .'

Fred looked at me, puzzled. Edith was engrossed in her plate of cake. He seemed about to ask me what was going on, but did not.

He said to Edith, 'Come, we're going outside.'

I pushed the chair, as Edith's hands were occupied, and Fred kept his hand on my arm.

As we went through the door, the light came slanting in, lighting up the three of us. Edith looked up at me and then back down at her plate. She had the feeling that Alice was vomiting. She put the piece of cake down and then there was the sound of a volley of loud pops and the wheelchair was released abruptly from my grip and rolled towards the steps.

The gunman waiting for Joe and Conti saw us instead. I can see how it happened so clearly. A simple mistake.

I looked like Conti, Fred was tall and dark like Joe, and we were with their crippled child. I knew it was happening as it was happening. It was unavoidable because we were in that particular spot just at the moment of wrong identification. And as I fell, it was not of that I was thinking, but of Lionel and all my dreams and hopes, the things I had put off and now would never have time to do, of the life I would not have and my terrible sadness that I would not be there for Lionel . . . Lionel . . .

There was no pain, just a sound and a flash and the sense of light splitting and splintering. I thought I saw a sunset, light changing in the west, reds and yellows and then a whole prism of the rainbow descending into a black horizon.

I am under the umbrella tree even as I hear voices shouting and a face in front of mine. 'Hold on, Helena. Stay with me. Helena, look at my eyes and stay with me.' Voices and sounds, sirens in the distance then up close. I can see and hear, but from a great distance.

In the ensuing mêlée as Joe cradled Edith in his arms, Conti crouched, hidden down the side of the hall with Alice, who had now curled on the ground in a mirror image of Edith, whom she could not see.

Conti had no doubt what had happened. It was that moment

of retribution she had feared, and somehow Fred and I had managed to be at the receiving end. She felt horror but also a sort of relief. If Fred and I had been shot in her and Joe's place, maybe it was over. But maybe it was not. Anthony had shown what he was capable of, and maybe she would have to tell Joe. And then, slowly, she took in the fact that she had seen the wheelchair moving forwards towards the steps and she got to her feet and began to run.

Ambulance sirens heralded our way to the hospital. In one ambulance, Joe and Conti each held one of their daughter's hands.

Conti tried to say something, but the words were strangled.

Joe shook his head. 'Don't talk. It's going to be okay. We'll talk later. It's going to be okay.' She could not decide if he meant what he was saying or if he was trying to convince himself.

In the hospital, both girls were taken from them. Edith's forehead was split from her fall down the steps and her face was covered in blood. Her parents still did not realise that she too had been shot. Alice just lay curled up, and while Joe tried to convince the doctors that she had not in any way been hurt, it was not the impression she was giving.

'She wasn't hurt in the incident,' he said. 'She was ill before it started.'

We were wheeled into the hospital on gurneys and Conti watched in horror as Edith, Alice, Fred and I were whisked away.

It wasn't possible. Conti could hardly bring herself to think about what had happened. The police were there now, trying to talk to both her and Joe. She wanted time to think, but everything was happening so fast.

Joe made her sit down and he did the talking. 'I think that the Wolffs were not the targets,' she heard him say. 'I think it was my wife and I who were meant to be hit. My wife, Conti, and Helena Wolff look very alike. And Fred, well, we're about the same height and we both have dark hair. And Fred and Helena were pushing our disabled daughter in her wheelchair.'

Conti wasn't sure if he would have seen it so clearly and so quickly. She no longer cared. All she could think about was Alice and Edith. Anthony had done his worst. She prayed, beseeching Babbo to intervene and to give her back her girls.

They were in a private room now, being interviewed, and Conti sat crying as Joe tried to handle the questions. Mistaken identity had taken out the wrong couple; there seemed to be no doubt of that.

'I think it was some kind of revenge,' Joe continued. 'There was an incident last year at a barbecue; we were interviewed at the time. There is a link . . . Once it's announced who was killed, obviously they're going to know they got the wrong people.'

'Does it matter?' Conti asked.

Joe put his arm around her. 'No,' he said. 'It doesn't. Nothing matters.'

The police tried to assemble the facts as sensitively as they could under the circumstances. 'We'll release a statement saying that there was a shooting outside a church hall and we'll work from there.'

Further decisions would be made as soon as it was clear how the twins were doing. 'But Alice is fine,' Conti kept saying. 'She was just feeling sick. A stomach bug maybe, I don't know.'

'She and Edith are very close,' Joe said to the doctor who had come in to ask them about her. 'Despite appearances, they are identical twins and they share feelings and thoughts. Please just believe me on this. Just concentrate on Edith.'

'I see,' the doctor said. 'I'll be back as soon as I can. Edith is in surgery now.'

Joe and Conti were now sitting close together. She was shaking.

'Oh, God,' Joe said. 'Lionel. He stayed home this morning I think.'

'Lionel is the son of Fred and Helena Wolff?' he was asked.

'Yes. He's at home, I think,' Joe said.

'Don't worry. He is being taken care of right now,' the police officer said. 'Two of our officers have gone to the house. We will look after him and that will buy us time here.'

Joe went over and over the events of the morning, the threat from the previous summer and the case he had turned down, which he felt had brought about the shooting. Conti sat there shivering. Everything was unravelling and she wanted to talk to Joe alone, but there was no time now.

The doctor returned and said that they had not managed to save Edith.

Back at our home, Lionel had woken and made his way to the kitchen to get something to drink. It was almost one o'clock and he wondered what time we would return. He rang the Martins to see if Alice was there, but there was no reply. He did not leave a message. He drank juice from the fridge and then he put on coffee. It had just finished percolating when there was a ring at the door.

He thought of not answering, but then, looking out, he saw the police car and so he went slowly to the door, running his hands through his hair, aware that he looked like someone just out of bed.

'Are you Lionel Wolff? The son of Fred and Helena?' There were two officers there, one male, one female.

He found himself being brought inside and told to sit, which he did reluctantly, almost in a dream. He feared he knew before they said anything what it was, but he sat and watched their faces and tried to understand the words.

He heard 'shooting'. And still he sat and looked at them.

'Both were shot?' he asked. He had the feeling he had already asked that. His voice did not appear to be his own.

'Yes, both were shot.'

Then one of the officers was making him tea. He wanted to

314

say that he would prefer the coffee, but it didn't make sense that he might actually have a preference under the circumstances.

'Are they all right?' he asked, bewildered. 'I need to get to the hospital. Are they in a hospital? Did you bring them to hospital?'

'Yes, they are in hospital. We don't know how they are,' the officer said. 'We'd like to call someone for you. You need someone with you.'

'We better call my grandparents. No, maybe we should call Freyn. He's my uncle.' He could not think what would be best. Best would clearly be if this had not happened.

'Shot?' he said again, as though he was only now taking in the word.

'Yes, son. Now can you give me your uncle's number?'

Freyn lived in a flat in Dublin, close to where he was working at the newspaper. Lionel had the feeling he should know if Freyn was actually there this weekend, but he couldn't remember. He got up and started dialling.

'Would you like me to do that for you?' he was asked.

No, he didn't think so. He didn't think anyone should be doing it. He felt it was a mistake, but that Freyn would sort it out. None of what the officers had said made much sense. People went to church on Sunday. They didn't get shot. At least not people you knew. Not your parents.

There was no answer from Freyn's number.

'We could try my grandparents,' Lionel said. He did not want to tell them though. He decided that if Freyn was not at his parents' house, then he would not tell them. But Freyn was there.

'Hey Lionel,' his grandfather said. 'We're sitting here watching the game. Your grandmother is making popcorn.'

'Hi, Grandfather. I wonder is Freyn there.'

'Sure thing. I'll pass you over and when you're finished with him you have to talk to your grandmother.'

Freyn came on the line. As Lionel tried to speak, the words

315

stuck in his throat. One of the officers was there, though, and took the phone while the other brought him back to the chair.

'It's all right,' she said to him, passing him a cup of tea. 'Drink this. You've had a shock. We'll deal with everything.'

He could hear the other officer telling Freyn the same thing he had heard already. He reckoned Freyn's reactions were pretty much the same as his own because he heard the officer saying, 'Yes,' and then 'Yes, both were shot. I'm sorry, sir, both. No, we've no further news at this time.'

Then the phone was passed back to him and it was Freyn's voice, strong, like his own father's, 'I'm on my way. I'll be with you in just over an hour. Go to the hospital with the police and I will meet you there. Just hang in there, Lionel. I'm coming.'

All things change and yet life goes on. I lie in the hospital bed with tubes attached to every part of me, and monitors beeping in rhythm with my pulse. I float in and out of awareness.

My dreams don't stop.

The past is clear to me and very real. I feel the rough cotton of my shorts and the hard ground under my bare heels beneath the umbrella tree. I sit with a book with my back to the tree and Horace is lying on the ground. He sits up and passes me the flask of water and I can taste the clear, cold liquid in my mouth and throat. I pass it back. He rubs the top of it and puts the lid back on it.

In the same instant, I can feel the soft Indian cotton of my wedding dress and the new sandals I bought for my wedding. They are hard on my feet. They rub along the side of my toes. I will get blisters. I look down and my toenails are painted. Daisy painted them the evening before my wedding as we sat on my bed in Trinity.

'I will miss you, Daisy,' I say to her.

'I'm going to miss you too,' she says, looking up from my feet.

'Meeting you has been such incredible fun.'

She's right. It has been fun. We grin at each other. She moves closer to me and puts her arms around me and I lean my head against hers and I can feel her hair on my cheek and we hug. Best friends.

In the same instant comes another memory. It is so long ago. I am lying in my basket in the shade on the veranda. I can see the awning above me. I am a baby. I move my hands in front of my eyes and I see the tiny pearly fingernails on each finger. There is a face moving in close to mine.

Not a face I know. Another one. Long and hairy with a high collar of fur around his neck.

I look into his eyes. I smile. He bares his teeth. He reaches into the basket and then I feel myself being lifted and my face can feel the rough fur of his body as I am held close. He doesn't smell like Mama.

I hear a trumpeting and then there is a scream from somewhere. Someone doesn't like what's happening. I hold his fur and then I let it go. Everyone is screaming. He is cornered on the veranda and Kulu and the other men are there, shouting. I am crying now. He does not want to let me go, but somehow he is forced to release me.

'Miss Helayna, Miss Helayna.' Kulu has me in his arms. He is soothing my screams. 'It's all right now, Miss Helayna,' he says.

My mother comes out of the house. She is crying and crying. She cannot stop. She looks at me in Kulu's arms. I want her to take me. I want to smell her perfume and feel her clean hair on my face. My father comes and he takes me from Kulu.

'It's all right, Carolina,' he says. 'She is safe now.' He is shaking. I can hear his heart pounding.

'I cannot even keep my own child safe,' she says. Her face is wet with tears.

'No, no, you're wrong. Look, she is safe. He didn't hurt her.

317

He held her tenderly. Kulu said the baboon did nothing but hold her, and when he was cornered he handed her back. Look,' he says.

My mother is afraid to look.

I float in time and space. Events unfold. I seem to see the future and the past in such a way I cannot tell which is which. Sometimes I see Lionel's face in front of mine.

'I love you, Mum,' he says.

I love him too. I love him with all my heart. I love Fred with all my heart. The human heart is enormous. It can carry so much love, an unending burden and an unending joy.

Jackson and Marjorie are here. Marjorie is crying and Jackson touches my hand. 'Fight,' he says to me. 'Fight. Fred would want you to fight.'

I know then, if I did not already know it, that Fred is dead. He has gone to the other place. Lionel would say, 'The real he, the one who laughed and loved and cared for us.'

Fred is buried.

It is raining and Jackson and Marjorie stand huddled together with Freyn towering over them and Lionel holding his grand-mother's arm. Their tears mix with the rain until it is impossible to discern which is which. 'Ashes to ashes, dust to dust...' Lionel rubs his face with the back of his hand. Freyn has his arm around Lionel's shoulders.

I cannot bear his grief. I cannot think of my own. Grief is a weight. It's too heavy to carry now.

Beneath the trees I see a shadow. A face emerges, pale and sad. There are tears on her cheeks, or is it just the rain? Lorina bows her head. I think she is praying. She slips away into the mist.

Time shifts.

Lorina is walking the streets of Dublin. She stops in her tracks in the middle of Grafton Street and Freyn is standing in front of her. He opens his arms and she steps into them. They hold each other so close, like they will never let go. They will never let go. His heart is big enough for two and she has a place in it.

Alice is learning to live without Edith in an echo of another time and another place, another twin who lost her sister and who has to live with loss. She cannot bear the taste or smell of alcohol. She sits with Lionel at the river one last time, their feet in the water. The beavers have a new lodge, a second one, further upstream. Life goes on in an endless, forward-moving repetition. Lionel and Alice hold hands.

'Best friends,' she says.

'Best cousins,' he says.

Neither can remember how to smile. 'Mum and I are going to live in England,' she says.

'We'll keep in touch,' Lionel says to her. 'Friends.'

'We've been like brother and sister,' Alice says.

'Yes, and that will last,' Lionel says. There is determination in his voice. He knows her grief. 'We will survive,' he says to her. 'My grandfather told me that. He said that with time, we will be able to see things clearer, that life goes on. He said life is precious.'

Alice stares at the water.

Joe stares in disbelief when Conti tells him about Anthony's threats. 'How could you not have told me?' he asks. 'How could you not say? Edith and Fred have died. Helena is lying there attached to drips and they say she probably won't survive.'

Conti sits and shakes her head. She is too tired. She cannot listen to him. She will not listen to him. She will never learn.

The Sphex wasps will not learn for another thousand million generations or more.

The baboons are making their journey from the forest. A new hunt for food begins. They stop at the gates and they look across at the veranda where once I lay in a baby basket. They hold their little ones by the hand and they trek onwards on their never-ending journey.

'We will take her out of the coma tomorrow,' a voice says.

'I came to see how she is doing.' It is Doctor. I would recognise that voice anywhere.

There is another voice. It is American. Not Marjorie. Another American and the past is here again. 'You look beautiful,' Daisy says. 'You make a beautiful bride.'

'The swelling in her brain has gone down. We are very hopeful,' the first voice says.

'Can I be here when she is coming round?' Daisy asks. It is Daisy. I would like to hear her whinnying laugh. Dear, funny Daisy.

'Can I stay with her?' It is Lionel. My wonderful son, my light, my joy.

'Can I sit with her?' It is Simon. Lovely, artistic Simon who wandered in and out of my life.

'Can I hold her?' It is my mother. Mama, I want to say. Mama, will you hold my hand? Please hold my hand. I smell her perfume. She is leaning over to kiss me. For some reason I can see the back of her head, and then she is sitting beside me and my hand is in her hands. She is stroking it over and over. 'I love you, Helena,' she says. 'I love you.'

I love you too, Mama.

'Kulu says you are to get better fast and to come back with us. We will sit together on the veranda and stone the mangoes. You will get strong again. I love you, Helena.'

My father is there. He is standing at the end of the bed. 'It will be all right.' He says it fiercely, as though he is addressing someone.

Tomorrow is another day.

They will go home and sleep. They will struggle with the demons in their nightmares. They will dream and waken and come back. I am holding a tiny leopard cub in my arms. So soft. So tiny. Like a baby kitten. Blue eyes. So wrong of Horace and me to take him. Some things belong in the wild and should be left there. It is dangerous to remove animals from their natural habitat.

The baboons wanted me.

The humans kept me.

One by one, machines are switched off. Slowly, drips are removed and I re-emerge.

Life begins over.

For a while, I have no voice, and I lie and listen to their stories. I smile and nod and close my eyes. Sometimes I sleep. I piece together the things I know and the things I don't know.

My parents are staying in our house with Lionel. When I am well enough, the house will be put on the market and we will go back to Kenya. I will learn to miss different things. Just as I once missed the height of the sky and the warmth and the taste of Kenya, I will now miss the damp days and the green fields, and the Sugar Loaf rising to the south. I will miss the constancy of the river flowing beyond the meadow and the soft voices of Irish people. I will miss Fred, beyond words.

Joe, forever decent, comes to visit my parents and to talk to them and Lionel. I don't remember who told me about that visit. They sit on our sofa and Joe puts his head in his hands and tries to talk, to explain and to give some meaning to the totally meaningless.

He takes my father aside and they go out on the deck.

'I need to tell you something, but then you have to decide what to do. Some time ago, I found my wife's missing mother; Lena is her name. She is in a sanatorium in the north of Italy. She lives there, and I'm on my way to see her . . . '

My father steps back and looks at him. 'I see,' he says slowly. 'I think I see. Do I understand you? Are you saying . . . ?'

'Yes, I am. It's incredible, but it's true. For years we lived here next door to Helena and her family, knowing nothing about her past other than that she was raised in Kenya. Like most people you ever meet, you only hear certain things, the things they choose to tell you. I knew nothing about Helena, really, just that she loved her childhood home. I knew she had parents, and that last year you came to visit. We were away on holiday at the time.'

'Yes, I remember. Helena spoke of your family. The link is extraordinary.'

'Now I don't know what to do. I don't know what is the right way forward. I'm flying to Milan in two days' time. My intention is to visit my mother-in-law. Shall I tell her . . . ?'

'Tell her?'

'About her sister and you? Everything? Her own daughter, who doesn't want to know her?'

'I don't understand why her daughter, Conti, why she does not want to know her,' my father says. He is trying to piece together all the different aspects of this story.

'I think it is some kind of snobbery. Conti came from a very wealthy and privileged background. I believe that she's unable to handle her mother's origins or what has happened to her.'

'But there was nothing wrong with her mother's origins. We cannot help where we come from. I married her mother's sister. Does this demean me in some way?'

'I'm afraid I have insulted you.'

'No, but Conti's attitude is an insult.'

'I'm aware of that, and I apologise for it. The irony is that my own background is nothing to boast about.'

'And how did your wife handle that?' my father asks, cold irony in his voice.

'She ignored it. It suited her simply never to acknowledge it.'

'I am having a problem understanding why a woman would dismiss her own mother because her mother was orphaned during a war and then used by a wealthy man who subsequently stole her child. I would feel that any anger I had would be directed towards him.'

'Me too. But right now I am less concerned with Conti than with her mother. Your wife's sister.'

'I will tell my wife. Come back inside. I need to talk to Carolina. We will talk afterwards.' My father hesitates in the doorway. 'What about you? What plans do you have?'

'My wife and I have separated. She's going to move to England. I will stay here and continue working.'

'You and your wife, is it irreparable?'

'Yes, it is. I suspect it has been for some time, only I didn't see it.'

'I am sorry. Is it safe for you to go on working here?'

'I have to. If ever I saw meaning in my work, I certainly see it now.'

'They haven't caught them,' my father says.

'No, but it will be part of my life's work,' Joe says.

My father talks to my mother and their voices drift down the corridor, sounds of distress and animation, of weeping and laughter.

Eventually my mother emerges back into the living room. 'Is this true? You have found her?'

Joe nods, but looking into her eyes, he wonders if she had any idea that this might not be such a happy occasion. Does she understand that her sister is now in a sanatorium? That she is considered unstable, if not demented?

He tries saying as much, but my mother says, 'I don't think that matters. To find each other again, that will be enough. I have been given a second chance on many fronts.'

To find, to love, to hold, to care, to give succour and warmth and shelter, to learn to live with life, to accept, to seize the day, the hour, the moment; I have tried to do these things. We learn by example and from experience. As I write this story, I am sitting, once again, beneath the umbrella tree dressed in an old white

Indian cotton dress. My feet are bare, and my heels feel the hard dry soil.

I was given another chance and I have sat with my mother on the veranda and stoned mangoes, our fingers sticky with the juice. We have talked together, shared smiles and confidences.

I was given time and I wrote my story for Lionel.

He is growing up to be a fine young man. Fred would be as proud of him as I am. He rides out with my father and oversees the farm. Just as my father taught him to hold the reins on the horse, now he is handing him the reins for the farm. In the distance, on horseback, he looks so like Horace.

'Miss Helayna.' Kulu's hair is white now. He stands at the foot of the hill. 'It is time to go home,' he says.

The sun is sinking, a huge red orb in the western sky, and the light is fading.

He is right.

It is time to go home.

Epilogue

My name is Lionel Wolff and today I finished reading the book my mother wrote. She died peacefully last year beneath the umbrella tree. She never really recovered from the shooting, although she hid her wounds and the pain she suffered.

In the distance, I can see the farmhouse and my elderly grandmother, my mother's mother, is sitting there on the veranda, rocking backwards and forwards on her chair and holding her sister's hand. They are in the shade, with the slanted roof protecting them from both the light and the heat. I suspect they are both looking over here towards this tree, where my mother and Horace are buried.

When I first arrived here, my eyes were drawn to this place on the horizon, and sitting here on the dry ground. I can feel the presence of Helena and Horace and I imagine them telling their animal stories, their voices low in the stillness of the day with the sun above and hats on their fair heads. I can hear their laughter. It echoes here under the tree. There is no wind to carry it away.

My mother deserved more than she got. Doesn't everyone? I think, though, that she lived with hope. She was the gentlest person I ever met. There did not seem to be a mean bone in her body. She always gave everyone the benefit of the doubt. She often said, 'It doesn't matter where you live; it's how you live.'

There are photos and pictures around the house of both my mother and her brother. And there is a portrait of my mother above the mantelpiece; it is a truly beautiful painting of her. She is sitting with the light coming in on her face and a dove is resting on her shoulder.

Life is not fair. I remember my mother telling me that. She

told me that we have no right to expect things and that we are lucky to have what we have.

I think I know now what she meant. It wasn't that I didn't feel lucky growing up. I never really thought about it. I took things that came my way and sometimes I aspired to things I couldn't have for whatever reason. But to accept the limitations of life and to be fulfilled by what one has creates contentment.

Of course, it is easier said than actually done. For the Martins to live all those years with Edith's impending death was terrible. For my mother to live with Horace's murder, for my grand-mother to live both with Horace's death and with the loss of her own sister; these are things that are not easily accepted. It's like me; I must live with the loss of my parents. And yet if I do accept, if I do not rail against what life throws at us, maybe that is how I can find happiness.

Grieve? Yes. But accept too.

I think that was the unusual thing about my mother. I think she understood acceptance. My grandmother did not. Nor did Conti Martin. And because of that they were the ones who lost out. My grandmother lost years of potential love with Helena through grieving for her sister, but in the end she found both again.

Somehow my mother's stories brought me to love this place. I can feel the magic she spoke of. It's here in the dust and the heat.

The answers are here. They are in my grandparents' minds and memories. I think of my mother and her quiet persistence, not just with me but also with those around us – my father, Conti, Lorina, Alice, Edith and all the people with whom she came in contact.

It was her strength. Like the strength of water. The type of strength you cannot see because its effect is so slow, but it is there at work, all the time, gradually breaking rocks into sand.

She was there for us all.

Her life was small and quiet, but it was a decent life. By that I mean she lived decently. She was kind and loving and she never stopped trying. And that, I think, is her gift to me. I learned from her how to live decently, with kindness and love.

That is all you can ask from a parent.

My Lionel turns the page and then closes my book and puts it into his bag. In a moment he will look up at the blue sky far above the dark branches of the tree. He will look around, down towards the farmhouse and then to the north, where he will see a herd of elephants approaching from beyond the scrub. There are about twenty of them in varying sizes. They move across the rough ground and stop at the foot of the hill where he is sitting. They stand and watch him.

One moves forwards and slowly approaches, his trunk swinging gently from side to side.

Ode on Solitude

Happy the man, whose wish and care
A few paternal acres bound,
Content to breathe his native air,
In his own ground.

Whose herds with milk, whose fields with bread,
Whose flocks supply him with attire,
Whose trees in summer yield him shade,
In winter fire.

Blest, who can unconcernedly find
Hours, days, and years slide soft away,
In health of body, peace of mind,
Quiet by day,

Sound sleep by night; study and ease,
Together mixed; sweet recreation;
And innocence, which most does please,
With meditation.

Thus let me live, unseen, unknown;
Thus unlamented let me die;
Steal from the world, and not a stone
Tell where I lie.

Alexander Pope (1688–1744)